TITLES BY BRENDA JOYCE

NOVELLAS BY BREND

DEADLY
LOVE

BRENDA JOYCE

St. Martin's Paperbacks

DEADLY LOVE

Copyright © 2001 by Brenda Joyce Dreams Unlimited, Inc.

ISBN: 0-312-97767-0
EAN: 80312-97767-2

Printed in the United States of America

St. Martin's Paperbacks edition / January 2001

St. Martin's Paperbacks are published by St. Martin's Press, 175 Fifth Avenue, New York, NY 10010.

10 9 8 7 6 5 4 3

To all of my Bragg fans,
with the utmost thanks and appreciation.

DEADLY
LOVE

CHAPTER
1

There was a soft rapping upon her door. Francesca Cahill recognized the knock and she froze, hunched over her desk, a Waterman fountain pen in hand. Electric lighting, installed when the house was first built eight years earlier, spilled over the vellum she was writing upon. She felt like a crook caught with his hand in the bank safe.

Her sister did not wait for her to answer, and she entered Francesca's large, beautifully appointed bedroom. Outside, it was snowing heavily; inside, a fire roared in the dark green marble hearth. "You're not even dressed!" Connie cried, eyes widening so vastly that the effect was almost comical.

Francesca forced herself to smile as she jumped to her feet, effectively blocking Connie's view of the desk. She stole a guilty glance at the grandfather clock standing in the corner of her room. Eight o'clock already? Guests would be arriving at any moment, if they hadn't begun to arrive already. "I'm sorry," Francesca said, unable to breathe properly. Darnation! She had an examination in biology on Monday morning, and she had yet to even begin studying for it. She had been too busy organizing this latest endeavor of hers, and now time had run out.

But then, there was never enough time in the day for

her to do all that she had to do. It was so frustrating.

Her sister faced her with exasperation, clad in a pale pink evening gown, her throat encircled with diamonds, her pale blond hair pulled loosely back and piled on top of her head. Diamonds fell from her ears and a diamond and ruby necklace decorated the expanse of bare skin between her shoulders and her bosom. She was a very beautiful woman. "Fran, how could you do this?" Connie implored. "You know what Mama has in mind for you tonight. She begged you not to be late and you promised. I know. I was there." Connie shook her head.

Francesca did feel a bit guilty, because she most certainly had promised their mother, Julia, that she would not be late, that she would be well dressed and on her best behavior. Francesca remained standing in front of her desk. On occasion, Connie was the biggest snoop. Francesca did not want to get into an argument now, even if her older sister did mean well. She smiled, far too brightly. "I was writing letters, the time escaped me," she said, crossing the fingers of her right hand behind her back and silently apologizing for the very small white lie.

"I don't believe you," Connie said, and she marched right past Francesca and lifted the sheet of parchment that Francesca had been working on, ignoring Francesca's exclamation of protest. "What is this?" she cried. And while she read, Francesca silently recited the words she had written, over a hundred painstaking times.

Next Meeting of the Ladies Society for
the Eradication of Tenements
Time: Saturday, January 25 at 3 o'clock P.M.
Place: The Library at the Waldorf-Astoria Hotel
For further information, please contact
Miss Francesca Cahill at No. 810 Fifth Avenue

Francesca folded her arms. "Connie, you know as well as I that the tenements are a disgrace to this city—a disgrace to you and me," Francesca said fervently.

Connie's brows arched impossibly—and it did not detract from her stunning beauty. "What I know is that you are an eccentric, Francesca Cahill. And what I also know is that you are late and that no matter how you think to try, eventually, Mama will have her way." She gripped Francesca by the arm and dragged her to the window. "Look!" she cried.

Through the velvet draperies, which were open, snow could be seen dancing through the night in tiny swirling points of brilliant white light. Francesca's bedroom was on the second story of the family's five-floor, Fifth Avenue mansion. The snow had already blanketed the front lawns and the poplar trees, as well as what could be seen of the sidewalk and street, which lay just beyond the wrought-iron front gates.

Francesca looked down on the circular front driveway, the lawns, and Fifth Avenue. Had the evening been clear, she would have been able to make out the tall iron street lamps with their double-headed white bulbs and the even taller trees of Central Park. Already two four-in-hands, a hansom, and a very dashing motorcar were coming up the driveway, the effect almost magical, the vehicles spookily emerging from the mistlike clouds of snow and electric lights. Beyond the drive, the lamplit street was eerily deserted. Because the Metropolitan Club was two blocks down, there was usually a high degree of traffic on the avenue. Tonight the weather was causing most of the city to stay home.

"Francesca, don't you belong to enough societies?" Connie's hands found her slim hips.

"Are you interested in coming to a meeting on Saturday?" Francesca returned, as quickly as a shot. She saw that Connie was about to make an excuse in order to refuse. "Please, Connie, please, please come. And bring a dozen of your friends. You know the cause is a good one!"

"I will come if I can," Connie said reluctantly, with

resignation. "I must check with Neil to make sure we do not have plans for the day."

Lord Neil Montrose was Connie's husband; they had married four years ago. Although he had a home in Devon, they spent most of the year in the States, preferring to summer in Great Britain. Francesca knew she would have to press her sister to join her next Saturday even if she was free. Not that Connie was opposed to charity and good works; like their mother, she was quite active in such affairs. But her idea of active and Francesca's varied dramatically. Connie preferred lavish balls, the tickets to which cost hundreds of dollars.

"Please try to come. If I give you a dozen flyers, could you hand them out this week at Montrose's dinner party for Livingston?" She was prepared to beg if need be. "Please? I am desperate for attendees." She smiled hopefully at her sister.

Connie merely gripped her arm again. "Can't we discuss this another time? I will help you dress. Good God, look at this mess!"

Francesca glanced at the big four-poster bed in the middle of her room. Half a dozen evening gowns were strewn there amongst all the green, blue, and gold pillows and shams, along with the appropriate undergarments and accessories. "How about the black?" she suggested dryly.

Connie scowled. "Amusing. How about the pink?"

Francesca shrugged. "Why does she insist on tormenting me so?" she asked as she stepped out of her white shirtwaist and fitted dove-gray skirt.

"I doubt Mama thinks she is tormenting you," Connie returned, while Francesca lifted a corset. "She has your welfare at heart. We all do, Fran."

"If she truly had my happiness at heart, she would allow me to do as I please and I would not have to suffer through this kind of evening," Francesca said grumpily. "I am not ready for a suitor."

"I said 'welfare,' not 'happiness.' " Connie began pulling on the ties. "And I do believe Mama has given up on the idea of a suitor. You are twenty years old, my dear. She is going directly for the husband." Connie's smile was serene.

Francesca scowled. "I am not getting married. Not at any time in the near future."

Connie had to smile again. "You are so funny, Fran. Look at the bright side. Maybe your future husband will be a radical reformer with a capital *R,* like you yourself!" Connie started to giggle.

Francesca saw nothing amusing about the fact that her mother was determined to marry her off, sooner rather than later. "How can you make fun of reform? When there is so much poverty and injustice in our midst?"

Connie ceased pulling on the corset. She turned Francesca around. "I am not making fun of reform, Fran. I would never be so callous. But you are so serious! Study, reform, study, reform, study, reform. It *is* funny. *You* are funny!"

"I am thrilled to be such a source of entertainment," Francesca grumbled.

"You do know that Mama suspects something?" Connie dropped the pink gown over Francesca's head.

Francesca stiffened. And because she and her sister were so close, she knew exactly what it was that her sister was speaking about. "But how could she? I am so careful."

"It is the hours you are keeping. Why don't you just tell her the truth? That you are a bluestocking and that you have enrolled at Barnard College? It will make your life so much easier."

"She will insist that I withdraw," Francesca said, as her sister was buttoning up the back of the brilliantly pink dress. "I am not going to withdraw. I am going to attain my AB degree. I am determined."

Connie finished and she smiled. "And God strike down whoever might dare stand in your way—unless it is Mama."

"Ho, ho, ho," Fran said sarcastically. But Connie was making a valid point. Julia Van Wyck Cahill was as determined as Francesca was—if not more so. It was a rare day indeed that Julia did not get her way.

"This color suits you, Fran, you will be ravishing tonight," Connie said with admiration in her blue eyes. "Mr. Wiley will be smitten," she added slyly.

Francesca groaned. "Onward, then, to my sordid fate."

"Oh, no! You have no shoes, no rouge, and no jewelry."

"Good! For then he will deem me madder than a hare." Francesca grinned.

"No such luck," Connie said cheerfully, producing a pair of beaded silver slippers.

"I have so much to do, and instead of being occupied in a useful endeavor, instead of being intelligent and using that intelligence, I must spend the evening being paraded in front of society's most eligible and dull bachelors," Francesca complained, meaning her every word.

"I just do not understand you," Connie said flatly, moving into the bathroom. Reluctantly, Francesca followed.

"I mean, there are no female journalists. Which you well know. Ah. Rouge. So you do have a vain streak," Connie said triumphantly.

"Mama bought that," Francesca returned calmly, taking the small pot of rouge and dropping it into the wastebasket. "And there have been no female journalists up until now, therefore I shall be the first when I graduate, unless another woman blazes the way for me."

Connie gave her a look. It was somewhat patronizing. But then, her entire family refused to believe that she truly meant what she said and what she intended.

Francesca loved to write. But it was more than that. For she was a passionate reformer, just as her father was; she had joined the ladies' auxiliary of the Citizen's Union Party when she was seventeen. What better way to bring about reform than to write scathing articles about poverty and corruption? The reporter Jacob Riis was her idol. She had read his book, *How the Other Half Lives*, five years ago, twice. Like most of those who had read that shocking account of life in the slums of New York City, Francesca had been appalled and shaken. That book had changed her life.

For she herself had so much. It was almost shameful. She *had* to do something to help those less fortunate than herself.

Connie retrieved the pot of rouge, placing it safely on the sink. After Connie had helped her put up her hair and don a small pearl cameo and matching ear bobs, Francesca allowed her sister to pose her before the mirror. Their eyes, both the exact same shade of blue, met in the looking glass.

Francesca had to admit that the gown with its fitted waist and flowing skirt was beautiful. The sleeves were two small caps just covering the points of her shoulders. "Have I ever worn this before?" she asked, puzzled. The gown seemed vaguely familiar.

"You wore this to my birthday," Connie said with exasperation as she rumbled through Francesca's toiletries. "Just before Christmas, remember?"

Francesca made a face at the mirror. "My memory is returning." She made another face, a pouty scowl. That might put off Mr. Wiley, she thought.

Connie chuckled. "I know what you are thinking, Fran. Forget it. You are beautiful and you cannot change the fact, no matter how you might, ridiculously, wish to try." The two sisters strongly resembled one another. Connie was fairer; Francesca's skin and hair were tinged with rich hues of peach and gold.

"Beauty fades. Character lasts forever." Francesca was firm.

Connie rolled her eyes heavenward and she guided Francesca out of the bathroom, through the bedroom, and out of the door, keeping a grip on her all the while.

The ballroom was on the mansion's third floor. But

guests would be arriving in the hall on the ground floor first. The sisters descended the wide white alabaster staircase, which led to a huge marble-floored hall with Corinthian pillars set at intervals, marble panels on the wall, and a high ceiling sporting a magnificent mural depicting a pastoral scene. The Cahill home had been dubbed "the Marble Palace" from the moment its construction had been completed.

At least two dozen guests had already arrived, with several groups arriving through the front door, handing their cloaks, hats, and umbrellas to the doormen. The sisters paused on the last landing. Julia stood poised between the hall and the reception room, greeting guests as they entered. She was resplendent in dark red silk and black lace and more diamonds than anyone had the right to wear. Francesca suddenly shivered. Whom was she fooling? She was no match for her mother. Her heart seemed to sink like a rock at the very thought.

"Thanks for the help, Connie," she finally said.

Connie squeezed her hand reassuringly. "Chin up. There are some dashing rogues present. If Wiley's not the one, tonight might very well be your lucky night anyway." She smiled and sailed off.

Francesca glimpsed Montrose across the hall, chatting with a group of men. Her heart seemed to stammer to a halt briefly, before resuming its beat. He was tall, dark, and dangerously handsome, especially in his evening clothes, and he did not glance her way, not even once. For one moment she watched him as Connie joined him, slipping her arm around his waist. Montrose smiled fondly down at his wife, briefly pulling her even closer. Resolutely, Francesca turned away.

She might feel very differently about marriage had she been presented with Montrose, and Francesca was well aware of it. But Connie was older than she was, and it had only been right that he had been presented to Connie. She was very lucky. Montrose was not just handsome and distinguished, he was intelligent and sincere and a very noble man.

Francesca's temples had begun to throb. He was also the father of their two small children. She loved her sister and her nieces, and she worked very hard not to succumb to jealousy and envy. In fact, she was so happy for Connie, who had such a perfect life. Her sister had a heart of gold and no one deserved a husband like Montrose and two such beautiful little girls more.

She took a deep breath, to regain her composure and prepare herself for the evening ahead.

But Julia had espied her daughter. Their gazes met.

Francesca recognized the look, which was a summons, and having little choice, she made her way through the growing crowd, nodding at those she passed.

"Francesca, do come here. Darling, I have someone you must meet." Julia smiled. She was a beautiful woman who was just a few years past forty, and she was also one of the city's leading socialites. In fact, her daughters resembled her in no uncertain terms. She also came from the most reputable Dutch stock; her father had made his fortune in banking, her grandfather had been a shipbuilder and city alderman. Julia was as proud of her heritage on the maternal side: her mother was a Georgian Southern belle who could trace her roots back to the French aristocracy before the Revolution.

Julia knew everybody with blue blood, wealth, or power. That is to say, she knew everybody who mattered. At times, it was daunting—at least for Francesca. Now she reached for her daughter's arm and then refused to release it—as if she knew well enough that otherwise Francesca would bolt and run.

"Mama." Francesca kissed her cheek, and dutifully, she extended her hand toward the man who must be Mr. Wiley. Inwardly, her heart sank even more and she cringed.

"Mr. Wiley has asked specifically to meet you, Francesca," her mother said, an edge to her tone. It belied her smile. "He remarked you at Delmonico's the other night, and of course, I have done nothing but sing your praises," Julia continued, facing a thin young man with the outstanding feature of his being very, very tall. He had to be at least six inches over six feet.

Francesca's smile felt wooden.

Wiley beamed, blushing hotly.

"My daughter is a saint, my dear Mr. Wiley. There is no woman here with a more benevolent heart. She ladles soup to the working poor and the destitute on Sundays, she visits the orphans at St. Mary's Asylum every other week, if not more frequently, and just the other day, she stopped by the city hospital on lower York Avenue to bring flowers to the ill." Julia beamed. "Mr. Wiley's family is in banking, darling. Mr. Wiley works for his father; they have a company on Wall Street."

Francesca stared at her mother in disbelief.

"Wiley and Sons," Mr. Wiley offered eagerly. He had light brown hair and bright blue eyes. He was smiling but his cheeks remained brightly pink.

Francesca barely heard him. And her mother, who had to know why her temper was escalating with the passage of every second, merely smiled at her. "I do believe Mr. Wiley might be pleased to take you for lunch on Monday, darling, if you would go downtown."

Francesca was so upset and angry she could not speak. She and Julia had fought for hours over her activities, too many times to count. Her mother hated her charities, insisting that a financial donation was far more appropriate than Francesca's highly individualized approach. If it were not for her father, Francesca knew she would not be allowed to visit the ill, the poor, and the destitute—not ever. But now, of course, she was singing a completely different tune.

"Oh, yes," Wiley gushed, turning a deeper shade of red. "Please do come downtown. And Monday would be so fine."

"Monday, then," Julia said, smiling at them both.

Francesca found her voice. Her examination was at eleven o'clock Monday morning. "Monday? I am afraid—"

Julia cut her off with a single glance. "Darling, you cannot possibly refuse such an invitation. And do save Mr. Wiley a dance," Julia said, smiling and kissing her daughter's cheek. She excused herself from the group, turning to greet other guests.

And suddenly the two of them were left alone.

Francesca was trembling. She felt as if the rug had just been pulled out from under her, and she had landed on elbows and knees on the hard marble floor. Of course she could not go. Not on Monday. Yet her mother had put her in a terribly awkward position.

Of course, this was not the first time her mother had outmaneuvered her. But this, this was beyond the pale. It truly was.

"Miss Cahill? Are you all right? You seem distressed."

Francesca jerked and met his concerned gaze. "I am fine, truly I am." She forced a smile. He reminded her of a gangling puppy, eager to please, yet somehow so awkward he could not help but do the wrong thing.

"There are some fine restaurants downtown," he offered.

"I'm sure," Francesca murmured, thinking she would send him a note tomorrow. And not really intending to be rude, Francesca glanced around.

Eliza and Robert Burton were just entering the hall. They were her neighbors, inhabiting the mansion adjacent to the Cahill home, which they had moved into two years previously. Francesca had to stare, because the moment the Burtons had handed off their cloaks, an animated crowd surrounded them. Eliza, who was not really beautiful, made a comment, and suddenly everyone was laughing. Even her husband was smiling, and holding so lovingly onto her arm.

"Ah, the Burtons. They are neighbors of yours, are they not?" Wiley said, following her gaze.

Francesca tore her gaze away from the striking brunette, who fascinated her. She blinked at Wiley. "Yes, they are. They live right next door."

"Wonderful people," Wiley said in a rush. "Very lively, that Mrs. Burton."

"Yes, she does seem to regale those around her with her wit and conversation," Francesca said truthfully. Francesca had always secretly wondered how she did it. When Eliza Burton entered a room, she drew admirers of both genders to her like honey drew bees. She was one of the most interesting women Francesca knew. For she was always speaking her mind, voicing her opinions, and she wasn't afraid to offend and be outrageous. Yet the world seemed to adore her.

Francesca could not help glancing her way again, even though Wiley was saying something. Eliza was wearing a dark red gown that was very bare; truly, it was almost scandalous, for it showed off her lush figure to perfection. Her dark hair was piled high, and her lips were dark red. But somehow, she was elegant in the daring gown and the dark red lips. And she was saying something about their newly elected mayor. Francesca strained to hear.

No, she was making a comment about the city's last mayor, something to the effect of his being not Croker's lapdog, but his snapping turtle. "After all," she smiled, "there was no bark and no bite, just the tiniest of ineffectual snaps."

Everyone roared.

Francesca had to smile. Eliza was far more original than the press.

And Wiley had heard, because he was chuckling, too.

She glanced at him, and thought she saw admiration in his eyes as he stared at the other woman. Francesca found herself watching Eliza as her husband escorted her across the hall and to the reception room. Eliza was smiling, but there was nothing artificial about it. She seemed genuinely happy. Her gaze met Francesca's, and she smiled again.

Almost shyly, Francesca smiled back.

"A very nice turnout, don't you think?" Wiley said, tugging nervously on his mustache.

Francesca drew her attention back to her suitor. The one thing she was not was rude. "I suppose so." She inhaled, aware that etiquette demanded that she attempt small conversation. Then she faced her suitor, feeling grim. "So, what do you think of the break in ranks between Platt and Odell?"

Wiley blinked at her. "I beg your pardon?" He didn't seem to have a clue as to what she was speaking about; it was as if he had never heard of Thomas Platt, the most powerful man in the state.

"Surely you are aware that Senator Platt and Governor Odell have broken ranks. Odell was assumed to be Platt's man. Perhaps Platt has finally fallen, what do you think?" Francesca could no longer restrain herself. "Perhaps his days of power are finally over," she added eagerly.

He stared at her as if she were sporting two heads. "Of course I am aware of the rift growing between them," he finally said, eyes wide.

"And I doubt it will be healed," Francesca added. But Wiley remained silent and suddenly Francesca's frustration soared to new bounds. He was not for her. Why did Mama have to do this? Why couldn't she understand that Francesca had more important things to do than to meet suitors who expected her to be coy and flirtatious, who did not care that she had a brain inside of her head? Why were most men afraid to have an intelligent exchange of opinion with a woman? How did Eliza Burton do it? Francesca suddenly felt despair descending over her like a heavy black cloud. "I had better mingle with Mama's guests. It was a pleasure meeting you," Francesca said with a brief, strained smile.

"Until Monday, then," he called after her eagerly.

Francesca found herself nodding, for there was little else that she could do. But she would send Wiley a letter of apology first thing on the morrow. And as for Julia, well, they would have to have a very serious discussion, indeed.

The idea was quite terrifying.

Suddenly Francesca stumbled and stopped short. Just ahead of her was her father, a short man with iron-gray hair, a beard, and huge sideburns. He was in the midst of conversation with a gentleman Francesca had never before met but whom she recognized immediately from all the press he had received since New Year's Day. Her heart flipped oddly and suddenly Andrew Cahill saw her and he beamed.

"Darling."

Francesca heard her father but did not look at him, meeting the dark, golden gaze of a man with tawny hair and swarthy coloring instead. He was extremely attractive, although in a rougher way than Montrose, at once tall and broad-shouldered, and like most of the gentlemen present, he wore a black tuxedo with satin lapels, a fine satin braid sewn down the side of his evening trousers. Andrew Cahill grabbed her arm, pulling her close. He was, Francesca knew, the newly appointed commissioner of police.

"There is someone you must meet," Cahill said, for he knew his daughter better than anyone and, in fact, Francesca's passion for reform had been inherited from her father's own, similar passion.

Francesca met his smile with one of her own. And even though her gaze was now on her father, she was acutely aware of Rick Bragg, standing there beside them. "Don't chastise me for being late," Francesca said affectionately, but she could hear that her own tone sounded odd—breathless and high-pitched. And her mind raced at lightning speed. The city police department was notoriously corrupt. So many efforts to reform the institution had failed. Bragg was expected to bring about much-needed reform. But could he do it? She stole another glance at him.

He had been studying her, and politely, slightly, he bowed.

His eyes, she noticed, were amber, and flecked with gold. Francesca felt herself flushing.

Cahill did not notice. "How can I not chastise such a delinquent daughter?" he was saying. He smiled, kissing her cheek, his salt-and-pepper beard scratching her skin.

Francesca was the apple of her father's eye and she knew it. Yet it was so hard to respond right now; instead, she was trying to recall everything she had read about Bragg in the papers since his appointment by the newly elected mayor on New Year's Day. "Please be gentle with me, then, Papa," she said. She had to steal another glance at Bragg.

And she could not decipher his penetrating gaze.

"We shall see." Andrew winked. "Darling, you must meet the police commissioner."

Francesca managed a smile that felt unnatural and tightly stretched; how odd. She was aware of a tension she had never before been faced with, and she did not understand it.

"Rick, this is my younger daughter, Francesca," Cahill said proudly. "And my daughter may be the youngest member of the Cahill family, but she is without a doubt the most intellectual—I would go so far as to say that she is brilliant." He beamed.

Francesca was embarrassed. Usually she was proud of her education and intelligence, but just then, she could only hope that her father's words had somehow impressed him, and finally, she gave in to sheer confusion. His taking her hand and bowing over it did not help. "Charmed," he drawled, and there was something laconic in his tone that startled her even more. His accent was slightly Western.

Her mind raced.

Rick Bragg was related to the Texas Braggs, a wealthy family with holdings in mining, railroads, banking, and beef. Apparently, he was a great-great-grandson of the founder. Hadn't she read somewhere, though, that he was originally from New York? She did recall that he was a graduate of Harvard Law School, and that he had had his own firm in Washington, D.C., until recently. But what Francesca remembered the most was that one and all wished to know if Bragg had been given carte blanche to administer the police. Seth Low, whom her father had supported heavily, was a Reform mayor, and his appointment of Bragg had raised a flurry of hopes and expectations among the city's progressive-minded liberals.

Francesca trembled. Could he do it? Would he do it?

Bragg was laughing briefly at something her father had said. The sound was warm and rich. He had his back to her. He said, "I saw the cartoon. I only object to the fact that the horse they put me on was a nag instead of a fiery steed."

"I liked the six-shooters, myself," Cahill chuckled.

Francesca wondered what cartoon they were referring to. Obviously, she had missed the caricature of the city's newest police commissioner. She wondered if it was in today's paper. She must check immediately and find out.

His gaze had turned slightly, allowing her to study his nearly classic profile. "I cannot reiterate enough what your support has meant, Andrew," he said.

"I have every confidence in you, as I do in Seth," her father said jovially, referring to the city's newly elected mayor.

"He has his work cut out for him," Bragg returned. His back was now to Francesca. "But I shall do everything in my power to see to it that my department eases his way, instead of adding to his burdens."

As her father responded, Francesca realized she had been dismissed. She stared at Bragg's broad shoulders, shocked.

For even though she was not looking for a suitor, and even though she was not a flirt, she was used to being admired. She was used to being ogled, if she dared be frank. It had been a fact of her life ever since she was a small child.

This man was impervious to her charms? But . . . how could that be?

"So, will Low make a public policy declaration regarding the police department and its affairs?" Cahill asked Bragg, apparently not even noticing the slight upon his daughter.

Francesca found herself crossing her arms tightly over her chest. An image of Connie retrieving the pot of lip rouge from the wastebasket came to mind. And she snapped silently to herself, *Do not be an absurd ninny!*

"I'm afraid you'll have to ask the mayor that," Bragg responded, smiling slightly at her father. His smile softened the distinct planes of his face.

Francesca wet her lips. Her pulse accelerated with her almost conscious intention. "So. Do you intend to enforce the Raines Act?" she heard herself ask.

His shoulders stiffened ever so imperceptibly and he turned to face her. His amber eyes locked with hers, wider now with some surprise. Francesca's tension had escalated dramatically—oddly, she felt as if she had just baited the bear in its den and she somehow felt threatened. She expected him to ask her what she had just said. He said, evenly, "I am afraid you will have to wait and see, just like the rest of the city, Miss Cahill." And his regard remained upon her, unwavering in its intensity.

She wasn't sure why she was so nervous. She wondered if she had made a mistake to so captivate his attention. But she could not seem to stop herself. Breathlessly, she said, "The law should be enforced or it should be repealed." And to her own ears, her normally husky voice came out high-pitched, like squeaky carriage wheels in the need of a good oiling.

He stared, becoming extraordinarily still. Francesca did not feel even a moment of triumph; if anything, she was stricken with anxiety and incapable of all movement.

An endless moment ensued before he spoke. "Again, I am afraid I must decline to make a comment," he said. But his gaze had sharpened like two lead pencil points.

Cahill slid his arm around Francesca. "My daughter is not only intelligent, she is very interested in the welfare of this city," he said proudly. "The district attorney is a friend of ours, as well."

Francesca managed, "He had supper with us Thursday night."

"I see," Bragg said, his gaze still on her, and Francesca had the feeling that he did. Had she made a mistake to engage him so? She could not tear her gaze away. "He can be a loose cannon," Bragg said flatly.

"He is the district attorney, and a man of the law," Francesca said, hoping to sound mature and calm when her heart was fluttering uncontrollably within her breast. "I respect most of his opinions."

Did she remark the briefest and faintest of smiles flitting across his face? Had she somehow amused him? For that was not her intention, oh no. "So you mime his opinions?" Bragg asked.

Suddenly the crowd around them disappeared. Francesca heard nothing and no one but her own deep, labored breathing, her own pounding heartbeat; she saw nothing and no one but the man standing before her; she even forgot that her father stood beside her, so closely that her skirts brushed his trousered leg.

Francesca's instinct was to flee. She did not. Undoubtedly because she was so oddly incapable of most movement. "I mime no one's opinions, sir. The only ones to gain from the failure to enforce the blue laws are the saloon and brothel keepers." She was amazed that her intellect did not fail her.

And suddenly he smiled. It transformed his face, already attractive, to one rather devastating in a rough, male, almost cowboy-like way. "Shall we debate?" he asked. And there was a twinkle in his gaze.

Francesca felt her eyes widen and she was also overcome with relief. "I am not trying to debate you, sir," she began. "But I have very strong feelings upon this subject."

Cahill threw his arm around her. "My daughter would be the Reform mayor herself, if she were a man. Isn't that right, Francesca?" he said.

Francesca somehow managed to tear her eyes away from Bragg. "But I am not a man, so the question is moot, is it not, Papa?"

"My daughter will not give an inch, Rick, I warn you on that. She is devoted to her many causes. Do you know that she is an active member of four leagues?"

Bragg had not removed his gaze from Francesca, and perhaps that was why her cheeks continued to feel as if they were on fire. "No, I did not. That is a large number of clubs, Miss Cahill."

She wet her lips again. "Actually, I belong to five." She glanced at her father. "I just began a new society, Papa. The Ladies' Society for the Eradication of Tenements."

"A terrible blot upon our city," Cahill said grimly.

"And where will the tenement dwellers go if the tenements are torn down?" Bragg asked with a calm that she was realizing was characteristic of him. But there was nothing calm about his intent eyes.

Francesca refused to fidget. "We are a rich city." She took a deep breath, hoping to recover her composure. "Surely you are aware of the fact that one half of the country's millionaires live here?"

He smiled again. A dimple appeared in his right cheek. "Will the funds then come from the pockets of men like your father, or from the city's coffers—assuming the politics of such a budget might be mastered?"

Francesca told herself that she was not in over her head.

But was he now amused? "Both, I hope. In fact, now that we have an honest and determined Reform mayor, my hopes have never been higher." She smiled briefly. It felt brittle. If she had become a source of amusement, she might very well die. "Commissioner Bragg, there is always a way to accomplish a worthy end." And by God, she did mean it.

He was silent for a moment. "I admire your enthusiasm," he said, then ruined the compliment with, "How old are you, Miss Cahill?"

She tensed again. "What does my age have to do with my ideas? I am no child."

"The young tend toward optimism," he said flatly. "*Not* realism."

Francesca had just received an ungentlemanly setdown, and she could no more stop herself than she could stop the snow from falling outside. "And you are so very elderly?" she asked.

He chuckled.

Was he laughing now at her?

She was about to point out that, throughout history, the greatest strides made by mankind were precipitated by the young and the restless, when her father took her arm. "The commissioner is right, of course. But it is the enthusiasm of the young that drives society to debate and action and ultimately the best of all possible conclusions." He kissed his daughter's cheek. "I must introduce Bragg around, although I would love to listen to the two of you debate all night. Have a good night, dear."

"Thank you, Papa." She somehow smiled at him, and then she looked at Bragg again. Right in the eye.

He had been studying her; his eyes immediately changed, making them impossible to read, and he nodded politely. Too politely, as if they had not just had the most scintillating exchange of opinions and ideas. Still, there were hidden layers there, and as he walked away with her father, Francesca watched them go. She felt rooted to the spot.

Whatever had she been thinking, to debate a man like that? And had she been adversarial? For that had not been her intention, not at all.

Did he think her odd? A fool? Or did he, at least, respect her for her intellect?

And had he not noticed that she was blond and blue-eyed, with a prettily sloped nose?

Francesca closed her eyes, replaying their conversation in her mind. Had she pressed too fervently? Did he think her outspoken? Outrageous? And why should she even care?

Francesca opened her eyes and found herself standing alone in the midst of the festive, animated crowd; worse, Wiley was smiling at her from across the reception room. It was just too much to bear.

She fled down the hall, brushing by someone in her haste and somehow apologizing, and then she dashed into her father's library, and finally, she was alone.

For one moment she could not move, oddly out of breath, leaning against the two huge oak doors, now solidly closed behind her. And as she took a few deep breaths, she began to relax.

Whatever was wrong with her? she wondered. She shook her head, as if to regain her senses. For the life of her, she could not understand what had just happened. In fact, even now, a sense of confusion remained.

She sighed, glancing around. Her father's library was her favorite place in the entire world. A gold tapestry cloth covered the walls, the pastoral scenes hand-painted. The ceiling was arched, and ribbed with the same rich, dark wood that ornamented the rest of the room. Stained glass covered the windows. There was a huge fireplace with a beautifully carved mahogany mantel, and a fire roared within it. Francesca walked over to his massive desk and plopped down in the chair behind it. She felt exhausted and drained.

Francesca stared at the desk but did not really see the papers and books there. Instead, she saw Rick Bragg. Her father liked him, he seemed intelligent and determined, and she realized that she hoped he was not a crook like so many of the city's previous police commissioners. Unfortunately, one could never tell.

Francesca shook her head to clear it again. Enough. How had she become so undone? She began to smile and she sighed again, tension draining away from her. The quiet and solitude were so welcome, but she did have a ball to return to, and Julia would remark her absence and complain loudly on the morrow if she stayed away. But Francesca did not move, taking another moment to recover the last vestiges of her composure and to enjoy her peaceful surroundings. She toyed with a pile of mail on the desk. Hadn't she known this evening would be dismaying? If only she was a bit more like Connie—just a bit.

Her sister was intelligent, well educated, and interesting. Yet she loved social affairs.

Francesca wondered if Bragg would have noticed Connie in a way that he had not noticed herself. For all gentlemen noticed Connie. Their admiration was always so frank and remarkable.

Francesca frowned slightly. Her entire life, she had been told that she and her sister might have been twins. Yet he had turned away from her after her father had introduced him.

As Francesca contemplated this last thought, she shoved the pile of mail aside. It worried her that Bragg kept intruding upon her thoughts.

And then she noticed one cream-colored envelope that had slipped free of the pile of mail. It wasn't addressed to anyone, in fact, one word was scrawled on the envelope's

front where the address should be and it caught her eye.
She blinked.

Urgent.

This was strange. Francesca picked up the envelope,
turned it over, but there was no return address either, nor
was there a postmark. Had a guest left it on the desk?
Curiosity seized her. Francesca picked up an ivory-handled
letter opener and immediately slashed it open. It said:

> *A is for Ants*
> *If you want to see the boy again, be at Mott and*
> *Hester streets at 1 P.M. tomorrow.*

CHAPTER
2

Francesca blinked and read the typed note again.

"A is for Ants . . . If you want to see the boy again, be at Mott and Hester streets at 1 P.M. tomorrow." My God— what did this mean?

She was standing, the note in her hand. Her mind raced with dizzying speed. She could not seem to think clearly. The note made no sense. What boy did it refer to? And what did "A is for Ants" mean?

This was a prank, she decided. Because the note had clearly been left on her father's desk by one of the guests. Or had it been slipped into their mail somehow, and brought by the mailman with the rest of their mail?

No, she decided firmly, this was a strange prank. Evan was a prankster. Could the joke be his doing?

But it wasn't very funny, she thought, shaking her head in confusion. In fact, it was so odd it was maddening. What if it wasn't a prank?

Francesca decided she would show the note to her father the first chance she had.

"Miss Cahill?"

Francesca shoved the note back in the pile of mail and leapt as if she were a thief with her hand caught in a master safe. And her gaze locked with the commissioner's.

Bragg seemed every bit as surprised to see her as she

was to see him. And then he recovered, and he nodded politely at her.

Francesca felt herself flushing, and she could not summon up a smile in return. She wanted to say something witty or amusing. Instead, she breathed, "Commissioner?"

"I did not mean to intrude," he said, his gaze steady upon her. "I merely wished to use the telephone. Unfortunately, I must leave early, as there is another affair I must attend."

Her heart was beating like a drum. The prospect did not seem to please him, but Francesca did understand the politics of a job such as the one he now had. She nodded. "And I shouldn't be cloistered away like a nun," she said, hoping for some levity in her tone. She moved away from the desk. "Please feel free to use the telephone."

"Thank you," he said, his gaze on her. His scrutiny was careful.

She knew she was acting strangely, like a witless idiot, if the truth be known, but did he know? Francesca smiled again and walked past him, making sure to give his body a safe berth—as if brushing too closely by him might be a criminal offense. And then she reached the door. She half turned.

He had picked up the telephone receiver. But he was looking over his shoulder at her and their gazes collided.

Francesca did not know what his look meant and she fled.

"Fran!"

Francesca whirled to face her brother, Evan. Tall, dark, undeniably dashing and almost too handsome, he grabbed her hand. "There is someone I want you to meet," he said, his blue eyes twinkling.

Francesca could not smile. Why was she so undone—again? What was happening to her? Surely she was not flustered and breathless because she found Rick Bragg rather attractive? She was a mature, grown woman, and more importantly, she was an intelligent and thoughtful person. She was far above succumbing to a silly infatuation.

"Fran? Hello? Are you even listening to me?" Evan was tugging on her hand. He was just under six feet tall and his hair was pitch-black and curly. He had always reminded Francesca of a classical rendering of a Grecian poet or god.

"I'm sorry," Fran cried, jerking her hand free. She rubbed both temples, then smiled at the brother she adored. "I am sorry. I do not know what is wrong with me."

"Too much studying," Evan said teasingly and he dragged her through the hall, past numerous sculptures and paintings, and into the reception room, filled now with dozens of guests. Evan smiled at her as he guided her across the room. "I am anxious for your opinion," he said with his usual enthusiasm. "There is someone you must meet."

Francesca realized that he was moving her toward three women her own age, and most of the comely faces were familiar. Still, Francesca knew no names; she had no friends outside of those ladies in her clubs and at college. She had trouble conversing with the young women who attended her mother's affairs. They wished to discuss fashion and men; she wished to discuss the most current of events and issues. Their giggles suddenly ceased as she and her brother paused before them. And it was comical the way the women turned their cow-eyed gazes upon her brother.

But of course, he was a catch with a capital *C*. He was *the* Cahill heir and all of society knew it.

Evan smiled, and Francesca followed his gaze, rather amused. For even though her brother was a very eligible and preeminent bachelor, she knew him too well, and his liaisons were not the kind sanctioned by society. Of course, she pretended not to know about the string of gorgeous mistresses; even Mama turned the other way. Therefore,

Francesca could not believe Evan was introducing her to a proper and available young lady. What could this possibly mean?

And she was also just noticing that one of the three young women hadn't turned cow eyes on her brother.

"Fran, this is Miss Marcus, Miss Berlendt, and Miss Channing. Ladies, my sister, Francesca Cahill."

There was a chorus of hellos and giggles. Two of the three women blushed hotly. Francesca thought it comical. They were so terribly obvious.

Except for Miss Channing. Francesca stared at the one woman who neither spoke nor laughed and who did not blush; she stared at a pale, petite brunette with huge brown eyes that could only be described as soulful.

Sarah Channing stared back. Like Francesca, she wore no rouge; unlike Francesca, her gown was terribly overdone with frills and flounces and a huge lavender bow. The gown would have been a disaster on the most beautiful and seductive of women. On Sarah Channing, it was absurd.

Francesca felt a pang of pity.

"Miss Channing and I met the other day at Sherry's. I was having lunch with a friend, and she was dining with her mother." Evan smiled, stepping closer to Sarah Channing.

Francesca had assumed the stunning brunette to be the object of her brother's interest, and she felt her jaw drop and her mouth open wide. Quickly she rearranged her expression. "A wonderful restaurant," Francesca managed, looking with real surprise at the young woman who had yet to speak and who was rather plain for a man like her brother, if she dared be frank.

Sarah smiled slightly.

"I have eaten there frequently, in fact," Francesca said politely, hoping to draw Sarah out.

"Yes," Sarah said, low.

"It is the most wonderful of restaurants," one of the

other women gushed. Francesca thought it was Miss Berlendt, the dark brunette with the amazing green eyes and the even more amazing figure. She was so obviously the kind of woman her brother enjoyed flirting with. But Evan hardly spared her a glance.

"I do so love it," agreed the pretty blonde, Miss Marcus. "The other day after shopping, Mama and I had the chance to stop there. Have you been to the bargain counter at Macy's? I bought the most wonderful pair of kidskin gloves and a marvelous facial cream."

Her friend instantly turned and the subject of discussion went from shopping at Macy's to shopping at Lord and Taylor's and then Bergdorf Goodman's, some of the city's most exclusive stores. Francesca shut out their chattering, because Evan had ducked his head and was asking Sarah if he might escort her upstairs to the ballroom. Of course, she should not eavesdrop; she strained to hear.

Sarah glanced at her brother, holding his gaze only briefly. Clearly she was shy. "Of course."

Francesca could only stare. Did her brother harbor some serious affection for Sarah Channing? The woman could not seem to utter a word, and it was clear she had the most meek of characters. Francesca just could not believe her eyes and ears. This was so surprising!

Evan had tucked Sarah's arm in his. "We are going on up. Do come." He hesitated. "Fran, why don't you call on Sarah sometime?"

Francesca blinked. "Well . . ." She could not refuse her brother, ever. But what on earth would they talk about?

Francesca imagined confessing to Sarah that she was an undergraduate student at Barnard College. Or inviting her to join her for a charitable visit to Blackwell's Island. Sarah would swoon. She had no doubt.

Sarah murmured, "That would be lovely." She seemed as reluctant as Francesca—or was that just her timidity?

"Of course I will call," Francesca said valiantly. For here, clearly, was a woman in need of a friend.

Smiling, Evan led Sarah away.

Francesca took a few steps after them in order to continue to watch them. Evan kept up a stream of conversation; Sarah listened, her head ducking slightly, and finally, once, she smiled briefly at him.

Francesca did not know what to think. Her brother was a man of high intellect and even more passion—in fact, passionate natures were a Cahill trait. Even her mother could form the most vocal and fervent of opinions, when aroused to do so. Francesca thought about all the debates she had shared with her brother, she thought about his passions and convictions. And he was also a very active man; he loved to motor, to hunt, sail, play polo, and to ski. Was he truly interested in such a mild-tempered woman?

Francesca thought about the notion that opposites attract.

"She is so odd," a voice said, from behind her.

The remark was made in such a tone that Francesca stiffened. She was certain that the speaker, one of the young women she had just walked away from, referred to timid Sarah Channing. Francesca didn't really know Sarah, but she was about to turn, ready to defend Evan's latest love interest—if that was what Miss Channing truly was—should the need arise.

"She is quite eccentric," whispered another of the young women—the blonde, who did not sound silly or frivolous now. The two ducked their heads and moved away, but not before Francesca became alarmed and heard the brunette say, "I think it is so strange, don't you? She is miserably aloof. Perhaps she thinks she is better than we are because she is a Cahill. It certainly seems that way. She looked right through us as if we were, why, worms! Well, if she wasn't a Cahill, she would not find many doors open to her, I am certain of that. And she might be beautiful, but she would not have a single suitor with her mannish opinions and ways."

Francesca was paralyzed.

The brunette turned and gave her a cold glance and then the two women wandered off. The shock began to abate.

Mannish ways?

Worms?

Very deliberately, Francesca crossed the reception room, reminding herself that she did not care what those marriage-mad women thought of her, as they had not one whit in common. Tears blurred her eyes.

She reminded herself that she was proud of her education and intelligence and her desire for reform.

Angrily, she rubbed the tears away.

She had not meant to be aloof. She had not meant to look at anyone as if they were a worm. Had she really done that?

She left the room, moving slowly down the corridor, shaken to the core. She told herself again that she did not care what those two frivolous women thought of her. Francesca paused, leaning against the wall, knowing that she must go up to the ballroom. She took a deep, steadying breath.

Did all of society think her odd? Rude?

Suddenly she thought about Bragg. Had he thought her odd? Had he thought her opinions mannish? Oh, God! If he had, she would die, right then and there.

Francesca blinked back a few more wet, recalcitrant tears. "Oh, balderdash," she whispered aloud. "I am an intellectual and they want nothing more than to marry and shop. We are worlds apart. Of course they would think me odd. It is not important, not at all."

"Francesca? Are you going up—dear! What is wrong?" Julia cried.

Francesca stiffened, caught in the act of brushing another absurd tear of self-pity aside. Julia was the last person she wished to face. "Of course I am going upstairs, Mama," she cried too brightly.

"You are upset," Julia said, pausing by her side. "Whatever has happened, Francesca?"

Suddenly Francesca looked at her mother and heard herself say, "I don't know why you make me do this. I am a bluestocking, Mama, and I have nothing in common with anyone here!"

Julia studied her and then smiled, tucking Francesca's arm in hers. "You are young and beautiful and you have plenty in common with every other young lady in this room. You are no different from the other young ladies present, Francesca, and stop telling yourself otherwise, as it will do you no good. Please, Francesca, just this once, listen to what I am saying. I am your mother, and no one loves you more—or wants the best for you more than I." Julia smiled again, as if certain she had made her point and made it well.

Her mother would never understand. Francesca summoned up a weak smile. "I am different," she whispered. "And I am very tired . . ."

"Let's go upstairs, for the dancing will soon begin. And just wait until you see the buffet," Julia added, guiding her to the door.

Francesca had no choice. But then, that was hardly unusual when it came to her mother. And as they left the reception room, she felt eyes upon her, and she flung a glance over her shoulder, slipping free of her mother as she did so.

She stiffened, meeting Montrose's gaze.

It was the first time he had looked at her that entire evening. Francesca did not know what to do, so she did nothing.

He bowed as any gentleman would and then he turned away.

"Good morning, sleepyhead."

Francesca was awake, but she was drifting in that soft, cozy cloud where sleep vied equally with consciousness, enjoying the warmth of her bed. She opened her eyes and gazed across the room. Evan stood grinning at her from the doorway.

Suddenly she was fully awake. A quick glance at the parted velvet draperies told her that it was not seven o'clock—the time she usually awoke. The sun was too high in a cloudless blue sky. Francesca threw off the covers, leaping to her feet. "What time is it?" she cried in a panic. The biology examination loomed in her mind.

He laughed. "Whoa, there. It's ten—but it's Sunday, Fran. No school today."

She had forgotten. Francesca briefly closed her eyes in relief, and then she rushed to the door and slammed it closed. "Do you have to announce my affairs to the entire household?"

He smiled at her with affection and concern. "Were you up all night studying?"

Francesca went to the closet and donned a warm flannel robe. "Yes, I was. I have an examination Monday morning."

He leaned against the door, his hands in the pockets of his tan trousers. "Fran, don't you think you should confess? This has gotten far too hard. Sneaking off to college by day, staying up all hours by night, and trying to still have a normal life! I think you should tell Mama the truth."

She just stared. "Have you gone mad? She will demand that I drop out of the program—and I am not going to do that, especially when it was hard enough to borrow the money from you and Connie for the tuition."

"How can you keep this up?" he said flatly. "I have never seen you sleep this late—you are exhausted."

"I'm not," she said, a half-truth. "Evan, I know you are concerned for my welfare, but I am so happy. Please, don't even think of telling Mama about my having enrolled at Barnard College." She lowered her voice. "In fact, I'm nervous even discussing this subject in the house."

He was wry. "She never leaves her apartments before noon."

"There's always a first time."

He shrugged. "Suit yourself, then. So, shall we ride after breakfast? The park will be beautiful after all the snow we got last night."

"I'd love to but . . ." She hesitated. She had intended to spend the entire day studying.

He scowled. "I understand."

She watched him swing open the door. "Wait! Evan, what is going on with you and Sarah Channing?"

He turned to smile at her. "She is sweet, isn't she?"

She gaped at him. "Sweet?"

He nodded, winked, and left the room, closing the door behind him.

He seemed smitten. Sweet? Francesca shook her head as she went into the bathroom to wash up and brush her teeth. Evan did not know it, but last summer she had happened upon him and his mistress one weekday afternoon. They had been strolling down Broadway; she had been running an errand. Francesca had taken one look at her brother and the gorgeous redhead he was with, and she had known that they were lovers.

Francesca had never said a word. But a little research had revealed that the woman was a somewhat renowned stage actress named Grace Conway, and in any case, her bright and worldly manner had been apparent. If Evan had been in love with the actress, how could he now be falling for her complete opposite? It was amazing.

Francesca went downstairs, having quickly donned a navy blue skirt and a white shirtwaist, the former flaring attractively at the hem. She had twisted her hair into a neat chignon, and for some reason, as an afterthought, had dabbed a speck of rouge on her cheeks and lips. She was trying not to remember last night.

As she approached the breakfast room, which was cozy and intimate compared to the formal dining room where her mother routinely had dinner parties for forty or fifty guests, she realized that something was amiss. Her father and Evan were conversing with loud, raised voices. But they did not seem to be arguing.

Francesca stepped onto the room's threshold.

"What are the two of you shouting about?" Francesca asked without undue concern.

"Look at this, Fran!" Evan cried, pointing at the page in front of his father's nose. They were both reading the *Times.*

Cahill stood, and as Francesca came forward, he handed her the paper. "Burton's boy has been abducted," he said grimly.

And Francesca stared at the headline on the front page.

BURTON HEIR ABDUCTED

Francesca gasped, then read the subtitle aloud. " 'Boy disappears in middle of the night.' " She looked up, stunned.

"I am sure the police are already handling this," Cahill said, crossing the room, Evan on his heels. "But I feel compelled to do what I can. Perhaps we should notify the office of the U.S. Marshal. Undoubtedly the Burtons will want all the help they can get."

"Are you going over there? I will come," Evan said grimly, at their father's side.

"We must offer them whatever aid and support we can. This is an abomination," Cahill exclaimed.

Francesca stared at the words swimming on the front page of the *Times* as her brother and father left the room. The article stated that Jonathan Burton had disappeared from his own bed in the middle of the night, that he was six years old and had a twin, and that the Burtons had been attending a ball at their neighbor's home, the house of the millionaire Andrew Cahill, when the crime had occurred. They had not realized one of their children was missing until their return. The article had nothing else to say about the disappearance, so it then went on, laboriously, about the Burtons and their life.

She put the paper down.

Oh, God. Last night while Eliza had been laughing and dancing, some criminal had entered her house, snatching one of the twins.

Francesca felt ill. Which twin had been taken? She knew them both, and well. They were such sweet, mischievous boys. Jonathan and James. In fact, it was only a few days ago that she had given Jonny a ride on her hack in Central Park—they had ridden double, the little boy in front of her. She was always giving them penny candies.

Was it last summer that James had put a beetle in her lemonade?

Eliza must be in hysterics, Francesca thought, near tears.

A is for Ants . . .

Francesca froze. And then she ran to the library.

The note in hand, Francesca raced back through the house, her mind whirling at impossible speeds. The note she had discovered last night—which she had entirely forgotten about—must pertain to the missing Burton boy. But why had it been left on her father's desk? Why hadn't it been left at the Burtons'?

In the front hall, Francesca skidded to an abrupt halt. The thought struck her with stunning force. Whoever had abducted Jonny, either he or his accomplice had been present last night at the ball.

Francesca was about to dash through the front door, when it occurred to her that the envelope was also evidence. She ran down the corridor, burst into the library, rushed to the desk, and hurried through the mail scattered there. Where, goddarnit, was it?

She espied the envelope with the single word "urgent"

typed on its face, grabbed it, and bolted back down the hall.

"Miss Cahill!" one of the doormen cried as she wrenched the front door open. Francesca paid him no mind. She dashed down the imposing limestone front steps of the Cahill mansion, careful not to slip and fall on her face.

"Miss! Your coat! Your hat! Your gloves!" the doorman shouted after her.

Francesca ran. As she ran down the drive, which had been shoveled free of snow, the frigid air blasted her. She hit Fifth Avenue as a trolley was passing by, but she paid it no mind. The Burtons' property abutted the Cahills'. Unlike her own home, they had no grounds in front, just lawns in the back, and the four-story house sat directly on the street. And standing before the wide staircase leading up to the front door were three uniformed policemen in their brass-buttoned blue serge coats and blue-black helmets.

Carriages were triple-parked in front of the Burton house. So was a handsome Daimler motorcar. And two officers on horseback seemed to be patrolling the entire block from Sixty-first to Sixty-second Street. Already a crowd of pedestrians was gathering to point and speculate.

Francesca rushed forward, breathing hard. The three patrolmen immediately barred her way, preventing her from taking more than one step up the staircase.

"Sorry, miss," the short one said. "No callers today." But he eyed her warily.

Francesca guessed he thought her insane, running about without any outer clothes. "I am a friend of the family's," she cried. "I must go in!"

"Orders from the commissioner himself. No callers today." He was firm.

"But I am Francesca Cahill, I live right next door," she cried, her teeth chattering. "My father is a personal friend of Bragg's, why, he was at our ball last night. I must go inside. Is the commissioner here? I must speak with him! I have information vital to the case," she cried.

The three turned to look at one another, then stepped back, whispering. Francesca was losing her patience, and she was freezing. The short patrolman stepped forward and told her that he would take her in.

"Thank you!" She dashed past him, eager to get inside.

Once inside the hall, a spacious wood-paneled room with a high, domed ceiling and marble floors, she looked around. She had been to the Burtons' house many times, and on either side of the hall where she stood, the doors were open, to show off the beautifully appointed drawing room and a reception room similar only in function to that of her parents'. If memory served her correctly, there was a parlor at the far end of the hall, which seemed to be where the patrolman was leading her. The double doors were open, and immediately Francesca glimpsed the occupants inside.

Eliza sat on a settee with her husband, Robert. She was sobbing into a handkerchief, and Burton had his arm around her, although he was as pale as a newly laundered sheet. Her father and Evan stood on their right side, their expressions terribly grim, while a shabbily suited gentleman with a huge belly and thick whiskers stood on their left. Behind him was another detective, also clad in a poor brown worsted suit, but sporting a badge. Bragg stood facing the Burtons, his back to Francesca.

"Commissioner, sir." The patrolman spoke with unease, as if afraid of having his head taken off by the interruption.

Bragg turned, and saw not the policeman, but Francesca. His gaze sharpened impossibly.

He did not appear to be in a good humor. In fact, he looked rumpled and unshaven, as if he had not had a very good night's sleep. Francesca was almost sorry she had come. "Commissioner," she began.

He strode forward. "Miss Cahill, good day." He was curt to the point of being rude, and she knew the slight courtesy of his greeting was an effort. "I am afraid you will have to come back at a later time. This is the scene of a felonious crime." He turned an ice-cold stare on the policeman. "Escort her home. No one is to enter these premises—or have I not made myself clear?"

The policeman blanched. "Y'did, sir, 'n' yes, sir. Let's go, miss."

Bragg reached for the door, apparently about to close it in her face.

"Bragg!" Francesca also gripped the door, forestalling him. His eyes widened. "I have a clue!"

"What?" This not from the commissioner, but from her father.

Francesca held up the now crumpled note and envelope. "I found this last night in the library," she said in a rush, "just before you came in to use our telephone. I think this pertains to Jonathan."

He snatched the note and envelope and Francesca watched him read, and then she watched him pale beneath his natural golden coloring. She thought he cursed beneath his breath.

Burton was on his feet. "What is it? Is it a ransom demand?"

Bragg held the note and his gaze locked with Francesca's. "No, it is not a ransom demand, but it appears that Miss Cahill is right. Come in, Miss Cahill," he said.

It was hardly an invitation; it was a command. Francesca stepped inside, aware now of just how hard her pulse was pounding.

He slammed the doors closed behind her.

CHAPTER
3

Bragg was no longer facing Francesca. "Robert, please read this," he said quietly. But there was no mistaking how strained his expression was.

Robert Burton took the note and read it silently with shaking hands.

"What does it say?" Eliza cried. Her eyes were swollen, the tip of her round nose red. "Dear God, what does it say?!"

"It makes no sense," Burton said, handing the note back to Bragg.

Francesca could not help herself. She was hardly close to Eliza, but she stepped to her and laid her palm on the other woman's shoulder. Eliza did not notice. "Please, may I see the note?" Eliza asked.

It was handed to her. "Robert, can you think of anyone with a grudge against you or your wife, who might leave this kind of note in the wake of the abduction?" Bragg asked grimly, with a sidelong glance at Francesca.

Burton shook his head. "I have a few enemies, I suppose. From past business dealings, but dear God, my answer is no. I know of no one who would be so insane as to steal my child from his own bed right out from under our roof!" His face collapsed as if he too might burst into tears. ·

"Miss Cahill." The words were like a whiplash.

Francesca stiffened and met his dark eyes. "Yes?"

"Describe to me exactly how—and where—you found this note."

She swallowed. Having this man's full attention did odd things to her. It caused an almost unbearable tension within her; or was she imagining it because of the horrid predicament they all faced? "I already told you. It was perhaps ten in the evening, and I was sitting at Papa's desk in the library. I was thinking." She hesitated, recalling exactly why she had closeted herself in the library, and she avoided his gaze. Francesca stared at the floor and continued. "The entire day's mail was in front of me. I saw the envelope with the word 'urgent' typed upon it. It was so odd that I opened it." He stared, and she added quickly, "I suppose I shouldn't have. I didn't think twice about it."

If Bragg felt that her behavior had been erroneous, he gave no sign. But then, he was thoroughly preoccupied with the matter at hand. He paced. His strides were tight and hard and filled with anger and urgency.

Her father patted her shoulder. "That's all right, Francesca," he said reassuringly, diverting her attention.

Francesca smiled a bit in return. "I suppose I should not have opened it. I'm sorry."

Bragg looked at Cahill. "I will need a list of guests who were at the house last night, as well as a list of the entire staff in your employ, including those who had the night off."

Cahill nodded. "My wife will see to it."

Bragg turned to the portly man with the heavy whiskers. "Murphy. See to it that no one enters or leaves the Cahill premises until I say so."

"Rick," Cahill began.

Bragg did not give him a chance to continue. "I am

sorry, Andrew, but there is no choice in the matter. I must interview everyone who is in your employ—no one shall be allowed to leave the grounds." He faced Murphy. "No one is permitted to leave these premises, either. And Robert, I need a staff list from you, as well."

Francesca found his authoritative manner impressive. She realized her eyes had been glued to him again and she looked away, with reluctance. If any man could locate Jonny Burton, it was this man, she thought. His determination would know no bounds.

"I don't understand," Eliza suddenly whispered. "Why would someone do this? And why leave such a note? What does it mean?" More tears slid down her face. Her chignon was coming undone. Dark curls were beginning to fall about her round shoulders.

Bragg suddenly knelt before her, taking her hands in his. "Mrs. Burton. I will find the boy. I promise you that," he said softly. As abruptly, he stood again. "Murphy. Take this note and envelope to headquarters. To Heinrich. Put a dozen men, no, two, on the detail. I want to know the kind of typewriter that was used; that is, I want to know the company and the model. Then I want to know every single store in Manhattan that carries or has carried the particular machine. Do I make myself clear?"

Murphy's eyes were wide. "Commissioner, no offense intended, sir, but that's an impossible task."

"Is it, Inspector?" Bragg asked so coldly that Francesca could have sworn the temperature in the room had dropped a good ten degrees.

"We will do our best."

"Do more than your best. You can also tell Heinrich I suspect a shift-key machine was used. The five capital letters in this note seem to be imprinted more deeply on the page."

Francesca's brows shot up. She wished she could look at the note again, but knew better than to ask. Bragg was very impressive, indeed.

"The paper is of high quality. Find out what kind of paper was used—and which stationers here in Manhattan carry the stock."

Murphy did not look happy. "Aye, sir."

Francesca could not help herself. "Are you thinking a servant has abducted the child?"

Bragg whirled. His eyes were wide. And there was no mistaking his expression—he did not appreciate the question.

Francesca held her ground, silently applauding herself for doing so, for the commissioner could be daunting, indeed. "Commissioner, I only want to point out that a servant could have stolen the paper from this household—as it does seem to be a job done from within the Burton home."

His gaze narrowed. "I would be remiss to draw any conclusions at the beginning of this investigation. I would also appreciate your leaving the analysis of evidence to the authorities. That is, to myself and my detective bureau, Miss Cahill."

Francesca nodded, though she wanted to say more. She wanted to tell him that if a servant had taken the child, then surely there would have been a ransom demand. Still, ransom was probably the motive—for surely a ransom demand would be forthcoming.

For if it was not forthcoming, they were dealing with a madman.

"I still do not understand this note," Eliza said, finally standing. She paced, dabbing at her eyes. Watching her, Francesca tried to imagine how she felt, with one of her children missing, taken out of his bed by some criminal, but she failed to do so. How could she? She was not a mother. She could only empathize. How she wished she could help.

"The note is bizarre," Burton cried angrily. "Maddening!"

Eliza nodded, appearing about to burst into tears again,

and she sank back down on the settee, hugging herself hard.

Francesca went over to her again. She knelt. "Can I bring you some tea? Or better yet, a sherry?"

Eliza finally looked at her for the first time. "No, thank you, dear," she said, and suddenly she took her hand and squeezed it. Then she wept, hard and uncontrollably.

Francesca was at a loss. "We will find him," she whispered unsteadily, tears coming to her own eyes. And then she felt eyes upon her back, and slowly, she looked up.

Bragg's brows slashed upward. "We?" he asked, at once incredulous and harsh.

She stood, releasing Eliza's hand. "A mere figure of speech." She backed away, realizing she must be careful not to tread upon his toes in the future, then wondering just when the boy had been taken. "When was Jonny abducted?" she heard herself ask.

His temper looked as if it were being ratcheted up to frightening degrees, so she added, in a rush, "Bragg! I know them both so well! I have known them ever since the Burtons moved in next door two years ago."

There was a moment of silence. Bragg seemed somewhat appeased, either that, or he was resigned. Then Burton said, agonized, "We don't really know. Jonny was in bed when we left for your ball; we returned just before one, and he was gone."

An image of big brown eyes, a round, smiling face, and a mop of brownish hair filled Francesca's mind. On her birthday last year, Jonny had presented her with a bouquet of roses—unceremoniously cut from his mother's gardens. Briefly, Eliza had been angry with him for cutting down half of the blooming bush.

He could have been abducted at any time between eight and one in the morning.

And everyone knew it. Francesca looked around the room. Eliza wept anew. Burton sank down beside her, to cradle her in his arms. She sobbed on his chest. Evan's mouth was downturned; her father was as grim. Bragg stood staring at everyone, his fists clenched. Murphy shifted uneasily, as did the man standing with him.

This was terrible, Francesca thought. This was a terrible, needless, outrageous tragedy. But surely they would find Jonny. Clearly Bragg was a very capable man; in fact, he looked as if he were on his own private warpath. And suddenly Francesca was stricken by the most stunning insight. "Bragg!"

He had been handing Murphy the evidence; he whirled. "Miss Cahill?"

"I have just realized that you seek two men, not one," she gasped.

He opened his mouth but she barreled on. "I mean, the note was left on our desk, in our house, which makes absolutely no sense. It had to have been left there during the ball, that is, while the Burtons were still present. Which means someone left the note while *another person* was abducting Jonny." Francesca paused, out of breath.

Bragg stared at her and his eyes literally turned black.

"Good deductive reasoning, Fran," Evan said admiringly. "But why the hell was the note left at our house and not here? It would be so easy to just drop the note right on Jonny's bed."

He had a very good point, the answer to which eluded her, but she couldn't turn to look at him—he was standing behind her—because Bragg looked as if he wished to strangle her. He said to Murphy, "Please escort Miss Cahill home." And then he said, directly to her, "Unless this criminal is extremely bold, Miss Cahill. In which case he abducted the child, stashed him somewhere, and then went to your family's ball."

Francesca's eyes widened.

"Or perhaps the note was somehow slipped into your mail on Friday," Bragg said.

Francesca met his gaze. Their eyes briefly held and she thought, admiringly, he is very clever, indeed.

Bragg turned to her father and brother. "Andrew, Evan, I am afraid I must ask you to leave, as well, as I have a tremendous amount of work to do. I must speak with the Burtons privately."

"We understand," Cahill said, and he paused before Bragg, slapping his shoulder. "Good luck, Rick. If anyone can solve this case, I am confident that it is you."

Bragg nodded, but he did not smile, in fact, he was deathly grim. And in that single moment, it occurred to Francesca just what Bragg was up against, and the amount of pressure he faced.

Francesca felt no small amount of compassion for Bragg then. She did not know Bragg's complete employment history, but he had been the commissioner of police for exactly eighteen days—if one included today. And he was being presented with a scandalous criminal case; one that would be in the newspapers until it was solved. He could hardly know the men in his command, which might become a damaging drawback to his efforts to solve the case. And was he at all familiar with investigative work?

He caught her staring and said, "Miss Cahill. Do not go out today. I should like to interview you as well when I am finished with my business here."

Francesca blinked. Why would he wish to interview her? He had already interviewed her, just moments ago. Trepidation filled her instantly, but so did an odd little fluttering of excitement. For she wanted nothing more than to help him solve the ghastly crime. "Very well," she said earnestly. And her plans to go to the public library were instantly revised.

A pair of patrolmen escorted her, her father, and Evan home. Shortly afterward, their house was also blocked off from the public by half a dozen uniformed guards.

Julia had descended from her apartments, and in the drawing room, she, Evan, and Francesca's father discussed the terrible abduction.

Francesca walked into her father's library and stood by the door, staring at the massive desk where she had, last night, found the bizarre note.

A is for ants. What could that mean?

An image of the tiny creatures marching in the sand toward their nest filled her mind, and she dismissed it. Why had the note been left on her father's desk in the Cahill home and not at the Burtons'?

Had the criminal been so clever as to hope to be misleading?

But there was another possibility. What if the note had not been left on this desk? What if it had been deposited earlier in the day through their mail slot on the front door? Erroneously, as Bragg had suggested?

Her hands flew to her head and she paced. But wouldn't that mean that the note had been left *before* the abduction? Francesca found that unlikely; still, it was possible. If so, it meant that the criminal was very confident—but it also meant that he was very *stupid*. Because he had erroneously put the note in the wrong mail slot!

However, it would not be the first time such an error had occurred. Occasionally the Cahills received the Burtons' mail and vice versa.

Francesca was excited. The latter seemed to be a plausible explanation—but that meant they were dealing with one criminal, not two. Didn't it?

She couldn't wait to share her theory with Bragg.

Then, as she was about to leave the library, she paused. Maybe she had better keep her suspicions to herself, for now. He did not seem to want her help.

Suddenly she glanced across the large, luxurious room, in the other direction. A number of sofas and chairs were assembled in various seating arrangements. Her father's favorite chair faced the massive hearth at a right angle. Next to it was a round, leather-inlaid table. At the table's claw-footed base was a newspaper and magazine rack.

Francesca wandered over, sat down, and pulled out half

a dozen papers, including *Harper's Weekly*, the *Times* and the *Herald*. Instinct made her open *Harper's*, which they received on Mondays.

It took her less than a minute to find the cartoon and she almost giggled, despite the tragedy of the abduction.

Rick Bragg was dressed like a cowboy, in cowboy boots with spurs, chaps, a vest, bandanna, and cowboy hat. He was riding a nag—but the nag was bucking wildly. Somehow holding the reins, he was also holding and firing two six-shooters. But more importantly, the nag was attached to a police wagon, and it seemed to be pulling the wagon along on a wild, frantic ride. And in that wagon was the mayor, wide-eyed and panicked, another man with a badge that said "Chief of Police," and two uniformed patrolmen with their leather helmets. Their expressions of wide-eyed fear and dismay were comical.

But even more comical were the bundles of money sprouting out of all three police officers' pockets.

The caption read: "Will Commissioner Bragg drag the police department with him? To reform or not is the question!"

Bragg's expression was so perfect, it was blazingly fierce, as if he did intend to drag every reluctant policeman right along with him, come hell or high water.

She laid *Harper's* on the end table, her thoughts going back to Jonny Burton. Now what?

There hadn't been a ransom demand. Not yet, she reminded herself. But she just could not get that fact out of her head. And the note was so strange . . .

Her mother's guest list would undoubtedly be upstairs in her parlor on her secrétaire. Francesca hesitated for a single heartbeat, and then she took off.

A maid was changing the bed, Francesca saw through the open door, which attached the parlor to the bedroom. Francesca ignored the girl, going right to the eighteenth-century desk. She sat down, rummaged among the letters there, and found the list. Quickly, she scanned it.

She could not rule out that the culprit had been a guest, even though probability dictated that it was some poor servant seeking a ransom. Or even a crook from the Bowery, coming uptown to prey upon the wealthy. Still, how could she not make a copy of her mother's guest list? Just in case she might find it useful in the future . . .

Francesca calculated that Bragg would be at the Burton home for many hours, for he had clearly stated his intentions to interview the entire household and staff. She could copy the list within an hour—last night they'd had perhaps a hundred and fifty guests. Taking the list, Francesca hurried to her own room. Excitement filled her.

But she had hardly begun the task she had set herself when the grandfather clock in the corner of the room began to chime. Francesca started and turned. It was noon.

A is for Ants. If you want to see the boy, be at Mott and Hester streets tomorrow at 1 P.M.

Francesca stared at the clock as it finished chiming. She was on her feet.

She did not know exactly where Mott and Hester streets were, but from some of the city guidebooks that she had read—in the wake of Jacob Riis's book—she knew they were downtown, in an unsavory and unsafe neighborhood. She also knew she should not be thinking what she was thinking—which was that if she left now, she could be at Mott and Hester by one o'clock.

What was she doing?

Francesca's heart raced with alarming speed, and now she paced. She knew Jonny. She knew him far better than she did Eliza, but she admired the other woman greatly. What if she could help the little boy?

What if she got in the way?

Francesca shook her head angrily. She was an intelligent and resourceful woman. What if she *could* help? God knew, Bragg had his hands full, being the new commissioner, with the city's hopes running high that he would finally make a difference and reform the city's police department. Besides, he would undoubtedly be there, along with a number of patrolmen and detectives. It wouldn't be that terribly dangerous.

He would kill her at first sight.

She would need a disguise.

Her decision was made, and Francesca had no intention of thinking twice. She ran out of her bedroom, and saw a maid passing in the hall. "Betsy! Come here."

And she dragged the passing housemaid into her room, locking the door behind them.

"Miz Cahill," Betsy said, eyes wide, appearing confused and somewhat surprised. "Did I do something wrong?"

"No, not at all. Give me all your clothes!"

She had left her carriage two blocks away from the corner where she now crouched in her disguise, on Mulberry Street, almost but not quite comforted by the fact that it was a mere three blocks from police headquarters. Francesca's heart felt as if it were wedged in her throat. Excitement filled her, but so did fear.

She was crouching against the wall of a tenement building, the kind which she wished to eradicate. In fact, she was in the kind of neighborhood she had only read about; it was one thing to ladle soup to the poor from the kitchen of a church, and it was another to stand where she now stood, in disguise, without a servant, surrounded by every imaginable type of person. The crowd moving up and down both Mott and Hester streets were bundled up in ragged clothes, oblivious to the cold. The reason for the general indifference to the frigid winter weather was immediately obvious; there were six saloons crowded around the busy intersection and their business was robust, indeed. It was Sunday, and it was illegal to serve liquor until midnight, except in hotels, during meals, but working men, mostly of German descent, were stumbling in and out of the various establishments, in various degrees of inebriation. Some of them were openly swilling beer from their

cups. Women were drinking, too, but on the street; one of
them even had a pail filled with beer. Hoodlums loitered
on every stoop, as did beggars, both male and female,
some young, some old. Vendors were hawking various
wares on Hester Street—earmuffs, mittens, and pharma-
ceutical remedies—mostly to hordes of Russian women,
their heads wrapped in scarves. Raggedly clothed children
raced through the crowds. Francesca actually watched one
little girl slip her hand into a man's coat pocket, extracting
his purse and running away without the man's ever noticing.

Other vendors were hawking "hot" meat pies and "delicious" pigs' feet. Meanwhile, ladies of ill repute sat in
the windowsills above the ground-floor establishments,
shockingly clad, loudly taunting and ridiculing those passing below.

On the street, the occasional buggy or dray passed by,
empty of wares.

Francesca felt as if she had entered a very strange and
foreign land. It was the land Jacob Riis had described so
accurately in his famous book.

She was cold and she shivered. To further her disguise
she was wearing a huge hooded cloak, with the hood
pulled up so no one might remark her face. But Betsy's
cloak was threadbare; Francesca had already decided to
buy her another one. She had also placed a pillow in her
dress, as Betsy was quite plump.

There were some old men on the stoop near where she
stood, swilling ale and playing dice, but Francesca ignored
them. She was starting to regret her decision to come to
the Lower East Side. For even in her disguise, she felt as
if she stood out like a sore thumb.

And Bragg waited on the opposite corner in his suit,
bowler hat, and long brown overcoat, making no attempt
to blend into the crowd.

Passersby gave him a wide berth. And far too many

wary glances to count. He had "policeman" written all over him, Francesca thought nervously.

He was impatient and it showed as he paced back and forth in a very tight space, looking around constantly. His gaze was everywhere. Too many times he actually looked directly her way, making Francesca duck and hide.

Of course, Francesca was quite certain that even though he was looking in her direction, he was not gazing at her. There was no way that he could discern who she was while in her disguise.

But where was the criminal responsible for Jonny Burton's abduction and the odd note?

Francesca had arrived about twenty minutes ago, and although she had no watch, she was certain it was at least ten past one. Bragg was even now pulling out his own pocketwatch, snapping it open and snapping it closed. And then he paced again. Even from a distance, his expression was fierce.

Francesca suddenly realized that she was not merely cold, she needed to answer nature's call. Blast it, she thought, resolved to ignore the growing discomfort.

"Mum. Can you spare a nickel or two? Or maybe even a half-dollar?" A small boyish voice came from behind.

Francesca flinched and met the dark, sloe-eyed gaze of a dark-haired boy with a pinched white face. He grinned at her. The tip of his nose was dark with soot. So were his cheeks. "Please? Me mum's sick an' we ain't got nuthin' to eat."

Francesca stooped lower. "I'm sorry, but I cannot get into my purse now," she said, meaning it. For if Bragg happened to see, she would be unmasked immediately.

His eyes widened. "I thought you was a rich un. You be a lady, huh? An' why are you crouchin' like that? An' why do you have a pillow in your coat?"

Francesca blinked, then, flushing and furious, said, "Go away!"

He came closer, no longer holding out his hand. And

he stared at her face, still hidden by the hood. He finally said, "The pillow's comin' down just like a baby." And he grinned.

Francesca looked down just in time to see the pillow land between her feet. "Blast," she ground out, kicking it behind her. She crouched lower. "Boy, go away this instant, and I mean it!"

He smiled at her, revealing two deep dimples. He was probably ten or eleven years old. "Not unless you give me a dollar or two," he said slyly.

He had raised his price and she could not believe it. "I may give you a wallop," she finally said.

"Just try," he retorted, and locked gazes with her. " 'Cause I'll scream my head off 'n' the fox will come and then what will you be, lady?"

"Fox?" she finally managed. This was not going well.

He tossed a glance at Bragg. "Over there. Gent in the suit and bowler hat. Leatherheads everywhere, yes, ma'am." He seemed very satisfied.

Briefly, Francesca closed her eyes, filing away the boy's street slang. Then her eyes snapped open. "Does 'leatherhead' mean what I think it means?"

He was cheerful. "Yep. Flies thicker than bees," he said.

"Flies? As in 'policemen'?"

He nodded. "All over the place, today. But—uh-oh. Here we go," he cried.

A police wagon was coming up the street. The four grays pulling it were being whipped along at a ferocious pace. Bragg's head whipped up, and there was no mistaking his shock. Sergeants and patrolmen spilled from the wagon, rushing to one of the saloons. One policeman kicked the front door in, so hard that it sagged off most of its hinges. Bragg started shouting. The policemen in uniform raced inside the establishment, clubs upraised. And Francesca realized what was happening.

She was witnessing a crackdown on the violation of the Sunday blue laws. The police were closing down the saloon for serving liquor illegally on the Sabbath.

And Bragg was throwing the sergeant against the wall, shouting at him, his face flushed with rage. Francesca could imagine why. The police raid would ruin contact with the crooks responsible for Jonny's abduction. Apparently, lines of communication had been seriously crossed.

And suddenly a huge man was standing not far from Bragg, who had apparently finished shouting at the sergeant. Francesca stared at the man, clad in a poor baggy brown jacket and dirty brown boots. He looked as disreputable as anyone she had thus far seen that morning, and she just knew that he was the criminal intending to make contact with Bragg.

Bragg also saw him.

But the big, dark man in the loose jacket and gray trousers turned and walked into another saloon.

"Darnation," Francesca cried in consternation.

And she thought she heard Bragg shout, "Get that man!"

Which was precisely when she realized that the boy who had been so annoying was racing into the street. She suddenly comprehended what he was doing—he was making a beeline for Bragg, while two patrolmen were entering the saloon where the big hoodlum had disappeared. Francesca's eyes widened even more. The beggar boy pressed something into Bragg's hand, and then he turned and fled.

Bragg looked down at a crumpled piece of paper. Then he glanced up, and took off after the boy. The two of them disappeared from Francesca's view on Mott Street.

"Oh, dear God," she said, straightening now and tossing off her hood.

That blasted little boy, the one who had tried to blackmail her for a few dollars, had been the contact with whoever was responsible for the abduction. He was working for the criminal responsible for the abduction! And she had been conversing with him . . . Francesca just stood there, not able to believe it.

Cries and shouts were coming from the saloon across the street, as was the sound of furniture being tossed around or broken. Apparently, there was opposition to the forced closing, and a fight had broken out.

Francesca couldn't care less. She was still in a state of shock, and she turned, to head down Hester Street and then across to Mulberry Street where her carriage and driver were waiting.

The big, frightening man smiled down at her. "Hello, lovey," he said.

It was the hoodlum who had seemed to want to approach Bragg, but who had instead walked into an adjacent saloon. Francesca's heart felt as if it would burst right out of her chest. Her every instinct screamed at her that this was not a welcome circumstance.

He grinned at her, revealing yellow, slimy teeth. "Now what is a rich lady like you doing down here with the likes of us poor folk?" he asked.

Francesca did not have to think twice. She produced her purse, shoving it at him. "Here," she said, and she turned and ran.

But she only took two steps. For he had caught her hood, and he yanked her so hard back around that she fell against his huge barrel chest.

"I think it's my lucky day," he said, laughing.

His breath stank. But not of beer, gin, or rum, nor even of tobacco, it just stank of rot and decay. Francesca tried to press herself away, but his grip tightened on her arms, and she screamed.

He smiled, pulled her close, and pressed his stinking mouth to her face.

Francesca jammed her one-inch heel as hard as she could into the top of his foot, and he pulled back with a cry. She was still trapped in his grip, and she screamed again and again, as loudly as she could.

There must have been a hundred people on the sidewalk

and in the street. No one appeared to hear her, which was impossible, and if they did, no one cared.

And all of the police were inside the damned saloon they were trying to close down. It sounded as if a riot were taking place there.

"That wasn't very mannerly of you, little lady," the hoodlum said, and his mouth was downturned.

Francesca looked into narrow black eyes and it truly hit her then—she was in very serious jeopardy, indeed.

When he cried out.

Francesca looked down as he grunted again, and was confronted with the sight of the beggar boy kicking the bejesus out of the ruffian's shins. The little boy would not stop.

Francesca lifted her knee, hard, into the man's private parts.

He finally released her, howling, dropping to the ground.

"Run, lady, run," the boy shouted, grabbing her hand.

"No, this way." Francesca pulled him around and they set off through the throng, pushing past women and children, mindless of everything except escaping that horrible man.

Francesca had to look over her shoulder. He was following them!

"Blast it," she panted, for she thought his intentions had now changed. Rape was not on his mind, revenge was. Revenge, and maybe even murder.

"Faster, lady, can't you run faster?" the boy shouted, ahead of her now, but then, he was an expert at weaving his way through the crowded street—clearly, he had done this many times before.

They turned right on Mulberry Street, which was no improvement from Hester—if anything, it was worse. Saloons, brothels, opium dens . . . they ran past every imaginable establishment of illegality and ill repute. And then Francesca espied her carriage and driver.

"There," she shouted, but she had to look back again, and he was almost close enough to reach out and seize her by her hair—which had come loose and was flying behind her like a cape.

The boy leapt into the carriage first. Francesca gripped the squabs, shouting, "Go, Jennings, go, go now!" She was still on the running boards as the coachman whipped the bay in the traces; the boy reached down, grabbed her arm, and pulled her up into the safety of the box.

Francesca turned and looked down and saw one thick hamlike hand on the door, and she met his black, furious eyes. And then the carriage sped away, leaving the thug standing in the middle of Mulberry Street, staring after them.

Francesca collapsed against the leather squabs, panting and shaking like a leaf.

"Whew," the boy said, wiping his brow. "That was close! That Gordino, he's no good, a real rough, yes sirree."

Francesca turned and suddenly grabbed his ear, hard. He cried out. "Who are you and do you know that man and who is he?" she shouted, furious with herself and thoroughly shaken. In fact, she remained shocked. For she had been assaulted.

"You're hurting me," he squealed.

"Answer me this instant!" She pulled on his ear, with very little mercy, her insides now churning dangerously. *She had been assaulted.* That disgusting man had kissed her.

"Me name's Joel and he's Gordino an' he's real mean, he'll pop off his own mother and never think twice!"

Francesca's heart was still pounding so hard that it hurt. But now she began to shake uncontrollably, while fighting the terrible urge to vomit. Oh, God. That horrid thug had actually tried to stick his tongue inside of her mouth! She released his ear. "Pop off? What does 'pop off' mean?" She must not vomit now.

He rubbed his red ear, grimacing. "You know. Knock off. Kill. Murder."

She stared, hugging herself and trembling. "He *murders* people?"

Joel nodded, still massaging his ear.

"He murders people and he is not in jail?" Francesca could hardly believe it. She was shocked anew, and it eased her distress.

He looked at her as if she were not in possession of any degree of normal mental ability. "He's been in the Tombs more times than a body knows." He shrugged. "Guess them flies got more use fer him on the street."

Francesca was staring when she realized that she was being stared at, as well. She lifted her gaze and saw a larger carriage keeping pace with her brougham, and sitting in the passenger seat was Bragg. Her heart sank like a rock.

He gestured at her. "Pull over," he said.

Francesca stared, then hurried to obey. "Jennings." She tapped on the window partition. "Please halt the carriage." This was not good, she thought. No, this was definitely not good.

Bragg's carriage pulled over, angling in front of them in such a way as to block her carriage from moving forward—should she even try to do so. Francesca's apprehension increased.

"Damnation," Joel cried, and he was suddenly scrambling across Francesca's lap in a mad dash to leap out of the other side of the carriage.

Bragg jumped in, caught him by the shoulder just as he gripped the door handle, and pushed him down into the seat. "Sit," he said.

Joel sat. In fact, he sat as still as a statue. His white cheeks were now red.

Bragg calmly sat down opposite Francesca. "Good afternoon, Miss Cahill."

Francesca could not summon up a reply.

He did not turn, but he tapped on the window partition. "Driver. Three hundred Mulberry, please."

Oddly, Jennings did not hesitate. He moved the carriage backward and then around the commissioner's carriage, and back into the street.

Francesca did not like the way events were developing, oh no. "Where are we going?" she asked with great trepidation.

He finally smiled at her. "Police headquarters," he said.

CHAPTER
4

Francesca sucked in her breath, loudly. "Why are we going to police headquarters?" she asked. As if she did not know. He was furious with her; how could she have thought, even for a moment, to help solve the abduction?

His gaze was benign. "We have matters to discuss."

She tried not to fidget. The five-story brownstone, which she had passed earlier on her way to Mott and Hester streets, was already in view, just up the block. Of course, she had never before seen the police headquarters, although upon occasion, there had been a drawing in the *Times*. Now she stared with open curiosity; a curiosity that could not ease her nerves. Several patrolmen were loitering on the sidewalk in front of the building, and there was some activity as gentlemen and patrolmen entered and left the premises. "Commissioner, I would love to discuss whatever it is that is on your mind, but I am afraid I am running late and I must be getting home." She managed a smile, hoping against all odds to avoid an unpleasant interview with him.

He smiled in return and said nothing as Jennings braked the carriage directly in front of the entrance to the building.

Francesca glanced at Joel, her trepidation rising. She reached for his hand, perhaps to comfort herself as well as him. The boy was clearly restless—Francesca had the feeling that he would bolt and run given the slightest opportunity to do so.

Bragg leapt down from the carriage, then held his hand out to help her down. Francesca accepted it, acutely aware of his touch. She drew uneasily away as Bragg's own carriage halted behind hers. Two detectives were already escorting Joel from the brougham, as well.

Bragg gestured for her to precede him up the stairs and into the building. As she did so, she asked, "What are you going to do with the boy?" For one of the detectives, a tall, husky man, had his hand clamped down hard on the thin child's shoulder. Joel was complaining vocally about it, too. "Damn blast tarnation!" he shouted.

"He has information that I want," Bragg said, as if he had not heard the child's cursing.

Francesca did not like the sound of that. Her worry increased. Bragg was so grim. It did not bode well for either of them. And they paused in the front reception room.

Francesca glanced around, wide-eyed, briefly forgetting what might lie before her. She had never been inside a police precinct before, much less police headquarters. Several officers stood behind a desk, faced with rows of benches and a milling crowd of men, some in uniform, some not. Francesca could hear the occasional sound of a typewriter, the constant pinging of the telegraph, and the intermittent ringing of telephones. One very scruffy and dangerous-looking man was standing in manacles between two roundsmen. And suddenly every horror story that she had read about the police department came to mind.

Innocent passersby being brutally clubbed by roundsmen. The innocent being jailed for days on end in the most wretched of conditions, for crimes they had not committed. But surely, that was not her fate. After all, she was a Cahill and Bragg was friendly with her father.

She imagined the worst that would happen was that she would receive a polite setdown. Yet another glance at his face caused her anxiety to spiral upward. And what about poor Joel?

"Bragg," she began valiantly, returning her attention to Joel. She smiled at him reassuringly. "He is a little boy—"

"Thompson, escort Miss Cahill to my office." He looked at Francesca. "I will be a few moments, and you may wait for me until I return." Clearly there were no ifs, ands or buts about it and he turned and signaled his men, who followed him up the stairs with Joel.

Joel flung one last glance over his shoulder at Francesca, and his plea was obvious.

Francesca tried to smile at him, but her expression felt weak and feeble.

"Miss Cahill?" The detective smiled at her, gesturing her toward the elevator.

Francesca was hugging herself. Bragg had been curt and brusque—not a good sign. She realized she had no choice. She entered the cage, and a moment later found herself alone in Bragg's office on the second floor, the door closed firmly behind her.

Her trepidation began to vanish in the face of her growing curiosity. She looked eagerly around, trying to remind herself that curiosity had killed the cat and that in the past, at times, her snooping and prying had engendered some disagreeable conclusions.

Her mental battle failed. She smiled and studied his desk, approaching it. His desk was about half the size of her father's, and every inch was covered with books and papers and folders; a telephone sat on one end, as well. Clearly he was a prolific reader; clearly he did not shy away from a huge workload. A swivel chair with a woven cane seat and back was behind the desk, but it was turned away, as if he had last been looking out of the window onto the street. Francesca smiled, imagining him sitting there, lost in thought and deliberation. She turned. There was a fireplace on the adjacent wall, a clock above the mantel. Numerous photographs were propped on the mantelpiece.

Facing his desk were two rather sorry-looking chairs;
once, she supposed, they had been a pleasant shade of
green, now they were brown and stained. The small rug
between the desk and the chairs was threadbare and torn.

His office needed a woman's touch.

Francesca walked over to the mantel and could not re-
frain from picking up a photograph of Bragg and Seth
Low. They were smiling and shaking hands; they were
standing on the steps of City Hall. She suspected the photo
had been taken on New Year's Day, the day of Low's
taking office and the day of Bragg's appointment.

She glanced at the other photos. Bragg with Carnegie,
Bragg with her father and two other gentlemen she did not
recognize, Bragg with Platt and Theodore Roosevelt—undoubtedly before he had become President of the United
States. Francesca was impressed.

There was also a photograph of him standing with a
dozen gentlemen on the wide front steps of the Union
Club, and another of him with an elderly man standing
across the street from the Fifth Avenue Hotel. The last
picture at one end of the mantel held Francesca's attention
the longest. He stood with his arm around the waist of a
very attractive woman, behind three smiling, freshly
scrubbed children, two boys and a little girl.

His family? She felt an unfamiliar pang. She really
knew nothing about him; she assumed he was a bachelor
because she hadn't read anything about his being married,
or she didn't recall having read that he had a wife, and he
had been at the ball last night alone. She stared at the
photograph for another moment, trying to find a resemblance between the woman and Bragg. She couldn't find
any, but what was worse, she thought the children did re-
semble him more than a little bit.

Suddenly disturbed, perhaps even dismayed, she walked
over to the window behind his desk, chastising herself for
snooping into his private affairs—which were none of her
concern. She stared down at Mulberry Street.

Snow still clung to the curbs, but it was already blackened from dirt and manure. It was so little different from Mott or Hester streets, she thought, amazed. For the crowd below looked like an assortment of ruffians and scoundrels, beggars and pickpockets. How could so many scoundrels go about their illicit if not illegal affairs right in view of the police department? For even as she stared down, she watched two men brawling violently, fists flying. One finally landed in the gutter in a heap, causing a bevy of pigeons to take flight—directly at the feet of a pair of patrolmen. They looked the other way, pretending not to see.

Francesca turned away, but not before she saw a woman open her coat and flash her mostly naked body at a man. She shook her head in disbelief.

Then she had to look again. The woman was accepting something from the man—cash, Francesca assumed—and she was then leading him across the street. Eyes wide, Francesca watched them walk down into a basement-level establishment. She could guess what would happen next.

Her thoughts returned to Bragg. What did he want? If only he had evinced the slightest degree of compassion or even friendliness earlier. But he had not, he had been brusque and abrupt. He had been all business. He had been the commissioner of police.

Of course she knew what he wanted. He would demand to know just what she had been doing on Mott and Hester streets. And what would she say? What excuse could she make? Especially as he knew that she had read the note left for the Burtons?

Francesca closed her eyes. If only she knew what the second note had said! If only she could speak with Joel herself. In fact, she would give an arm and a leg to be a fly on the wall right now, listening to Bragg question the boy.

She *had* to know what the second note said. It *had* to be a ransom demand.

And as Francesca thought about it, her gaze fell on the notes left on the very top of all the papers and books on Bragg's desk.

Her heart began to pound.

She looked at the door of the office. The top half was glass. But it was so thick and opaque that it was creamy white and one could not see out of the room, or into it, either. Francesca wet her lips, *knowing* she should not snoop, and then she walked right over to the desk. She hesitated.

If he walked in while she was searching his desk for clues, she would be in very serious trouble, indeed. Was it a crime to search a police commissioner's desk? She imagined it might be.

Careful not to touch anything, Francesca edged closer, until Betsy's cloak brushed the edge of the desk. She stared down at the handwritten notes left carelessly atop the mess.

"Ants," she read. "Ants, sand, woods, park, Central Park? Fields, dirt, grass." The words were scribbled haphazardly across the page. Also scribbled, off center, were two additional words: "Burton" and "enemies." Heavy slashes underlined them.

And that was all.

"Darnation," she breathed. Francesca quickly reached out and flipped the page. The page below was blank.

She scanned the desk. Nothing else seemed pertinent to the Burton case. Just to be certain, after another quick look at the closed and unmoving door, she opened one beige folder, saw names that she did not recognize, and then she flipped it closed.

She tried to think. No one knew what time Jonny Burton had been abducted from his bed. She would have to find that fact out, as precisely as possible. She wondered if Bragg had narrowed the window from eight P.M. to one A.M. If only she could interview the Burtons' servants herself.

Bragg would have been summoned from his bed shortly

after one A.M. He had been at the Burton house at ten that morning. Francesca couldn't imagine when he had been able to stop by his office to make the few notes that he had, but perhaps he had done so just before the one o'clock appointment on Mott and Hester streets. In any case, he hadn't spent very much time in his office since the abduction, which would explain the paucity of notes and related material on his desk.

Francesca could not help herself. Frightened now, she quickly moved a few books and folders aside, but found nothing at a glance. She wet her lips, debated opening up at least one drawer. And that was when he stepped inside.

She smiled at him; he stared. She was merely standing behind his desk, thank God. Had he walked in even an instant earlier, he would have caught her with her hand in the cookie jar, indeed.

His gaze went from her brittle smile to his desk. He closed the door behind him, slowly. "Are you looking for something?" he asked, staring as he came forward.

He was in his shirtsleeves and vest, having taken off his suit jacket; his sleeves were rolled up to his elbows, revealing muscular forearms dusted with dark hair. His tie had been thoroughly loosened, as well, revealing the strong hollow of his throat. "Of course not," Francesca cried, and she smiled brightly again. Do not overdo it, she warned herself. He was astute and he was no fool. He could sense what he had not seen. "I was merely looking at the view." She was amazed at how easily she lied.

His eyes narrowed as he approached his desk, and then he settled one buttock on the edge, facing her at an angle. "The view? Oh, let's see, you mean the wonderful view of pickpockets, hooks, and crooks?"

She straightened. He was not being particularly nice right now. "I have never been to this part of the city before, and you do not have to be mocking."

He started. "I apologize." Then his gaze moved from her face to his notes. "Find anything you liked?"

Francesca felt her cheeks heat dramatically. "Your notes caught my eye," she finally admitted. "I apologize," she added guiltily.

And suddenly he sighed, rubbing his temples. With his gaze downturned, Francesca could stare openly, and she found herself doing so. He seemed terribly tired, terribly worn. His face was drawn, his tie was askew. No small amount of compassion moved her. "I'm sorry," she whispered softly. The last thing she wished to do was to add to his burdens.

His head snapped up and their gazes locked, and then he was on his feet, and any vulnerability that she thought she had seen was gone. "Sit down, Miss Cahill," he said. And the tone was very similar to the one he had used with Joel in her carriage just half an hour ago.

It was a tone that caused her anxiety to spiral anew. Francesca sank down in his chair. She found herself gripping the edge of the desk. "I can explain."

"Really? I cannot wait. Please feel free. Feel free to tell me what possessed you to go to Mott and Hester streets."

She looked into a pair of uncompromising golden eyes. "I wanted to help," she said, low.

"Help? Help?" His voice was rising. "Is getting yourself raped by that rough Gordino helping? Is it?" He was shouting.

She was thoroughly taken aback. "How—how did you know?"

"Our little friend told me," he said, having recovered some degree of composure, but not all of it. He was standing now, his hard legs braced apart, and he was clearly angry. "I am still waiting for an explanation."

It was hard to speak. "I am so fond of that boy," she said, and they both knew she meant Jonny Burton. "This is an outrage. I thought he might be present, I thought you might need my help if he was present," she cried. His brows lifted with more disbelief. Francesca did not pause and give him a chance to speak. She too was on her feet.

"The note Joel gave you. Was that from the wretch who abducted him? Is it a ransom demand? Did Joel tell you who he is working for? Do you know or suspect who abducted Jonny?"

His eyes went wide. And then he snapped, "Sit down."

Francesca did not think twice about it; she sat.

And he was leaning over the desk, leaning over her. "There is a recently enacted statute on the books," he said, low. "Are you aware that it is a felony to obstruct a criminal investigation?"

She stiffened. "What?"

"You, Miss Cahill, could be charged with obstructing a criminal investigation. Are you aware of that?" He leaned closer.

She shook her head no, drawing back.

"So then you are not aware of just how serious those charges are?" he pressed, still leaning over her. Their faces were not very far apart. Yet her spine was already digging into the back of the chair; if she leaned back any further, she might very well topple over. She was afraid to breathe.

And did she detect the slightest whiff of whiskey on his breath, mingling with his musky cologne?

"Well?" he demanded.

"No, I am not," Francesca whispered, shaken to the quick.

"You have committed a crime, Miss Cahill," he said, holding her eyes with his. She did not dare even blink. "A very serious crime. If one were convicted of such a crime, one could serve up to ten years in a *federal* penitentiary."

Francesca felt rather faint. She had never intended to commit any crime. "Are you intending to prosecute me, Commissioner?" she finally heard herself say.

It was as if he had not heard her; either that, or he was so agitated that he ignored her. He straightened. "As commissioner of the police department, I could put you in jail right this very minute, and leave you there, until I decided whether to proceed against you." His eyes were as dark as storm clouds.

She blinked frantically, then somehow found the last shreds of her courage and dignity. She stood so abruptly that her chair scrapped nosily back, toppling over at last. Neither one of them even looked at it. "Commissioner," she said, as firmly as possible, given the fact that she was not used to being shouted at by attractive men. "Should you do so, should you even try, I doubt you would have this position for very long." And she imagined her own eyes flashed because she was scared—but now she was also angry. How dare he threaten her.

His eyes widened dramatically. And then he choked, "You threaten *me*?"

Francesca was afraid she had made a mistake. But no one, ever in her life, had set her down and threatened her the way that Bragg had. Of course, he did have some right. But on the other hand, she wasn't one of the prostitutes on the street just below them. She wasn't a shop girl or a sales clerk. She was Andrew Cahill's daughter. She deserved respect. And her father was a friend of Platt's. In fact, he was an even better friend of Roosevelt's. Should he choose, Francesca had no doubt that Bragg's head would roll, sooner rather than later.

Francesca said, "It was hardly gentlemanly to threaten *me*, Commissioner."

Their gazes had locked, and it seemed irrevocable. He said, "I never claimed to be a gentleman, Miss Cahill."

Francesca did not like the sound of that. Every man she knew was a gentleman—or outwardly seemed to be. She could not think of a response. She could only stare—or, perhaps, gape.

"You may go home," he said finally, folding his arms across his chest. "And I am certain that in the future you will let police affairs alone."

She had to nod. "I will try."

He shook his head in amazement. "Please, do more than try." Then, seriously, "I have no time to look after you, Miss Cahill. I am afraid that my hands, currently, are quite full."

Francesca was beginning to feel bad for adding to his worries. "I am sorry," she said, meaning it with all of her heart. "I really had no intention of interfering with your investigation."

He seemed to accept that, and this time, when their gazes met, it was without anger on his part, and without anxiety on hers. Immediately they both looked elsewhere, anywhere but at one another.

His office suddenly seemed *very* small. Too small, in fact, for the two of them.

"Can you find your way down?" he asked, moving behind his desk and reaching for the telephone.

"Of course." But Francesca hesitated.

His brows lifted as he began to speak.

"The boy. Joel. What is to become of him?" she quickly asked.

Bragg set the receiver back on its hook. "Do not concern yourself with Kennedy."

"Is that his last name?"

"Yes, it is. Now, if you will excuse me?" The receiver was in his hand again.

"Please tell me that you are not tossing him into some wretched cell with a group of thugs."

He set the receiver back on its hook. "Miss Cahill, Joel Kennedy might appear to be a child, but he is far more jaded than either you or I."

"What does that mean? He is only a child," Francesca cried, worried now. "Where is he? Are you going to arrest him for his part in this—his tiny little part?"

"Kennedy is a well-known pickpocket," Bragg returned with exasperation. "Here." He opened a drawer and tossed a book on the desk.

"What is this?" Francesca said, picking it up. As she opened it, she saw photographs filling up both pages. Each man had his name printed below each photo, with words like "cracksman," "pickpocket," "pennyweighter," and "sandbagger." The next page contained the photographs of eight women. Every single one of them was a "shoplifter."

"That is a mug book, developed by one of my predecessors. I find it useful, although the last commissioner did not, and we are intent upon updating it immediately. Keep turning the pages," he instructed.

She did. And there was the exact likeness of Joel, with his full name printed below, and below that, the word "kid." "I thought you said he is a pickpocket?"

"He is. A 'kid' is a child pickpocket. Kennedy is in trouble more often than not, and if I were you, I would not feel sorry for him."

She closed the book and set it down on his desk. "He saved me from that ruffian, Commissioner."

Bragg stared.

Francesca stared back, allowing him a moment to absorb what she had said. "What will happen to him, now?"

"He will spend the night at the Tombs, and perhaps tomorrow he will be released."

She folded her arms. She was afraid of what might happen to the boy in a jail filled with men like Gordino. "Are you charging him with a crime?"

Bragg's jaw was tight. "Good day, Miss Cahill."

"He is just a boy," she said fervently, "and he was only the messenger!"

He sat down in his chair, lifted the phone, and spoke to the operator. A moment later he was speaking tersely to someone on the other end. As if Francesca were already gone.

Having no other choice, she left his office.

Jennings had barely taken her two full blocks when Francesca spotted a very familiar small figure weaving amongst the crowds on Lafayette Street. She actually stood up, in order to to get a better view. It was the kid, Joel Kennedy.

And the way he was rushing along, flinging glances over his shoulder, it was clear that he was in fear of being pursued—it was clear that he had, somehow, run away from the police.

"Jennings!" Francesca turned and banged hard on the window partition; as she did so, the carriage hit a pothole and she was thrown against the front of the cab. "Pull over," she cried.

The brougham had not even been braked before Francesca flung open the door, leaping out and falling on the slick, icy cobbled street. She glanced backward, but did not see any policemen at all. Then she rushed after Joel Kennedy. "Joel! Stop! Joel!"

He paused and turned and saw her, then ran on.

"I want to help!" she screamed, running after him. "Let me help! Joel, come back!"

Suddenly he halted in his tracks, and an instant later, Francesca was hustling him up into her carriage. And still there was no sign of blue uniforms in pursuit. "Jennings! Home, and quickly, please!"

The carriage took off, tuning north onto Fourth Avenue, racing alongside the New York and Hudson Railroad tracks. Francesca sat facing forward, facing Joel, who bounced along in the opposite seat. "Are you all right?" she asked, her gaze sweeping over every visible inch of him. And she meant her words.

His thick dark brows, as jet-black as his hair, slashed together. And then he shook his head.

"What happened?" she cried.

"That big beefy spot, he hit me, he did. Hard." He looked grimly at her, and his mouth began to tremble.

Francesca stared, appalled. "What!"

He scowled at her. "I hate them *po*-lice," he spat. "Every single stupid-brained one of them."

She saw no bruises on his face, but he was otherwise

covered from head to toe, huddled in his worn and grimy overcoat. "I cannot believe it. Where did he hit you? Do you need a doctor?"

He looked at her. "Miz Cahill, an' if'n I did need a doctor, jest how would I pay him?"

She did not hesitate. "You would not have to worry about that," she said.

He seemed to deliberate her words, and then he seemed to relax. "He hit me on the back. Betcha it's all red. An' you?" he said cautiously. "Guess they didn't hit you."

Francesca might have laughed under other circumstances. "No, but I was threatened with being thrown in jail for committing a crime."

He was incredulous. "No! That sly fox, the commissioner, he threatened *you*?" Joel was clearly disbelieving.

Francesca smiled a little and nodded as a train raced past them, heading south. Momentarily, the noise of steel wheels on the steel tracks was deafening. When the train had passed, she said, "How on earth did you escape?"

He smiled proudly then. "It was easy. I knocked over a cigarette and started a fire, and with all the ruckus, I just ran out. Them oafs can't catch me!"

She had to smile. "Let me take you home. Where do you live?"

He looked at her as if she had gone mad. "Anywhere. Everywhere," he said.

She started. "But—where are your parents? Are you an orphan?"

He nodded somberly. "Me dad died when I was a babe, of the pox." Francesca winced. "Me mum died when I was six. Tu-bur-cu-ly-o-sis," he said.

"Tuberculosis," she corrected automatically, her heart going out to him and no mind that he was a thief. "But where do you live? Where do you sleep?"

"I don't live anywhere," he said with an indifferent shrug. "I ain't got nothin', anyways. An' I sleep where I feels like it. Mostly on stoops, sometimes in garbage,

'cause it's warm"—he was briefly defiant—"an' sometimes I even climb in people's houses." He smiled then,
as if proud of the feat.

"Well," Francesca said promptly, "how would you like
to sleep in a nice warm bed, with a roof over your head?"
She did not even have to reflect upon her decision. "How
would you like three hot meals every single day?"

He blinked at her. Then his eyes narrowed with suspicion. "Miz Cahill," he said, "I ain't going to no orphans'
asylum. No sirree."

She shook her head and reached out to pat his small
hand. He wore rags wrapped around the palms, and his
bare fingers were red and icy cold to the touch. "You'd
have to work, honestly, for the bed and the meals. But I
am sure we can use you in the stables. You'd even be paid
a small wage for your efforts." She smiled. "What do you
say?"

He looked at her and did not reply at once.

"Surely you would not prefer to go back to living on
the street?"

"I hate living like a dog," he said passionately.

"Then it's settled."

"Mebbe."

She was startled. "What is it, Joel? I won't tell the commissioner where you are, if that is what you are thinking."

"No, that's not what worries me. What worries me is
that you want somethin' from me, but I don't know what."
His black gaze was unswerving.

He was right. And Francesca laughed uneasily. "I want
to help you because you are a little boy and I have the
ability to help you," she said. "I do want your help, but
only if you will give it freely."

"Mebbe. What do you want?"

He was awfully blunt, she thought. But maybe she
would be too if she lived in his circumstances. "Who gave
you the note?" she asked. "The note that you gave to Commissioner Bragg?"

"That's easy," he said with obvious relief. "That rowdy, Gordino."

"Gordino!" she exclaimed. "That dirty man who tried to kiss me and . . ." She could not continue.

"Yep. That's him."

Francesca did not believe, not for a moment, that Gordino was smart enough to even plan an abduction, much less execute one. "Do you know who his partner is?" she asked hopefully.

"Nope."

She sank back against the seats, then strained forward again. "Surely you looked at the note. What did it say?" And she found herself holding her breath.

"I can't read," he said simply.

CHAPTER
5

SUNDAY, JANUARY 19, 1902—4 P.M.

Francesca paused after stepping out of the kitchens. Joel had been left there in the hands of the Cahill housekeeper, Mrs. Ryan, with explicit instructions. He was currently being fed from a potted roast—and eating ravenously—and afterward, he would be shown to his cot in the attics above the stables, adjacent to the newly constructed garage. Tomorrow he would begin his employment as a groom, never mind that he knew nothing about horses—having never even petted one in his entire young life.

Francesca's brief moment of satisfaction vanished. She stood just outside the kitchen door, which was closed, still clad in Betsy's black dress, Betsy's cloak over her arm. On the drive home, she had tried to twist her hair up into a knot, but she had lost all of her pins, and it had proven impossible. As a result, her hair was still hanging down her back to her waist. She imagined she was quite a sight.

A challenge faced her. Could she make it undetected through the house to her room? Leaving had been easy enough—her parents and Evan had been in the drawing room, debating the Burton affair. It was hours later now, and it was also a Sunday afternoon. Evan was undoubtedly out and about. But her parents often spent Sundays at home, especially in this kind of weather. Currently she was in a back hallway, but it did not go upstairs to her room. The back stairs only led to the servants' quarters.

She had no choice, and she dreaded running into her mother. But she had to change; she had so much to do. She wanted to interview the staff about last night's affair; in fact, tomorrow she would confront the mailman. She also wanted to peruse the guest list she had taken from her mother's secrétaire as soon as she had finished copying it. But most importantly of all, she had to find out what the second note said.

Francesca started forward, refusing to recall Bragg's warnings, hurrying down the corridor, passing the empty dining room, its solid doors closed. When she reached the very back of the entry hall, which was in the center of the house, she glanced around. It was empty. Francesca strained to hear and heard nothing and no one.

Everyone must be out. Either that, or upstairs in their private apartments.

Francesca darted for the stairs. She was on the landing midway between the first and second floors when she heard someone in the front hall behind and below her. She ducked flat against the wall, certain that it was Julia.

"Francesca?"

It was too late, she had been remarked, and it was none other than Connie's husband, Montrose.

Francesca managed a smile, turning, as he came toward her.

Connie and Montrose lived around the corner on Sixty-second Street. They often stopped by to call, and as frequently dined with them. Montrose was a very big man. He was a few inches over six feet tall, and Francesca had seen him in his polo clothes, his swimming costume, and his golfing tweeds—there was no fat on his large, muscular frame. She was five feet five, but he dwarfed her—around him, she felt feminine and petite. He was also extremely attractive. His hair was thick and black, his eyes brilliantly blue, his cheekbones high, his nose straight, his jaw strong. He had a cleft in his chin.

The ladies adored him. He was always the object of their whispers and stares.

He and Connie had married four years ago. He had been widowed for some time; his first wife had died in a carriage accident just a year after their marriage. It had been a terrible tragedy. Francesca would never forget the first time she had met Montrose. He had been presented to Connie, who had been just seventeen at the time, and everyone had known the match would be made. For he needed the Cahills' wealth and Connie needed the Montrose heritage. It was as simple as that.

She had been fourteen and utterly tongue-tied. She hadn't even been able to say hello properly and it had been mortifying.

Montrose paused below her, clad in a leisure suit, his gaze sharp, taking in every inch of her appearance. "Good God. Francesca, what is going on?" he exclaimed.

Francesca felt her mouth stretch wider. She opened it, but no words came forth.

"Are you all right?" he said, eyes intent upon her, and suddenly he was on the very same landing as she was.

Francesca nodded. Why did she have to become a speechless idiot in his presence? It was still mortifying. "Hello . . . Neil." Not only did she rarely speak to him, she hardly ever uttered his name. "I'm fine . . . uh . . ."

His gaze moved over her again. Francesca felt herself flush—she hated his having caught her wearing an ugly black housemaid's dress. He might be married to Connie, and she might not be vain, but around him, she did want him to think her somewhat pleasing. Instead, undoubtedly, he thought her homely, and probably he also thought her to be a dolt.

Flustered, wanting to escape, she suddenly realized he wasn't looking at her dress. Before he glanced aside, she caught him staring at her mane of wild, golden-blond hair.

He was grim. His eyes seemed to shutter, hiding whatever he was thinking.

"What has happened, Francesca?" he asked, in a tone of voice he had undoubtedly used many times before. It was a tone of voice few who were not blue-blooded British aristocrats could ever emulate; it was the kind of tone that made one want to stiffen and salute. His regard found hers again.

Francesca wanted to come up with an elaborate lie, but her mind was failing her now, because she wondered if he had been admiring or despising her untamable hair; Connie's hair was much shorter, just to her shoulders, and it was as fine as silk. Connie had the most beautiful hair. She avoided his eyes. Determined to fabricate, she opened her mouth, but all she did was inhale. "Nothing," she managed.

His jaw tightened. "Just tell me that you are all right. Otherwise, I am going to have to speak with your father."

"No!" she cried, gripping his arm without thinking about it. As instantly, as if burned by a hot iron, she dropped her hand. Desperation fueled her words. "Please, Neil, do not mention to my father that you have seen me like this!" For Andrew would tell Julia everything.

He gripped her arm. "I thought so," he said, his face darkening.

Francesca looked down at his huge hand engulfing her wrist. She was trembling. An image of her sister crossed her mind. And she thought, helplessly, life is unfair. What if she had been the older sister?

"Are you certain you are all right? Have you been hurt?" he demanded.

"I am not hurt," she said, amazed at the extent of his concern.

He nodded and then seemed to realize he was holding her wrist. He released it. His cheeks flushed. "Francesca, you cannot do this again."

She stared. Why was he blushing? She drew back a bit,

crossing her arms tightly beneath her breasts. His gaze followed her movements. And he could not possibly know what she had been up to, could he? "I won't," she said carefully. What was he talking about? She decided to play along. "Not ever again."

"I want your promise," he returned steadily. A slight pink flush still mottled his cheekbones.

She stared and their gazes collided yet another time. She could not deceive him. She could not make a promise that she might not be able to keep. Yet she felt certain that they were not communicating clearly with one another.

"Good God!" he cried, flinging his hands up. And when they found his hips, they were fisted. "Francesca." He leaned close. "You are very young. I must tell you, and you must listen to me, whoever he is, do not rendezvous with him again."

It took Francesca a moment to realize just what he had said and just what he meant. She blinked in shock. He thought her disguise was the result of her having met a lover for a tryst!

"Well?" he demanded.

Francesca managed to shake her head. "Neil. This is not what you are thinking." But now she was aware of just how hard her heart beat. In a perverse way, she was glad he was thinking she had met a man. Perhaps he might think of her as a more interesting woman than merely Connie's odd little sister who was never coherent in his presence.

"Francesca. If this . . . bastard . . . was a gentleman, he would be courting you openly. I can only assume he is some ill-bred sort, with the worst of intentions. Look at you!" His eyes flashed.

Gentlemen did not use such language in front of a lady, and Francesca realized he was genuinely concerned for her welfare. But then, he thought of her as a sister, which was natural and right. She knew she must correct his mistaken assumptions, but instead, impulsively, she said, "Neil, I will never meet my *lover* again."

And the moment she had uttered the words, Francesca did not know who was more shocked, he or she herself.

For he just stood there staring at her as if she had spoken Greek.

Whatever had come over her? Francesca could hardly think. Absurdly, she wanted him to think her womanly enough to have had a lovers' tryst. Absurdly, she was elated because he thought her womanly enough to be someone's paramour.

Suddenly he said, "Tell me his name."

She felt her eyes widen. "What!"

His smile wasn't pleasant. "Someone needs to beat him into a bloody pulp. And clearly, that someone is myself."

Her hand covered her chest. She knew she was gaping; she could feel her mouth hanging open. He would beat this legendary lover of hers into a pulp to avenge the loss or near loss of her innocence? Francesca felt as if she had somehow entered a fairy tale.

His smile was a baring of teeth. "Francesca, the day I married your sister you became my sister, and I must tell you, right now, I am in shock."

"Nothing really happened," Francesca managed.

He tilted up her chin, forcing their eyes to meet. Francesca could not move. And finally he nodded. "I can see the truth in your eyes."

Francesca pressed back against the wall. He let her go. There was an odd, electric tension between them.

But she had never really spoken to him, and they had never, ever, been alone before.

"This is the end of it, then, as far as I am concerned, but you must abide by your word." Montrose cut into her thoughts.

She nodded. Speech escaped her once more.

His jaw flexed. "You had better get upstairs. Before Andrew or Julia remark you in such dishabille."

Francesca nodded, and she started cautiously past him. He stepped back so that her skirts would not touch his legs. She was very careful to walk as far to the side of the landing as possible, also intent to avoid contact. But on the next step she paused and looked back.

He was staring at her. His expression might have been carved in granite, and it was impossible to read.

"Thank you, Neil," she said with what she hoped was vast dignity and a matching maturity. And then she felt her face turn beet-red, ruining the effect.

He merely nodded, then he turned, and she watched him enter the hall and stride through it.

She watched him until she could see him no more.

She changed with lightning speed. Then she glanced at the guest list, which remained upon her desk. The biology textbook was there, as well.

She could not study now. Not with Jonny Burton missing. But she would fail biology if she did not study soon, and hard—the examination was tomorrow. And she could be tossed out on her backside if her grades were not above average, no matter that there were only fourteen girls in her class. The president of the college had been very clear when he had spoken to the entering class earlier in the fall. Barnard College aspired to be one of the finest institutions in the country for the higher education of women. He expected all of the freshmen women entering that year to uphold those very high academic standards and to set an example for all those women courageous and determined enough to follow in their footsteps.

It had been a terribly rousing speech. Francesca had been stirred, as had all the other young women in her class. But that had been months ago, in September. That had been before the terrible abduction of Jonny.

He must be frightened to death. She hoped he was being well cared for. She hoped he was safe, unharmed, well fed, and warm. Every time she thought about him, she felt sick inside, imagining his fear and loneliness.

And what about poor Eliza and Robert? She had been

grief-stricken earlier, what condition must she be in now? And Robert did not seem to be in much better form. Francesca decided she must speak to Julia; they must at least bring the Burtons some supper and cake that evening.

Of course, if the note Joel had given Bragg had been a ransom demand, Jonny would be home very soon—wouldn't he?

Francesca rubbed her temples. She could not go visit Eliza, not yet, because Bragg had promised to interview everyone at the Cahill mansion, and he had yet to do so—preoccupied as he had been all day with the blossoming Burton affair and, recently, that risky business on Mott and Hester streets. Her bedroom was at the corner of the house. She walked over to the windows there.

Both windows faced south, and Francesca found herself looking directly at the Burton house. An expanse of snow-covered lawn separated the two residences, as did a high limestone wall. Francesca had excellent vision, but she couldn't see very much even though the other home was but a football field distant.

She turned, raced to her armoire, found her opera glasses, then ran back to the window. She trained them intently at the Burton house. She ignored any guilt she might feel for being so crass as to invade the Burtons' privacy.

She could see into a room on the ground floor, and it was empty. She thought it was a small, intimate parlor. She raised the glasses to the second story. And she was faced with a clear view of a lavish bedroom that was also set at the corner of the house. It also seemed to be empty. Was it a guest room? It seemed far too large to be intended for guests. She wondered if it was Eliza's room.

"Blast," Francesca said. Yet what had she hoped to see? She stood there, dismayed and impatient, when something flickered and caught her eye. She raised the glasses again. A light had gone on in the second-story bedroom. Francesca was rewarded with the sight of Eliza Burton moving about the room. An instant later she saw Robert Burton, pausing before Eliza, and then the two of them seemed to be talking, Robert gripping Eliza's arms.

They seemed to be in love, Francesca thought, lowering the glasses, not wanting to see any more. Every single time she had seen them while out, he doted upon her. Earlier, he had been kind and caring. She wondered what it would be like, to have someone love you so much—to always have someone there.

She couldn't help thinking about Connie and Montrose. Then, as always, she shut off her thoughts, because her sister deserved Montrose.

A moment later Francesca saw a handsome motorcar stopping in front of the Burton house. She did not have to raise her glasses to recognize the figure in the tan overcoat and brown bowler hat with its satin band as he got out of the car. But she did.

Bragg walked up to the house, followed by a detective. Francesca began to prepare herself for the audience that would surely follow. Trying without success to remain composed.

Francesca edged over to the threshold of the library, so she could glimpse her father and Bragg, standing and carrying on a conversation. The tall, beefy detective from earlier that afternoon—the one who had hit Joel—stood aside, taking notes. "I'm afraid that is all I know," Andrew Cahill was saying. "I cannot imagine any of the guests being involved in such a base affair."

"I cannot dismiss the possibility, not yet. Please have the entire staff summoned to the hall. I will interview everyone independently, one by one," Bragg said. "Which room may I use?"

Francesca crossed her arms uneasily as Andrew told him he could use the dining room for the interviews. Francesca took a small breath, more for composure than courage, and stepped inside.

He did not seem surprised to see her. He nodded, as if they had not been at headquarters earlier that day. "Good afternoon, Miss Cahill."

Francesca murmured an identical greeting.

"Show me exactly where you found the note," he said.

Francesca nodded and hurried forward while her father excused himself to round up the staff.

"Hickey, go with him," Bragg ordered.

The big detective obeyed.

Francesca walked over to the desk, aware of the two of them being awkwardly alone together in the library—just as they had been so awkwardly alone in the very same room last night. "There is nothing more for me to say," she said, looking at the desk while sliding her hand over the smooth, worn wood. "I found it here, amidst all of the mail." She looked at him eagerly. "You know, it seems more plausible that someone slipped it into our mail slot. That makes more sense. It would have been an easy mistake to make."

"Only for an intolerably stupid man," Bragg returned evenly. He seemed exhausted. She had the urge to reach out and comfort him.

Instead, she hugged herself.

"Are you certain you did not see anyone leaving this room, or in the hallway outside, as you were entering?" he pressed.

Francesca was about to say no, and then she stopped herself. She replayed the moment of the night before in her mind. She remembered how unbearably tense she had become when first meeting Bragg. Could she have somehow failed to notice someone leaving the room? She slowly lifted her gaze and found him staring at her with a scrutiny that was unsettling. Francesca felt herself flush. "The truth is," she said, so hoarsely that she had to clear her throat, "I was upset when I came in here, and it is possible I did not notice someone leaving the room."

She strained to recollect exactly what had happened after leaving the reception room. Had she brushed someone upon entering the hallway?

He moved closer to the desk. Francesca found it impossible not to watch him, dreading his asking her why she had been distraught, but he did not, much to her relief. She realized that he was staring, and she followed his gaze.

He was staring at the typewriter on the smaller desk set off to the side of her father's desk. Francesca's eyes widened. Surely he was not thinking what she thought he was.

He sat down in the small utilitarian chair behind that second desk, saying reflectively, as he placed a sheet of paper in the machine, "This is a Remington, and a new one, I think."

She wet her lips, excited in spite of herself. "It is new—we purchased it last year. It is the latest model, a Remington 5. But Bragg, it is a double-character machine. Papa's secretary uses it," she added as an afterthought.

He began to type, slowly, painfully, using his two index fingers.

Francesca rushed over. "May I?" she asked.

He stood and their gazes locked. "Absolutely," he replied.

She sat down, trembling, and quickly typed, "A is for Ants. If you want to see the boy again, be at Mott and Hester streets at 1 P.M. tomorrow." Then she scrolled the page out and, with a flourish, handed it to him.

He studied it.

"You said you thought a shift-key machine was used," Francesca said.

"It is only a guess," he said. Then, "You have a good memory."

She was pleased. "Will you compare the notes? Do you really think someone was so bold as to type the note on *our* machine?" She was not just incredulous, she was absurdly thrilled, as well.

He eyed her. "This is not a game, Miss Cahill."

"I am aware of that. And I do not think our machine was used, of course. I am only going by my recollection of how the first note appeared."

He smiled slightly. "Very well, Miss Cahill," he said. "I will also be frank with you. I do not think your machine was used."

Francesca felt somewhat deflated. Then he said, "I was also hoping that you had seen someone lurking about this room or in the corridor." His smile was brief and self-deprecating. "I appreciate your efforts, and if you do happen to recall anything, please call me directly either at home or at headquarters."

Francesca realized that the interview, as brief as it was, was over. "Of course I will call if I happen to remember anything."

That seemed to satisfy him. She watched him fold the page she had just typed and tuck it into his interior breast pocket. He then said, "Have you recovered from the afternoon's events?"

She had been about to leave; she faltered. His words were not harsh, nor did they insinuate any condemnation or judgment on his part based on her earlier behavior. He seemed to be implying that he held some degree of gentlemanly concern for her welfare. In fact, his voice was rather warm.

"I do believe it will be some time before I venture onto the Lower East Side again," she said hesitantly, an image of the foul Gordino flashing through her mind.

He smiled. "I hope so, Miss Cahill. I do hope so."

She smiled back.

His gaze fell onto the table in front of her father's chair, where he was now standing. Francesca followed it, and her smile faded; she winced.

He picked up *Harper's* and chuckled. "Is my nose really so big?"

She laughed, glad he had a sense of humor. "Hardly. The cartoonist did his best to detract from your attractiveness." The moment she had uttered the words, she wished she had said something else, anything else—something entirely noncommittal.

His smile faded. He did not look at her as he set *Harper's* down, exactly the way it had been, folded back and revealing the caricature of himself.

When he looked up, it was as if he had never heard her. "Shall we?" He moved toward the door.

Francesca preceded him into the hall, relieved that he had not noticed that she found him rather handsome, when a fact struck her. She seized his arm. "Bragg!"

He halted. "Now what, Miss Cahill?" he asked, but quietly, without censure.

She wet her lips. Did he know that Gordino had given Joel the note? Had Joel told him while being questioned at police headquarters? Of course, she could not tell him the entire truth, either, for then he would know that she had found Joel after his having escaped the police, and he might even surmise that Joel was present in the house now. But she could not keep such a clue from him. "Commissioner," she said quickly, "just before you waylaid my carriage when we were leaving Hester Street, the boy told me that the thug Gordino had given him the note to deliver to you."

He studied her. Something flickered in his eyes, and for an instant, she was uneasy, afraid he suspected the truth was not wholly that, but embedded with a small lie. "Thank you, Miss Cahill, for sharing that fact with me. But our mutual friend, Joel Kennedy, quickly confessed that bit of truth while you were waiting for me in my office."

Francesca stared. Did he know that his detective had struck the boy? And would he condone such violent behavior on the part of one of his men? She could not confront him now, for then he would know she had seen Joel afterward. Francesca swallowed all that she wished to say, with difficulty.

She refused to believe that he knew about Hickey's behavior.

He took her arm, firmly. "And that is, of course, the end of your involvement in this terrible affair."

"Of course," she said demurely, avoiding his eyes.

She must have been far too sweet and far too meek, for his gaze shot to her, filled with alarm. But Julia interrupted them before he could speak, hurrying toward them from the other end of the house.

"Commissioner," Julia said, perturbed. "This is very strange! My guest list was on the secrétaire in my sitting room, and now it is gone."

Francesca froze.

"Gone?" Bragg stepped to her. "You mean it is missing? Misplaced?"

"I left it right on my secrétaire," Julia said firmly. "I last glanced at it yesterday before the ball, just to remind myself of those few names that were new to me. Letitia is the only one who cleans my apartments—she swears she did not touch it. And she also thinks she saw it there yesterday, as well." Julia hesitated. "So much happened today but . . ." She paused.

"But what?" Bragg asked quickly.

"But I could almost swear that I saw it this morning, right on the secrétaire where I had left it."

Francesca felt sick.

Bragg stared. And when he spoke, he was grim. "Someone stole the list. Well."

And Francesca did not have to be a mind reader to know what he was thinking. He was thinking that one of the guests had stolen the guest list to hide his identity; he was thinking that one of the guests was involved in the dastardly affair.

Francesca felt her cheeks flaming. She must tell them the truth. But then what would happen? Surely he would not charge her with obstructing a criminal investigation.

He had been very angry with her for her foray to Mott and Hester streets.

In that instant, Francesca succumbed to cowardice. She decided she would furtively return the guest list to her mother's secrétaire without admitting to what she had done. No one would ever know and tomorrow Bragg would get his list.

She did not feel better. Perhaps she really *was* obstructing his investigation.

"Hello, Mrs. Burton, I do hope I am not intruding, but I thought you might like this." Francesca managed a friendly smile as she stood on the threshold of the small parlor she had been escorted to.

She was holding a boxed raspberry tart in her hands. The Cahill cook was not pleased, but Francesca had cajoled him into making another one to serve at supper that night.

She had also cajoled her way into the Burton home. For two patrolmen remained on the Burtons' front steps. It had been a rather laborious task.

Eliza sat in a huge armchair, wrapped in a woolen blanket. Her face was exceedingly pale, her eyes remained swollen, the tip of her nose red. A fire roared in the hearth in the center of the small drawing room, but the room still remained cold. Eliza looked at her with very little interest.

"It is a raspberry tart, and it is delicious," Francesca tried.

Eliza bit her lip. She nodded. "You are very kind. I have always thought so." She looked away, dabbing her eyes.

Francesca set the tart in its box down on the table in front of the couch. "Can I get you anything? Have you eaten today?"

Eliza looked at her. "If it were your child who was missing, would you be able to eat?"

Francesca sat down hard on an ottoman, not far from

her hostess. "I guess not. I am so sorry! But we will find Jonny, I am so sure of it."

Surprisingly, Eliza reached out to pat Francesca's knee, and then she wept, briefly.

Abruptly Francesca stood. She walked over to an open bottle of sherry. Its presence on the table in front of the sofa was very conspicuous; Francesca had noticed it and the empty glass beside it the moment she had crossed the threshold of the room. The sherry bottle was nearly full, though, and Francesca thought it might be better if it were mostly empty. Francesca poured a full glass, and brought it over to Eliza.

Eliza waved it away. "I have had two glasses. I cannot even get drunk."

Francesca did not know what to say. She knelt beside Eliza. "Are there any clues? What does Bragg think?"

"The clues are insane!" Eliza cried, standing. "Insane! 'A is for ants, B is for bees.' " Suddenly she doubled over, hugging herself, as if in the worst pain.

Francesca threw an arm around her. "What is it? Are you in pain? Is it your stomach? Should I get a doctor?"

"No, no, I am fine," Eliza gasped, although clearly that was not the case.

Francesca helped her back into the big chair, then covered her with the blanket. Eliza continued to clutch her midsection. She was so starkly pale, except for two very bright pink spots in the center of her cheeks.

When it was clear to Francesca that the stomach ache, if that was what it was, had subsided, she sat down on the ottoman again, this time pulling it close. "There has been no ransom request?" she asked, with acute dread.

Eliza looked directly at her. "No. Just that second, horrid note."

Francesca stared. "Is that what it said? 'B is for bees'?" She was whispering, and she did not know why.

Eliza nodded, and briefly her eyes closed. When they

opened, she cried, "And that is all it said. But there was a lock of Jonny's hair glued to the page!"

"Dear God," Francesca said.

"Who is doing this?" Eliza cried into her hands, covering her face. "Why is he doing this? Why won't he ask for a ransom? When will I get my child back?"

Francesca had no answer to make. And Robert Burton suddenly came into the room.

He did not look at Francesca. Indeed, perhaps he did not even notice her presence. His expression stricken, he raced to his wife, pulling her into his arms, holding her there, trying to hush her. He rocked her as he might their missing son.

Francesca knew it was time to leave.

CHAPTER
6

MONDAY, JANUARY 20, 1902—11:30 A.M.
*Please describe the difference between the nervous system
of a toad and a human being.*

Francesca thought she knew the answer to the fifth
question on the examination. She sat at a large table with
the twelve other women in her class. Beth Brooke was
absent, and Francesca hoped she had a note from her doctor; otherwise she was in serious trouble, indeed. Francesca
began to write, then she paused.

A is for ants, B is for bees.

Sunlight was streaming into the classroom. It was one
of ten large rooms in the brick-and-mortar building that
had been finished the previous year. In fact, it was only
last year that the college had moved to 119th Street and
Broadway from its previous location downtown. The college occupied an entire acre and consisted of a library, an
administration building, and this hall. All of the students
lived off campus, most of them at home.

Francesca stared at dust motes dancing in the air. There
had not been a ransom demand, and whenever she dared
to think about it, she was overcome with dread. The feeling
made her ill.

What was happening? Why were the Burtons being
toyed with? What if ransom was not the intention of the

crook responsible for the abduction? But if that was the case, then what could possibly be his intention?

Bragg had asked Robert Burton if he had enemies. Francesca shivered, recalling that moment yesterday morning at the Burtons' home.

Had it only been yesterday that Jonny's disappearance had been remarked, making headlines? It felt as if it had been weeks ago.

"Miss Cahill?"

Francesca started and looked up at the professor, who happened to be a woman not much older than herself.

"Are you having trouble with the examination?" Professor Wallace asked. She was a small, plain woman with a severe expression that lightened only when she was lecturing upon her favorite subject, biology.

"No. I am not." Francesca smiled, ducked her head, and began answering the fifth question. Fortunately, she had stayed up most of last night studying, and she knew the material. Unfortunately, she was exhausted. She had overslept that morning and had barely made the class on time.

A is for ants . . . Ants were busy creatures; they built, lived, and traveled in tunnels in the ground. They could be found beneath rocks, in fields, and in the woods. Was the crook they were seeking directing them to a tunnel? Or was he directing them to fields, or the woods? Was he even directing them at all?

And what about the second clue, "B is for bees"? Bees were also very busy creatures, and they worked hard to harvest honey, and they were ruled by a queen bee. Francesca laid her pencil down. She was at a loss. Was there a significant connection that she was failing to see?

Ants and bees were both busy workers, she decided. Busy workers were everywhere in New York City, but especially downtown, where no one lived, but where everyone worked, whether it was as a professional on Wall Street or a laborer on South Street. But how in God's name would they find Jonny if the crook intended for them to go and search downtown?

Francesca rubbed her temples. Rocks, fields . . . she suddenly froze.

And for one moment, she did not breathe.

Fields . . . busy workers. And she stood up.

"Miss Cahill? Are you finished?"

Francesca did not even hear Professor Wallace. The field behind the Burton house was a construction site. A lawyer was building a new house there, and right up until it had snowed on Saturday, a crew of workers had been laying the foundation and frame of the house.

Ants were found in fields. So were bees, if the field was full of flowers. That field had been a carpet of wildflowers last summer, and now it was filled with busy workers . . .

"Miss Cahill?" Francesca sat back down. What if she was right? What if the crook was directing them to that field?

Finishing the examination was the hardest thing she had ever done.

She did not expect to be right. New York City was full of fields, and maybe the clues indicated Central Park, which was filled with ants and bees in the appropriate season. Or maybe the clues did refer to downtown, or even to a tunnel. Francesca had done nothing but think as she had traveled south on the Ninth Avenue El before getting off at Fifty-ninth Street and taking a trolley across town. The busiest tunnel in the city was the one where the trains on Fourth Avenue went underground from Fifty-seventh to Ninety-sixth streets.

But the envelope was nailed onto a wooden beam that was rising out of the concrete foundation of the yet-to-be-constructed house.

Francesca stood there in the snow, huddled in her fur-lined coat, her hands in a fur muff, staring, wide-eyed. She was almost disbelieving.

But the envelope was there, and it was frozen solid.

Francesca hurried forward, slipping as she stepped up onto the foundation. She dropped the muff and took off her gloves. And very carefully, she jimmied the envelope free of the nail and the beam.

And the moment it was in her hand, she saw the frozen blood.

Nausea overcame her. Francesca opened the envelope with stiff, frozen fingers, extracting a frozen, bloody page.

C is for Cub.

Francesca ran into the house and through it to the library where the telephone was. The envelope was thawing, and it was becoming sticky in her hands. She was shaking as she put it down and reached for the telephone.

"The police commissioner at police headquarters," she told the operator tersely. An image of Bragg came to mind and she imagined just how surprised he would be when she told him that she had found the third note.

As she waited impatiently for him to come onto the other end of the line, she stared at the envelope. There was blood on her fingertips and blood all over the note. She thought that the page had been literally soaked in blood. She felt like throwing up.

"The commissioner is out to lunch," a man said on the other end of the line.

"Out to lunch!" Francesca cried.

"Who is this?" The policeman's tone was sharp.

"Francesca Cahill. Where is he?" she demanded.

"He's at the Fifth Avenue Hotel," the officer returned. "Should I take a message?"

"When will he be back?" Francesca stared at the bloody envelope, feeling perilously close to tears. How could Bragg be eating now! How?

Was the blood Jonny's?

Oh, God! Was he alive?

"He just left," the officer said.

Francesca hung up the receiver. "Darnation," she said harshly. Then she picked it up again. A moment later she was speaking with the hotel operator. "Please, Commissioner Bragg is having lunch in your hotel, this is an emergency, and I *must* speak with him."

"I will see if we can locate him," the operator said. "What is your name, miss? Are you certain everything is all right?"

"Of course everything is not all right," Francesca shouted. "Please, just put Bragg on the line."

She wanted to pace, but she could not, otherwise she would yank the phone from the cord. She could only stand there and fidget, breathing harshly, wishing that this were not happening. *Why was there so much blood on that note?*

Fifteen minutes went by. And then he said, "Bragg here. Who is this?"

"Bragg! This is Francesca. I found another note!" she cried.

There was one moment of stunned silence, and he said, "Where are you?"

"At home."

"Don't move. I'll be right there."

Francesca had been pacing in the hall for a half an hour when she saw his motorcar coming up the driveway. Her relief knew no bounds. She ran to the door and opened it before he was even out of the car. She began jumping up and down.

He hurried up the steps and into the house. When he was on the threshold she cried out. "This is terrible."

He held her shoulders. "Calm down. Where is the note and where did you find it?"

She stared up at him. "It's on the desk in the library," she said, and finally she gave in. Tears slipped down her face. "There's blood, Bragg, so much blood, all over it."

He cursed and ran. Francesca ran after him. She was so frightened.

He reached the desk before she did. He lifted the page, which was now thoroughly wet. "God damn it," he cried.

She stared at his rigid back, wiping the tears away.

Bragg turned. His eyes were wide with shock and the very same fear she herself felt. Francesca wished that she had never seen such an expression on his face. She wanted to be reassured. She did not want to know that the commissioner of police was as frightened as she was for the little boy's safety. "Where did you find this, Francesca?" he said grimly.

She told him. "I was in an examination and it just struck me that maybe the crook was directing us to that field," she added.

"You shouldn't have touched it," he said, coming forward.

She started. "I—"

"This is evidence and you should have left it precisely as you found it." His eyes blazed with anger. He was waving the bloody note at her.

"I'm sorry," she whispered, backing away.

"It's too late to be sorry," he snapped.

Francesca stiffened.

And suddenly he stared. "Good God, Miss Cahill, I apologize."

She met his stare. "You do not have to apologize, I understand," she said, touching the sleeve of his black suit jacket. And she did. He had lost his composure because of this latest, frightening development in the case. This was not about her; it was about Jonny.

He stepped away and her hand dropped to her side. "No, I doubt that you do. But there is no excuse for me to lose my temper, when, in fact, you have helped this investigation enormously."

Francesca crossed her arms. He was still agonized. He could not hide his anguish. She was anguished, too, but absurdly, she was so pleased that he had recognized her efforts to help solve the ghastly crime. "What do you think this means? Is the blood Jonny's?"

He met her gaze, nostrils flared. "Your guess is as good as mine."

Francesca hugged herself. "It's his blood, isn't it? Do you think he's dead? Are we dealing with a madman and a murderer?"

"He isn't dead," Bragg ground out. "The boy is not dead."

Francesca inhaled, her eyes tearing yet again. "I hope you are right. For his sake, for the Burtons' sake, for James's sake."

"I am right," he said tersely.

Francesca knew him a little by now. She knew he was an intelligent, capable, and determined man. She suspected he was also very ambitious; why else would he accept the position as Seth Low's police commissioner? So she could not understand why he would so fiercely insist upon something that might or might not be true. Did he think to delude himself? "This criminal, he doesn't want a ransom. This is not about ransom, is it?"

"Clearly this is not about ransom," he agreed.

"Someone wants to taunt the Burtons."

"Yes. At the least," he said.

Their gazes met and held. It was a moment before she could speak. "Why, Bragg? Why would someone hate them so? They are nice people. I've known them for two years and, I must say, I cannot imagine either one of them having made such an enemy."

"We will know the answer to that when we find the criminal behind the crime," he said flatly.

Their gazes remained locked. Francesca shivered. "So we are dealing with a madman. Only a madman would do something like this."

"I am afraid so."

He looked at her and, for one moment, she almost

thought he might reassure her, even with a simple touch. Instead, he said, "You will have to get your coat. I wish to see exactly how and where you found the note."

She nodded. "Will you tell the Burtons?"

"I have no choice," he said.

They stood side by side on the cement foundation, shivering. Francesca watched Bragg run his bare hand up and down the beam, around the nail. She could not imagine what he was looking for.

"What are you doing?" she asked.

"I was foolishly hoping to find some trace of whoever put the note here. Perhaps a piece of fabric, or even a hair."

Her eyes widened as he stooped low and sifted through the snow with his bare hands. Francesca continued to shiver. "Have you had the other notes compared with the one we typed last night on our typewriter?"

"The notes were not typed on your Remington 5. They were typed on a shift-key machine, as I originally suspected." He stood, brushing the snow off his hands on his overcoat. "And they were both typed on the same machine. At least, that is what we have determined."

"My mother found the guest list last night," Francesca volunteered, knowing that if she did flush with guilt he would not notice, as her cheeks were undoubtedly red from the cold.

"It was delivered to me at my office last night." He took her arm and helped her down from the foundation.

He must have worked late. She admired his stamina and his ambition, but she couldn't help thinking that he looked as exhausted as she herself felt. As they crossed the lot, she suddenly thought about the photograph in his office.

If that woman were his wife, if those children were his, wouldn't he have gone home at a reasonable hour? "Do you always work at night?" she asked, and this time, she knew she flushed.

"Frequently," he said. "It is odd, isn't it, how that list

briefly disappeared, and so suddenly reappeared—exactly where your mother thinks she last saw it?"

She looked away as they found the more firm footing of the sidewalk. "It was probably on her secrétaire the entire time, but buried beneath other papers."

He made no comment. She could feel him studying her, and she prayed her expression would not give her hand in the matter away. He said, "I am becoming more and more convinced that someone very close to the Burtons is behind the child's disappearance."

"Can you find that ruffian, Gordino?" Suddenly she halted, excitement rising within her. "Surely he knows just who the dastardly crook is!"

He smiled at her then. "Good detective work, Miss Cahill. In fact, Gordino has gone underground, so to speak. But my men will find him, and when they do, I shall be the first in line to give him the third degree."

"The third degree?" she asked, but her mind was racing. Joel might know where to find Gordino. The possibility elated her—as soon as Bragg had left, she would seek Joel out and ask him.

"That is police terminology for a serious interrogation. You've heard of Thomas Byrnes?"

"Who hasn't?" she said mildly. "He was such a corrupt chief of police that when he retired he had amassed a fortune of millions of dollars. He resigned when Teddy Roosevelt had your job, for he was afraid to have to explain his actions in a court of law. I am a great fan of Roosevelt's," she added with a smile. "McKinley's assassination was a terrible tragedy, but we do have a wonderful man and a determined reformer in the White House now."

His brows lifted as they paused before the front steps of the Burton mansion. "I had forgotten," he said, "that you are a woman of not just intelligence and education but the most vocal and impassioned opinions and convictions."

She stared. There was no possible way she was mistaking his meaning. He was praising her character. He did not think her mannish after all.

Francesca could not move. She felt heat warming every inch of her face, and she realized she was flushing with real pleasure. "Thank you, Commissioner," she said finally.

He hesitated, smiled briefly, and then became grim as he faced the front door of the house. Francesca realized she should leave and return home. But she did not. "Can I be of help?" she asked hesitantly.

He took her arm again. "I think so. Eliza may need another woman when she realizes there is a third note."

"I wish this could be avoided," Francesca said uneasily as he rang the bell.

"So do I. But I do not intend to show the note to her. Burton, however, will have to see it."

The door was opened and they went inside.

They were shown into the same drawing room they had been in yesterday morning. It was not the room that Francesca could see from her bedroom window with the aid of opera glasses.

Burton and Eliza appeared at the exact same moment, their faces pale with fear and dread, Eliza wearing a heavy cashmere shawl upon her shoulders. Immediately, Francesca moved closer to her.

"What has happened?" Burton cried. "Please tell me you have found our son and that he is fine!"

"We have not found the boy," Bragg said. He gestured. "Please sit down."

Neither Burton moved. And then Eliza strode forward, grabbing Bragg's arm. "Something has happened! I can see it in your eyes. Something terrible has happened!"

He took her elbow. "Please, Mrs. Burton, sit down. We have found another note, that is all."

But Eliza would not budge. "A ransom demand?" Hope filled her tone and her expression.

"I am afraid not."

"Let me see it." Burton came forward, paler now than before—if that was even possible. He looked ghastly. Clearly he had not slept at all, he was terribly unshaven, rumpled, with the coloring of one becoming ill. And Francesca realized he was trembling.

"I will show it to you in a moment." Bragg told them where the note had been found and what it said. Francesca flushed when the Burtons turned to look at her. But they did not ask her how on earth she had managed to deduce just what the first two notes had meant.

"What does 'C is for Cub' mean?" Eliza whispered in anguish. "What does this bastard want!"

Francesca flinched but went to her and took her hand. "If anyone can solve this case, it is the commissioner," she said softly, meaning it.

Eliza did not seem to hear her. "And he was here, right next door, in that vacant lot!"

" 'C is for Cub,' " Burton murmured. And suddenly he whirled to face them. "My God! I think . . . I think I know what that means!"

"What?" Bragg demanded.

"The boys' treehouse. They named it 'the Den.' "

Francesca stared. Cub, bears, cave . . . den. And she looked at Bragg.

"Francesca, stay here with Mrs. Burton. Robert, please get your coat and show me to the treehouse."

The two men hurried from the room, but Eliza ran after them—and therefore, Francesca did, too. "I am coming, too!" she said.

Francesca suddenly had a horrific thought—what if the boy was in that treehouse, bloody and dead? She gripped Eliza's arm. "It's not a good idea."

"Stay in the house," Bragg ordered without looking back at them.

Eliza wrenched free of Francesca. "Do not tell me what

to do," she shouted. "Not when my son is missing." And she lifted her skirts and ran.

No one bothered to retrieve his or her coats. Francesca had to run hard to catch up to Eliza, who trailed the two men as they crossed the gardens in the back of the house. Clouds had moved in, threatening more snow. The sun had disappeared. A gusting wind had picked up, and in general, the area was desolate and bleak, whereas in the spring it was riotously colorful and in bloom. And the oak tree loomed ahead.

It was just off to the side of the half-acre property, not far from the wall dividing the Burtons' land from the Cahills', as bare as the gardens, its heavy branches covered with snow. A boxlike structure with a slanting lean-to roof was built into its center branches, a ladder leading up to it.

Francesca slowed as Bragg reached the ladder, commanding Burton to stay where he was. He began to climb up. She did not like this. She did not like it at all. In fact, she was more than uneasy now; she was filled with dread.

She prayed this would not be the end of their quest. She prayed they would not find the boy in that treehouse, frozen, bloody, and dead.

Bragg disappeared, ducking into the low, squat structure.

Eliza was shivering uncontrollably. The freezing cold hit Francesca then, and she put her arm around the other woman, who did not even notice. She wanted to reassure her, perhaps with the most simple of statements, such as, "It will be all right." But she could not get such an inane phrase out.

Because she wasn't sure she believed that it would be all right anymore.

"What's up there!" Burton shouted frantically from below.

At first there was no reply. Then, "Another note."

Francesca felt her knees buckle with relief. She smiled

at Eliza. Tears slid down the other woman's face. "Where can he be? Why is someone doing this to me?" Eliza whispered.

Francesca's smile faded and she stared. What if Eliza was the target of this madman's efforts?

Her mind sped with dizzying speed. And images of Eliza filled her head. The other woman riding in an open carriage in summertime, through Central Park on a Sunday afternoon, gentlemen calling greetings to her ceaselessly. Eliza being rowed across the lake, resplendent in billowy white, a white parasol open above her head—the oarsmen young rakes. Eliza at the ball Saturday night, surrounded by men, each and every one of them filled with admiration for her. She thought about the way Wiley had looked at her Saturday night. She thought about the way she had seen Evan look at her on too many occasions to count.

Was the madman love-struck?

Had he been rejected?

Was this his insane idea of revenge?

Bragg was climbing down from the treehouse. Francesca craned to see what he held in his hand, and then she relaxed, because the envelope was pristinely white. Thank God.

Then she whipped her gaze back to Bragg—to his face.

Something was terribly wrong. He was turning green, as if he might actually become sick.

"Bragg?" she whispered.

Somehow he heard her. His wide, stunned gaze went to hers, and their eyes held. And Francesca felt far uneasier than she had before. Something was in that note, something terrible, it was there in his expressive amber eyes, and she did not want to know.

He cleared his throat. "Everyone back into the house," he said, but his tone was hoarse and unclear.

"What does it say, damn it?" Burton demanded.

"Let's adjourn to the house. I wish to speak with you

privately, Robert, and afterward, I wish a private conversation with your wife."

"What does it say!" Burton shouted.

Clearly Bragg was not going to compromise and reveal the contents now. "Francesca," he said.

She understood. She gripped Eliza's arm. "We are all freezing. We must obey the commissioner, Eliza, we must. He is in charge of this case. He is the authority here."

Eliza looked at her and Francesca had never seen such an expression on a human being before. It was one of utter defeat and hopelessness; it was an expression of absolute resignation. She nodded and seemed to collapse against Francesca, who managed to support her weight.

"No, goddamnit," Burton shouted and he tore the note from Bragg's hand.

"Burton, don't!" Bragg shouted, gripping the other man's arm.

Burton made a sound that did not seem human and he somehow flung the commissioner off. Later, Francesca would say it was his desperation that gave him the strength, as he was a much smaller man than Bragg.

And he opened the note, and reached inside.

Producing half of a small human ear.

CHAPTER
7

Francesca sat on a chair in the entry hall, her hands rigidly clasped in her lap. Bragg had disappeared to speak with the Burtons individually; it seemed hours ago since they had discovered the fourth envelope. Francesca closed her eyes. Again, she felt as if she would retch up the only meal she had eaten that day, her breakfast.

There was no longer any point in pretending. Jonny Burton was not fine. A piece of human ear had been in the envelope, and Francesca had not a doubt that the ear belonged to a child and that it belonged in particular to Jonny.

What kind of madman were they dealing with?

She curled over, eyes closed, fighting tears and the urge to vomit uncontrollably.

The doorbell rang. Francesca watched as a servant answered it, allowing a bearded older gentleman in a heavy black coat and top hat to enter. She recognized him at once.

"I'm to show you upstairs to Mrs. Burton," the houseman said with the slightest Scots accent.

"Please," the gentleman returned, his physician's black satchel in hand.

"Hello, Dr. Finny," Francesca said.

He started upon seeing her. "Francesca! What are you doing here?"

She got to her feet. She felt as if she had aged precariously in the past hour. "I had hoped to comfort Eliza Burton," she said. And she was also waiting for Bragg. Although she could have returned home, she wanted to speak with him before she did so. She wanted to share her latest theory.

"Then they have not found the little boy?" Finny asked with genuine concern.

Francesca shook her head. Instinct warned her not to share any facts of the case with the doctor.

"Well, I think it was a good idea for the Burtons to send James to Eliza's parents during this crisis." He patted her arm. "You look tired, my dear. I will give Eliza something to help her sleep. Why don't you go home?"

"I intend to." She knew her smile was wan. As Finny and the servant started up the polished teakwood stairs, covered with a Persian runner in delicate creams and golds, Bragg appeared, descending.

He paused on the steps to speak to Finny. Francesca strained to hear. He kept his voice low, but she heard his every word. "The case has taken a very bad turn, Finny. Give her laudanum. I'd like her to sleep away this night."

"I understand, Commissioner," Finny said, heading upstairs.

Bragg entered the hall and his amber eyes found Francesca. There was no censure there. He just seemed terribly tired and terribly strained. While another servant brought him his coat, Francesca donned hers, which she had been holding, and together they crossed the hall on their way out.

"Will you be able to get any rest?" she asked as they stepped outside. The wind was howling now, and it was snowing. Snowflakes swirled through the air.

He glanced at her. "How can I? When a child's life is at stake?"

They had not yet descended the front stairs to the sidewalk; Francesca gripped his arm. "What does this madman want? What does he intend?"

"Clearly he seeks to wound the Burtons." Their gazes held.

"And this time, there was no note. There was no clue, nothing, nothing but . . ." She could not continue.

His jaw seemed so tight she imagined it would snap. Still, he reached out and steadied her by holding both of her arms. The gesture was so reassuring. She looked up, into his eyes. "Now what?"

"We will hear from the madman again. Have no doubt."

She had no doubt. Because the madman wished to torment them with uncertainty over the boy's fate. "There will never be a ransom demand, will there?"

"I think it unlikely."

"So that would rule out a servant having committed the abduction."

"Not necessarily. There are servants who despise their employers. However, I cannot imagine a servant being so creative." He paused. "Where are you leading, Francesca? I mean, Miss Cahill?"

She smiled at the sound of her name on his lips. Then her smile vanished. "Unless this person takes pleasure in inflicting pain, his motive must be revenge."

"I have assumed so."

Francesca was quite certain he had thoroughly questioned the Burtons. "Did they come up with *anyone* who might hate them enough to do this?"

He hesitated. "Francesca, you do realize that this remains official police business, no matter how helpful you have been?"

"I do," she whispered. And she already knew that the Burtons had come up with someone, otherwise he would have merely said no.

"I cannot share that information with you." He stared.

It was hard to look away from his worried eyes. It was

the most absurd moment to think of it, but Francesca recalled the photograph of Bragg with the three small children and the beautiful woman. She shoved the recollection
aside. "I have thought of something."

"Indeed, I would, at this juncture, be shocked if you
had not."

Had they not been in the midst of an unfolding tragedy,
Francesca would have smiled. "Perhaps, just perhaps, this
madman seeks to hurt Eliza—not Burton."

His only reaction was a flicker in the depths of his eyes.
She grew dismayed and she plucked yet again on his
coatsleeve, her fingers quite numb now from the cold. "She
is the most admired of women! Perhaps the madman has
been in love with her—and was rejected?"

He sighed. "Fran . . . Miss Cahill. You have thought of
nothing I have not already thought of. There is one problem. Eliza Burton has not rejected any gentlemen. She says
there have been no inappropriate overtures, no inappropriate suitors, and that she has not conducted herself in any
inappropriate manner."

Francesca grew uneasy. "What if she is lying? To protect her marriage?"

He stared. "You accuse her of what? Lying? A lack of
morals? Infidelity? Or merely callous self-absorption?"

"No." Francesca shook her head, taken aback by his
somewhat angry reaction. "No. I am sorry. I admire her
so! I just . . . I just want to find the boy, alive."

Bragg turned away. But not before she saw the despair
in his eyes. And she stood there, unmoving, watching him
tread down the steps, already dusted with snow.

He was taking this almost personally, she thought. But
then, so was she.

On the sidewalk he turned as a horse-drawn omnibus
passed by. "I will walk you home," he said.

Francesca nodded and hurried to catch up to him. A
moment later they passed through the wrought-iron gates
that opened onto the Cahill property. They walked in si-

lence, each absorbed with their own thoughts. And finally they reached his roadster.

Francesca had shoved her gloveless hands into her coat, as she had not had the time to grab gloves, a hat, or even her muff. She watched him produce leather gloves from his coat pockets and dust off the windshield of the Daimler. When he was done, he faced her one last time. "By the way," he said, "a new thought is occurring to me."

Eagerly, she said, "What is it?"

"You said you were taking an examination when you pieced together the first two clues. What did you mean?"

She looked at him and went blank.

"Miss Cahill?"

Evan and Connie were the only ones who knew she was studying at Barnard College. She managed a smile. "I meant . . . it was a self-examination. I study various subjects . . . and test myself from time to time."

He looked at her as if she were very odd, indeed. "I see." He tipped his dark bowler. "Good day, Miss Cahill."

"Good day, Commissioner," she said, inwardly wincing and hardly relieved.

Francesca stepped into the warmth of her home, handing her coat to a passing houseman. She shivered and rubbed her hands together, hoping to warm them. Her mother sailed into the hall, apparently coming from the yellow salon. "Francesca." Julia smiled and Francesca knew her mother had been waiting for her. "How was your lunch with Mr. Wiley?"

Francesca froze. Wiley! She had forgotten all about him, and not only had she forgotten, she had also failed to send him a note that morning explaining that she could not make their appointment. She stared at her mother, appalled.

"Francesca! Just what does that look upon your face mean?" Julia's hands found her hips. She was marvelously dressed in a fitted gray skirt and jacket with cream-colored stripes. Her blouse, adorned with lace, was a pale cream color, as well. A pearl necklace, brilliant with interspersed diamonds, winked above the collar of her blouse. And her curled blond hair was pulled neatly back.

Julia Van Wyck Cahill was still an extremely beautiful and elegant woman. She never failed to make an entrance, no matter what the establishment might be.

"I forgot," Francesca whispered.

"You forgot?" Julia exclaimed, wide-eyed. "How on earth could you forget? And where have you been all day?"

Francesca clasped her hands to her cheeks. "Mama, I will send Mr. Wiley a note with both an explanation and an apology! This exact minute!"

"I would like to hear that explanation," Julia said, her blue eyes turning a stormy gray. "Francesca, you have gone too far. How could you?"

Francesca bit her lip, then blurted, "Mama, I found another note."

"You what?"

Francesca grabbed her mother's arm and her words tumbled over one another as she explained how she had found the third note, and just where she had been since then. Of course, she did not breathe a word about her class that morning at Barnard College.

"Oh, dear," Julia said, becoming pale. Francesca followed her mother back into the salon, where they both sat down on a gold brocade couch with gilded arms and legs and red trim. "This is terrible," she said. "Eliza . . . she must be going insane."

Francesca had not told her about the ear; describing the bloody note had been enough. "Yes, I think so. Dr. Finny came to tend her."

Julia looked up. "That's good." She reached out and patted Francesca's hand. "Well, I never denied that I have an extremely intelligent and capable daughter. I am glad you were of help, Francesca."

Her mother's praise was rare. Francesca was absurdly pleased and she had to smile, aware that she also flushed. "Thank you, Mama."

"Of course, I expect you to go downtown this moment and apologize to Mr. Wiley—in person," she said firmly.

Francesca wanted nothing more than to crawl into her bed and take a good long nap. But she looked at her mother, saw the warning in her eyes, and knew better than to refuse. "All right." The fastest way downtown was by the Second Avenue El, but Francesca could not deal with the crowds on the elevated, considering all that she had been through that day. "May I take Jennings? Maybe I can nap on my way."

Julia patted her knee. "Of course." She stood up. "And do not forget that we have been invited to Connie's, Francesca. Supper will be at eight."

Francesca was dismayed even though the Montrose home was just around the block on Madison Avenue. "I prefer to rest in my room—"

"It is an intimate dinner, just twenty guests, and it should be lovely. Your sister is a magnificent hostess. I would like you to come."

Francesca had to study for her French literature class; she also desperately needed a good night's sleep. An image of the piece of tiny frozen ear filled her mind. How would she ever sleep after the horrors of the day?

"Francesca? Are you all right?"

Francesca stood. "I am so worried about Jonny Burton."

Her mother grimaced. "We all are, dear. But the police are on the case, and doing, I presume, the best that they can. Wear your green gown tonight, please. And that cameo pendant." She started from the room, then paused. "This will perk you up. Dr. Parkhurst is one of the guests."

Francesca's eyes widened. Parkhurst was the founder and president of the Society for the Prevention of Crime. Dinner no longer loomed as an intolerable affair. To the contrary. "Why didn't you say so?" she said.

"I think the commissioner of police will also be present." Julia left the room.

Francesca reached for the back of a chair to steady herself. What did the small series of skips of her heart mean? She ran after her mother. "Mama, wait."

About to cross the hall, Julia paused. "Yes?"

"What do you know about Rick Bragg?"

Julia's eyes widened with surprise. "Why, whatever do you mean? Surely you—Francesca! Surely you are not interested in the police commissioner?" her mother cried, with obvious dismay.

Francesca felt her cheeks heat with embarrassment. "I did not say that," she said slowly. "But why would it be so terrible? After all, he comes from a good family. The Texas Braggs are a match for the Vanderbilts. Or—he's not married, is he?" She felt the heat in her cheeks ratchet up a few more miserable degrees.

Julia faced her, hands on her slim hips. "I do not know what is going on in that incomprehensible mind of yours, Francesca. But any interest you might have in the commissioner should be laid immediately to rest."

He was married. Francesca felt her heart sinking, hard and fast.

Julia faced her. "You know I do not like to speak ill of anyone," she said, lowering her voice. "But I would never approve of a match between you and Rick Bragg."

Francesca stared, bewildered. "He's not married?"

"Married? Hardly! He is illegitimate, my dear girl. As illegitimate as one can get."

Francesca felt her mouth drop open and her jaw hang. "What?"

Julia was actually turning pink. "Your father told me. The other night before bed."

Francesca's eyes widened, for she could not imagine her mother and father in a private conversation, much less one in the bedroom.

"I do not believe it is common knowledge," Julia added.

"And that is the end of that." Her brows lifted.

Francesca stared, speechless. She did not know of anyone in good society who had such a stigma attached to him. Illegitimate men just did not move about in quality circles. "He seems very well educated," she finally said, at a loss. "He went to Harvard Law School."

Julia was grim. "What does that matter? He is also well connected. Your father thinks he will one day run for the Senate. But that does not change the fact"—and she looked all around them as if afraid of being overheard, before dropping her voice to an almost inaudible whisper—"that his mother was a woman of ill repute."

Francesca gasped. She was in a state of shock.

"Do not ever repeat what I have told you, it would not be fair to the commissioner," Julia said. "But if you have any romantic inclinations, I suggest you forget them this very minute." She softened and touched Francesca's face. "Now, I see you are as stunned as I was. Do not give Bragg another thought. When will you be ready to go downtown? I will tell Jennings."

Francesca managed to say, "In half an hour."

Julia nodded, pleased. She caressed Francesca's cheek one more time and left the hall.

Francesca felt as if she had been hit over the head with a huge wooden board. The day just kept getting worse.

Francesca had taken a few minutes to freshen up, all the while thinking not about Mr. Wiley, but about the missing child and his parents—and Rick Bragg. Her earlier feeling of dismay had intensified, but she wasn't quite willing to acknowledge why. She told herself that it had nothing to do with Bragg. She also wished she would not have to make the long and tiresome trip downtown.

But of course, she had done Wiley a terrible disservice and her mother was correct, she must apologize immediately, and in person. A note would not do.

Downstairs, Francesca told Jennings to bring the

brougham around. Then she walked into the kitchens and asked for Joel Kennedy.

Mrs. Ryan appeared from the pantries where she had been instructing several kitchen maids upon their duties. She was a tall, gaunt woman with fading red hair and faded blue eyes. Spectacles, which she never wore, dangled upon her narrow chest. Her hands found her hips. "Miss Cahill, the boy is not to be found. Anywhere."

Francesca blinked at her. She was always a bit intimidated by the woman, who ran the house with an iron hand. "I beg your pardon?"

"Joel Kennedy is gone." She was very grim—but then, such an expression was characteristic of her. "And not only is he gone, so is a good portion of the silver."

"What?" Francesca cried, stunned.

"He's stolen the silver, Miss Cahill. And I am not happy about telling Mrs. Cahill the sad fact."

Francesca could only stare in shock. Joel had stolen from her family when she had been so kind as to give him a job and a roof over his head! But more importantly, he was her only connection to Gordino and whoever was truly responsible for Jonny Burton's abduction. Dismay crushed her then. "But how could he steal the silver? It's kept under lock and key. And you have the keys, Mrs. Ryan," Francesca said.

"Come with me," Mrs. Ryan said, and she marched off. Francesca hurried to follow.

In the dining room was a huge piece of furniture, almost as high as the ceiling. It was a seventeenth-century piece that was exquisite to look at. But Francesca knew that the locked drawers and cabinets were where her mother's most valuable silver, crystal, and china were kept. Mrs. Ryan pointed to a lower drawer. Francesca followed her gaze.

The mahogany drawer was badly scratched around the brass keyhole. "He picked the lock," Francesca whispered.

"Indeed, let us hope he did no more than that, for it

will be just our luck should he be a bedchamber sneak."
Her hands had found her hips again.

For a moment, Francesca wondered if she enjoyed the
drama of what had occurred, either that, or Francesca being
the one responsible for the theft. "We must be alert in case
burglars try to enter the house at night while we are all
asleep." Bedchamber sneaks made wax impressions of
bedroom locks, and came back with their cohorts to rob
on a more massive and premeditated scale. It was not a
pleasant thought.

"Yes, we must," Mrs. Ryan said. "Shall I tell your
mother, or will you?"

Francesca inhaled. "I must go downtown, Mrs. Ryan.
Why don't you keep this to yourself for a bit, and I will
tell her later tonight?" She would delay that event as long
as was possible.

"Very well." Mrs. Ryan turned and left the room with
brisk, efficient strides.

Francesca was grim and angry as she went to get her
coat. She had been trying to help Joel Kennedy. He was
an ungrateful little thief.

Wiley and Sons was actually located on the corner of
Broad and Wall streets. It had taken Francesca an hour to
get downtown, as it continued to snow, although lightly.
But the snow underfoot was enough to cause traffic jams,
and now the sky was darkening—soon it would be twilight. Francesca asked Jennings to wait for her where he
had double-parked alongside rows of carriages and a few
motorcars, and she stepped carefully down to the curb.

Francesca had not been to Wall Street in several years;
there was little reason for her to do so, although her father's offices were also in the area. The last time she had
been downtown, the street had been busy with pedestrians
as well as hansoms, coaches, and trolleys, all of the passersby male. Today, due to the weather, she supposed, only

a few gentlemen were hurrying about their business, most of them holding open black umbrellas.

Francesca glanced at the directory in the granite lobby of the building, then went upstairs to the second floor. A receptionist pointed her toward a corner office. Anxious now, Francesca proceeded to the office and knocked hesitantly upon the solidly closed door.

Wiley called out for her to enter and she did.

He was seated at a large desk, in his shirtsleeves, which were rolled up. He seemed to be very busy with paperwork. He glanced up and his eyes widened. A second later he had jumped to his feet. "Miss Cahill!"

Francesca entered the room more fully, closing the door behind her. "I have made a terrible mistake," she said softly, smiling in apology. "I forgot all about our luncheon date."

He came forward, having now turned quite red. "That is quite all right . . . let me take your coat . . . this is a delightful surprise!"

Francesca did not want to linger, but she had already been rude enough, and she handed him her coat. "Please allow me to explain," she said.

"Of course—although no explanation is necessary," he said, his gaze earnestly upon hers. "I cannot believe you would come downtown now, in this weather."

Francesca only smiled as he hung her coat up on a wall peg, then opened the door and called for his assistant to bring them tea and cake. He closed the door, saw that she remained standing, and he hurried forward to drag one of the room's spare chairs forward. "Please, do sit."

Francesca smiled and sat. She felt worse now than before. He seemed to be smitten with her, and she had so callously disregarded his feelings. "You have heard about the Burton affair," she said as he pulled another chair out to face her, settling his too-long frame there.

"A terrible tragedy," he said gravely. His cheeks had

paled now, their coloring almost normal. Only a slight pink flush remained.

"That is what distracted me. I know both twins, quite well, and I am sick over Jonny's disappearance."

"I am so sorry," he said fervently, leaning forward as he spoke.

For the first time, Francesca looked at him. He seemed to be a nice man. "Thank you."

"How is Mrs. Burton? Mr. Burton?" he asked. "They must be in a panic."

She studied him. "They are. But there is little to be done except wait for the police to solve the case."

"Poor Mrs. Burton," he said.

Francesca started and stared at him again. She instantly recalled how he had looked at Eliza with such frank admiration on Saturday night. She reminded herself that so had dozens of other gentlemen, but still, she had to wonder if Wiley was somewhat infatuated with Eliza. "Have you known them long?" she asked.

"Not only have I known them for some time, but Robert Burton and I golf together in Saratoga Springs, where we have our summer home." He smiled. "The Burtons are only three miles down the road from us."

"I see," Francesca said, her heart speeding. "I hadn't known." She estimated Wiley as being a few years older than herself; he was close to Evan's age. Evan was twenty-four. Eliza Burton was perhaps a few years older than that. "The Burtons have had their home in Saratoga for just a year or two, haven't they?" she asked, having no idea at all.

His brows rose. They were the same light brown color as his hair. "Actually, they have had that house for many years. I remember first meeting the Burtons in the summer at the lake when I was but a boy. I think I was fourteen years old or so at the time. They were newly wed."

She gripped her hands. She sat up even straighter. Her pulse raced at a faster pace. Wiley might be an important source of information, as he clearly knew the Burtons well. "You must know the boys very well, then?" she said, but it was a question.

"I have known the twins since they were born." His smile disappeared. "This is terrible. Whoever is responsible should be shot."

"In this case, I think I might agree. Can you think of any acquaintance of the Burtons' who might secretly despise either Eliza or Robert? Who might secretly hold a grudge against one or the other or both of them?" Francesca asked.

Wiley's pale brows furrowed. "No, I am afraid I do not. Miss Cahill, Commissioner Bragg has already asked me a number of similar questions. Unfortunately, I was hardly of any help."

There was something in his tone that made her sit up straighter and suddenly she wondered if Wiley was a madman. Of course, that idea was far-fetched. Still, someone who was close to the Burtons, someone who appeared gentle and innocuous, had done this. There was a person out there who was not at all what he—or she—seemed to be.

She must share this theory with Bragg. She stood. "I would love to linger, but I am afraid the weather will worsen, making it a terrible drive home."

He had already leapt to his feet. "I would not want you to get stuck in traffic on an afternoon like this." He guided her to the door, retrieving her coat and helping her put it on. "Miss Cahill?"

She buttoned it up. "Yes?"

"Might we reschedule lunch?" He flushed wildly again.

She was about to put him off. Instead, she thought about how well he knew the Burtons. "Of course," she said, feeling a twinge of guilt for accepting his invitation for the wrong reason. "Could we wait until Saturday?" she asked. There were no classes on the weekend.

"That would be perfect," he said happily. And then, at

the door, which he held open for her, "I will walk you down, if you do not mind."

"Of course not," Francesca replied.

In the lobby of police headquarters, Francesca asked if Bragg was in. The sergeant behind the desk told her that he was, and asked her what her business was.

She hesitated, in the midst of unbuttoning her coat, her gloves and muff in one hand. "He is a friend of the family's," she said. "The Cahill family. I am Francesca Cahill."

The sergeant raised a brow and barked out to a younger policeman to go see if the commissioner would see Miss Cahill. Francesca watched the patrolman take the stairs. She wondered if Bragg would turn her away. But she had not dared state her real business.

Suddenly there was a cough behind her and Francesca turned, to face a gentleman perhaps thirty years old with a long, twirling mustache. His hand shot out toward her. "I am Arthur Kurland, with the *Sun*. Did I hear correctly? You are Andrew Cahill's daughter?"

She found herself accepting the journalist's hand. "Yes, I am," she said, taken aback.

"So what brings you to Mulberry Street?" he asked, point-blank.

She wet her lips. "The commissioner is a friend of my father's."

"And he's a handsome fellow, eh?" Kurland grinned.

Francesca drew herself up. "I do not think my business here is any of your concern."

"Just nosing around," he said quickly. "No need to get in a huff, Miss Cahill. I meant no offense. Do you know the Burtons? Aren't they neighbors of yours? Weren't they at your house when their son was abducted?" he asked.

She blinked at him. What nerve! she thought. "Yes, they are friends," she managed stiffly, when the patrolman returned and told her that Bragg would see her now. Relief flooded her. "Excuse me," she said, following the officer to the elevator.

"May we speak when you come down?" Kurland called after her.

Francesca entered the elevator and waited for the door to close. The wait was interminable, but she refused to reply. And finally she was ascending to the second floor. "What a forward man," she murmured, more to herself than to the patrolman.

"They're all that way, if you don't mind my saying so, miss," he said. "Like vultures, they are, waiting for a scoop."

She smiled at him. "A scoop?"

"A story." He held the door open protectively and she went out first. Bragg's door was wide open. As Francesca approached, she could clearly see inside.

He was at his desk, in his shirtsleeves. They were rolled up, revealing strong, muscular forearms. His tie was askew, the first few buttons of his dress shirt open, revealing the hollow of his throat. He was on the telephone, with a stack of folders in front of him. The rest of his desk looked as if a hurricane had passed over it.

Francesca truly admired his work ethic. For one more moment, she took the liberty of staring. Had he been more cleanly shaven, he truly would have been a devastating man.

He glanced up, motioning her in and motioning the patrolman to shut the door. The officer backed out, doing so. Bragg gestured for Francesca to sit. "Thank you. And keep me apprised," he said.

He replaced the receiver in the telephone and looked at her. "Hello again, Miss Cahill," he said. And he smiled.

Francesca smiled back, finding it impossible to look away, unable not to think about what her mother had said. Did it really matter that Bragg was illegitimate? It was hardly his fault, after all. And he was certainly well educated and a gentleman. Suddenly, she fervently wished that he had not suffered from the fact of his birth.

She sighed. "I have just come from downtown. Bragg, I may have a suspect to add to your list."

His brows lifted and he steepled his hands. "Do go on."

Francesca told him about her visit to Wiley, omitting nothing.

Bragg shook his head. "Francesca, you are jumping to conclusions—false ones, I fear. There must be dozens—no, hundreds—of young men in this city who openly admire and perhaps secretly love Eliza Burton. The fact that he has known her for years does not qualify him as a suspect."

Francesca was somewhat dismayed by his tepid reaction to her news; on the other hand, a part of her was relieved. "But do you not agree that there is a wolf out there in sheep's clothes? Surely we must keep that in mind."

He leaned back in his cane-backed chair. The window behind him was open, in spite of the cold, allowing in fresh, icy air. "*We* must keep this in mind?"

She flushed. "I am sorry. I just cannot stop thinking about that . . . that ear!"

His expression changed. It became so dismal that it more than dismayed Francesca, but he was on his feet, moving away from the desk, turning his back to her. He paced and she could not see his face.

"Have you located Gordino?" she asked hopefully, thinking now about Joel Kennedy.

He faced her, his features composed once more. "We are working on it around the clock. Francesca," his tone softened, "I understand that you are a woman of extreme compassion. But please, allow me to manage this investigation—alone."

"I only want to help," she whispered, her gaze on his.

"I know you do. But it would be more helpful if you did *not* help," he said firmly.

She felt terribly deflated. How could she not help, if

there was something that she *could* do? It felt like such an impossibility.

"Is there anything else?" he asked.

She wet her lips and stood, clasping her hands nervously. "I have a confession to make."

He looked at her. "I am almost afraid to hear it."

She winced. "But I think you should."

He folded his arms. "And?"

She inhaled for courage. "Sunday afternoon when I was leaving police headquarters I saw Joel running on the street. I picked him up and gave him a ride."

Bragg groaned. Then, "Will you never learn?"

"I thought he might be useful and I felt sorry for him. His mother died of tuberculosis, his father of . . . well, never mind. I offered him a job and took him home and fed him and found him a bed." She paused, realizing she was hugging herself, as well.

His smile was a grimace. "I assume there is a moral to this story?"

"Unfortunately."

"Let me guess. The little bugger made off with the family jewels?"

She met his nearly golden eyes. "No. He stole some of our silver. The ingrate," she cried, dreading her mother's reaction to the theft.

Bragg shook his head. "Francesca, I hate to tell you this, but you have been conned. Kennedy's mother is very much alive, although who and where his father is, I have no idea. Maggie Kennedy is a seamstress who works for Moe Levy. In fact, she is an honest, hardworking woman, and she has three other, younger children whom she struggles to feed. She lives in a tenement on Avenue A, just off Tenth Street. Unfortunately, Joel does not take after his mother."

Francesca stared in disbelief and dismay. "I believe the terminology is, I have been suckered."

He laughed, but the sound was brief. "I've been round

to Maggie's twice since Sunday afternoon, in the hopes of finding Joel. At least now I know why she hasn't seen him, although she tells me he rarely comes home."

"I'm sorry," Francesca finally said.

"Perhaps you have learned your lesson?" Bragg asked.

Francesca met his gaze. There was no mistaking that he was hoping that was the case. "I think I have," she said.

He smiled.

So did she.

There was a knock on the door and a head poked in. Francesca saw a fleshy face and a balding pate. "Heinrich, what do you have?" Bragg barked, moving toward the other man.

"Not the best of news," Heinrich said, opening the door wider. He was a hugely obese man. He handed Bragg a page. "This is my report, Commissioner."

Bragg took the page and scanned it. And then he seemed to stagger slightly, as if struck by a physical object.

"What is it?" Francesca whispered, almost afraid to know.

But Bragg did not seem to hear her. To Heinrich, he said, "Are you certain? How can you be certain?"

"It's my job to know the difference between the living and the dead. That piece of ear came off a corpse that's been dead at least eighteen hours. Sorry, sir."

Francesca looked from the one man to the other and slowly she sank into her chair. This could not be happening. This could not get any worse.

She was wrong.

CHAPTER
8

Heinrich and Bragg stepped outside of his office in order to speak privately. Francesca realized she was shaking uncontrollably.

Jonny Burton was dead.

Bragg stepped back into the office. He did not seem to be aware of her presence. Francesca managed to get to her feet, holding on to the chair for support.

In that one moment, he looked as if he had aged a good ten years. The few crow's-feet around his eyes suddenly seemed pronounced, as did the laugh lines around his mouth. His brow was deeply furrowed. He walked to his desk, but clearly he too was in shock.

She went over to him, laying her hand on his back. "This is not your fault!" she heard herself cry vehemently.

He started, meeting her gaze with wide eyes; clearly he had forgotten that she was present. "If he is dead, it is my fault," he said evenly. Too evenly.

She was about to refute him but instead she breathed, "*If?*"

His jaw flexed and he moved away from her, so that her hand fell to her side.

Francesca grew uneasy. She crossed her arms, wondering if he had rejected her in a way that was distinctly disturbing. "*If* he is dead? Heinrich said—"

He cut her off. "I know what Heinrich said." His tone was cool and sharp. "But this is a city filled with corpses, including those of children."

It took her a moment to realize what he was saying. She gasped. "You think that perhaps Jonny is alive? That the ear came from a different child?"

"It is certainly a possibility," he said. Abruptly, he moved behind his desk and sat down so hard that the chair groaned.

But was it a possibility? Or was it very unlikely? Was the commissioner of police indulging himself in wishful thinking, in hope? Francesca continued to hug herself. "Well, let us assume the ear is Jonny's," she said.

He had been staring out of the window; he whirled in his chair, his gaze flying to hers.

"In which case, the perpetrator of this deed is clearly insane, cruelly so. Clearly he wishes to inflict the gravest torture, psychologically speaking, upon the Burtons. Am I right?"

He was grim. His temples throbbed visibly. "Go on."

She swallowed. He was making her even more uneasy. "And if the ear does not belong to Jonny, if it was taken from a dead child, then this madman is also bent on the cruelest kind of torture. But that would also mean that he has some interest in keeping the boy alive." Her last thoughts, which had arisen while she was speaking, excited her. Perhaps there was hope after all!

"The only point in either case is that we are dealing with a madman. In the first case he is an insane killer, in the second, merely insane." He stood. "I am sorry that you have overheard this latest development." He was suddenly standing in front of her. "Under no circumstances are you to reveal what you know to anyone. Am I clear?"

"I would never say a word," she said, hesitating.

"What is it? What have you already said?" he shot.

She must never forget that he was astute, she reminded

herself. "I did tell my mother about the third note," she said reluctantly.

He grimaced. "I wish you had not done that."

"She will not tell anyone," Francesca cried.

"Please stress upon her that she must keep her knowledge to herself. You have no idea, Miss Cahill, of just what these reporters are capable of. They somehow sniff out the details of all that they should not know. I do not want the details of this case blasted throughout the city on the front pages of every newspaper. It will, I believe, only incite the madman to further extremes—while making it even harder to locate him."

She thought about Kurland, downstairs, waiting for her to descend so he could pounce upon her with more questions. "I will speak to Mama as soon as I return home."

"Thank you. Now, if you will excuse me?" He waited impatiently for her to leave.

But Francesca did hesitate. "Will you tell the Burtons?"

He looked at her, but not with exasperation. "Let me share something with you," he said. "Something it has taken me twenty-eight years to discover."

Francesca nodded.

"Words are so easily spoken. But once spoken, they can never be changed, and they can never be taken back."

She stared into his eyes. "I understand," she said.

"Good day," he returned. He was already out the door, shouting, "Murphy! Hicky! Newman!"

Francesca left and he did not seem to notice.

The Montrose home was at 698 Madison Avenue. Francesca entered the drawing room with her parents. It was a large room with a huge green, blue, and gold Oriental rug covering most of the floor. Numerous seating arrangements were interspersed throughout the room, the furniture a collection done in various shades of gold and green, in damasks, silks, velvets, and brocades. The lower half of the walls were paneled in wood, the upper half a fantastic mu-

ral depicting various classical scenes from Greek and Ro-
man mythology. Two huge chandeliers hung from the
ceiling, which was frescoed in colorful, tight pink and gold
squares.

Francesca paused on the threshold, gazing at the crowd
of dinner guests already gathered together there. She immediately espied the short, slender form of Parkhurst,
whom she had met on several prior occasions. He was
immersed in conversation with Montrose and two other
distinguished gentlemen.

They were all listening to Parkhurst. Many subjects impassioned him, and she wondered which one he had em-
barked upon. She couldn't help but study Montrose, who
was outstanding in his black dinner jacket. She recalled
the brief conversation yesterday upon the stairs, and the
gallantry he had evinced toward her. She knew he would
never breathe a word of that conversation with anyone,
even with Connie.

Or would he?

Suddenly he turned and looked right at her, as if he had
felt her staring. Francesca quickly looked away, but not
quickly enough—he had caught her watching him. Why
was she behaving as if guilty of a crime? Of course, he
now thought her a woman of the world. Whatever had
possessed her?

Turning away from Parkhurst, Montrose came over to
her. "Hello, Francesca. I had hoped you would join us."
His eyes seemed searching.

"Mama insisted," Francesca said quietly, avoiding his
brilliantly blue eyes. Then she instantly regretted not thinking through her choice of words—while simultaneously
wondering if she should tell him the truth.

But he smiled. "Yes, I imagine so. I imagine that you
would prefer to spend the evening studying at the library."

Francesca's gaze flew to his. For one moment, she
thought that he knew why she was always at the library.
But she had sworn Connie to secrecy, and surely Connie

had not told him about her enrollment in college. "I am a hopeless bluestocking," she managed.

He studied her. "Do you know that sometimes I wonder at how different you and my wife are? And it never ceases to amaze me."

Francesca was growing more uncomfortable by the moment, and what was worse, not only was she somewhat breathless, her pulse was racing. "Connie is so perfect." She was the perfect wife, the perfect mother, the perfect hostess. Francesca shrugged. "I am highly flawed."

He laughed. "You are both unique, and my wife, as much as I adore her, is hardly perfect."

"What is so amusing?" Connie asked, approaching them with a smile. "I'm so glad you came, Fran," she said.

Montrose smiled at his wife. "We were discussing just how imperfect you are," he said fondly, slipping his arm around her waist and pulling her close.

Connie smiled at him and then he released her. "What a challenging subject," she said.

Francesca tried to ignore the gesture of affection. "Actually, we were talking about my flaws," she said.

"Flawed? You?" Connie hugged her. "Fran, you are stunning tonight." She gave her a look that said, Just what is going on? Why are you wearing lip rouge and powder? Who curled your hair? Why are you wearing ear bobs and the cameo and rings? She stared, smiling, the questions evident in her eyes.

Francesca wasn't about to say a word. "Not as stunning as you," she said, meaning it. Because Connie was one of the most beautiful women Francesca knew, especially in the evening, when she did not restrain herself with either her wardrobe, her jewelry, her makeup, or her hair. Connie had the same glamour Julia had, and it was as effortless as it was inherent to her nature. Her low-cut red gown was daring but so beautifully and simply designed that no one could possibly find fault with it. A huge diamond choker covered her throat. A matching bracelet, as wide as her wrist, adorned one arm. Her lips were rouged the shade of red wine, and her curls, piled atop her head, made her look very Parisian.

"I am in absolute agreement with Francesca," Montrose said. "Darling, you are stunning tonight, as always. Now, if you ladies will excuse me?" He smiled at them both, bowing, and he returned to the rest of their guests.

Connie plucked on her hand. "What is going on?" she asked in amazement. "Is this my sister I am looking at, or an impostor?"

"Obviously I am an imposter—your sister is at the library, studying." Francesca was about to ask Connie if she had said anything to Montrose, when she blinked, staring across the room. "Sarah Channing is here, as well?"

Connie followed her gaze. Sarah Channing stood with Julia and another woman, listening, apparently, to the two older women chat. "Evan is courting her, and I do believe it is serious."

Francesca shook her head. "How can it be? She never says a word. She is so shy and timid; they seem awfully mismatched."

"I don't know her well." Connie shrugged. Evan suddenly detached himself from a group of young gentlemen and a moment later he was at Sarah's side. He was so much taller than she was, and he stooped in order to speak with her. Francesca watched him smile at her; Sarah eventually smiled back.

"Just how serious do you think it is?" Francesca said, disturbed.

"Perhaps you will have to ask him that?" Connie said with an arch smile. Then she glanced all around, checking to make sure they would not be overheard. No one was about. She took Francesca's arm and pulled her closer to the threshold of the room—away from everyone else inside. "Mama told me *you* found the third note this morning," she whispered.

Francesca stared at her, recalling Bragg's warning. "She

told you?" she cried, but low, and in dismay.

"And that it was covered in blood! Dear God, Fran, is there any more news? Please tell me they have found that sweet little boy."

Francesca bit her lip. Bragg would not be thrilled to know that her sister now knew about the third note, too. "Connie, don't tell anyone, please, I shouldn't have even told Mama."

"I won't tell anyone," Connie assured her. "Of course, I already told Neil."

Francesca groaned.

"And Beth."

"What! How could you tell Beth Anne Holmes that!" Francesca nearly shouted.

"She is my best friend," Connie returned. She patted Francesca's arm. "Have no fear. Beth is not a gossip, and Neil will certainly keep this to himself. Now, let's go in to dinner."

Beth Anne was not a gossip? No one loved to talk more! Francesca stared after her sister as she began to round up the dinner guests. Then she hurried after her.

But Parkhurst was speaking, the entire crowd of guests gathered around him. "The mayor cannot choose which laws to enforce."

"Here, here," were the murmurs of agreement.

"That was a wonderful sermon you gave yesterday," Andrew Cahill said. "Simply superb."

"Thank you," Parkhurst replied. Because he was such a powerful orator, and so passionate about his causes, his sermons, given at the Madison Square Presbyterian Church on Twenty-fourth Street, were among the most widely attended in the city.

"Of course, I understand Low's position," Cahill continued. "It will be the kiss of death if he directs the police to crack down on the saloons on Sundays. Still, Bragg is a man of high moral fiber. I believe he is a reformer at heart."

Francesca edged closer, so she could hear better, her pulse accelerating. Bragg was a reformer. Nothing could please her more.

"I wonder what Commissioner Bragg will do? Is he Low's man, or his own man? If he is truly bent on reform, he will have to enforce the Raines Act, sooner or later," someone said.

"Bragg is caught in a very bad position, indeed," Cahill returned. "Should he crack down on the saloons, he will ultimately damage Low's chances for reelection. But should he not do so, he is failing in his duty as a reformer and a moral man."

"I would not want to be in his shoes," someone said. "Especially not with this terrible Burton affair. Already the press is accusing him of incompetence."

Francesca gasped so loudly that everyone turned to regard her. She felt herself flushing. Good God, how could the press be critical of Bragg when he was working round the clock to solve the Burton affair? It was so unfair!

"Everyone, into the dining room," Connie said quickly, during the brief lapse in the conversation.

And as the crowd obeyed, filing out of the salon, still discussing Bragg's efforts to solve the abduction, Francesca felt her heart sinking with dismay. What would happen to Bragg if, somehow, he failed to find Jonny—alive?

It was a terrible notion. Francesca also realized that he would undoubtedly lose his post as police commissioner.

She caught up with her father. "Papa? Isn't the commissioner coming to supper tonight?"

"He has sent his regrets," Cahill said, tucking her arm in his. "May I escort my beautiful bluestocking daughter in to dine?"

Francesca nodded glumly. She realized that she was very disappointed—and it added to all of her other worries.

She had a French literature class at ten A.M., and Francesca was dressed and downstairs in the breakfast room at a quarter to eight. Her father was already seated at the head of the dining table, sipping coffee and reading the *Times* while waiting for his breakfast. "Good morning, Papa," Francesca said with a smile, taking a seat beside him.

He glanced up, smiling only briefly. "Good morning. Francesca, look at this!" He handed her the paper, his face grim.

It was the front page of the *Times*. And the headline in the center of the page screamed, "More Notes But No Sign of Missing Burton Heir."

For one moment, Francesca froze, recalling Bragg's warning yesterday not to breathe a word of anything that she knew to anyone, and simultaneously, she thought about her mother telling her sister, and Connie telling Neil and Beth Anne. She started to read, her hands beginning to shake, when she almost fell off her chair. She read, "A third and fourth note were found yesterday within hours of one another, the former soaked in blood, the latter with a piece of a human ear." She looked up at her father, stunned.

"Can you believe this . . . this . . . monster?" Cahill cried. He slammed his fist on the table. "While the commissioner has refused to comment, it does appear as if the poor Burton boy has been murdered!"

She had only told her mother about the third note. Who had revealed the existence of the fourth? And what about the Burtons when they saw this newspaper? Oh, no! They would be devastated and terrified. "This is terrible," Francesca whispered.

"It is far more than terrible," her father said. "Your mother told me that you found the third note, Francesca."

She blinked. So much for confidences. "Papa—" she began.

"No." He held up his hand. "I know you inside and out, my dear. I know you undoubtedly wish to help find the boy. I do not want you involved. Is that clear?" He was very serious, indeed.

Francesca's pulse was racing. She nodded as Evan entered the breakfast room and took a chair opposite Francesca. "Good morning. Why is everyone so grim? And what must Fran stay out of this time?" He grinned, then saw the headlines. "May I?" he asked grimly.

Francesca handed him the newspaper, rubbing her temples as platters of toast and marmalade, scrambled eggs, sausages, and bacon were placed upon the table. She no longer had an appetite.

"Your sister found the third note," Cahill remarked, helping himself to eggs and bacon.

"Leave it to Fran," Evan said, shoving the paper aside. He stared at her. "Father is right. Stay out of this, Fran. Leave this blasted business to the police. They are experienced when it comes to dealing with this sort of thing."

Francesca poured herself a cup of tea with trembling hands. "I am not trying to be involved. I just happened to put the clues together. Anyway, Jonny might still be alive." The moment the words were out she regretted them.

But no one made the connection between her and the police commissioner. "I suppose it's possible," Evan said. "But perhaps it might be best if he is dead."

"How can you say that!" Francesca cried, appalled.

"Because the little boy's ear was cut off, Fran," Evan said grimly.

"Perhaps the ear did not belong to Jonny Burton." She drew herself up stiffly as she repeated Bragg's words of the day before.

"An interesting theory," Cahill said. "Shall we change the subject to one more pleasant?"

The siblings nodded. Francesca served herself eggs without much interest while Cahill said, "Evan has news. Why don't you tell your sister?"

Francesca looked up.

Evan smiled. "Sarah and I are getting engaged. Mama is throwing a big fête this Saturday, and Father will make the announcement while I publicly give her a ring."

Francesca was dumbfounded.

"Fran!" Evan got up, moving around the table. "Why so white? Did you just see a ghost?" he joked. "I expected a much warmer reaction. Aren't you going to congratulate me?"

She blinked at him. "Isn't this happening a bit quickly? How can you be so smitten!" she cried.

"He's twenty-five, twenty-six this June. It's high time he settled down," Cahill remarked mildly, now immersed in the *Herald*.

"High time," Evan said cheerfully.

Francesca felt as if she had just received a bodily blow. "How long have you two known one another?" she finally asked.

"A few weeks," he said, standing beside her, his hand on the back of her chair. "She is very sweet, Fran. And she comes from a fine family. I am hoping the two of you will become friends." He was no longer smiling; in fact, his gaze was dark and searching and deadly earnest.

"Sweet," Francesca whispered. "Would it hurt to delay the public announcement? Until you are truly certain that this is the woman you wish to spend the rest of your life with? The rest of your *entire* life?"

Evan shrugged and his smile flashed. "But I am certain. You know, Fran, sometimes it just happens. Le coup de foudre. That lightning bolt, sent from Cupid himself. And there isn't very much one can do about it."

She nodded, but she could not smile and she did not believe; nor did she believe what she was hearing. "Evan, as your sister, your loyal, loving sister, I beg you to wait a few more months before getting engaged."

Before Evan could respond, Cahill rustled the paper, putting it down. He stood, most of his breakfast uneaten. "I approve wholeheartedly," he said. "Children, I must be off to the office. Evan, will you come with me now or are you leaving later?"

"I'll ride downtown with you now, Father." Evan

winked at Francesca. "It will be all right, Fran. Trust me," he said.

She swiveled in her chair to watch him as he strolled from the room with their father. Suddenly he looked back and said, "You promised you would call on her."

Her smile felt sickly. "I shall," she said.

When they were gone, she pushed her plate away and with her elbows on the table—a pose her mother would murder her for—she laid her head on her hands. Last night she had tossed and turned restlessly, dreaming about pieces of ears and Rick Bragg and finding Jonny Burton—but when they had found Jonny, he had been Joel Kennedy instead, and it had been a huge mistake.

Bragg had said he'd been to the Kennedy home twice since the abduction. Where had he said Maggie lived?

Hadn't he said Avenue A, just off Tenth Street?

They needed to find Joel. Because they needed to find Gordino even more desperately. He was their only link with the madman behind the abduction and the terrible, sadistic notes.

God. What if that ear did belong to Jonny? What if Jonny had been alive when it had been cut off?

Francesca leapt to her feet, pacing. Do not even think such terrible thoughts, she told herself frantically.

She laid her hands on her throbbing temples. Maggie Kennedy was a decent, hardworking woman. She worked at Moe Levy. Moe Levy was a famous men's apparel maker. How many factories could he have? Francesca doubted there was more than one. What if Maggie had not wanted to really talk with Bragg, because he was the police? What if she would talk to Francesca, woman to woman? Francesca knew she had to go speak to the other woman. Otherwise, they were very much at a dead end.

She turned, thinking to skip breakfast after all, go uptown to school, attend class, study for an hour or so, and then try to locate Maggie. But a flash of bright light outside the window made her pause.

She watched Bragg's long roadster park on Fifth Avenue, just past the Cahill front gates—in front of the Burton house.

He had certainly seen the morning papers. He must be going to the Burtons to explain, and perhaps try to make them understand that Jonny was not necessarily dead. Francesca didn't think twice. She rushed upstairs while he was getting out of the car, as fast as her feet would go. She was panting when she reached the window in her bedroom, opera glasses in hand. She trained them on Fifth Avenue; Bragg had already entered the house.

She looked into the first downstairs window—the front hall. It was empty.

She looked at the next two windows, into the smaller drawing room. It too was empty.

No, it was not. She stared, seeing Bragg standing there, silhouetted against the window. He wasn't moving, and she had a perfect view of his profile.

He stood and stood and she realized his mouth seemed to be moving. He was speaking to someone she could not see. Darnation!

Francesca assumed it was Burton or Eliza. And then Eliza came rushing forward.

He had been speaking to Eliza, she thought. And then she froze.

Eliza did not stop. She walked right into his arms.

He held her tightly, cradling her against his body, her face flat upon his chest.

There was no doubt she was crying, just as there was no doubt that he was comforting her.

There was also no doubt that Eliza Burton and Rick Bragg were far more than mere acquaintances.

CHAPTER
9

They were lovers.

Francesca stared through the opera glasses, her hands shaking so badly that the glasses wobbled up and down, hardly giving her a clear view. But Bragg had stroked Eliza's hair. She was certain of it.

And a man and a woman just did not hold one another the way that they were doing, not unless they were intimate.

Suddenly they leapt apart, and there was no mistaking the guilt associated with the action. Francesca inhaled hard, steadied the opera glasses, and saw Eliza walk away from Bragg. She was speaking to someone, and a moment later Francesca's suspicion was confirmed. Burton had entered the room.

She was sick. Sick enough to think about trying to retch.

How cozy, she managed to think.

Then, Did Burton even suspect that his wife and the commissioner of the New York City police were having an affair?

Francesca could not seem to think straight. How *could* this be happening? Given all of the circumstances? She walked away from the window to sit down on the first piece of furniture she came to. She had never been this upset, it seemed. What was wrong with her? Who cared if Eliza was Bragg's mistress?

Tears came to her eyes. She cared. Goddammit, she did.

She covered her face with her hands and then surprised herself, for briefly she wept.

She hardly ever cried. She was a sensible sort. Crying accomplished little; besides, Francesca hardly admired those women who seemed to have water spigots in the place of eye ducts. Francesca wiped her eyes with resolution, when suddenly absolute and complete comprehension struck her. She was on her feet.

There must be dozens—no, hundreds—of young men in this city who openly admire and perhaps secretly love Eliza Burton.

Wasn't that exactly what Bragg had said?

And suddenly she recalled the way he had insisted the boy was not dead when they had found the fourth note. She recalled how he had insisted that the ear had come off a corpse that was not Jonny Burton's. And she recalled how angry he had been with her for suggesting that Eliza might be lying about inappropriate suitors in order to protect her marriage. Suddenly, Francesca knew why he was taking this case so personally, why he refused to believe the boy dead, and why he had protected Eliza's reputation so fiercely.

All of his behavior thus far indicated just how involved he was with Eliza; every word, every action, signified that he was the one who was in love with her.

And now here was the proof, proof she had witnessed with her very own eyes.

Francesca wondered just how long they had been carrying on.

She wondered how Eliza could live with herself, deceiving her husband the way that she was doing.

And what about Bragg? Francesca stiffened. She could hear her mother's voice in her mind as if she were actually speaking. Julia would say, "Did I not tell you? An apple, my dear, does not fall far from the tree!"

Francesca almost clapped her hand over her ears, as if that would shut off her mother's smug voice, taunting her in her mind.

There was a knock on her door. Francesca called out, "One moment, please," and rushed into her bathroom. Her eyes were a bit red from that sudden burst of tears. She smiled grimly at herself, pinched her cheeks, and tucked some tendrils of golden blond hair behind her ears. It did not help. The curls jutted free instantly. And her eyes remained suspiciously pink.

Worse, she remained nauseous, with a horrible hollow feeling in the pit of her stomach—or was it in the center of her chest?

Francesca opened the door herself, to find a housemaid standing there.

"The commissioner is here to see you, Miss Cahill," the young woman said.

Bragg had been shown into the drawing room adjacent to the much larger reception room. Francesca paused on the threshold and had one instant in which to study him without his knowing it. He was staring unseeingly into the fireplace. He appeared exhausted, and although freshly shaven, he looked as if he hadn't slept in days. His anguish was so tangible she thought that she could feel it.

She felt a twinge of sympathy for him and shoved it determinedly aside. He was a liar himself. God, he had appeared such a noble, moral man. She was so disappointed. She had every right to despise him now. And he must take her for a fool. Actually, he must take most of New York society for fools.

"Francesca," he said, coming forward.

She moved back a step, causing him to pause with surprise. "Miss Cahill," she heard herself correct him, as if she were a prude, as if they had not spent hours together discussing the case—as if some kind of unspoken partnership had not evolved during the investigation. She flushed upon hearing her own curt tone.

"I beg your pardon," he said, his gaze searching her face. "Is something wrong?"

"No. Yes. Of course something is wrong." Her smile felt brittle. What would he say and what would he do if she accused him of being Eliza's lover? And it was at that precise moment that she thought of Evan and his last mistress—who had not been the first. She grew uncomfortable. She adored her brother. She did not consider him an immoral man, not in the least. In fact, now that he was about to get engaged, she knew he would abandon his love affairs.

She reminded herself that there was a huge difference between Bragg and Evan. Bragg was carrying on with someone's wife. Evan was not.

"Fran . . . Miss Cahill?" He approached her, golden eyes filled with concern.

"Is there any more news?" she asked, crossing her arms tightly over her fitted shirtwaist. Somehow she did not back away when her entire being screamed at her to do so. She was aware now of feeling betrayed. It was a horrid feeling to have.

"No." His mouth firmed. "Have you seen the papers?"

She hesitated. "Unfortunately, I have." How could she feel betrayed? They were almost strangers; he owed her nothing, nothing at all.

His eyes darkened. "So has all of New York City. So have the Burtons."

"Eliza must be in hysterics." How wooden she sounded to her own ears.

"I have just come from the Burtons," he told her, studying her frankly and with some confusion again. "She is convinced her son is dead." He added, "Are you certain something is not amiss?"

Francesca's heart was wrenched uncontrollably by his

last words. How dare he be so kind and compassionate toward her now. And even though Eliza was not what she appeared, that did not change the fact that she was a mother with a missing child, one who might very well be dead. Francesca could not despise Eliza. "Have you called Dr. Finny?" she asked. "Should I go over to see what I can do?"

He seemed relieved by her response. "She has retired to her rooms. I doubt she will take any callers," Bragg said.

Ah, but she has seen you, Francesca thought uncharitably.

"I have called Finny. Whom did you tell about the fourth note?" he asked. "Or rather, the envelope with the ear?"

She was taken aback. "No one," she said firmly.

He studied her and nodded, relaxing. "I'm sorry. I had to ask. I am very angry about the *Times* running such an article, one with the vast potential of damaging my investigation."

His investigation, she thought. Never mind that he was the police commissioner and the ultimate authority on this and any case. "I swear to you, I never breathed a word about what was in the fourth envelope," Francesca said.

"I believe you." He sighed. "Unfortunately, I have little doubt the leak—both of them—came from within my own department." He sighed again.

She continued to hug herself. "What makes you so certain?" Francesca felt quite certain herself that Beth Anne had told the world about the third note.

"Although this is a high-security case, which means that only a handful of detectives are working on it, sworn to absolute secrecy, there are technicians involved. Any one of whom might take a bribe." He frowned. "I handpicked the detectives, but only three of them are men I recently promoted for their honesty and character. I cannot even be certain that the leak did not come from one of the detectives."

"I'm sorry," Francesca said, and she did mean it.

There was a moment of silence then. It quickly became awkward, heavy. Francesca had no comment to make—she kept replaying the scene she had just witnessed at the Burtons' in her mind's eye. He kept studying her, his scrutiny far too intense for comfort. He seemed bewildered by her behavior. Clearly he had noticed that she was dismayed and oddly put off. He should not care.

Finally he said, "I must be going. Francesca, if something is wrong, please feel free to raise the subject."

Her smile was arch. Too arch. "Why ever would you think that something is wrong? Other than the fact that one innocent child is missing under ghastly circumstances?"

"We have only just met," he said with a slight smile, and it seemed rueful, "but I do believe we have become friends, of a certain nature, in a manner of speaking. And I am quick when it comes to understanding and judging character. Something is amiss. I am certain of it."

She smiled and said, "Nothing is amiss. You have made a mistake, this time, Commissioner."

He eyed her, for her tone was too sharp to be sociable. Then, "I do hope it is not something that I have somehow, inadvertently, done."

Francesca almost gaped.

"Well, good day."

"Good day," she said. And she did not walk him to the door.

She would skip her class. There was simply too much to do and a little boy's life was at stake. Francesca had realized that until they discovered otherwise, she must assume that Jonny Burton was alive.

She slipped on a fitted charcoal-gray jacket, one that matched her custom-made skirt. Both garments were beautifully detailed with black soutache at the cuffs and hem.

She adjusted a black hat with jaunty ostrich feathers, grabbed her purse, and hurried downstairs. She was determined not to think about Bragg's affair with Eliza Burton.

She had not even set foot on the ground floor when the front door opened and Connie came inside, her infant daughter bundled up in her arms, followed by Mrs. Partridge and three-year-old Charlotte.

Charlotte looked exactly like her mother, except that her blond hair was still so pale that it was almost white. She saw Francesca and her blue eyes lit up. "Auntie! Auntie!" she shrieked.

Francesca grinned and held out her arms. "Come here, Cinderella."

Cinderella was Charlotte's favorite fairy tale, and somehow, the nickname had evolved from that and stuck. Charlotte tugged her little gloved hand free of her nanny's, and still shrieking, she hurled herself at Francesca.

"Hello," Connie cried happily. "We decided to come over and have breakfast with you, Fran."

Her short navy blue coat, skirt, and petticoat flying above her knees, Charlotte leapt up as Francesca caught her and lifted her high into the air. Charlotte laughed. "Higher, Auntie Fran!" she ordered.

"Any higher and you'll be up in heaven, sweetie pie," Francesca said, hugging her a bit too hard and then letting her down to the floor. She eyed her sister in surprise. Then she glanced at her sister again. Connie looked tired, indeed. "Con, you had a dinner party last night. We left at midnight! Why aren't you still loitering in bed? Maybe with hot chocolate and *Harper's Weekly*? Better yet, the new catalogue from Sears?" Her intuition told her that all was not as it should be.

Connie gave her a look. "Since when I have ever slept late? Or have you forgotten? Besides, the girls are up at seven, little sister."

Francesca walked over to her sister, to peer past the bundles of blankets at the tiny sleeping infant. Lucinda was only eight months old. She smiled at the sight of the perfect, chubby face. Oddly, Lucinda had red hair and the alabaster complexion to match. "Dinner was wonderful, Con. The food, the company, everything was perfect." She stroked Lucinda's smooth little cheek.

Connie smiled then. "Thank you. I really appreciate that. You know, Mama never said a word." Her smile faded.

Francesca patted her back. "Mama told *me* that it was a lovely affair," she said truthfully. "You know how she is. It is not her nature to praise us, Con."

"I know, but I wish she would have told me," Connie said with a sigh, shifting Lucinda in her arms.

"May I?" Francesca said eagerly, and a moment later she was cradling the baby to her breast. But even as she relished the moment, an image of Eliza in Bragg's arms came to mind. How was she ever going to forget about their affair?

"Francesca, why are you scowling?" Connie asked.

Francesca started. "I am not scowling. Connie, I cannot recall a time when you came over at such an hour to have breakfast with us."

And she also wondered how she would get out of the house in order to find Maggie Kennedy if Connie stayed. Because she had a plan. She would go to the Moe Levy shop on Broadway, and learn the location of the factory.

"Has Papa left yet?" Connie asked, handing her fur coat, hat, and gloves to a houseman while ignoring Francesca's comment.

Charlotte, who had run out of the hall, came running back in. She was still wearing her navy blue coat and matching hat. "Grampa isn't home," she wailed.

"Miss Charlotte, come here and remove your coat and hat," Mrs. Partridge said firmly.

Charlotte scowled but obeyed, walking over to the short, plump woman with the unruly gray curls. "And you act like the lady your mama is," Mrs. Partridge scolded in a whisper.

Charlotte nodded then shouted, "Auntie Fran! Let's go shopping! Can you buy me a doll? Today?"

Before Francesca could begin to reply, Connie took her daughter by the hand. "You have two dozen dolls, Charlotte. You may wait until your birthday for another one."

Charlotte gave her mother an annoyed look.

Francesca caught her eye and gave her a wink. Later, she told her silently.

Charlotte grinned, clapped her hands together, and then looked up at her mother guiltily to see if Connie was aware of the conspiracy forming behind her back. Connie sighed. "Oh, Fran. I wish you would not spoil her. You need one of your own. Trust me."

"I'd love one of my own," Francesca said, handing Lucinda to Mrs. Partridge, "but I don't want all that goes with it." She smiled. "I am too young to get married."

Connie smiled serenely at her. "Now that Evan is getting engaged, you have about six months' respite. Once he's wed, my dear little sister, you are next."

Francesca looked at her for a long moment without speaking. "Don't tell me. A June wedding?" She was almost but not quite disbelieving.

"If Mama has her way."

Francesca rolled her eyes, but she was more than dismayed. Because Connie was right, and because she still had not adjusted to the fact that Evan was getting engaged, much less married. And in such a rush!

"Have you eaten?" Connie asked.

"Actually, I have. I was on my way out," Francesca said, her thoughts veering to Bragg, Eliza, Maggie Kennedy, and the case.

"At this hour?" Connie lifted both pale, groomed brows. In fact, her hair was pulled back into a flawless chignon, she was wearing the simplest pearl necklace above the collar of her blouse, and her lips were delicately rouged. Francesca wondered if she looked as perfect when she went to bed and when she first woke up in the morning. She had the feeling that she did.

Connie said, "And pray tell, Miss Up-to-Something-Once-Again, just where are you going and what are you up to, this time?"

Francesca smiled. "I am hardly up to anything, Con. I was going to go to the public library to read. That is all." She lied as easily if she had been born a liar. But she hated deceiving her sister.

Connie clearly did not know whether to believe her or not. Then she grabbed her arm. "Well. Keep me company for a while. Let's have waffles with pounds of maple syrup and hot chocolate with whipped cream and let's get so deliciously fat no man will look at us again."

Francesca stared after her sister as she walked away. What an odd comment to make.

"Miss. Are you going to get out of the cab?"

Francesca stared out of the window of the hansom. The Moe Levy and Company factory was on the fourth floor of the building she was regarding, on Thirty-second Street between Seventh and Eighth avenues. The four-story brick building seemed terribly run down, but so did the entire street. There were potholes everywhere, the buildings had broken windows, and the few workers passing by looked as worn down as the world they lived in. "Of course I am getting out," Francesca said, already having handed the cabby his fare. As she stepped down to the sidewalk, taking care of her footing on the frozen, blackened snow, she wondered how she would ever find a hansom to take her home. The street was empty except for two passing wagons, loaded with merchandise Francesca could not identify.

The hansom departed. Francesca clutched her muff in one hand, her purse in another. Two men in baggy, poorly made jackets and caps eyed her as they passed. A stray dog urinated on the wheel of a parked wagon. Shouts were emanating from one of the buildings—it sounded as if a huge fight were breaking out. Francesca's heart pounded far too swiftly for comfort.

What am I doing here? she wondered uneasily.

Then she shook her head, as if she might shake herself free of fear and doubt. This was where Maggie Kennedy worked. Francesca had no choice but to confront her there, for time felt as if it were running out. And having Jennings or another coachman drive her was far too dangerous. One question from her mother and he would dutifully spill all. Francesca imagined that if Julia ever learned where she had gone that day, or the past few days, she would not be allowed to set foot out of the house for the next six months.

The front door was unlocked, its heavy, rusting bolts unlatched. Francesca pushed the heavy, scarred and scratched door open, peering into a shadowy, unlit hallway. Dark, nearly black stairs faced her.

She had no choice, she reminded herself. She slipped inside and went up two flights of stairs that smelled suspiciously of urine.

On the second-floor landing she thought she could hear the whirring of machinery and the occasional sound of a human voice. There were only two doors on the hall, at opposite ends, and Francesca moved toward the one farthest from her, which would face Seventh Avenue. She pushed it open.

The room was extremely large, which explained why there were only two apartments on the floor. Wooden tables piled with fabrics were everywhere. Tailors and seamstresses sewed and stitched steadily at the tables. Three walls were covered with windows, and natural sunlight spilled into the room. But it was amplified by the glare of the electric light coming from the hanging lights that were suspended from the ceiling. After the darkness of the hall and stairwell, the bright glare of the lights made her blink repeatedly.

A few heads, male and female, were turning her way. As Francesca's eyes finally adjusted to the bright light, she scanned the room, wondering who Maggie Kennedy was—and if she was present that day. A man was approaching her.

He was a heavyset man, but he was wearing a suit and tie, even if his garments were askew. "Miss? May I help you?" His accent was heavy. Francesca thought him to be either a German, a Russian, or a Jew.

"I am looking for Maggie Kennedy. I understand she works here." Francesca smiled. "It is extremely urgent that I speak to her."

"She works here, yah, but she is very busy," he said, studying her.

"I am desperate," Francesca said.

"Why do you not come back at six? She will be leaving to home then," he said.

"I have come all the way downtown to find her. This really cannot wait," Francesca said, beginning to despair.

He shook his head grimly. "No, no."

Suddenly something Bragg had said registered in her mind. Flushing, Francesca reached into her black satin purse and handed the man a silver dollar. He smiled at her. "She is the red one in the back," he said, pointing. And he walked away.

Francesca stared after him. She had just bribed someone for the first time in her life. She did not know whether to be thrilled or dismayed. Then she gave it up. Sunlight was glinting on bright red hair at the far end of the room. Francesca made her way through the tables and workers until she was facing Maggie over the pile of fabrics on her table.

Maggie had stopped sewing. She sat on her stool, blue eyes wide, staring at Francesca.

Francesca could not help but stare back. Maggie was probably Connie's age. She was still pretty, but she had that odd look of someone young who is also so very old. Her fair skin was lined, her lips chapped, but maybe it was the light in her eyes that aged her so. It was a light that was dull and flat, a light that cherished no dreams, a light without any hope.

She had four children, Francesca thought grimly. And Joel was ten or eleven. She must have had Joel when she was no more than thirteen or fourteen. Francesca had never before faced a woman in such circumstances—or at least, she was not aware of ever having been face-to-face with someone who had lived this kind of life before. "Mrs. Kennedy?"

"Maggie will do," the redhead said, ducking and beginning to stitch again. Her movements seemed labored, unlike those of the rest of the seamstresses around her. Her concentration seemed forced. There were a few freckles splattered on her small nose.

"May we speak?"

Maggie did not look up. "Why?"

"I am desperate," Francesca said simply. "Because a six-year-old boy is missing, and Joel might be the key to finding him."

Maggie's sewing stopped. For one moment she did not look up, and Francesca saw her hands tremble. Then her tired blue eyes lifted. "I am sorry about that little boy. The policeman told me all about it. But it happens all the time in the city. Children disappear. And worse. I am sorry. But I cannot help. I do not know where Joel is."

Tears seemed to fill her eyes and then she was sewing again, with hard, fast movements.

Francesca reached out instinctively and covered her palm with her own; Maggie's sewing ceased. "I know you are scared for Joel. Don't be. He can be of help, Maggie. Please, I beg you, as a woman to another woman. I don't have children. But I have two nieces. I cannot imagine what I would do if one of them had been abducted. Eliza Burton—the boy's mother—is sick to death with grief and fear. Please. I must find Joel. He can help, I think. Please."

Maggie regarded her. "I don't know where he is," she

said, eyes wide and intense. "I never know. He comes and goes as he pleases, always in trouble, he is, been in and out of boarding school so many times I lost count. He's like his father, he is, 'cept Daniel was a bloke buzzer and Joel he's on the molls. But they're one of a kind, them two, and I've had enough, I have, trying to keep a roof over the other three, trying to feed the little ones, and I just can't take it anymore!" Tears suddenly spilled from her eyes. Her hands were shaking terribly.

Francesca was quite certain boarding school did not mean boarding school, and she had no idea what bloke and moll buzzers were, but she had got the gist. "He's not a bad boy," she whispered. "He saved me from a terrible situation."

Maggie swiped at her eyes and stared up at Francesca. "I just can't take it," she said, and she wiped her eyes again. "I can't, a body can only do so much."

Francesca gripped her hand. "You must be very strong," she said, meaning it. She could not even imagine the kind of life this woman had.

"I ain't strong. I'm weak and tired, and I yell at the little ones all the time," she said. Then she looked up, her eyes moist. "He saved you from a terrible situation?"

Francesca nodded, her smile slight. "I was in a place I had no right to be, and a terrible thug accosted me." She shivered. "Joel attacked him and we ran away together. I owe him, Maggie."

She smiled a little, sniffled, and said, "He's not always bad."

"Have you seen him since Sunday?"

Maggie looked away, shaking her head no.

She was lying. Francesca had seen the lie in her eyes just before she turned away. "Please, Maggie. Joel will not get into trouble. I am not the police. I am a young woman, just like you." The moment her last words were out, she regretted them.

"You are hardly like me," Maggie said, eyeing her

defiantly. "You are rich, miss, and I bet you never went hungry a day in your life." She laid down her needle and opened her hands, palms up. "See them calluses?"

"Yes," Francesca said, and she was beginning to realize that either Maggie did not know where Joel was or she would never help because they were from different worlds, a gulf between them that could never be crossed. "You're right. We are nothing alike, except that we are both women. But I will not stop, Maggie, not until I find that little boy who is missing. I only pray that he is still alive, and every moment that passes makes that more unlikely. He is in the hands of a madman."

Maggie stared.

Francesca stared back. Tears of desperation had risen to her own eyes, but she refused to let them fall.

Maggie said, "He will not get bagged?"

"Bagged?"

"Bagged," she repeated. Then apparently seeing Francesca's confusion, she said, "Pinched. He won't get pinched by the spots?"

It was like speaking a foreign language, Francesca thought. "You mean, caught by the police?"

Maggie nodded. "An' bagged."

"No, he will not," Francesca said firmly. "I am not a policewoman. There are no women on the police force, Maggie. I am, in fact, a college student, that is all."

Maggie wet her lips. "He's staying with me neighbor. We're at number 201 Avenue A, at Tenth Street. He's in the fourth apartment. Letter C."

"Thank you," Francesca cried, clasping both of her hands. And impulsively, she kissed her on the cheek.

Francesca had taken a hansom across town to 201 Avenue A. The only difference between this neighborhood, she thought, and the one she had just come from was that this one was primarily residential. The tenements were sandwiched between shops selling groceries and grog, and there were two or three bars and saloons on every block.

The day had grown warmer, enough so that the dirty snow underfoot was turning to slush. The sun was high, the sky almost cloudless, and pedestrians were numerous, mostly women going about their daily errands and shopping for their families. A few street vendors had put out their wares and carts. Francesca bought a bag of hot roasted chestnuts with the intention of eating them on her way home. She passed the Greenwood Memorial People's Bath. There was a line of men and boys on the street, waiting to enter the premises. A few of the boys were playing stickball in their sweaters, careless of the dirty snow and slush, their coats piled up on the bathhouse stoop.

Her spirits were high. She was smiling—she was going to find Joel!

She paused before number 201, glancing up at the front door. The stone stoop was empty, but she could hear voices coming from the basement apartments. She glanced down. The windows were open. A woman was humming a ditty and she could smell a roasting chicken.

Her stomach growled, reminding her that she had forsaken breakfast that morning. Francesca felt a twinge of trepidation as she went up the stoop and inside. What if Joel was not home? What if he saw her and ran away? She crossed her fingers—he had to be home, and he had to talk to her.

This time, she was not surprised by the lack of lighting and the odors of urine in the hall. But she cried out when a mouse leapt out in front of her, scurrying across the hall floor. She hurried up the four flights of stairs.

Outside apartment C, she banged on the door. A moment later it was cracked slightly and Francesca glimpsed a heavy woman with iron-gray hair, clad in a dark day dress and a faded apron that had once been white and was now gray. Behind her she could make out some shabby furnishings in a dark, ill-lit apartment.

"Maggie told me I could find Joel here," Francesca said.

"He ain't here," the woman said, eyeing her with outright suspicion.

Francesca handed her a silver dollar. "May I wait?"

The woman pocketed it and unlatched the chain on the inside of the door and let her enter. She turned. "Joel! Someone to see you." Then she looked at Francesca again.

She made a sound, perhaps a harrumph, its meaning indecipherable. And she walked over to the kitchen counter—the apartment's living area included the kitchen— as Joel came out of the bedroom, three children trailing behind him. His eyes widened with apprehension when he saw Francesca.

She told herself not to even think about the stolen silverware now. "Hello, Joel. Your mother told me I could find you here. How are you?"

His eyes widened even more. "She told you?"

"She did. Your mother is a fine lady." Francesca looked at the three children, two little boys, one with pitch-black hair like Joel's, the other a flaming redhead like his mother, and a girl perhaps Charlotte's age, also with jet-black hair. The three children were wearing faded, worn clothes with many patches, the boys' pants were inches too short, revealing skinned knees, but the clothes were spotlessly clean otherwise—as were the children. The three little faces peering at her with open curiosity were all freshly scrubbed and glowing.

"My mother ain't no lady," Joel said flatly. "She works." He had a spot of soot on his nose. He also had a patch of dirt on his left elbow.

"She has the character of a fine lady," Francesca said.

He looked at her. "She does?" He seemed pleased, but tried to hide it.

"Absolutely. Will you introduce me to your brothers and sisters?"

He hesitated. "Why?"

"Why not?"

He sighed and turned. "This here is Lizzie, an' Paddy an' Mat." He turned his back to Francesca, facing his siblings. The boys, Francesca thought, were probably five and seven. "Scoot! Go into the bedroom and wait for me until I say otherwise," he said sternly.

"Who's the lady and what does she want?" asked the red-haired boy, Paddy, who was five.

"Not your business," Joel warned.

With many protestations, the three finally trooped off, disappearing into the other room. Within seconds, Lizzie was shrieking and the boys were laughing. Francesca could not help but be concerned.

"They're just playin'," Joel said, digging his hands into his pockets.

"Joel, I need your help."

He shrugged. "Don't know if I can."

"We must find Gordino. Do you know where he is?"

"No."

Francesca was about to reach into her purse—bribery, perhaps, was becoming a bad habit—but then she thought about the silver. "Joel, how could you?" she heard herself say.

He looked wary. "How could I what?"

"How could you take my mother's silver!" Francesca cried.

He stared. "I didn't take no silver, lady."

"Please. You ran away after stealing our silver—after I gave you a hot meal, a warm bed, and a job."

"I didn't take no silver," Joel said harshly.

Francesca started, because he seemed angry, and she was bewildered. "Joel, you were the new employee. You are the one with a police record. My mother will kill me when I tell her what has happened."

He stared belligerently. "I thought you wanted to know about Gordino."

Her heart skipped. "I most certainly do," she cried, but she was also filing away the fact that by pressing him on a matter that made him uncomfortable, she had actually gotten him to address the subject she wished him to.

"He's been hiding since Sunday. That's the word on the street," Joel said.

"But where? We must find him!"

"No one knows where, lady."

Francesca pursed her mouth, then, "Joel, you do know why we want to locate him?"

He made a face. It seemed to say, Do I look like an idiot? " 'Course I do. That Burton boy. It's about him."

"You wouldn't know where he is, would you?" Francesca cried suddenly. "I mean, is there 'word' on the 'street' about the abduction?"

"There's some talk, not much." Joel shrugged.

"What kind of talk?" Francesca sat down on the room's single small sofa. Joel was standing beside it and she took his hands in hers.

"I don't know." He pulled his hands away, flushing. "Just that it's a strange business, it is, an' everyone thinks so."

"How so? Please?" Francesca pressed.

He hesitated. "Ain't no ordinary crook, Miss Cahill, who done this. It was an inside job, an' the street knows it. Word is, someone out there aims to do as bad as he can to Burton. That's the word. Burton's the mark."

So it was an enemy of Robert Burton's, Francesca thought. "How can we find Gordino? And will you help me?"

He hesitated another time. "I guess so. Because you gave me a job an' all, even if I decided not to keep it."

She suddenly wondered if he had been telling her the truth—if he had not stolen the silver after all. "Didn't you run away because you had stolen the silver, Joel? In order to sell it so you could help feed your brothers and sister?"

His eyes flashed. "I didn't steal nuthin' from you, lady! Someone works for you is a real rook, an' he went an' used me, seein' the opportunity to steal for himself. See what I mean? You been swindled, good."

Francesca stood up, uneasy now. If he was right, then one of the Cahill employees was a thief. "I would understand if you had stolen the silver, Joel."

"I didn't. I can cut ten purses a day," he said heatedly. "I don't need your silver!"

She believed him. She laid her hand in his thick, wavy hair, wincing because it was dirty. "I apologize," she said softly. "I do."

He jerked away, eyes wide. "You apologize to me?" he gasped.

She smiled then. "Yes. Is it such a surprise?"

He flushed and looked away. And mumbled, "I might know where to find him."

"What?" Francesca cried, turning him back around to face her.

"I might know where to find Gordino." He looked up at her.

"Where?" she gasped.

"Tonight. Meet me here around eleven. I'll take you to this place. He might be there."

Francesca stared, filled with anxiety now. "Tonight? At eleven? You want me to meet you *here,* tonight, at *eleven* P.M.?"

He nodded.

She folded her arms across her chest. "I have to know, Joel. Where will you be taking me?"

He stared, eyes narrowed. "You workin' for that fox?"

Fox. Policeman. "No."

"You be here at eleven an' maybe we can find Gordino," he said.

Francesca stared. And finally, her heart sinking like a rock, she nodded.

She did not have a good feeling about this.

CHAPTER
10

The Channings daringly lived on the West Side. Their residence, just a block south of the Dakota, so nicknamed for its remote location from the rest of the civilized world, was brand-new. Francesca eyed the mansion, which was horrendously Gothic, as she alighted from her carriage. She could not imagine what the architect had been thinking by designing so many turrets and towers, not to mention the numerous gargoyles clinging to the building's façade.

Sarah Channing's father, as it turned out, was deceased. Her mother had inherited his millions and had promptly built the West Side house. Sarah, Francesca had learned, was the only child. One day she would inherit the entire Channing fortune.

It was very hard for Francesca to focus on the task at hand—which was befriending her brother's soon-to-be fiancée. The rendezvous later that night with Joel Kennedy was haunting her. Every time she thought about it she got butterflies; how could she even be thinking of sneaking out alone at such an hour to one of the worst neighborhoods in the city?

Slowly, pensively, she climbed the front steps. She had debated telling Bragg about locating Joel and his offer to take her to find Gordino, and she had dismissed the notion.

Joel was wary of the police, as well he should be. Francesca felt that Joel would bolt the moment he realized Bragg was involved in their scheme. But she was truly afraid for her own personal safety; not for a minute had she forgotten how foul Gordino was, or the way he had kissed her. Now, of course, Joel's past words also kept haunting her. Gordino was a murderer, and for a reason she just could not fathom, he had gotten away with his crimes and was not behind bars.

Francesca rang the doorbell, fretting and worrying.

What if Gordino accosted her again? What if, this time, he was successful? The very thought was enough to make her dizzy and faint.

What if she told Bragg and they conceived a way for him to be present at the scene of the rendezvous, without Joel ever knowing?

The problem was, Francesca hated being deceitful. To make matters worse, in an odd way, she was somewhat fond of the "kid." He might be a pickpocket and a thief, but she could certainly understand how poverty and desperation had driven him to such a livelihood. In the end, she just could not blame him for being what he was.

He had seemed genuinely fond of his brothers and sister.

She did not want to betray his trust.

A footman suddenly opened the front door, startling Francesca, who was so immersed in her thoughts.

She stated her business, presenting her personal card, and was told that Sarah was at home, but occupied. However, she was led inside, and the footman told her that he would inquire as to whether Miss Channing was currently receiving callers.

Francesca handed over her fur-lined coat, her hat, muff, and gloves, and was left alone inside a huge drawing room that was seriously overdone. Cherubs floated amidst puffy clouds on the ceiling, and every bit of wood trim, as well as every piece of furniture in the room, was gilded. She did not sit. She paced.

Would it do any good to honor a confidence with Joel, a boy she hardly knew, if she became badly hurt, or even worse, by the night's upcoming shady affair? Francesca shivered.

But Jonny Burton's life was at stake. *If* he was still alive. And they desperately needed to locate Gordino and make him reveal his connection to the abduction. But how in God's name could she even hope to do that? The only possible way, Francesca had earlier concluded, was to bribe him—and handsomely. She was prepared to offer him an outrageous sum in exchange for the name of whoever had given him that second note.

A houseman appeared. "Miss Cahill, if you would not mind the informality, Miss Channing is in her studio, but she will see you now."

Her studio? Puzzled, Francesca followed the servant through the large house. It, too, could have been dubbed "the Marble Palace" as her own home had. But nothing seemed to be in good taste, she thought. Every inch of space was occupied with chairs and tables, sculptures and vases, mirrors and paintings. Mrs. Channing, apparently, had very lavish tastes, indeed.

The manservant led her deeper and deeper into the house. And when he opened a door, allowing her to enter first, Francesca's eyes went wide.

The large room was at the very back of the house, and two walls were nothing but windows. Even at this late afternoon hour, the room was flooded with light. The views of the frozen Hudson River and the snowy Palisades were fantastic, especially with the sun just beginning to set. But that was not what amazed Francesca.

She was in an artist's studio. Every available space along the walls was covered with propped-up canvases, some larger than Francesca herself. They were almost all portraits, with very few exceptions. Some of the oils were finished, others in various states of completion. And standing with her back to Francesca, studying one large canvas upon an easel, was Sarah Channing herself.

She was wearing a plain pale blue day dress with an apron. Even the back was smudged with splotches of red, blue and brown paint. Sarah turned, holding a brush, and she smiled slightly. There was a smudge of ochre on her cheek. "Hello, Miss Cahill. This is a surprise."

Francesca was momentarily speechless. The timid little Sarah Channing was an artist? And a superior one at that, if Francesca was any judge. Superior, and clearly devoted to her work.

For painting could not possibly be a mere hobby for her. Her work was too professional—any one of the portraits could have been hanging on a wall in the Cahill home. There was a dreamy quality to her style of painting, as if each subject were seen through a fine veil, and as Francesca looked from portrait to portrait, she realized that every subject had a completely different expression.

There was a portrait of the mayor. He was unsmiling, and his eyes were burning with his characteristic fervor. A portrait of a pair of young girls showed absolute innocence and gaiety and one child was obviously mischievous. A painting of Sarah's mother featured a slight, lopsided smile, and her eyes had that faraway quality that Mrs. Channing had in real life, as well. Sarah's mother was a bit absent-minded and unfocused, and Sarah had caught that quality brilliantly.

"I had no idea," Francesca heard herself say, unable to keep her eyes on Sarah. There were just too many beautiful paintings to admire.

Sarah laid down her brush and wiped her hands—covered in paint—on her apron. "Few people do. Mother prefers it that way."

Francesca finally looked directly at Sarah, who had now captured her complete attention. Maybe they had more in common than they had first thought. How deceiving, she thought, appearances were. "Your art is superb."

Sarah flushed. "Not really," she demurred.

"I am no art critic, but I do think it is fabulous."

Sarah smiled again, and her eyes were bright, shining.

Francesca stared. This woman, she thought, loved her work the way Francesca was devoted to the cause of reform. Her eyes had never been this bright on either of the two previous occasions Francesca had seen her.

And suddenly she had an image of her brother, so dashing and jaunty in his evening tails, announcing that he was off for the night—on his way, undoubtedly, to one of his clubs, to wine and dine the night away, with a little gaming thrown in.

She could also see Evan in his goggles and duster, preparing for a speedy drive in the country.

Or in his tennis clothes, on the court, his body covered in sweat, hitting ball after ball, determined to best his opponent. Hopeful ladies were cheering him from the sidelines.

This was, Francesca decided, the most awful of mismatches. She could not imagine Sarah giving up her studio time to cheer him from the sidelines during a tennis match, or joining him for an afternoon outing on the yacht or for a drive in the country.

"I am sorry you have caught me in such dishabille," Sarah said quietly.

"It is my fault, let me assure you of that," Francesca said with a quick smile. She took a better look at Sarah, who seemed flushed with the exertion her work had cost her. She was so much prettier caught this way, although her big brown eyes remained her best feature. "I have come to offer you congratulations on your impending engagement to my brother," Francesca said.

"I thought so. I have some lemonade over there on the table. Would you care for some?" Sarah asked, already leading the way to the one seating area in the room, which was in front of a fireplace with a wooden mantel. It consisted of an old green sofa and two plush yellow-striped chairs, worn and comfortable, and a small table covered with a lace cloth on which was placed a tray containing the pitcher of lemonade and several glasses.

"That would be lovely," Francesca said.

They sat down and Sarah poured the lemonade, her fingers leaving spots of green paint on the crystal pitcher. She did not seem to notice.

The two women sipped their drinks in silence. Francesca could see why Sarah had fallen in love with her brother—she would not have many suitors, and none like Evan. But she still could not comprehend how and why Evan had fallen in love with her. He was always dancing attendance on the most beautiful and coy women. He loved a good flirtation. "How long have you known my brother?" Francesca asked, just to make conversation—for she already knew the answer.

"Just two weeks." Sarah did not smile.

"What a whirlwind romance," Francesca exclaimed.

Sarah smiled, just a little, and did not reply.

"Evan seems besotted," Francesca finally volunteered. "There will be hundreds of ladies insanely jealous of you."

Sarah looked up at her, her brown eyes steady and unwavering. "I am sure there will be many broken hearts in the city; your brother is both handsome and charming."

Francesca stared. She was quite certain there was an unspoken "but" about to follow that statement. When Sarah did not continue, Francesca said, "And you must be walking in the clouds."

Sarah set her glass down, which was now covered with green and beige paint, and did not look up for a long moment. When she did so, her face was sober, as it usually was. Except for that moment when Francesca had first entered the studio. Then her expression had been dazzling with animation. "I am very pleased to be marrying your brother," she said.

Bells went off in Francesca's mind, bells of warning.

Something was just not right here. She stared. "It is certainly a good match," Francesca said.

Sarah nodded. "Yes, it is. My mother is thrilled, as are your parents."

It almost sounded as if Sarah were not thrilled. But she had to be thrilled, didn't she? Francesca knew she was prying, but she said, "Sarah, is anything wrong?"

"Of course not," Sarah said.

"Do you like motoring?" Francesca asked impulsively. "Evan has a new roadster. In good weather, he loves to spend entire afternoons driving about Long Island. It is great fun."

Sarah hesitated. "I suppose I shall learn to like it," she said.

"He also has a yacht. We have had the most wonderful boating parties in the summertime." Francesca smiled. "Surely you like boating?"

Sarah hesitated again. "In truth, I get seasick."

It was as she had suspected. They had nothing in common, except that they were in love. "Well, I was so surprised when Evan told me he had taken the 'fall,' so to speak."

"The fall?"

"You know. The fall into love." She smiled encouragingly.

Sarah looked at her and said nothing. Then she glanced longingly over her shoulder at her canvas.

It was a work in progress. It showed a young woman in a beautiful peacock-green evening gown, her red hair piled atop her head, and she was looking archly at the viewer. Darker green velvet window treatments were behind her, and she had her hand on the back of an object, which Francesca supposed would emerge into a chair.

"She is very beautiful," Francesca said.

Sarah brightened, facing Francesca. "Yes, she is. She is my cousin, and she is the black sheep in the family. She is already widowed and she is not even twenty-three, and she has been living most lavishly in Paris since last summer. I began this just before she left—with her husband's fortune." Sarah laughed, the first time Francesca had heard her do so. "Her name is Bartolla Benevente. Her husband was an Italian count. She reminds me of Eliza Burton."

Francesca's eyes widened. Indeed, she did, but not through any physical resemblance, as Bartolla was a true beauty. But it was there in her saucy, confident expression, and she shared the same vitality that Eliza Burton had.

Francesca sobered, thinking of the missing child and the night to come. Her stomach lurched unpleasantly. If Bragg ever found out . . .

"I do hope they find the boy, and soon," Sarah whispered.

"So do I." Francesca stood abruptly. "I hope I haven't kept you from your glorious art."

Sarah flushed and it made her pretty. "You overflatter me, I think."

"You are too modest," Francesca said firmly.

Sarah walked her to the door. "Thank you for calling, Miss Cahill."

"Please call me Francesca, as we will one day be sisters."

"Only if you call me Sarah," Sarah said.

Francesca smiled and agreed.

Then Sarah said, surprising her, "I would love to paint you sometime. May I?"

Francesca started. "Well, I . . . I do not see why not . . ."

"You are so beautiful, but you have so many interesting layers to uncover. It would be a most exciting project," Sarah said, smiling fully now, her eyes sparkling. "Please think about it."

Francesca stared. Her eyes had not sparkled that way when they had been discussing her brother and the marriage. "I shall," Francesca assured her.

"Thank you." Sarah dutifully walked her through the house and to the front door.

Francesca remained deep in thought during the brief ride across the park. Sarah was a far more interesting woman than she would have ever thought.

Her parents were at the opera for the evening. Evan was out, as well. He had cheerily announced that he was off to the Metropolitan Club. Things could not have worked out better.

Now, if only the rest of the evening would turn out as well.

Francesca had not bothered with a disguise. She hailed a hansom and within twenty minutes—there was no traffic at such a late hour—she was at 201 Avenue A. Joel was waiting for her, lingering on the front stoop, a brown scarf wrapped around his neck, a worn plaid cap on his head. He jumped into the carriage before she could even call his name.

" 'Evening, Miss Cahill." He grinned.

Francesca's stomach was upset; she was a bundle of nerves. She could not return his somewhat mischievous smile. "How did you know it was I?"

He guffawed. "How many cabs do you see in this part of town?" He leaned forward and knocked on the glass partition. "Twenty-third, off Broadway."

The hansom rolled forward.

Francesca could hardly see Joel in the shadows of the cab's interior. The fact that the street lighting downtown was so poor did not help. "Joel, please tell me where we are going?" she asked, and she could hear the faint note of desperation in her tone. She was now regretting her decision to be so brave. She was regretting her decision not to tell Bragg what she was up to. And now she was wondering if she should have left a note on her bed, just in case something did happen, just in case she did not return home that night.

Joel did not respond. He was on his knees on the seat beside her, peering through the hansom's back window.

Francesca glanced backward and saw only an empty cobbled street, covered with patches of black ice. And then she realized what he was about. "I have told no one about this . . . this adventure of ours," she said tersely.

"Just makin' sure no spots are shadowing us."

"Shadowing?"

"Shadowing," he said, sitting down. "Following us," he exclaimed with exasperation.

"Where are we going?"

"You don't need to be so afraid. It's just a small saloon. Gordino likes cards and dice. If he's out, he'll be there."

A saloon. It was as she had thought. How on earth was she going to enter a saloon?

"I'll go in first," Joel assured her. "To see if he's there. You pay the cabby to wait. It will be fine, lady. I'll bring him out to talk to you." He smiled.

She was hardly relieved. "I hope so," she murmured, aware of perspiration gathering along her hairline and at her temples. She reminded herself that this was not a casual lark. This was about Jonny Burton. Gordino obviously knew who was responsible for the second note, delivered by Joel to Bragg at Mott and Hester streets.

Ten minutes later Joel directed the cabby to stop. The street just off the avenue was lined with bars and saloons and what Francesca feared were houses of ill repute. One glance upward at second-story windows, fully illuminated from within, showed her too many scantily clad women to count. "I think I am going to be sick," she whispered.

"I'll be right back," Joel said. "Give the driver a fiver." He opened the door and jumped down from the cab.

Francesca fumbled with her purse and then with her money. She handed the driver the coins. Her knees were shaking and knocking together. How could she do this?

Suddenly she could taste Gordino's kiss, and the recollection was so tactile it was enough to make her gag. She was an instant from rapping on the window partition and demanding that the cabby take her home.

But an image of Jonny's impish grin came to mind. Tears came to her eyes. How could she not go through with this?

But now she knew, she just knew, she should have told Bragg.

Five minutes seemed to pass by. Then five minutes more. And then another five minutes. Francesca peered out of the window at the brilliantly illuminated entrance where Joel had disappeared. What was taking so long? Had something happened to the boy?

"Miss." The cabby interrupted her thoughts. "I can't stand here all night."

"It hasn't been all night," Francesca managed. She shoved another dollar at him.

And suddenly Joel was standing outside of the cab, his hands in his coat pockets, shoulders hunched against the cold. "He's there, all right," he said. "But he won't come out. He's playing stud an' he don't want to talk to you or no one."

Francesca inhaled hard. "Then I will have to go in." She had never before realized just how brave she was. She was more nauseous than before.

But before she could put one foot on the frozen ground, Joel plucked her sleeve. "Miss Cahill. I don't know. It ain't a posh place. Maybe we should wait a bit, see if he comes out later."

The street was bright with old-fashioned gaslights. Francesca silently debated the issue. She had to get home before her parents—and she doubted they would come in much later than midnight. The clock was ticking; time was running out. "How bad is it?" she asked.

"Ain't right for a lady," Joel said seriously. "It ain't."

"I'll wait ten more minutes," Francesca said finally.

Joel nodded, hopping back into the hansom. The driver demanded more money. Francesca gave him another silver dollar.

Five minutes later, Joel went back in while Francesca

fought nature's sudden call. She was shivering now, for
the cab was not heated and it was no more than twenty
degrees out, with a brisk breeze. Joel instantly returned.
"Maybe we should come back tomorrow," he said. "He's
still playin' cards, Miss Cahill. He wouldn't even talk to
me."

Francesca recalled his disgusting kiss. His fetid breath.
And worse, his smug, fearless eyes. She wet her lips. They
should come back tomorrow, but by tomorrow, Jonny
could be dead. Assuming he was still alive . . .

"I will go in." She handed the driver five dollars. "No
matter what, wait for us, we won't be long," she said.

"Will do," the driver said, smiling.

Francesca shut the door, slipping on the ice. Very carefully, she crossed to the curb, and then to the saloon's front
door. Joel looked unhappy as he pushed it open for her.

Once inside, Francesca was blasted with warmth—and
that, at least, was a relief. Then she stood there, staring.

The room was filled with men, all working-class im-
migrants, and none of them particularly reassuring in their
demeanor or presence. In fact, most of the patrons, whether
standing at the long wooden bar or seated at tables, were
clearly, boisterously, drunk.

There were women present, too. They were wearing
short dresses that revealed stockings and high heels. The
gowns were mostly red and cut extremely low. Francesca
had never seen such an abundant display of bosom before,
and so much long, wild, disheveled hair.

She was, obviously, facing prostitutes. She could not
tear her eyes away.

And suddenly, she was seen. There were hoots, whistles, and catcalls.

Francesca stiffened, suddenly aware of the remarks.

"Princess! Over here! Want some fun? I'm the one!"

Francesca felt her knees buckling; Joel moved in front
of her, protectively.

Oh, God, she thought. What am I doing? Am I insane?

"Lady." His voice was loud, so he could be heard over the cries and calls directed at her. "He's at that corner table. Let's do our business and leave."

She could not agree more. Francesca followed Joel's gaze and saw Gordino, who was sitting back in a chair at a poker table with four other men. His card hand was lying face down, and he was staring at her. Francesca's heart sank—she knew he recognized her.

Joel grabbed her hand and pulled her forward. The hoots and calls continued.

"Need some boffing?"

"Hell, no. The lady wants a fuck!"

Her face burned. Her heart was pounding its way right out of her chest. This was a terrible mistake—but damn it, she would get the information she wanted. Otherwise this nightmare would have been for nothing.

"Princess! Forget him! Over here!" Someone grabbed her skirt.

Francesca stumbled, weak with terror.

"Let her go, cocksucker," Joel snarled. And a knife flashed in his hand.

Francesca gasped. The man, whom she did not even look at—she did not dare—released her skirt.

"Fuck you, son of a bitch," he growled at Joel.

Joel pushed her forward. And Francesca found herself facing Gordino. He was grinning. "Hello, princess," he said, slowly standing.

He was a big, brawny man. Francesca smelled whiskey and tobacco on his breath. "Mr. Gordino, I must speak with you, and it is a most urgent matter!" she cried in a rush. "I will pay you handsomely for information!"

"Yeah?" His hands were on his hips. "You can pay me all right, princess. Let's go."

"Let's go?" she squeaked. Because he had jerked his head behind him.

"Upstairs. Leave the asswipe here."

She felt her cheeks flooding with heat again. Both at

his language and at what she realized he wanted from her in payment. She swallowed hard. A lump had formed in her chest. It burned and hurt. "I will pay you handsomely, with cash."

He grinned lewdly. "Only one form of payment I want, and that's a nice, rich piece of snatch."

Francesca inhaled. She could guess what that last word meant. "I will give you fifty dollars, sir, if you tell me who gave you the note that you gave to Joel on Sunday. The note pertaining to the abduction of the Burton boy."

"Maybe I will take the cash. Upstairs," he said, and he laughed.

Francesca realized she was shaking.

"She ain't goin' upstairs," Joel said savagely. "You tell her what she wants to know, right here, and she'll give you the money."

"Shut the fuck up, you little pisspot," Gordino said, not once taking his eyes off of Francesca.

"I am not going up those stairs," Francesca heard herself say. Unfortunately, she also heard her own tone, and it was high and filled with fear. "So you may tell me what I want to know and take the money, Mr. Gordino, or I will leave and you will be no richer tonight than you were today."

"I'm real good, honey," he said.

Francesca stared.

"All right," he said. "Give me the money and I'll tell you what you want to know."

In that moment, elation rose up fast and hard in Francesca. She began to open her purse; Joel restrained her. "No," he told her, then tossed at Gordino, "You tell her first, and then she pays you."

Gordino glared at Joel with such menace that her elation vanished instantly, and all Francesca could think about was that they had to get out of there, as quickly as possible. "It's all right," she said frantically, digging into her purse.

"Lady, don't!" Joel cried, warning her.

Francesca shoved the fifty dollars at Gordino, jerking back just in case he decided to grab her along with the money.

He grinned and counted it carefully, slowly. And then he pocketed it and looked up. "Well, thank you, princess," he said.

"Who gave you that note?"

He laughed. Hard. "I don't know what the fuck you're talking about," he said. "But we can still go upstairs," he added with a suggestive look.

Francesca felt herself gape.

"I told you not to give him the money first," Joel cried.

"You promised!" Francesca heard herself protest.

He laughed harder.

Joel had her hand. "He ain't gonna sing. Let's get the hell outta here."

"Mr. Gordino," Francesca began, refusing to budge. "Please."

"If you come upstairs, I'll tell you anything, an' more."

Francesca stared in disbelief, as Joel tugged hard on her hand. Gordino grinned. "Let's go,", Joel said, and Francesca finally heard the nervousness in his tone.

She looked around. Every single person in the saloon was staring, and none of the men looked much nicer than Gordino. "All right," she managed, a whisper.

Joel pulled her back through the tables. There were more whistles, and some extremely suggestive remarks, which Francesca somehow blocked out, perhaps by the noise of her deafening heartbeat. And suddenly they were outside on the street.

"That dad-blasted cabby!" Joel shouted.

Francesca suddenly realized that the street was deserted—the hansom was gone.

"No," she said, shocked and disbelieving. The driver had left them! Abandoned them! They were stranded.

"C'mon. We can find a hansom on Broadway."

"At this hour?" Francesca gasped.

"Well, we've got to go. C'mon." Joel dragged her down the block.

Francesca ran to keep up with him, stumbling on the uneven footing caused by the patches of frozen snow. How could this have happened? she managed to think as they raced toward Broadway. How? She had just suffered the worst night of her life—it had been a nightmare come true: those men, their eyes, those comments—and she wondered if she would ever be able to forget any of it. And it had all been for nothing. They had found Gordino. But all she had done was suffer a tremendous indignity—and she had lost close to seventy dollars as well.

And what had Gordino meant when he had said that he didn't know what she was talking about? Had he been honest with her? Or had he been lying—in order to protect himself and whoever was behind the Burton abduction?

They paused on the corner of Broadway. A hansom was coming toward them and automatically Francesca's arm shot up as she tried to flag it down. But it did not stop. It was occupied.

And suddenly she and Joel were standing there alone on the vast, deserted avenue. And looking up and down Broadway, Francesca was afraid.

"How will I get home?" Francesca whispered.

"We can always walk to my flat," Joel said. "An' you can stay there for the night."

Francesca briefly closed her eyes in sheer dismay. Her parents, should they discover her gone, would immediately call the police.

And suddenly a roundsman was coming toward them.

"Damn," Joel whispered, about to bolt.

Francesca grabbed his collar, detaining him. She had never seen a more welcome sight. "Officer!" she cried, "Please, please help."

The policeman saw her and hurried forward, eyes widening as he realized that she was a lady, and a fine one at that.

Francesca intended to explain. Instead, she burst into tears.

Francesca gripped the seat of the hansom, staring through the window in amazement, as her cab drew abreast of the entrance to her driveway. For three police wagons and Bragg's roadster were parked in front of the Burton house. The mansion was ablaze with lights.

Something had happened.

Francesca had not a doubt, just as she had not a doubt that it was something terrible. "Stop, driver, stop right here!" she shouted, banging on the partition.

The hansom braked hard. The horse danced in its traces in protest.

"How much?" Francesca was already digging into her purse. And even as the cabby answered her, her mind was racing. She had to know what had occurred. Yet could she just jump out of the cab and rush into the Burtons' home? How could she not?

Francesca leapt out of the hansom. She was in such a rush that she fell headlong onto her hands and knees on a patch of lumpy gray ice.

She inhaled hard and got to her feet. As she stood up, the front door of the house opened, and she had a clear view of Bragg standing in the hall, gesturing in that terse, commanding way of his. He was with a pair of officers and two detectives. Both detectives hurried from the house and outside to one of the wagons, where shivering patrolmen were standing.

Bragg was turning away. He shot back around, having seen Francesca.

The entire episode of that evening flashed through her mind. She desperately wanted to spill all. As Francesca hurried forward, she cautioned herself not to say a word. Hadn't he told her himself that words could never be taken back? She needed to think things through. She could always tell him about the interlude with Gordino if she thought it best to do so on the morrow. It wasn't as if she had learned anything useful, anyway. And she felt a twinge of guilt. Bragg would certainly want to know Gordino's whereabouts.

He was hurrying down the front steps. "Francesca?" He seemed incredulous, and his gaze went past her. Clearly he was stunned to find her without an escort.

Francesca forced a bright smile. But she wondered if the smell of whiskey and cigarette smoke and overpowering perfume was hanging on to her from the saloon. "Bragg," she heard herself cry. And she heard the odd note of relief in her own tone.

He felt like a safe haven, even though the horror of the evening was long past.

And then she looked beyond him at the brilliantly illuminated house. Or was it?

"What are you doing out alone at this hour?" he demanded, taking her by the arm. He drew her directly under a street lamp. And he stared at her face. "Are you all right?" Suddenly he leaned closer, eyes dark and intent, and he sniffed.

"I am fine!" she cried gaily. "I have passed the evening at Connie's. I often go there alone—it is just round the corner, as you probably know."

He stared at her.

Francesca continued to smile. How hard it was. How could he not believe her? Her tale was entirely plausible—except, of course, that no lady her age would ever travel home alone, even around the block, at such an hour. Francesca was quite certain that it was at least one in the morning.

"Francesca, you are a poor liar," he said flatly.

She stiffened. Then, "I cannot say."

He continued to hold her arm. It was a moment before he spoke, and when he did so, it was with deliberation. "If you tell me that you are all right, if you tell me that nothing has happened, then I will have to respect your decision to keep your affairs private." He was grim. There was a tic in his clenched jaw.

Her affairs. Francesca suddenly recalled the conversation she'd had with Montrose the other day. Oh, God. He didn't think she was out and about and up to no good with a *lover,* did he?

But of course he would think such a thing. After all, he behaved the same way and he must assume others did, as well.

She wished that she had not just recalled Bragg's affair with Eliza.

"Thank you," she managed. Never had two words been harder to emit.

His regard remained probing. The tic in his jaw did not go away.

"What has happened?" Francesca asked, suddenly noticing how close they were standing to one another—which was undoubtedly why she was not shivering with cold. But he did not even have his coat on. She glanced up at the house. "Maybe we should go inside, Bragg, before you catch pneumonia."

"I will have you escorted home. I am leaving in a moment, anyway." Something dark and weary—perhaps resignation—passed through his eyes.

Francesca grabbed his arm before he could turn away. "What has happened?" she cried fearfully.

"Another note." His gaze locked with hers.

She realized she was holding her breath. And that she had also gripped his hand. It was callused and hard, like Maggie's. It was not a gentleman's manicured hand.

She did not release it. If anything, she clung to him more tightly. "Oh, no."

He pulled free and ran both hands through his tawny hair. "Goddamnit," he said. "Goddamnit. God*damn*it."

She had heard worse that night, she could not be offended, and she felt tears forming in her eyes, tears for

Jonny, because she knew now, she just knew, that he was dead. "Tell me."

He looked at her and his eyes were moist now, too. "I should not."

Francesca wiped her eyes.

"Don't cry," he whispered.

She started, and their eyes collided and held.

He nodded. "His clothes. The pajamas he disappeared in. The note was pinned to them. The pajamas were covered with dirt, stained with blood, and frozen. And they were found on his bed. The note said, 'D is for Dog.' "

" 'D is for dog,' " Francesca whispered.

"James found the pajamas and the note," Bragg said harshly. "James found his brother's clothes when he was going to bed."

Francesca was appalled. Tears slid down her face. "I thought James had been sent to his grandparents'."

Bragg shook his head. "Eliza could not stand being apart from him. He came home this afternoon. It is understandable, I think." Then he added, "He is asking for his twin."

She felt a fresh tear welling up in her eye. Of course, it was understandable, she thought. If she were Eliza, she would not let the remaining twin out of her sight. She plucked his sleeve. "Bragg. You do know what this means?"

"We are analyzing the evidence," he said, sighing heavily and looking away from her. It was, she knew, because he had been briefly unmanned.

"D is for dog. Bones," Francesca said. "Bones, Bragg. Bones."

He looked at her. "Bones?"

She licked her lips. She was sick. "A grave."

CHAPTER
11

WEDNESDAY, JANUARY 22, 1902—8 A.M.

"Wake up."

Francesca vaguely heard her brother's voice. She did not want to wake up. In fact, she was so terribly exhausted that she doubted she could raise her eyelids, much less move a single muscle.

"Wake up, Fran. It's eight o'clock. Today is Wednesday. You have a class at ten."

Class. She had cut her French literature class yesterday, and she had three classes today. Evan was right. She had algebra at ten this morning. What a wonderful thought.

She still did not want to wake up. And as she became fully awake, she was stricken with the searing comprehension why.

Jonny Burton was dead.

The dirty, frozen, bloodstained pajamas that he had disappeared in had been found on his bed. By his twin brother. With the fifth note, "D is for Dog."

The monster was becoming obvious. Francesca sat up.

"Fran?" Evan sat down on the foot of her bed. He was grim. But one brow slashed upward. "Are you sick?"

She looked at him. Dog, bones, grave. How easy this last clue was. "He's dead, Evan. I am certain of it," she whispered, shaking and wondering if she was as ashen as she felt.

His eyes widened. "Who? Jonny?"

She nodded, pushing waves of hair out of her face. "There was another note . . . I'm afraid I can't go into the details, but it seems inescapable. That poor boy. Poor Eliza. Poor Burton," she whispered.

Clearly the monster wished to torment the Burtons. Yet who was he? Or she? Whoever it was, the person had access to the Burton home. The pajamas had been left right on Jonny's bed.

What kind of gesture was this?

How confident the monster must be, Francesca thought, to walk into their home and leave the pajamas in the boy's bedroom with another note.

"I am so sorry," Evan said, leaning forward. "God, what a horrid mess. I hope they find that madman and hang him by . . . well, never mind," he said.

She flushed. She could guess what part of the madman's anatomy Evan referred to. After last night she was afraid that very little in the way of vocabulary would ever stymie her again. Had she really gone into that saloon? Or had it been a nightmare? She felt her cheeks warm even more. If only she could forget those crude remarks and even cruder words.

"Are you sure there's no hope?" Evan was asking, cutting into her thoughts.

Her smile felt wan, as an image of Bragg as he had been last night flashed through her mind's eye. Still so undeniably attractive, but so defeated and resigned. He believed as she did, she knew. "I suppose there is always hope, until the body is found." She pushed aside the covers, about to slip from the bed.

Evan caught her wrist, restraining her. "Actually, we must talk."

His tone confused her. It was hard. She paused, seated

on the edge of the bed, staring at him. "Is something wrong?"

His expression hardened. "Where were you last night?"

She blinked and blinked again. And then she felt the heat of guilt invading her cheeks. "I . . . What?"

"You heard me, Fran. Where were you last night? I wanted to talk with you, and knowing that you are up so late most nights studying, I stopped by your bedroom. It was a quarter past midnight. Not only weren't you here, but your bed was untouched, and no one, Fran, not a single person in this house, knew of your whereabouts."

She was flushing so hard she felt feverish. The same lie she had told last night came unbidden and as naturally as the cold draft from her window. "I was at Connie's," she said, avoiding his eyes. She would have to go to her sister before she did anything else that day. Go to her and beg her to protect her in this lie. Connie would not be easy to convince.

"I don't believe you," Evan said, shocked. He stood up.

She stood, as well. "I was at Connie's, Evan." She wet her lips. She wanted to add, I wouldn't lie to you, but she could not. "Please," she added, instead.

"Please, what? Believe your lie?" He flushed with anger and paced. Then he faced her. "Do you know that I had the oddest conversation with Montrose a few days ago?"

Francesca froze, thinking, Oh, no.

"He was asking me all of these strange questions— about you. He wanted to know if you have been behaving strangely of late. Of course, my reflexive response was to say no. But then I started to think about it. You are an oddball, Fran. But lately your behavior has been even odder than ever."

"It's just college," she managed.

"He asked me if you had a sweetheart." Evan stared. "Of course, I knew the answer to that one, and I told him no, you do not. And when I said that, he had a look on his face that I did not fully understand at the time—but I just cannot forget it. Damn it, Fran, he did not believe me, and for some reason, he has been prying into your life!"

"It's nothing," Francesca said firmly. "And you, my big brother, are making a big to-do about nothing, as well. In any case, I must bathe and dress and get uptown before I am thrown out of Barnard on an unmentionable part of my anatomy." She managed a smile. "I will see you downstairs?"

He folded his arms, regarding her with a small, tight smile, and he did not budge. "Where were you last night, Fran? And more importantly, with whom?"

She regarded him carefully, then blurted, "Evan! I know you will not understand, but I am helping with the Burton investigation, and I cannot tell you where I was last night!"

His eyes widened. "What?" he exclaimed.

"It's true."

"Are you out of your mind?" he cried.

"No, I am not. Please, Evan, let this go."

He shook his head. "I don't know what to believe. Bragg would never let you help—"

"It's unofficial, of course, and he doesn't know," she said in a rush.

"As I was saying," he replied, "I do not know what to believe, but if you are sleuthing, that is exactly the kind of odd behavior you just might engage in! I know how passionate you are, Fran, and I have been waiting for the day when you discover love. With great anxiety," he added flatly.

"I have not discovered love," she whispered, and even as the words came forth, she had a flashing image of Bragg, seated at his desk at police headquarters. *That* was too disturbing to even speculate upon, and she dismissed the image immediately.

"I don't know what to believe," he reiterated. "But

whatever you are about, I advise you to stop. Isn't secretively going to college enough, Fran? How could you possibly entertain any other endeavors? Or should I say, affairs?"

"Good-bye, Evan," Francesca said firmly. "I am getting dressed." And without waiting for him to leave, she walked into her bathroom, closing the door behind her, locking it. And then she leaned on it for a good long minute, trying to recover her composure.

Her three classes came one after another. On a normal day, Francesca would have then gone to the library to study and do homework. But this was not a normal day.

She had important information. Information she must share with the police.

As the hansom she had found on Fifty-third Street, after getting off the Ninth Avenue El, stopped in front of police headquarters, she wondered if the commissioner would even be in his office. She imagined that the police were busy visiting cemeteries, looking for freshly dug graves. The thought made her ill.

She would have to call on Eliza later, as well. To provide whatever small measure of comfort she could. At least she no longer had to visit Connie; the notion of persuading Connie to go along with her earlier lie had not been a pleasant one. Now the lie no longer mattered, as she was on her way to fully disclose her whereabouts of the previous evening to Bragg.

She paid the driver and started up the steps of 300 Mulberry Street. As she did, she had to glance over her shoulder. It was another pleasant day, and a group of gentlemen in overcoats and bowlers were loitering across the street. One of them waved at her. She recognized Kurland.

She quickly looked away, pretending not to have recognized him, and she hurried inside. A desk sergeant she did not know was at the reception counter, a shackled man sat on a bench, guarded by two patrolmen, and one of the department's female secretaries was entering the elevator. Two detectives were coming downstairs, on foot. One was smoking.

Francesca approached the reception desk when another officer stepped out from a back office. "Yes, ma'am?" the first sergeant asked.

"She's here to see the commissioner," the second officer said. "He's in. Go on up, Miss Cahill."

Francesca flushed with pleasure; the second officer had been on duty the day before when she had come looking for Bragg, and somehow, he remembered her. As she hurried to the stairs—she did not feel like waiting for the elevator—she heard the sergeant say, "Who is that?"

"Dunno," was the reply. "But she's Andrew Cahill's daughter and a friend of the commissioner's. I think she has business with him."

Francesca smiled as she went upstairs. She did have business with the commissioner, indeed.

And then she thought about the fifth clue, and her smile vanished. If only she was wrong.

But how could she be? It was such an obvious clue.

Bragg's door was open. He was standing behind his desk, but with his back to the door—he was in his shirtsleeves, staring out of the window at Mulberry Street. There were papers all over his desk. Several folders were open. A newspaper was also on his desk; another stack of papers was piled on the floor.

She thought about the way he had been holding Eliza. A moment later she was envisioning herself in his arms. And she was so flustered that she halted right in her tracks.

Whatever was she thinking?

"Miss Cahill?"

Francesca suddenly realized that Bragg had seen her standing there in the open doorway and that he was speaking to her and trying to get her attention. She blinked. "Bragg."

And then their eyes met and he smiled, somewhat quizzically. "Good afternoon, Miss Cahill. What a pleasant surprise."

She could not smile in return as she stepped into his office. It actually seemed as if he were pleased to see her, and that notion did something funny to her heart. But then, as he gestured to one of the two worn chairs in front of his desk, she noted that he had not shaved that day, that the circles under his eyes were even darker than they had been yesterday, and that a lock of hair was hanging carelessly over his brow. The uncombed effect was rakish, but her heart twisted at the sight of him—he was exhausted and under extreme pressure, she realized. She prayed he did not blame himself for the failure of the police to locate Jonny Burton. Such guilt would be an intolerable burden.

Then she had to remind herself that this man was having an affair with Eliza Burton, and he did not seem to feel in the least bit guilty about it. Her confusion increased.

"Francesca?"

"I hope I am not intruding," she said, settling into the chair, trying to clear her mind and gather her thoughts. She now had to face the prospect of telling him the truth about last night. Francesca was no fool. She knew they would quickly engage in battle; she only hoped the battle would be brief, and that she would not be the one to lose.

He was smiling at her again. "The intrusion is a delightful one." Something dark and unhappy flitted through his eyes.

It did not matter that he was Eliza's lover, she thought fiercely. He was a caring man, a good man, and he was tormented by the Burton case. "Bragg? Have you found anything?"

He settled one slim hip on the edge of his desk. Francesca looked away from the hard line of his wool-clad thigh. "Have we found the body? No. And until we do, I refuse to believe that the boy is dead."

She nodded. "Have the police been canvassing cemeteries?"

He stood, hands on his hips. "Of course."

"Did Heinrich see the latest evidence? The pajamas, the note? Do you have any idea who is entering the house like that?"

His eyes briefly widened, and then he shook his head. "Francesca, we may be dealing with a murderer. I can no longer share any information with you—and it is for your own good. Not only that," he hesitated, frowning, "if the boy is still alive, it is best for his sake that the investigation remain highly classified."

She nodded, wondering who had called on the Burtons yesterday—that list would surely contain the name of the madman responsible for the abduction. And now Francesca was noticing the newspaper on his desk. She stood and pulled it free of the papers there. As she did so, she glimpsed the headline, which screamed, "Bragg Fails to Find Burton Boy." And a batch of papers fell to the floor.

She hadn't had time to glance at the papers that morning. The headline did not surprise her; what surprised her was that it was not worse. She stooped to pick up the other papers that had fallen, and at the exact same time, so did Bragg. Their heads knocked and their hands touched.

Francesca froze and looked up.

He was motionless, too.

Then he said, "Let me."

Francesca nodded, aware of the electricity between them, and she stood, allowing him to pick up the mess. But as she did so, her eyes fell upon one page. It was the original note, stuck there in the folder. "A is for Ants." "Did you ever find out what kind of typewriting machine was used for the notes?" she heard herself ask.

He replaced the folder on his desk. "Francesca."

She realized that she had trespassed. "I cannot help myself. I have a curious nature."

His smile was slight. "I know you do." Then, "An old Remington 2."

"A Remington 2?" she asked, perplexed. "I have never even heard of such a model," she said.

"That is because such a model first came into use shortly after you were born."

Francesca's eyes widened. "Why, that is a wonderful clue! A twenty-year-old typewriter—how many of them can there still be?"

He did not answer her, turning away, fingering the papers on his desk. Then he turned abruptly back. "Why have you come to call?" he asked.

She became still. She suddenly imagined a dozen unhappy scenarios ensuing after she told him about her adventure last night with Gordino. Then, she said, low, "We found Gordino. Last night."

His eyes popped. "What?"

"Please, please, don't be angry!"

His eyes remained wide. "Angry?" he said, as a huge flush covered his face. And then his jaw went tight. "Where is he?" he asked.

It was the most dangerous tone she had ever heard in her life. It was far worse than the tone she had heard Gordino use with her on Sunday. She trembled. "He was at a saloon on Twenty-third Street, off Broadway. Last night. Around midnight."

Bragg stared and stared while Francesca broke into a sweat. Then he said, "Sit down. Right now." She was already sitting. "And tell me just what the . . . just what the hell you were doing in a saloon last night, and why the hell wasn't I there instead?"

His eyes were ablaze. Francesca felt tears come to her own eyes—and no man—or woman—with the exception of her mother—could reduce her to tears. "I went to visit Maggie Kennedy," she cried. "I found Joel. He hates the police, Bragg. I wanted to tell you, because I was really afraid, but I knew Joel wouldn't help if the police were involved! Gordino was in this saloon and I tried to bribe him but he took my money and didn't tell me anything and that was why I got home last night so late, alone. There is 'word' on the street, though, that the motive is revenge against Burton. Oh, God. Are you going to tell my parents?"

"Yes, I will, but after I . . ." He stopped. "After I decide what to do with you myself!" he exploded.

Francesca shrank back in her chair.

He began pacing, then turned and fired questions at her. Francesca knew she had no choice but to answer them.

"Where did you find Joel?"

"Staying with neighbors on the fourth floor, apartment C."

"And he knew where Gordino would be?"

"He said that Gordino was in hiding but if he was out, he would be gambling at this place. In self-defense, Bragg, Joel did not tell me that we were going to a saloon until we were on our way there!"

He ignored that. "I want the exact name of the saloon, the exact location."

Francesca hesitated. "The entire street was nothing but bars and saloons and houses . . ." She stopped.

"Of ill repute. Go on."

"I . . . I would have to show you." She began to panic. She had been in such a nervous state last night, would she even remember which saloon she had gone into? "I think I would remember which saloon it was—"

"You think?" he shouted at her.

"I was so scared," she cried back as loudly. "I was so scared, I have never been so scared in my life and I did not want to go inside but I had to, because of the boy! I think I would remember if we went, but maybe not in daylight."

"I am not taking you there at night," he ground out. He began to pace. Francesca was quite certain he was silently cursing.

"What is it?" she finally asked fearfully.

"If we go looking for this saloon during the day, and we are noticed, that's the end of Gordino. I cannot risk it. If I go at night with my men, from saloon to saloon, the word will be out on the street before we have even left the first saloon, and again, Gordino will hole up like a fox in its den. Damn it." His face was filled with frustration.

"Oh, no," Francesca whispered, beginning to understand.

"Joel will have to tell me where the two of you were last night." His fists clenched and unclenched.

Francesca finally stood up. And their gazes met.

"What?" he barked.

"He won't. He won't help you, Bragg, I am certain of it."

"Oh, yes he will."

"What will you do? Beat him up the way your detective did?" she cried.

"My detectives never touched him."

"They did. He told me, and it is a travesty," she said angrily.

He stared her down. "I hate to tell you this, Francesca, that boy was in my sight the entire time we questioned him. He was never alone with the detectives. Once again, Francesca, he lied to you and you swallowed it hook, line, and sinker."

She stared back and she began to flush. "Oh, dear," she finally said. Then, "But Bragg. I am serious. He hates the police. He'll lie to you, then run away, and you'll never find Gordino."

He stopped in front of her and gripped her by both

arms. "I hate to do this," he ground out. "But a little boy's life is at stake. You will have to go back to Joel, now, and enlist him to take you there again tonight."

"What?" Her voice sounded like a squeak.

"You heard me. And I will follow you, Francesca. Now, sit down. And just listen carefully."

Francesca obeyed.

"I am sorry, Miss Cahill. Mrs. Burton is not receiving callers," the butler said.

Francesca was standing wearily in the foyer of the Burton home. She handed the slender servant her card, having already scribbled a short note upon the back. "Please tell her that if she needs anything, anything at all, not to hesitate to call me. Does she have a telephone?"

"I am afraid not," the man said.

"Well, I am right next door." Francesca smiled at him. "Good day." She left, unable to recall his name.

But before she had gone down the front steps to the sidewalk, she paused and faced the Burton home again.

Time was running out. Jonny Burton was probably dead, but on the slim chance that he was alive, that the monster was toying with them, he had to be found. Any clues to his abduction and whereabouts had to be in that house.

Francesca stared at the solidly closed front door.

Someone had left those pajamas yesterday on Jonny's bed. She had no doubt Bragg knew within a matter of hours just when the clothing had been left there with the pinned note. Bragg probably also knew exactly who had called on the Burtons during that period of time. But now Francesca wondered if it had been a caller after all. What if the monster was a servant? Because a servant would have even easier access to the Burton home at any time of the day or night than a mere guest.

Francesca felt a touch of excitement. A servant might

hate his or her employer, and if he was insane, he might also enjoy tormenting the Burtons so greatly. Of course, by now Francesca felt certain that the monster was a man. It was just a feeling that she had, but it was one that she could not shake.

Tonight Bragg was picking her up and they were hunting Gordino. The prospect was frightening; it was also exhilarating. But he was not picking her up until eleven o'clock. It wasn't even six in the evening.

Francesca could not even contemplate wasting time. She hurried back up the steps. She felt like a criminal as she tested the door, which was unlocked, as she had suspected. They did not lock their own door at the Cahill home until retiring for the night.

She pushed it open and peered inside—the front hall was empty.

Francesca darted in, shut the door as quietly as possible, and leapt into the doorway of the adjacent withdrawing room. Once there, she took a deep breath. She could hardly believe she was stealing uninvited into someone else's home.

She glanced around at the pleasant room with its several sofas and chairs and its wide-open gold velvet draperies. Eliza was probably upstairs in her apartments. Just what was she looking for? She supposed she would like to search Eliza's personal papers, but would her desk be upstairs, in her suite, or downstairs, in the library? Francesca could only assume the library was at the back of the house. It might be a good place to start.

She would also like to visit the twins' bedroom.

Francesca moved from the withdrawing room into the adjacent reception room, without having to go into the hall, as open doorways connected the rooms. She crossed it swiftly. A small, intimate salon was on the other side, larger than the withdrawing room, the blood-red curtains drawn, a grand piano in the center. The motif was Chinese—the walls were red, dragons creeping up them, the woodwork red lacquer, the furniture Oriental, as were the various vases and sculptures. It was a very seductive room, and Francesca was about to cross it to go to the door, when a flurry of movement on the other side of the piano caught her eye.

She saw a man on all fours on the sofa. Francesca darted behind a tall Chinese screen and heard a woman's soft, breathless cry.

She froze, in that instant realizing why the room was so dark, why the curtains were drawn, and just what was happening on the sofa. A man and woman were making love!

She did not mean to look. She assumed the couple to be servants. But Francesca found herself peering around the screen, unable to restrain herself.

The man was big and dark. He did not have his jacket on. The woman beneath him was a tangle of lace and black stockings. Francesca glimpsed white thighs.

She drew back as the woman cried out and the man grunted. Housemaids did not wear lace, or black stockings with rose-decorated garters, either.

Was that Eliza?

Francesca did not know what to think, in fact, she was stunned by the probability, and Bragg was, she knew, back at police headquarters where she had left him—wasn't he? It was so dark in the room, but that man was not Bragg, or was he?

"Oh, God, Eliza," the man said.

Francesca felt her knees buckle and she gripped the closest object—the top of the piano—to prevent herself from collapsing as she recognized the man's voice. But surely, surely she was mistaken!

Francesca stepped from behind the screen and stared, as the man drew back, lifted Eliza up, and began to nuzzle her breasts and test her nipples with the tip of his tongue. Eliza was spilling over her corset and out of her open shirtwaist.

She stared harder.

His head moved down her rib cage. And lower still, down her belly. As he continued to nuzzle and kiss her bare flesh, Francesca could not move, and she could not look away.

"Oh, God, Neil," Eliza gasped as she sank back on the couch and Montrose's head moved between her white, gartered thighs. Eliza began to whimper uncontrollably.

Was he doing what she thought he was doing? Francesca felt her knees buckle as she helplessly watched.

And Montrose reared up.

Francesca blinked at the sight of him in all of his swollen glory and then he was moving over Eliza and thrusting into her and the pair were bucking and twisting frantically. "Yes, yes," Eliza was crying.

Francesca suddenly realized just what she was doing and she jumped behind the screen, too stunned to form more than one single coherent thought. *Montrose.*

Their harsh, heavy breathing, their moans, Eliza's soft cries, filled the room. Francesca began to think.

Montrose and Eliza.

Montrose and Eliza.

Eliza began crying out.

Francesca did not mean to engage in further voyeurism, at least not deliberately. But the impassioned and fervent nature of Eliza's cries caused her to somehow move out from behind the screen.

Montrose was thrusting into her, again and again, his movements at once controlled and wildly passionate. "God, Eliza, God," he chanted, then, "You make me insanely jealous."

"Yes, Neil." Eliza was clawing his back. "Again, Neil."

"Yes," he said savagely.

Eliza suddenly cried out, even more loudly than before. Montrose clapped a hand over her mouth, collapsing on top of her with his own guttural grunt. And suddenly the pair was motionless.

Francesca took her cue. She ran.

And this time, when Eliza cried out, it was not in passion, it was in fear. "Neil! Someone was watching us!"

CHAPTER
12

Francesca ran blindly down the block and into the Cahill driveway. By the time she reached the house, she was panting harshly and her breath hung in big puffs of vapor in the chilly evening air. She staggered before the front steps, gasping for breath. To her own ear, those huge breaths sounded like sobs.

Montrose and Eliza were lovers.

Connie's husband was Eliza's lover.

Poor Connie!

Francesca sank down on the second step, aware of how wildly she was trembling. She remained in shock. How could Montrose be Eliza's lover? How?

He and Connie seemed so content, so perfect for one another.

Francesca did not know what to think or do. But while Eliza might be a very loose woman indeed, there was one thing she was certain of, and that was that she did not have a string of lovers dangling about. Bragg must have had an affair with her in the past. They had remained friends, and that explained the intimate embrace she had seen a few days ago.

Francesca felt no relief. Not now.

Did Connie know? Did she know that her husband was unfaithful? Did she even suspect?

Poor Connie! Francesca began to weep.

And as she wept, so many memories danced through her head. She recalled Montrose pulling Connie close, just last night, and Connie smiling up at him before disengaging herself. She recalled the first time she had seen Montrose, when she was fourteen years old.

"He's here," Evan had said, dragging Francesca out of her bedroom and downstairs. "His lordship is here, courting our sister, you must come see."

And on the lowest step, Francesca had stopped abruptly. Tall, dark, and broad-shouldered, his eyes brilliantly blue, he was quite the most handsome and masculine man she had ever laid eyes upon. He was speaking to her sister and smiling. Connie was gazing up at him and smiling back. It was, everyone said, the perfect match. A match made in heaven.

Francesca had watched them as they spoke for the very first time and she had felt her heart lurch wildly, uncontrollably, inside of her breast. The sensation had been terrifying, like leaping off a cliff and falling forever, with the ground nowhere in sight. She had secretly admired him from that moment on. And she had been so happy for her sister. But she had also, secretly, been so sad—for herself.

Francesca hugged her knees to her cheek and rocked, recalling the day they had made their wedding vows. Connie had been gorgeous in her frothy beaded white gown, and the moment they had exchanged vows, Montrose had pulled up her veil while pulling her close, and he had kissed her deeply. Francesca had watched, gaping; she had never seen a man kiss a woman like that before.

Someone in the crowded church had cheered. And then the applause was thunderous.

A match made in heaven.

How could he cheat on Connie? Didn't he love his wife?

Francesca recalled the way he had come barging into the house one summer eve, three years ago, haggard and drawn and afraid, waking up the household, shouting that Connie was having the baby. Even more vividly, she recalled the doctor announcing a safe birth for mother and child, and her father, with tears in his eyes, handing Montrose a cigar. Montrose had been ashen and red-eyed—he had kept an all-night vigil—and cigar in hand, he had sunk into the closest chair. An instant later he had bolted to his feet. "I am going to see my wife and daughter," he had cried, dashing from the room.

Francesca wept harder.

She did not know how long she sat there on the stoop, reliving too many memories of her brother-in-law and sister to count, but suddenly she was aware of being frozen through and through. The stone step she sat on was like ice, as was her derriere. She was shivering, and dried, frozen tears felt like plaster on her face. Slowly, Francesca got to her feet.

A huge and heavy weight had settled over her—the weight of grief. Hugging herself, she walked into the house.

How could he! Did Connie know? Those two thoughts replayed over and over again in her mind.

Suddenly Francesca stiffened. Should she tell her sister?

Francesca forgot to breathe. The starkly brutal importance of the question struck with violent force. What should she do?

"Francesca," Julia said, entering the hall from the dining room.

Francesca saw her mother approaching in a beautiful mauve suit with a determined stride she recognized too well. She prayed silently for a respite when she knew there would not be one.

Julia's expression changed, becoming bewildered. "Francesca?" Her strident tone had vanished. Her mother paused before her. "Are you ill? Have you . . . you have been crying!" she exclaimed.

Francesca turned away, removing her coat and hat and

handing the items, along with her gloves, to a servant. She wiped her face with her sleeve. "I am merely cold. I walked home," she said tersely.

Julia tilted up her chin. "What is it? You have been crying, Francesca. Tears are stained all over your face."

Francesca stared into her mother's concerned gaze and could not come up with a single thing to say. And then she wondered if Julia knew. Julia knew everything. She was the queen of New York society. But she would never allow Montrose to continue the affair if she knew. And Francesca had no doubt that Julia would somehow pull the proper strings to make him dance to her tune, perhaps through finances. The Montrose fortune had been squandered generations ago. His family, while titled, was impoverished and nearly landless. Connie had inherited a huge fortune upon her marriage. Still, it had been a love match. Hadn't it?

"I don't feel very well," Francesca finally said. "I have been at Sarah Channing's. I decided to take a walk in the park. I am very cold." She could hear how terrible her own tone sounded.

Julia hesitated and Francesca thought that she suspected her to be lying, but she said, "Then you should go upstairs to bed. Perhaps you will feel better in a few hours. We are having a small supper tonight, just family. Connie, Montrose, and the girls, and Sarah Channing and her mother, of course."

Her heart sank with sickening force. How could she face Montrose over a meal, tonight? "I don't know, Mama, I think I am feverish," Francesca said.

Julia laid her dainty hand on Francesca's brow. "You are never feverish," she said with real concern. "I am worried about you, Francesca." And, "Truthfully, I have been worried about you for some months now."

Francesca almost burst into tears again. Should Julia raise the subject of her comings and goings, she was too distressed to dissemble well and she would never succeed

in pulling the wool over her mother's eyes. "I will be fine."
And that was the truth. She would be fine, because it
wasn't her heart that was broken. It was her sister's heart
that was broken—or that would soon become broken,
should she ever learn of her husband's treachery.

"Francesca."

Francesca had been about to go upstairs and she paused.
"Yes?"

"We will discuss the matter of my silver when you are
feeling better."

Francesca trembled. "Thank you, Mama."

Julia smiled at her, but the worry in her eyes had not
abated. She turned and walked out of the hall.

Francesca leaned upon the banister, closing her eyes
briefly. Now she was aware of a tremendous headache
forming just behind both temples. And the truth was, she
did feel ill. Perhaps she was actually coming down with
the flu. It might just be a godsend if it would prevent her
from attending her family's supper that night.

Francesca was about to go upstairs when she heard a
loud and angry exclamation coming from behind the
closed doors of the library. Her brother had made the out-
burst. And now she could hear her father speaking in a
calm, measured tone of voice in response.

Evan was never angry. He had the most cheerful and
sunny of dispositions. Under normal circumstances, Francesca would have been concerned about whatever was
making him angry. She would have hurried to the library
and perhaps she might have eavesdropped. Now, she only
fled upstairs as fast as she could go. She could not handle
one more stitch of conflict.

It was only when she reached the sanctuary of her room
that she recalled words spoken in the heat of passion.

Words she wished she had never heard.

You make me insanely jealous.

Montrose was insanely jealous where Eliza Burton was
concerned.

"No," Francesca whispered, catching a glimpse of her ashen expression in the mirror across her room. She looked deathly ill. "No."

Montrose was not insane. Montrose was not a madman. Montrose was not the monster who had abducted Jonny Burton and was now so cruelly toying with Robert Burton because he hated his lover's husband.

It was impossible.

Francesca realized at the last moment that she must join the family for supper that night. She had to look Montrose in the eye, and try to comprehend him. She had to see him with her sister, and try to understand their relationship, as well. It seemed like a hopeless task.

She was late. But she could not hurry as she slowly descended the stairs, as if unsure of her footing, holding tightly onto the smooth brass railing of the banister. She was exhausted, but she also felt violated, the way she had after Gordino had assaulted her. That sense of violation gave her an anger that was welcome. How dare Montrose betray her sister!

And in betraying Connie, he had betrayed them all.

They were already taking their seats in the dining room. Her father smiled with pleasure at the sight of her. "Francesca! I am so glad you are feeling well enough to join us. Mother was just explaining that you did not feel well this afternoon." Her father pulled her close, his smile fading as he studied her with searching eyes.

Francesca forced a smile. She knew she still looked terrible—like death warmed over. Her eyes remained red from another, recent bout with tears. "I am better," she said so softly that she realized her tone was inaudible.

"Fran?" Evan wandered over, concerned. "I think you should go right back upstairs and get into bed. You look ghastly."

"I am fine." This time she was firm and she spoke up. And then she looked across the table, where Montrose was standing with Connie and the two girls. She hardly even noticed Sarah and her mother.

Connie and Neil were both looking at her with worry.

Neil! Someone was watching us!

Francesca found herself staring at Montrose, Eliza's last cry ringing in her ears so vividly it was as if she were calling out now, in the present. Images she wished she had never seen tumbled through her mind, almost too swiftly to decipher. And she felt ill, wretchedly so.

Montrose stared back at her.

His expression was impossible to read.

Had he leapt up after Eliza had cried out? Had he dashed after her? *Had he seen her?*

Did he know that Francesca knew about him and his rotten affair?

But he was not the monster who had abducted and maybe even murdered Jonny Burton, was he?

Their gazes locked.

"Fran." Connie handed the wide-eyed Lucinda to Mrs. Partridge, pausing to kiss her cheek, and then she hurried around the table.

"Auntie! Sit next to me!" Charlotte cried, jumping up and down.

Francesca had not moved. She could not tear her gaze from Montrose. He continued to stare back at her, as well. He might be an adulterer, but that was not the same thing as being insane. It was not.

A lot of men were jealous of their wives and mistresses. *You make me insanely jealous.*

She could hear her own heavy, deafening heartbeat in her ears. Surely the whole room could, as well. Francesca felt the tension arcing between her and Montrose as if it were actual currents of electricity. And the terrible tableau felt frozen in place and time.

I must not stare, Francesca managed to think.

Everyone is noticing the way we are regarding one another.

He was not smiling. And Francesca was quite certain that he knew she had been the voyeur.

"Francesca, what is wrong?" Connie asked, now at her side, and taking her hand.

And just as Francesca turned to face her sister, Montrose said worriedly, "I think Evan is right. I think you should go up to bed."

Francesca turned back instantly and met his worried blue eyes. Then she faced Connie, trembling, not knowing what to think now.

Joining the family for supper had been a terrible idea. Especially as she had an impending rendezvous with Bragg in just a few hours. She should lie down, she should rest.

But she would only cry again.

"Why don't we send supper upstairs to your room?" Connie asked.

Francesca was acutely conscious of Montrose walking deliberately around the table and pausing beside his wife. His wife; her sister. She saw his hand briefly touch the small of her back.

It was an intimate gesture, perhaps even an affectionate one; he had no right to make it. Not now, not ever again. Francesca felt like barging between them and slapping his hand away.

She felt like shouting out the truth about his rotten affair to everyone present.

"I think I will retire," Francesca said. She finally forced a small smile at Sarah and Mrs. Channing. "I am sorry. I am not well. I have forgotten my manners. Good evening."

"Oh, that is quite all right," Sarah's mother said quickly. "You must go to bed if you are ill. We truly understand."

Francesca looked at Sarah. Sarah smiled slightly but did not speak; however, there was a question in her eyes, and Francesca realized that of all the people in the room, Sarah, a stranger, comprehended that something was distressing Francesca and it was not the flu or another physical illness.

Francesca bade everyone good night, this time refusing to look at Montrose. When she had left the dining room, she began to breathe too rapidly, as if she had just run a long distance. By the time she reached the top of the stairs tears had risen in her eyes and she felt so exhausted she did not know if she could make it to her room. She lay down on her bed, hugging her pillow.

She had just washed her face, removing all traces of her tears, when there were two soft raps on her door—a sound Francesca recognized. She stepped from the bathroom as Connie opened the door and came into her room. She shut the door behind her.

"Let me help you undress," Connie said with a smile.

"Not right now," Francesca said, walking over to the moss-green sofa in front of the fireplace and plopping down heavily upon it.

Connie sat down in an adjacent chair. She reached out and pushed a tendril of Francesca's hair away from her face, back over her shoulder. She smiled. "Whatever you have been up to, clearly it is affecting your health."

Francesca smiled ruefully. "I just need a good night's sleep."

"I hope so." Connie smiled again, studying her. She had taken a pillow from the couch and was holding it in her lap. "Is anything wrong? Other than your catching a touch of the flu?"

"Well," Francesca said, her pulse racing now, "this Burton affair is haunting me." She was well aware of the double entendre in her words.

Connie grimaced. "I feel so terrible for Eliza. She must be sick with grief and fear." Briefly she closed her eyes.

She doesn't know. Francesca stared at her sister and realized that Connie had no clue that Eliza was Montrose's lover. Automatically, Francesca reached out and took her sister's hand and held it tightly. Connie opened her eyes, perplexed. "What is it?"

Francesca smiled back a little, feeling a fresh urge to

weep. She fought it. "I went to see Eliza today." She was aware of approaching treacherous territory. Should she tell Connie that Neil had called, as well?

"How is she?"

"She was . . . indisposed at the time I called. Have you called recently?"

"No, I haven't. I did on Monday, of course, to express my concern, but I thought it best to leave her alone, given the circumstances. If I were in her shoes, I would not want to be bothered with my neighbors, no matter how well-meaning they might be. I would want no one about but my family." Connie held the pillow more tightly.

"Yes, I think I would feel the same way," Francesca said. "You would want to be alone with Neil, waiting for news."

Connie glanced at her. "This is a terribly morbid conversation!"

No luck there, Francesca thought. "Con, Eliza seems to have a good marriage, doesn't she?"

Connie looked at her. "That's an odd question."

"Well, would you answer it?"

Connie stiffened. "I cannot imagine where you are leading, Fran. But yes, she does seem to have a solid marriage."

Francesca was disappointed. Until Connie said, "Fran. Appearances mean nothing."

Francesca stared at her sister.

Connie flushed and looked away. "I do hate to disillusion you, but you know the saying." She looked up again. "No one hangs out their dirty laundry."

"Of course not," Francesca said. Did that include her sister? And then she had an idea of how to proceed. "Is Burton a good father? You know, like Neil?"

Connie blinked. "I do not have a clue, Fran."

"Well, Neil is a wonderful father," Francesca stated emphatically. And it was true.

Connie smiled slightly, studying the pillow, toying with

its tassels. "He is a wonderful father," she said softly.

Francesca despised him then. She heard herself say, "He so admires you, Con. The other night at your dinner party he was teasing by claiming that you are imperfect; I could see he meant the very opposite." She was trembling. She hated manipulating her sister, but she wanted to draw her out and find out if Connie suspected that anything was wrong in their marriage.

It was a moment before Connie looked up. "Please. He was being a gentleman, that is all."

Francesca stared at her sister, whose tone remained calm and level. Then she said, shrugging, "He does admire you! He is in love." And she expected Connie to react by either agreeing with her—in which case she had not a clue about Montrose's sordid affair—or denying it. But Connie neither agreed nor disagreed.

Instead, her expression changed. She stood up. "What are you about? What are all these questions about? Is there something you wish to know about Neil?"

Francesca was also standing. Again, her heartbeat seemed deafening. And she thought, I should not say another word, not now, not tonight. Bragg's wisdom came to mind. *It has taken me twenty-eight years to learn that words once spoken can never be taken back.*

She said, "Does Neil love you?"

Connie went rigid. Her face paled and her eyes widened. She said, "Of course he loves me."

Francesca swallowed, hard. Clearly she had trespassed, clearly she had gone too far.

"What is going on?" Connie was flushing now with anger. "What are you after? Why are you prying into my private life?"

"I didn't mean to pry," Francesca said quickly, but of course she had.

"It is not your business," Connie said, and now she tossed the pillow to the chair. "But Neil and I happen to be very happy." She stared, her small face pinched, her nostrils flared.

"I am sorry," Francesca whispered.

Connie gave her an angry look and crossed the room. At the door she paused and turned. And when she spoke, she was calm once more. "Don't pry into my affairs, Fran."

Francesca hugged herself. "I am sorry. I won't."

Connie stared and finally nodded, softening. Then she left the room.

But not before Francesca thought she saw an anxious look in her eyes.

Bragg had wanted to ask her father's permission for her participation in the work at hand that night. Francesca had quickly convinced him that such permission would never be forthcoming. He had not been happy at the prospect of using her in a police operation without Cahill's consent.

Conveniently, her parents had just retired. Francesca had overheard the good-byes being said perhaps a quarter of an hour ago, opening her window to do so. The house had since fallen silent; Francesca did not know if Evan was in or out. He was the only one she was worried about. If he caught her now, sneaking out all wrapped up in her coat and hat, he would insist on knowing where she was going—and with whom.

She hurried silently downstairs, into the kitchen, and stepped out of the back door, closing it and leaving it un-locked as she did so. The night was filled with thousands of stars and it was extremely cold; Francesca's breath hung heavily in the air. She traversed the back yard, staying close to the house in case someone might go to a window and look down and see her. When she reached the drive-way she saw a hansom standing on Fifth Avenue. Here she had no choice and she dashed to the street.

The door swung open before she had even reached the curb. Francesca stepped up; Bragg caught her hand and helped her in. She settled down beside him as he reached over her to close the door. He knocked on the partition, and the driver moved the horse off.

The driver was a policeman in disguise as a cabby.

Francesca faced Bragg, unable to see him clearly because of the darkness of the hansom's interior. "Any trouble?" he asked. He looked odd in his shabby jacket and an even shabbier cap.

"No. Everyone retired twenty minutes ago. The timing could not have been better," Francesca said, noticing the worn, dirty boots he was wearing, as well.

"Good." He sank back in his seat. His knee touched hers, briefly.

Francesca quickly put a wider space between them. She stole a glance at him in the dark and suddenly she thought about Eliza. It *was* a relief that he was not her lover after all.

Should she tell him about Montrose?

She knew that she should. Montrose could not be the madman, but he rightly fell into the category of suspect. If only he had never uttered such incriminating words.

But what if she was the only one who knew of the affair?

She had thought about her conversation with Connie all evening and had not been able to draw any conclusions one way or the other. Sometimes she felt that Connie suspected something was amiss with Montrose, at other times she thought her sister oblivious, and as fond of her husband as she had ever been. But then she wondered if her sister's anger had been a crack in a nearly flawless façade. A façade that housed the truth.

Francesca had never felt more overwhelmed in her life. A little boy's life might well be at stake. But so too might her sister's marriage. For if Connie did not know, shouldn't she, Francesca, forever hold her peace?

Francesca closed her eyes tightly, acutely aware of Bragg seated just inches away from her. Besides, Montrose was not insane. He was not a madman. He might be insanely jealous where Eliza was concerned, but that did not mean that he was capable of the criminal acts that had thus far taken place.

She felt Bragg shift restlessly on the seat beside her.

Francesca glanced over at him. She told herself that any woman in her shoes would be filled with both trepidation and excitement at the prospect of facing Gordino again, with Bragg at her side. Yet was she being absolutely honest with herself?

She turned away from Bragg to stare out at the passing street. They were almost at Grand Army Plaza, at the southern tip of Central Park. Now was not the time to notice that it was becoming warm, almost uncomfortably so, within the confines of the cab, or that Bragg, even though tired and preoccupied, had an undeniable charisma and appeal. She must focus on the task at hand.

"Francesca? You are very quiet tonight." Bragg's soft voice interrupted her thoughts.

Francesca turned to face him and their gazes met. His eyes gleamed a bit in the slight illumination provided within the hansom by the stars and the streetlights. "It has been a very long day," she said as softly, quite unable to turn away now.

"Yes, it has." She thought he was thinking about the fact that she had paid a visit to Joel that afternoon, enlisting him to their cause that night. Of course, Joel had no idea that this time Bragg and a dozen handpicked men would trail him and Francesca. Francesca had come to terms with deceiving the boy. It no longer seemed to matter, not considering all of the turmoil that had suddenly appeared in the rest of her life.

"Hopefully, Gordino will be bagged tonight. I will give him the third degree, and he will lead us to the madman who has tried so hard to destroy the Burtons." Bragg was grim.

She took a moment to consider his words. If she were

Gordino, she would be very afraid. "What does 'bagged' mean, Bragg?"

He eyed her. "Imprisoned."

"And 'boarding school'?"

He folded his arms and she saw amusement flicker across his face. "Just a street term for 'jailhouse' or 'prison.' "

"I see." Poor Joel. Apparently he had been in jail.

"Your little friend?" Bragg asked.

"Yes."

"Let's go over the plan one more time," Bragg said. Like her, he was keeping his tone low, even though there was no reason for it.

Francesca nodded, her gaze riveted on his face, which remained cast in shadow and eerily sculpted because of it.

"You go in and locate Gordino. You leave instantly upon doing so. You raise your hand, no glove, as if to flag a hansom. That is the signal that will tell me and my men to enter the premises."

Francesca nodded again. "And if he is not there, I leave immediately, as well, but do nothing when I reach the street."

"Exactly." He turned his head away to stare out of his window. Then he faced her again. "I hate bringing you into this," he said with surprising vehemence.

She did not move. His words flustered her and pleased her immeasurably. "I will be fine," she whispered.

"Yes, you will. I shall make certain of it." He turned back to the window again.

Francesca huddled in her seat, knowing he intended to protect her from any harm from Gordino or any of his ilk at all cost. It was a thrilling comprehension.

She turned to study his hard profile and the strong line of his jaw. Even in his immigrant's clothes, he looked wealthy and powerful, she thought. He would not fool anyone dressed as he was, not for very long.

Then it occurred to her that if he was a bastard he might not be wealthy at all.

Of course, his background did not matter. Not to her, not anymore, not now, after all that they had thus far shared. Francesca felt herself shiver; yet she was perspiring. What *had* they shared thus far?

She wondered how he and Eliza had fallen into a love affair.

She had to wonder what it would be like to have this man hold her or even kiss her.

And she was appalled at herself. For goodness' sake, she was on a criminal investigation! Now was hardly the time to imagine Bragg as a . . . as a what?

In a way, they had become friends of a sort. But there was more than that to their relationship, wasn't there? Francesca would be the first to admit that when it came to this kind of thing, she was in way over her head. Bragg had once cared about Eliza; perhaps he had even loved her. His type of woman would be someone striking and intellectual. Francesca suddenly wondered if she might also be his type.

The hansom slowed and stopped.

"Are we here?" Francesca started, suddenly anxious. For now the night would truly begin.

"I am getting out. We are five blocks from the Kennedys'. I don't want to take a chance on Joel's seeing me. The kid is sharp." His tone was terse but it also washed over her like warmed honey.

Francesca nodded, filled with new tension, as he opened his door. But before he leapt out he faced her again. "Everything will be fine," he said reassuringly. "Trust me, Francesca."

Her heart leapt. "I know," Francesca said, but now she had butterflies, and she wasn't sure she meant her words.

His gaze slid over her face. "Do not worry. Just do as I have told you. This time I am here, Francesca. Let me do all of the worrying." He smiled a little at that, but the smile did not reach his eyes.

"All right." She managed a breathless smile in return, recalling what he had said. *Trust me.* How could two mere words be so sensual?

He swung away, and as he did so, his jacket opened and she saw the gun. And then the door slammed closed and he was disappearing into the shadows of the street. The hansom rolled forward.

He had a gun.

Of course he had a gun. It was just a precaution!

But Francesca remained immobilized, because she had never seen a gun like that before. It wasn't a hunting rifle. It wasn't a small, pearl-handled revolver, the kind that fit into a lady's palm. It was a big, deadly-looking handgun. It was a weapon designed to kill another human being.

It was only a precaution.

The hansom had stopped again. The driver, who was really a detective in the force, turned. "We're here."

"Please wait," Francesca managed, just as the door swung open and Joel hopped in. "Hello," she began, but all she could think about was the gun. Why was he carrying a gun? She had never noticed him carrying one before. Did he think he might have to use it?

Joel did not smile or greet her. "Are you sure you want to do this again?"

Francesca nodded, suddenly frightened. "Driver, Twenty-third off Broadway." The hansom moved forward.

"Don't know why you got to be involved," Joel muttered. He did not sit down. He was on his knees, facing backward—looking behind them to see if they were being followed.

"What are you doing?" Francesca asked uneasily, terrified he would espy Bragg or the other policemen and the entire operation would fail, then and there. If only Bragg had not felt it necessary to bring a gun. Clearly he expected the night to be one filled with jeopardy.

Joel did not answer, staring suspiciously down the street behind them. Then he scooted off the seat and went to the side windows, each one in turn, to stare out of them as well. Finally, he sat down.

Francesca almost said, "We are not being followed," but they were, and wisely, she held her tongue. Her heart continued to pound.

Finally Joel spoke. He was grim. "I got a real bad feeling about this," he said.

Silently Francesca agreed—completely.

CHAPTER
13

Francesca saw Gordino the moment she stepped inside the saloon. In fact, he was sitting at the exact same table that he had occupied the evening before, and like the other night, he was immersed in a game of cards with four other players, each and every man as hard and disreputable-looking as he was.

Joel glanced up at her grimly. He started to move forward, thinking, of course, that she intended to follow him to Gordino for a repeat of the previous night. Francesca gripped his shoulder. "I have to go back outside," she said, her voice thick and harsh with her fear.

"What!" he exclaimed.

She gave him no time to object, pulling him with her as she rushed out onto the sidewalk, somewhat relieved that everything had happened so quickly and that she had not had to suffer the same indignities as she previously had. She was already wrenching off her glove. She waved her hand wildly in the air.

"What are you doing?" Joel cried. "That bastard is inside. I thought you wanted to—" He stopped. "What are you doing?" And it was a suspicious demand.

But it was too late. Bragg had emerged from the shadows across the street and was already running toward them. Half a dozen men were following him, and as Bragg rushed past, Francesca saw that he was holding the gun. Her fear increased.

"Spots," Joel shouted at her.

Francesca grabbed him by both arms before he could bolt, crying, "Do not say another word!"

He fought to break free.

She fought to hold him, watching as the police ran into the saloon. Shouts filled the night. "Please, Joel, this isn't about you. This is about another boy, one who is missing!"

"You lied to me," Joel shouted at her, finally breaking free. "You lied to me, damn it!"

"I didn't want to," Francesca said, as a dozen patrolmen in their blue uniforms and leather helmets suddenly began converging on the saloon. It sounded as if a fight had broken out inside; she could hear wood splintering amidst the shouting and cursing. She prayed Bragg would capture Gordino, and she also prayed that no one would get hurt.

"Miss Cahill."

Francesca turned, recognizing the driver of the hansom. He was a big, bald man in his middle years with very bright blue eyes. She thought his name was Peter.

"I am to take you home now, miss."

Francesca was about to protest when she saw Gordino running across Broadway. And Bragg was ten feet behind him. Obviously they had left the saloon from a back door. Five other policemen, dressed as civilians, were following the pair. The policemen were waving their clubs.

"Miss Cahill, I have my orders."

Francesca didn't hear him, watching, paralyzed, as Bragg suddenly dove after Gordino. He succeeded in tackling him from behind, and the pair went down in the middle of the street.

A carriage veered around them, the pair of horses just missing the two men.

The driver shouted down at them furiously; Francesca cried out.

They did not hear. Bragg and Gordino were rolling around like boys wrestling in a schoolyard. And suddenly Gordino was on his feet. But so was Bragg, and he could only take one step before Bragg caught him by the shoulder, whirling him around, landing a vicious punch in his face. Gordino staggered backward but did not fall.

Bragg had to be stopped, Francesca managed to think, horrified.

Bragg leapt on him, and the two went down to the ground, hard.

"Someone should stop them," Francesca cried, lifting her skirts and running down the block toward the pair. The other policemen had formed a circle around the two men by the time she had reached them, but no one made any move to stop the fight.

Gordino landed a punch on Bragg's jaw. His head snapped backward and he almost fell, but he ducked the next oncoming blow. Francesca hardly saw what happened next. Bragg kicked with one leg, striking Gordino's knee. Gordino went down in a heap.

"Please, stop them," Francesca cried frantically, but no one seemed to hear her.

And Bragg jumped on top of Gordino and landed three blows to his face, each one more brutal than the one before.

Francesca was more than horrified, she was frightened, too. She turned to yank on Peter's sleeve. "Stop them!" she shouted. "Stop them before someone gets hurt! Please!"

The hansom driver who was really a policeman glanced oddly at her, his arms folded across his chest. He did not reply and he did not move.

Stunned, Francesca looked all around at the policemen watching the fight. Everyone seemed keenly interested in the outcome, and no one, apparently, had any intention of breaking it up. They seemed to be enjoying the spectacle.

Bragg was on top of Gordino, straddling him, about to

deal another blow. "Where is the boy?" he demanded. Blood was trickling from the corner of his mouth.

Gordino sneered at him.

Bragg punched him in the nose. Blood gushed. "Where is the boy? You have had it, Gordino. I promise you that. One way or another, I will make you talk. Where is the boy, and who the fuck is behind this? Who?" he roared.

"Fuck you, cocksucker," Gordino said.

Bragg hit him again and again.

Francesca had the horrible realization that he was not just enraged, he was out of control—and uncontrollable. It was as if he had become the maniac, the madman, himself. "Bragg! Please, stop!" she cried. But she knew that neither he nor anyone else heard her.

"I will kill you, but slowly, do you hear me? Where is the boy?" Bragg shouted, lifting Gordino up by his collar, his fist inches from one eye.

"Fuck off, asshole."

Francesca started forward without thinking, determined to stop Bragg before he killed Gordino. But someone seized her arm hard, detaining her. She looked up. Peter stared down at her.

"Want to lose an eye?" Bragg said very calmly.

"No!" Francesca screamed. "No!"

Gordino suddenly paled.

"You have one second," Bragg said.

"I don't know! I don't know where the boy is and I don't know who planned the thing," Gordino cried.

Bragg hit him. Gordino screamed. So did Francesca.

And then Bragg was on his feet, holding up the bleeding, battered Gordino, and he was shaking him. "Where is my son?" he screamed.

Francesca knew she had misheard.

"Where is my son, you son of a bitch?!"

Francesca stood on the sidewalk, shivering, vaguely aware that Joel had not left after all, and that he stood beside her.

Four police wagons had parked along Broadway where it intersected Twenty-third Street, and Gordino was inside one of them, his hands cuffed behind his back. He had been almost unconscious when he had been placed inside the cell in the back of the wagon; two officers had had to half drag and half carry him there and then physically push him inside.

Most of the occupants of the neighboring saloons and brothels had gathered on the street to watch the night's big event. Bragg was speaking with several of his men, standing only a few feet from the wagon containing Gordino. He seemed oblivious to his own wounds—one of his eyes was turning black and blue and his lower lip was terribly swollen. Blood flecked his shirt and stained his jacket. His knuckles were, not surprisingly, raw.

But mostly it was not his blood. The thug had not broken. Bragg had beaten him up badly; Francesca could only hope that he would be taken to a hospital and not to jail.

She could stand it no more. She rushed to the curb and retched up her dinner.

Then she started to cry.

She wished she had never witnessed such violence. She wished she had never seen Bragg beating up the other man.

"Here."

She was on her knees in the dirty snow, and the voice was kind and concerned. She looked up through her tears and accepted the ragged piece of handkerchief Joel was handing out to her. It was a scrap, but it was spanking clean. She could not get the words out to thank him, though.

Jonny Burton was Bragg's son. It all made sense now. God, it did.

She hurt for Bragg. Oh, she did. But she was never going to forget what he had done to Gordino. No matter the circumstances, such brutality was inexcusable.

She wanted to go home and find oblivion in sleep.

She knew she would never sleep a wink that night.

For she also wanted to go to Bragg and comfort him, desperately, if she could, and she also wanted to ask him half a dozen intimate and pointed questions.

How did he feel, having two sons whom he could not claim as his own? Did Burton know? Did anyone know? And dear God, should he even be the one to investigate the abduction, when he was so personally involved?

Her questions, if she ever dared ask them, would have to wait. She stood with Joel's help. And then she realized that Bragg was walking with determination toward her; the police wagon containing Gordino was driving away. Other patrolmen were instructing the gawkers to disperse. Francesca stiffened. She could not look away from his ravaged face.

He paused in front of her, his expression impossible to read. "One of my men will take you home." He turned away.

She grabbed his sleeve, forcing him to face her. She tried to search his eyes but he would not let her, for he looked aside. "Bragg." She had so much to say. She did not know how to begin. Instead, softly, with compassion, she whispered, "Bragg."

He flinched, his golden eyes wide, holding hers, filled briefly with surprise and anguish. And then he broke the moment, turning away. "Not now, Francesca. Not tonight." His tone was impossibly weary.

She wet her lips. "I'm sorry. I am so sorry."

His jaw tightened. "So am I."

He was leaving. But she had to know. She hurried abreast of him. "What are you going to do?"

"Not tonight," he said firmly.

She moved in front of him, blocking his way. And tears filled her eyes. "Tonight you almost killed a man. Don't you think if he knew something he would have told you?"

"This is not your affair," he said coldly. And then he barked, "Peter! I told you to take Miss Cahill home, now."

Francesca stared at him, and it felt as if her heart were

breaking. She felt a firm grip on her arm, knew it was Peter. She did not budge. "Don't hurt him, Bragg. Not anymore. You have done enough. I beg you."

His eyes grew dark, and he walked away from her, not saying a word.

Francesca let Peter escort her to the hansom. On the running board she turned before getting inside. But the street where he had been standing was empty; Bragg was already gone.

Francesca entered the house the way she had left it, through the back door, which led into the kitchen. No lights were on in that room, of course, and as she was hardly familiar with it, she had to proceed cautiously, groping her way past the center aisle, the sinks and icebox, to the door leading to the main part of the house. In the process, she bumped into a pot, left on the edge of the counter. It fell to the floor with a ringing crash.

The noise was enough to wake the dead.

She waited for her father, her mother, her brother, or Mrs. Ryan to come barging into the kitchen, flicking on the lights, demanding to know who was there. No one came.

She breathed easier.

And as she silently left the kitchen, she thought, The twins are Bragg's sons.

It was astounding. She was finally recovering from the shock. She wondered who else knew other than Eliza. She wondered again if Burton knew.

She had seen him with the twins too many times to count and he had appeared to be a doting father; she did not think he knew the truth.

And as she crept up the hall, it struck her weary brain that Bragg might be the monster's target, not Burton.

Oh, God. Was Bragg the maniac's intended mark? Did the madman want revenge on Bragg? Was Bragg the reason the little boy had been abducted, and maybe killed?

Her heart twisted and it was painful. She could only imagine that these suspicions had already occurred to Bragg, and that he was tortured by them and the guilt accompanying them. How helpless he must feel.

Francesca felt quite certain that Bragg was not a man accustomed to helplessness. That would, she thought, explain his uncontrollable rage.

She did not want to recall the way he had assaulted Gordino, not now, not ever again. She dismissed the memory from her mind and wondered when the affair between Bragg and Eliza had ended. It hardly mattered. It could have been seven years ago; it could have been days ago. There was no way of ever telling.

She knew she was wrong not to tell him about Eliza and Montrose. Yet Montrose might seek to hurt Burton; he would have nothing against Bragg. God, could the mystery become any more complicated? She still did not know what to do about her sister.

Francesca heard voices and she stumbled.

Who in God's name was up at this hour—other than Evan? She knew it was nearly two o'clock in the morning.

The voices rose in argument. They were coming from the library.

She had already recognized Evan's voice, for he was shouting, in a fine temper, indeed. Francesca was confused as she approached the door, knowing she did not dare open it. And then she heard, as clear as a bell, her father saying, "I shall not change my mind, and that is final."

Just what could they be arguing about—and at this hour?

"Fine." This from Evan. The door began to open and Francesca jerked away from it, shrinking against the wall. And Evan said, his tone nasty, "How proud of yourself you must be. To be blackmailing your own son."

Francesca somehow muffled her gasp.

"How dare you speak to me in such a manner!" Her father was now shouting.

"Oh, I suppose I should merrily walk down the aisle to the altar, pretending to love my bride, because that is what you have decided is best for me?" Evan shouted back.

"I will not discuss the merits of your marriage to Sarah Channing another time. My mind is made up. You are twenty-five and the most irresponsible of men. She is perfect for you. Should you wish to continue your irreverent lifestyle, so be it. But I will not pay another gambling debt, not one more, much less the thousands of dollars you currently owe. Good night, Evan."

Francesca tried to make herself smaller as the door was flung open and her father stalked from the library. As she stood on the side of the doorway closer to the kitchen than the stairs, he did not even see her. But she had gotten a single glimpse of him. He was livid.

Andrew Cahill was never in a temper. He was one of the kindest men she knew. He was also one of the most compassionate. How could she have just heard what she had?

He could not be blackmailing Evan. He could not be blackmailing his own son. Into marriage, for God's sake. It was an impossibility.

Francesca felt as if she were in the thick, foggy mists of an ever-worsening nightmare. She waited for Evan to leave the library, certain he, at least, would discover her. Minutes passed by, but he did not leave. Finally, she peeked quickly into the room, and saw him sitting on the sofa, a scotch in hand, his expression dark with his distress, and he was so immersed in his thoughts that he did not even see her.

She sucked in her breath and dashed past the doorway and down the hall and up into her room.

Once in bed, she threw the covers up over her head, and promised herself that she would sleep until noon.

She was up at six A.M.

* * *

She could hear her brother moving about his apartments. She had been up for an hour and a half, her mind spinning in turmoil, flitting from subject to subject—Bragg and his missing son, Connie and Montrose, Evan and Sarah Channing. She knocked lightly on his door.

Almost instantly, it was flung open. Evan's eyes widened as he saw her standing there. His shirt was hanging out and completely open; he flushed and turned his back to her to button it up properly. Of course, she had seen him in his swimming costume too many times to count. "Fran! It's half past seven. Do you have an early class?" He turned back to her.

"I don't even know," Francesca said truthfully. Classes were not on her mind now, and if she did not regroup and quickly, she would soon find herself expelled. She shook her head to clear it. She was so tired. "May I come in?"

"Of course." His brows furrowed together, expressing his bewilderment. "What is this about? Can't it wait until breakfast?"

Francesca shut the door as she stepped into his bedroom, leaning against it. He had a huge room done up in various shades of blue and green with pale beige accents. It was a master bedroom. When their father had built the house, there had never been any question that one half of it would be a separate residence for Evan and his future family. Although Evan rarely used it, he had a separate entrance farther down Fifth Avenue.

The adjoining homes had been Julia's idea. It was not unheard of.

"I prefer to speak to you privately," Francesca said.

Evan sighed. "I hope this is not as grim as your expression tells me it will be. I have had a hellish night."

Francesca hugged herself. "So have I." There was a mistake, she knew. Evan did not understand. Their father would never stoop so low as to blackmail Evan into a loveless marriage. It just wasn't possible. And if blackmail was at work here, Francesca had no doubt that Julia was the one responsible for it. "Evan, I heard you and Papa shouting last night."

He looked at her and said nothing.

"You don't love Sarah Channing?" Francesca asked.

"I see you heard quite a bit," Evan said darkly. "Fran, this spying of yours has to stop."

"I did not mean to spy," she said, reaching for him. He spun away, pacing. "Evan, you are my brother and I adore you. I must help."

He sat down hard on the emerald-green damask sofa. Francesca imagined that beneath his breath he was cursing. "Just what did you hear?" he asked cautiously.

"You accused Papa of blackmailing you. He would never do that, Evan." Francesca came forward, never taking her eyes from his face.

He stood. "No? I know you adore Father. But he is blackmailing me, Fran. In no uncertain terms. If I do not marry Sarah, he will not pay my debts and I shall have to leave town."

She could not believe it. "No. This is Mama's doing, then."

His gaze softened. "Poor Fran," he said.

"Poor me!" She was startled and she rushed to him and took both of his hands in hers. "On Saturday they are announcing your engagement. And it is the worst possible match."

He rolled his eyes. "Father thinks she will be good for me, in the long term." He shook his head grimly.

"Did you know that she is an artist? A painter, in fact?"

"I hadn't a clue," he said. "What does that have to do with anything?"

"It just points out that the two of you do not even know one another."

"I don't care to know her," Evan said unkindly.

"Evan, she is shy and timid, but she is nice."

"I apologize. Of course she is nice. But good God, Fran,

I should die of boredom married to a woman like that!" he cried. And he began to pace.

"Papa said something about gaming debts," Francesca said, watching him. "Perhaps we can find a way to pay them? And then you can back out of the engagement."

He eyed her. "I cannot pay them."

"How much do you owe?"

"You do not want to know."

"Evan! I am trying to help!" Francesca cried.

"Damn it," he said. "One hundred and thirty-three thousand dollars."

"What?" Francesca collapsed onto an ottoman. *"What?"* she said again.

He did not reply.

"How could you have lost such an excessive sum of money?" she cried.

"Now you sound like Mama. And I know you mean well, but I do not need another accusation just now."

She remained uncomprehending. "I just don't understand."

He flung his hands up heavenward. Then, "I know you think me some sort of hero. I am no hero, Fran. I like to gamble." He hesitated and closed his eyes. When he opened them, she thought she briefly saw despair flit through them. "It is like a sickness," he said. "Once you begin to win or lose, you cannot stop."

She managed to nod. "Oh, God. What shall we do?"

"There is nothing to do." He sat down on the sofa facing her, his elbows on his knees. "I shall marry Miss Channing, Papa will pay my debts, and I shall inherit my fortune—which I shall undoubtedly gamble away within a very few years."

"Don't say that!" She was furious. "Don't even think that! Surely you intend to stop gaming once Papa pays this debt?"

He cradled his dark head on his hands. "Of course I do," he muttered.

Francesca was relieved. And she saw his anguish. She touched him. "We shall find you a way out of this, now, before the engagement is announced. Poor Sarah. She must love you, and her heart will be broken."

"I doubt her heart will be broken, as come this June, I shall be exchanging vows with her." He glanced up. "Do not tell anyone about this, Fran," he warned. "Please."

"Of course my lips are sealed," she said. "I shall speak to Papa. You know how fond he is of me." Then she flushed. She was well aware that she was his favorite even though a parent should not have favorites. "I am sorry. I didn't mean that."

"It doesn't matter. No one is more truthful than you, Fran, and it is why we all love you so—it is why you are so refreshing. If anyone can sway Father, it is you. But I have no expectations that you will succeed."

Francesca stood. "I must succeed, Evan. Otherwise you will be miserably wed for the rest of your life. I intend to succeed," she said. "I want you to marry for love."

He smiled a little, for the first time since she had entered the room, shaking his head. "Only I know how romantic you are. Who marries for love in this day and age? Or any day and age, for that matter?"

She thought about Connie and Montrose, she thought about the Burtons. "I don't know," she finally said, suddenly grim and filled with despair. "I just don't know."

CHAPTER
14

Bragg was not at his office and it had not been hard to learn where he lived. Francesca had arrived at Madison Square by hansom; now she stared up at the brick townhouse with its wrought-iron curtain fence, wedged between other, similar homes on Twenty-Fifth Street and Madison Avenue. The house faced the snowy park with its stately trees and shoveled walkways. Madison Park was mostly deserted at this time of day—it was well before noon—although one ragged man with a heavy beard seemed to be asleep on a park bench. There was some activity on both avenues, which were filled with shops, mostly servants going about their business at this early hour. Francesca stared up at Number 11 Madison Avenue.

This was where he lived. Francesca could not imagine why she was so nervous.

Francesca had so much on her mind. Yet last night, Bragg had dominated her thoughts. She had slept only because of sheer exhaustion, but her sleep had been a restless one, more wakeful than not, with images of Bragg flooding her mind. Her compassion for him knew no bounds. And now she could understand his every action and reaction since the Burton tragedy had begun.

One question continued to haunt her. Did Robert Burton know about the twins?

It was not her business, of course, and the question remained, while logical, a highly sordid one.

Was Bragg the object of revenge? Or was it Burton—as Joel Kennedy claimed?

And as she stood there, debating whether she dared intrude upon him, with such a slight cause as her sympathy, she thought she saw a white curtain flutter in one of the windows facing the street.

Her heart skipped. Someone had seen her. A servant, perhaps, or Bragg himself.

How could she not go to him? For she was never going to forget last night, and now she was not thinking about his brutality in regard to Gordino, but the brief glimpse of anguish in his eyes just before he had turned and walked away from her, leaving that policeman, Peter, to drive her home.

Francesca started slowly toward the front steps. She wondered why he hadn't gone to the office. She knew a late night or even a series of them would not stop him.

She walked up the eight stone steps and used the door-knocker, aware of her nervousness increasing. She had rehearsed what she intended to say. Now she ran a few lines through her head as the door was opened.

I am so sorry. I had no idea. How can I help?

He would smile a little at her in that world-weary way he had, and tell her that she had already been of the utmost help, and he would decline any further assistance.

She would not, under any circumstance, ask any intimate questions. Not today.

And she would not reveal the fact that Montrose was currently Eliza's lover. She must, for the moment at least, protect her sister's marriage. Especially as she believed that Montrose couldn't be a madman.

"Good morning, Miss Cahill."

Francesca's eyes widened as she stared up at Peter's

strong, chiseled face. Then they widened even more, because he was not dressed as a patrolman or as a detective. In fact, in his starched white shirt and charcoal-gray suit, he was dressed as a gentleman's manservant. "Peter?"

He glanced past her, down the street.

She suddenly realized what he was doing, because she turned, and her eyes widened. Kurland had plopped down on a bench in the park. He waved at her, then shook out his newspaper to read it. Francesca groaned.

And then she was angry, realizing that Kurland must have followed her from police headquarters.

"I am afraid the commissioner is not receiving callers, Miss Cahill," Peter said very firmly, and before she could respond, he was shutting the door, quite in her face.

"Wait!" Francesca cried, to no avail, beginning to realize that Peter was not a policeman after all, but that he was Bragg's butler.

And as the door closed, she heard Bragg ask, "Who is it, Peter?"

"Miss Cahill, sir."

Francesca bit her lip as her heart skipped, while she wondered in the back of her mind what Kurland would make of her calling on the commissioner of police. Oh, well. He did not write a social column, so she supposed her reputation was saved. Not that it was unheard of for a lady to call on a gentleman at his home, but it was early, and she was without a companion. Julia would murder her directly should she ever learn of this.

The door opened. Peter gestured for her to come in.

Francesca did so, and as he quickly closed the door behind her, she instantly saw Bragg. All thoughts of Kurland and her mother vanished. Her stomach clenched with tension, and something else she couldn't name, at the sight of him.

He stood at the end of the short hall, on the threshold of a parlor with a fireplace. He was wearing a pair of shabby rough wool trousers—the same trousers he had worn last night. Clearly he had changed his shirt, for this one, while thoroughly rumpled, the top two buttons open, and both sleeves rolled up, was not stained and flecked with blood.

Every fiber of her being felt painfully alive; Francesca wondered why this man caused such an extreme reaction within her. Especially now, when he looked so disreputable and even dangerous, more like a ruffian or a rowdy than a gentleman. Even his hair was uncombed; several long gold strands were falling over his brow and into his eyes. His eyes seemed red, and there were circles beneath. And he had clearly not shaved in a day or two, the growth adding to his rather worn and scruffy appearance.

She hurt deep within herself just looking at him. Francesca had not a doubt that he had not slept a wink all night. Had he even tried to go to bed?

But if she were him, she knew she would never sleep, not until her child was found and the monster responsible for his abduction captured and placed behind bars.

"Francesca," he said very softly. Francesca started at his tone, a shiver passing over her. He was leaning indolently against the wall. He did not come forward. What had that smooth tone signified?

"I . . . I hope you do not mind." Her rehearsed dialogue escaped her memory now. Her nervousness had somehow increased. She glanced to her left, into a smaller parlor with a piano, the wood very dark, the furnishings Victorian, and then to her right, into a cozy dining room with green-flocked wallpaper. She guessed that there were two or three bedrooms upstairs.

"How could I mind?" he asked, his smile very faint and very slight. His slight Western drawl was more pronounced than usual, she realized. It was as smooth as honey. The effect was almost narcotic.

"It is hardly usual of me to intrude upon a gentleman at this hour," she began in a rush.

"There is nothing usual about you, ever, Francesca," he drawled, whisper-soft.

She became still.

His gaze remained fixed upon her, unwavering. His slight smile did not fade. "Have you brought me another clue?"

She could hardly think. She was trying to decipher just what he had meant by his previous words. Had they been a compliment? Was he out of sorts himself that morning? "Unfortunately, I have not," she said.

"I am disappointed," he said.

She blinked. Something was amiss.

He levered himself off the wall and began walking deliberately toward her.

Francesca felt her eyes widen as she stood and stared, tension rising so high and hard and fast in her that she could not breathe. His smile flashed, revealing his dimple, and then he reached for her.

Her knees buckled but he gripped her shoulders, steadying her, and briefly, she was in his arms. Oh, my God, she managed to think, as all kinds of crazy notions and even crazier sensations rioted within her mind and her body.

"Francesca," he murmured in his Texan drawl.

She looked into a pair of heated eyes. "Yes?" her voice sounded like a squeak.

"I am trying to take your coat."

She blinked and then realized that he wanted to remove her coat and hand it to Peter, who stood behind her—and whom she had thus far forgotten about. Francesca felt herself blush furiously and she practically jumped out of her coat, at the same time removing her hat and wrenching off her gloves. Two long hairpins somehow spilled to the floor. Francesca bent for them, but so did Bragg, and their hands collided on the floor.

She leapt upward to her full height.

He picked up the pins and handed them to Peter, who promptly disappeared.

Francesca decided she was as mature as a twelve-year-old schoolgirl. While he did not seem in the least bit undone. "You seem so tired," she heard herself say too quickly, trying to cover up her embarrassing lack of composure.

"I am tired," he said, and now he was staring at her, no longer smiling even faintly.

Why was he looking at her that way? What did it mean? Was something wrong with him?

"Would you like to come in?" He gestured behind him.

Francesca was about to agree, when she glanced into the parlor, and had to glance back again. Oh, no.

A bottle of scotch was on the table in front of the sofa. It was half-empty. A glass was beside it, with a finger of gold liquid within. She looked back at Bragg. He did not seem drunk, but clearly, he was drinking, and at this hour, that could only mean that he was trying to drown his sorrows. Furthermore, it now explained his honeyed drawl, his seductive smile, and his too-intent gaze. Didn't it?

She was hardly an expert on men, much less drunken ones.

"Please," he said, gesturing expansively and indicating that she might precede him in.

Francesca went cautiously forward. She decided to pretend she had not seen the shameful bottle and glass. For while she did not believe in drowning one's sorrows, Bragg certainly had just cause to do so. She sat down primly on a chair that was not quite facing the table. Bragg stood with his hands in his pants pockets, regarding her anew with a scrutiny that was uncompromising.

"Bragg? What can I do?" she heard herself blurt nervously. She reminded herself that, although she certainly found him quite attractive and even rather heroic, they were friends, and she could manage him when he was like this. Of course she could. The real problem, she thought, might be managing herself.

Francesca tried to tell herself that she was just overtired, and then she gave it up.

"Not much, I'm afraid," he said.

"I want to help," she said simply.

"I know you do." Another faint smile. His pain was there in his amber eyes, incredibly easy to read. "You are one of the kindest women I have ever met." He walked over to the table, filled up the glass, and took a long swallow. "Have I ever mentioned that?" And he gave her a long, direct stare.

She felt herself stiffen. And then, thank God, he turned away. She exhaled long and hard.

He poured himself another shot.

She watched. Now what should she do? He had no intention of pretending to be sober. "Bragg? Will it help?"

He held the glass in one hand, against his body. "Will what help? Oh, this? Yes, it helps, Francesca. Believe me, it helps."

She stood up. How could a few mere words, spoken under the influence of whisky, have such a sensual ring? "Have you slept at all?" she asked with concern.

"How can I sleep?" He drank again. Then his face tightened as he met her eyes. "How the hell can I sleep?"

"I am so sorry," she cried, moving to him.

"I know you are. But that won't deliver the madman to us, now will it? And it won't," he stopped abruptly and suddenly his expression became so hard and so grim that Francesca was alarmed.

"Bragg," she began.

The glass shattered in his hand.

Francesca cried out.

Bragg cursed, using a word no gentleman should ever use in front of a lady.

Francesca could not move.

"Damn it," he said, looking down at the broken glass on the faded Oriental rug.

"It was an accident," Francesca began, tears suddenly filling her eyes.

Peter appeared. He didn't say a word, but knelt and began cleaning up the glass and whisky.

"Don't cry."

Francesca had been watching Peter, who was very efficient and, within seconds, had whisked all the debris away. She started, as Bragg touched her face, and then she did not dare move.

"Don't cry for me," he said, and with his thumb, he swept the tears over her skin.

Francesca shivered. She found herself looking at his mouth. "Did you cut your hand?" Francesca asked, her nerves about to snap, her tone odd and husky.

He gave her a look that told her he didn't care. And abruptly, he dropped his hand and paced away, to the window. Tension riddled his shoulders and his stance. He parted the already partially drawn draperies, squinted into the morning light, and snarled, "Kurland." Then, "He is getting on my nerves."

Peter had risen to his full, amazing height, holding the dustpan filled with shards of glass in one hand. "I will take care of the situation," he said.

Bragg nodded without looking at him. "Thank you, Peter."

Peter left. Bragg turned back to Francesca, and she saw a smear of blood on his hand. "You could get an infection," she whispered, shaking.

His gaze steady on her, he walked back to her and stopped when they were face-to-face. Francesca became paralyzed.

He said, "You should not have heard what you did last night, Francesca."

She managed to draw a breath. She felt unsteady on her

feet, as if she were swaying like a young tree in the wind, toward him. "It's true?"

His jaw tightened so hard she thought he might snap the muscles there. Then, "Yes." And, "I prefer you to forget what you heard."

She knew she could not forget. "I am so sorry, Bragg."

"I know." He did not look away. With the back of his hand he brushed her cheek. Francesca froze.

He dropped his hand. "I should not be touching you," he muttered, as if to himself.

Had he just caressed her? Or had she imagined it? "Bragg? Others heard, as well. All those other policemen. This might be a secret that cannot be kept." Francesca was trembling. But she wasn't thinking about the policemen now, or even the case. How could she? She was thinking about what it would be like to be held by this man, to lose herself in his embrace.

She knew she should not let herself carry on so, not even in the privacy of her very own thoughts.

"My men will not speak up." Francesca was jerked out of her contemplation. "I have made it very clear, if this gets out, they are all without jobs."

She trembled, closing her eyes briefly, determined to control her wayward thoughts from that moment on. Then she looked at him. "Is that fair?"

He looked directly into her eyes, unnerving her again. "I am thinking about a little boy now, and Eliza."

She hugged herself. "Does Burton know?"

He was startled. "Francesca."

"I am sorry! This is just the most stunning turn." She turned away from him, trying to recover her composure, and doing a poor job of it. She remained shaken, undone. She should not have come.

Francesca walked over to a chair, took a deep breath, and sat down, finally facing him. She would focus on the investigation at hand. She swallowed and very briskly, in a nonsensical tone, she said, "Has a fresh grave been found?"

He was studying her and making no attempt to hide it. "Of course we have found several fresh graves—eight of them, to be exact. But every burial was legitimate."

Francesca smoothed down her skirts. "And you cannot go exhuming the dead upon a wild-goose chase." She remained brisk and businesslike.

"No, we cannot." He continued to stare.

Her mind raced. She knew he understood. What if the boy had been interred with someone else? How clever the killer would then be.

"Where do we go from here?" she asked, hugging herself again. If only he would break eye contact, even for a moment. "We have a handful of clues, but nothing to lead us to the killer," she cried.

Bragg's expression became ever more drawn, and he turned away.

She realized why and jumped to her feet without thinking twice about it. "Oh, I did not mean that! Maybe he is still alive, Bragg," she whispered, from behind him, not daring to reach out to him.

He faced her. "I cannot keep on fooling myself. The odds are against it. But the real question remains, who? Who did this to . . . my son?" The last words were a mere whisper.

"Who are your enemies, Bragg?" she whispered back. "You must have enemies."

"I have made a list. It is short. There are three men in my life who might wish to destroy me—and one of my sons." He gave her a hard, frightening look and walked back and forth across the small rug.

She watched him closely. "And they are?"

"My stepbrother. Calder Hart. He has always despised me, and the feeling is mutual." His smile was hard and ruthless. She had never seen such a frightening expression on his face before, not even last night, with Gordino. For there was something absolutely uncompromising and unforgiving about it.

"I do not know him," she managed, mesmerized.

"He is here in New York, actually. He is rather successful in shipping. But he does not know the Burtons, and he has never been to their home."

"And whoever did this, he has very easy access to the Burton home. Whoever did this is a close friend, or a servant."

"Or a relative," Bragg said. "In this case, I am ruling Calder off my list."

"Who are the other two men?" Francesca asked, wondering what could have caused such bad blood between him and his stepbrother.

He hesitated.

"Bragg?" Dread swept over her.

"Gordino."

"Gordino!" Francesca cried, shocked.

"We have a history, Francesca," he said. And then he flushed.

"I do not understand," she said. Her mind raced. "You have never been in law enforcement before—have you? So how could you and Gordino share any history at all?" She remained bewildered.

His high, ruddy color remained. "Let us just say that there was a time in my life when I knew him. We were boys. And we were enemies," he said. He continued to pace with long, hard strides.

It began to click. Bragg's mother was a prostitute. Bragg had come from a different class of society—the same class of society Gordino had. She did not dare ask, she did not, but a little boy's life was at stake. Francesca followed him over to the table where he stared down at the bottle of scotch. She ignored her own warnings to herself. "My mother told me," she blurted.

He barely glanced at her, walking away, only to return

with a fresh glass. His hand wasn't quite steady as he poured another drink.

"Bragg!"

He faced her, holding the glass tightly. "Indeed?"

"She told me about your family." Francesca felt a flush burning on her own cheeks. "It doesn't matter to me!" she cried fiercely.

He saluted her with his glass and drank.

"Please don't drink," she implored.

"Why?"

"Because the clock is ticking and we have a crime to solve."

He set the glass down carefully. " 'We.' You never cease to amaze me, Francesca. Never."

She thought she heard a note of bitter irony in his tone and she tensed. For she sensed he would lash out at her now in his hurt and confusion and grief. She was wrong.

"So beautiful, so intelligent, so vibrant, so determined. And so damnably kind and caring. But I already said that, didn't I?" He saluted her once again with the glass.

She could not tear her eyes away from him.

"How can a man resist?" he asked simply.

Francesca began to tremble. He was not teasing her. He was not being mocking.

He seemed deadly serious.

Bragg continued. "Gordino is smarter than he appears. He did not break last night, Francesca. And the question remains, is it because he does not know who abducted my son, or is it because he hates me so that he managed to remain silent, in spite of the beating I gave him?"

"Could he hate you that much?" she whispered, still reeling from what he had said about her. Did he really mean what he had said? Did he really think of her that way? Was it possible?

"When we were boys living on the Lower East Side, we belonged to different gangs."

Francesca could not believe her ears. But he was so

educated, so cultured! And then she thought about the way he had assaulted Gordino last night. "I thought you were from Texas."

"Oh, no. I was born here in the city. But my father is the son of Derek Bragg, the founding father of our family." He looked directly at her. "When I was twelve, my father appeared in my life, and he took me and my stepbrother in and we moved down south." His smile was brief. "His name is Rathe Bragg. He is a great man. But the woman who raised us is an even greater woman. Grace never treated us differently from the rest of her children." And as if he realized he had said too much, he looked away.

"I am glad, Bragg," Francesca whispered.

"The rivalry between the gangs was bitter and intense. And in one particular gang fight, Gordino's brother died. He blamed me. I was partly to blame." He briefly closed his eyes. "I was Joel's age. Ten years old."

"And he still hates you?" Francesca asked, reeling from all that he had said.

"Enough that he might have bribed a servant to have the kind of access necessary to have perpetuated this deed by himself," Bragg said flatly.

She stared for a moment. "Do we know where he lives? If he had an old Remington typewriter, then we would know he is the one."

"We found his flat days ago. There was no evidence linking him to the crime." Abruptly, Bragg sat down on the sofa, setting down his glass. He rubbed both temples.

Francesca sat down next to him, keeping a respectable distance between them and also trying not to think about that. "And the third man on your list?"

He did not look up. "Burton."

"Burton!" she cried. But then it made so much sense. "Oh, God! He knows the boys are not his, and he has secretly hated you for all these years! You have only just returned to New York City with your new appointment—and he decided to strike!"

He straightened. "Francesca. Eliza swears that he does not know. She swears he believes the boys are his. She swears that he adores them. And the truth of the matter is, I have seen him with the twins. I don't think he knows, Francesca. I think he loves the twins the way I do."

She was so disappointed. "Bragg, when did you meet Eliza?" The question, though cautious, just popped out.

"I attended Columbia University. We met eight years ago, and we had an affair." He hesitated. "For a year. We were young and in love, Francesca. Or so we thought." He hesitated. "When we broke up, neither one of us knew that she was pregnant. And she immediately married Burton. In fact, she was engaged to him toward the end of our relationship." He shrugged.

But Francesca had seen the look in his eye and she was dismayed and distressed. He had cared for her, even loved her, and he had been hurt when she had been affianced to someone else, someone more suitable than a bastard like himself. She cleared her throat. "Then it is Gordino—or someone out to get Burton."

"Or someone out to hurt Eliza."

She held his gaze. Her heart pounded now. "Why?"

He laughed, but not with mirth. "She has broken many hearts."

Francesca knew then that she had been right. She wet her lips. "What is it about her that makes men fall in love with her?" And she was thinking not just of Bragg and Montrose, but of Wiley, and even of Burton, who seemed to love her so. "I mean, if you really look at her, there are many women more beautiful."

"She is like you," he said, staring. "She is beautiful and intelligent and genuine. She is an original, and men find that mesmerizing."

Two compliments in one morning. Two vast compliments. Francesca held his gaze and could not, for the life of her, look away.

Abruptly, as if the couch they shared had become far

too small for the two of them, he leapt to his feet.

Francesca remained motionless.

He said, very grimly, "Eliza would not cooperate until yesterday, but I have a list of the men she has had affairs with. I cannot share it with you."

Her heart stopped. And when it resumed its beat, the pounding was frantic and all awareness of her attraction to this man briefly disappeared. He had spoken in the past tense. Was Montrose on that list? Francesca could not imagine any woman confessing to the identity of a current lover. "Did any of those men call on her Tuesday during the time that the pajamas and the fourth note were left?" she managed.

"No. She had three callers that day. Elizabeth Oscar and Georgina Hennessy."

She realized she was hugging herself. He was staring at her. She did not like the look in his eyes. It was suddenly highly speculative.

"Don't you want to know who the third caller was, Francesca?" he asked far too softly.

No. She did not want to know.

"Eliza did not tell me. I had to glean the information from a servant," he added in a drawl.

She sat there like a lump on a log. He knew. He was too damnably clever, and he knew all about Montrose and Eliza.

Bragg reached for her, took her hand and pulled her to her feet. Their gazes locked. He did not release her hand. Francesca did not pull free. "It was your brother-in-law," he said.

"Please don't tell anyone," she heard herself plead. And her hands slipped to his chest.

And briefly, she was shocked by how hard the slabs of muscle were beneath her palms, and by the feel of his drumming heartbeat.

His eyes widened. His hands covered hers and she

could not, did not, move. "Why does it not surprise me that you already know about this?"

"Please, Bragg." And suddenly she did sway toward him. Her thighs brushed against his. She had become a woman in that one transformative moment, and as their gazes locked, they both understood it. Her power felt fragile and it also felt vast. "No one can know, Bragg. Connie doesn't know, and it will kill her!"

He did not answer her for one long, heavy, awkward moment, during which time Francesca felt his heart racing even faster beneath her hands. "Francesca, I am going to have to speak to Montrose."

Francesca cried out. "But—"

He was grim. "Do you know that his first wife died under suspicious circumstances?"

Francesca gaped. "What?"

"He was heavily in debt and he married an heiress," Bragg said.

Francesca cut him off rudely. "Wait one moment," she said. "He inherited that debt from his family."

"I am well aware of that," Bragg responded evenly. "The point I am trying to make is that he paid off a large portion of that debt, and then a wheel fell off the carriage that was supposed to be carrying them both back to his estate. At the last moment, however, he decided to remain in London, and she went on alone. There was a brief investigation. The authorities concluded that it was an accident." His gaze was steady and dark upon hers.

"Well, then, you have your answer," Francesca said in a desperate rush. Now she tried to move back, away from him, but his grip tightened and she could not move. She felt her eyes widening. His stare darkened in return.

"Francesca, I am sorry," he said. And compassion filled his gaze.

"No. You are not," she said, but she no longer tried to wrestle herself free.

He pulled her into his arms.

Francesca did not stiffen in surprise. Because she was not surprised. She did not seem to have any control over her own body, and she melted against him, into him.

He was the one to tense briefly with surprise.

And then he wrapped his arms around her and held her hard, thigh to thigh and breast to chest. His breath feathered her neck and ear.

And suddenly Francesca became aware of desire for the first time in her life. He was a big, strong man, and he felt like a very safe haven from all of the world's evils; in his arms, with her cheek resting against his shoulder, she knew no harm could come to her, not ever. And he was all lean, long muscle, all hard, strong bone, every inch of him intriguing and arousing. Whom had she been fooling, to think he was just her friend? She had been smitten from the moment she had first laid eyes upon him.

If he did not kiss her, now, this instant, she might very well die.

He released her. "Montrose is a fool," he said gruffly. "But Eliza does that to men." His gaze was heated, wary, searching hers.

Francesca's knees seemed weak and about to buckle. She was so dismayed that he had released her, and she really did not hear what he said. She cupped his rough, stubby jaw, trembling. "You are very kind, too, Bragg. Did you know that?"

His jaw flexed visibly. He started to pull away. "I do not believe anyone has ever called me kind before."

"Don't, Bragg," she whispered. What was she doing? she managed to think as she slid her thumb over the hard, tensed-up muscle there.

And his gaze met hers, filled with brilliance and comprehension and hunger, and he pulled her forward again, and this time, he tilted up her chin and his mouth covered hers completely.

Francesca flung her arms around his neck, opening her mouth to receive him.

His arm, behind her back, tightened. His other hand slid around to her nape, covering it completely and anchoring her in place. And his mouth, which was warm and firm and tangy with the scotch whisky, plied her lips. The tips of their tongues tested each other and tasted and touched.

An image flashed through Francesca's mind, of Bragg going down on his knees before her, kissing her thighs, kissing her at the soft, aching juncture there, the way she had seen Montrose do to Eliza.

Francesca cried out, sagging in his arms.

Both of his arms went around her, hard. Francesca was drawn up against the entire length of his body while their mouths fused again, and there was no mistaking the huge arousal against her hip. Oh, God. So this was what a man felt like, this was what he tasted like. She threaded her fingers through his thick, silky hair. She tried to kiss him back. She tried not to think of him down on his knees, his face buried between her spread thighs.

He tore his mouth from hers only so he could rain kisses along her jaw and throat. His tongue touched her ear, penetrating it. His hand slid down over her breast, and then lower, over her hip, and lower still. Someone moaned wildly—it was herself.

Francesca's lower body collapsed.

He caught her in his arms, lifting her and carrying her to the sofa. As he laid her down on her back, Francesca managed to think in spite of the haze of heat unfurling within her. This was very wrong.

But Bragg was very right.

She did not, could not, care.

He moved on top of her and she embraced him with a cry, her mouth seeking his now, her tongue testing the seam of his lips. The sound he made came from the back of his throat. It was deep and guttural; sexual and male.

His arms lifted her even more tightly to his body and his mouth found her collarbone amidst the ruffles of her shirt collar. He licked the hollow there and drew the lower part of her body even closer to him.

"Bragg," Francesca whispered, clasping his face with both hands.

His heated eyes met hers and then his mouth was on hers, hard and insistent. And Francesca felt his erection against her pelvis. Somehow, without conscious volition, she was moving against him, and he was arching against her.

Mentally, she stripped him naked. He would be leaner than Montrose. Leaner, harder, more sculpted. Like Montrose, he would be huge. Like Montrose with Eliza, he would thrust into her, the way he was almost trying to do now, despite the barrier of their clothes. Francesca held him more tightly, crying out, frantically, desperately.

This moment must never end.

"Bragg," she moaned, and somehow, her palms found their way into his shirt, onto the hard slab of his chest.

Somehow, his hands were beneath her, clasping her buttocks. He was panting, and hard, as if he had just run a marathon. Then he reared up over her.

Francesca had never seen a man with such an expression upon his face before.

She did not have to be tutored in the ways of the world to understand. Bragg was consumed with the desire he felt for her. He wanted her. He wanted her in that savage, feral, carnal way that was as old as time itself. He wanted her the way Montrose wanted Eliza, the way that she wanted him.

Their eyes locked. Francesca prayed that time would stand still; she prayed that he would reach down and lift her skirts and touch her and ease the terrible longing of her tortured body.

He kissed her instead.

Long and hard, sucking on her lips, their bodies locked and rocking again.

There was a knock on the door.

Francesca vaguely heard it through the haze of heat and hardness and desire, and then the knock sounded again, more insistently, a hard rapping. Bragg, in the act of exploring her mouth with his tongue, froze. And she somehow thought, My God, someone is at the door, and then, Thank God the door is closed!

Bragg leapt to his feet.

Francesca blinked and opened her eyes and saw him standing there absolutely disheveled, his shirt open and hanging out of his trousers, his face flushed with passion. And then she looked past the sofa, confused, because the door had never been closed, and she was right. It was open, and Peter was standing there.

Francesca suddenly looked down at herself—her skirts were twisted well above her gartered knees—and she sat up as if struck by a lightning bolt. Her hair fell down in a wild mass over her shoulders.

If Peter was stunned to find her on his employer's sofa, if he had any clue as to what they had been about, he gave no sign. "Commissioner, sir," he said. "I think you had better come directly."

Francesca tugged down her skirts, aware of flushing feverishly, the ramifications of what had just happened beginning to sink in.

Bragg finished tucking in his shirt and he zipped up his trousers, his back to her. The fever in her cheeks increased. "What is it?" he asked grimly.

"Detectives Murphy and Benson, sir. There has been a fifth note."

CHAPTER
15

Francesca rushed after Bragg as he strode down the short corridor. Two detectives whom she recognized stood in the foyer by the front door. Francesca saw Bragg take the note. She saw him grow pale.

She knew better than to demand the note's contents. Bragg asked grimly, "Where the hell was this found? And when?"

She had reached his side and she peered over his arm at the note he held. It read:

E is for Eternity

Francesca cried out, grabbing Bragg's arm.

"Mrs. Burton found the note under her pillow this morning when she woke up," one of the detectives said. The larger one with the handlebar mustache.

"Under her pillow?" Bragg echoed, having turned as white as a ghost. "As in, under the pillow she slept on all night?"

Both detectives nodded, grimly.

E is for Eternity. Death. Oh, God, no. Francesca's mind raced in tandem with her heart. "Bragg. I think this means Jonny is still alive!" She was now aware of the two detectives casting frequent and interested if not highly speculative glances at her.

He glanced at her, then grew impossibly grim. "Peter, please show Miss Cahill to the powder room."

Instantly, Francesca realized why the detectives were regarding her almost lewdly. Her hair was down and undoubtedly a mess. It was probably obvious how it had gotten that way. She felt herself flush.

But she did not move. How could she? And if she was not right? Why, it was an unbearable notion. She said, "Bragg! Please!"

He moved aside so they could speak privately. Before she could begin, he said, "I know what you are thinking. You think he is alive because this note is a death threat. But this note may simply be another act of torture." His tone was so level and calm. Francesca could guess what the effort cost him. Yet there was nothing calm about his amber eyes. Anger vied there with fear and anguish.

It was so hard not to touch him. "I think he is alive," she said stubbornly. "Dear God, it is a feeling I have, Bragg."

He regarded her for a moment. Then he said, as if they were discussing a scientific experiment, "What interests me is just where this note was found. And how it was found." He turned away, then paused. "I will drive you uptown as I am heading to the Burtons'. But I suggest you make a few repairs before we go."

She nodded reluctantly. She wished to discuss the case. But Peter was waiting for her, in order to escort her out. Francesca turned.

"Francesca."

Her name was spoken so softly she almost did not hear it. She faced him, and their gazes locked.

And as they stared at one another, Bragg clearly hesitating, the astonishing kiss replayed itself in her mind. Francesca felt her tension renew itself, and now, it had little to do with the last note and the abduction.

"We will speak about what happened later," he said, and he flushed.

She nodded, her heart suddenly singing, at once elated and terrified and oh, so excited, and she smiled, but he did not see, for he had turned away.

Peter led her to the powder room, not batting an eye. His expression could have been written in stone, Francesca thought. Once inside, Francesca found that she was a far worse sight than she could have ever expected.

She stared at her own reflection, wide-eyed. She looked like a tart from the Bowery. Her hair was a wild, tangled darkly golden mane. Her lips were swollen from kissing. She was flushed—but in a spectacular manner. I am probably ruined, she thought grimly, recalling the way both detectives had eyed her. Then, never mind.

It was but one more worry to add to her ever-growing list.

She wondered what Bragg would say when they had the chance to speak privately. And she smiled. What if he declared his affections openly? Her heart skipped and raced at the thought.

Then she grew grim as she began to make some badly needed repairs to her hair. That note had been found under Eliza's pillow. Eliza had to be the madman's target. Not Bragg and not Burton. Someone wanted to destroy Eliza and drive her insane.

Francesca gripped the vanity, staring at her reflection in the mirror. The madman was getting very confident, indeed.

Confident enough to walk right into Eliza's bedroom and leave the note under her pillow.

Francesca wondered if Eliza was wrong. She wondered if Burton knew about the twins and hated his wife enough to use an innocent little boy to destroy her sanity and emotional well-being.

Montrose would also have access to that bedroom.

Francesca had known all along that she was coming to

this conclusion. As a result, she was shaking, and badly, and she was also breathless. She had to close her eyes.

Eliza insisted that Burton did not know the truth about the twins. Eliza insisted that he loved the boys completely, believing himself to be their father.

A servant could have also put the note under the pillow, Francesca told herself grimly. A servant who hated his mistress, or who was working for Gordino.

She still did not think Gordino clever enough to mastermind this entire affair.

Montrose's first wife had died under suspicious circumstances, after he had used her money to pay off a large portion of debt. But it had been an accident. Hadn't it?

There was a knock on the door. "One moment, please," Francesca called out, shaken to the core and so very ill now. She quickly tried to untangle her hair and pull it back into a bun. Fortunately, she kept a few spare pins in her purse, and she managed to make do. Poorly, but it was better than nothing.

It was not Montrose.

Bragg was waiting for her in a police carriage. Francesca climbed in beside him and they set off. He turned to her. "You might be useful, Francesca. I would like you to come over to the Burtons' with me. You are a woman, and right now, I think Eliza will need you."

Francesca's heart sank. She had another, more important call to make, but it would have to wait. She nodded.

But was she insane to be thinking of confronting Montrose?

"Bragg! It's about time," Burton cried angrily when Bragg, Francesca, and the two detectives entered the house.

Francesca had to stare. Burton was far more disheveled than Bragg had been earlier. Not only was his clothing rumpled, his shirtsleeves rolled up, his tie completely undone and hanging about his shoulders like a ladies' scarf, but he too appeared to have had a sleepless night. He was gaunt, unshaven, and unspeakably pale.

"I came as soon as I heard. I'd like to speak with you privately, Burton," Bragg said calmly.

"Privately! Why the hell do you want to speak to me?" Burton was shouting. "There's a goddamn madman on the loose, one who has my son! Why the hell aren't you out there finding my son? That's your job, isn't it?" He was gesturing wildly, too. If he noticed Francesca, he gave no sign.

Bragg touched his arm, but Burton shrugged him off. "We are all distraught," he said quietly. "But becoming undone now will not help anything or anyone, and it will not help us find the boy."

"The boy? He is not 'the boy.' Jonny is my son, and he has a name!" Tears abruptly filled Burton's eyes. He was shaking, Francesca realized.

"I know. I am sorry," Bragg said. "Please, I must ask you a few questions. Is your wife upstairs?"

"Yes! And you can imagine the condition she is in! Whoever did this, I swear, I will kill him myself once he is found!" Burton glared furiously at Bragg. "Maybe you are in over your head, Bragg. Are you capable of finding my son? Are you capable of running the police department? I seriously doubt you will keep this job if you do not solve this case and find my son."

"Time will tell whether I am competent or not," Bragg said without inflection. He firmly took Burton's arm, this time not allowing the other man to shake him off. "As I am in charge of this investigation, I expect your complete cooperation." He began leading Burton, who remained livid, actually resisting Bragg, across the hall. Bragg glanced back at Francesca. "Find someone to take you up to see Eliza. Sit with her until I come. Do what you can to calm her."

Francesca nodded. She understood Burton's anger, but was angry in spite of herself. Bragg did not need to be

shouted at and accused of incompetence now. Bragg and
Burton disappeared into the withdrawing room, Burton
raising his voice and shouting at Bragg again. Francesca
was rigid. Burton was hysterical with his fear and anger;
clearly, Burton had lost the last of his composure and perhaps his dignity, as well. Burton could not be the one responsible for Jonny's abduction and the cruel, taunting
notes. Not unless he was an actor worthy of the London
stage. Francesca was certain he was not acting. Francesca
would bet her life on it.

And as she crossed the hall, about to go upstairs, her
heart already sinking to a profound low, she heard Burton
sobbing in the other room. "I want my son back," he wept.

She could imagine Bragg speaking quietly, in a vain
attempt to comfort the distraught man.

She went upstairs, following a houseman. She had
never been this shaken.

It was not Burton.

The list of suspects was getting narrower and narrower.
But it could not be Montrose. His motive just was not
strong enough.

Unless he was insane and they had all been fooled from
the moment they had first met him.

Had he killed his first wife?

Francesca was shown into an upstairs sitting room that
was pleasantly but simply furnished, while the servant
went to inform Eliza that she had a caller. Francesca did
not move.

At the far end of the room was a desk. On the desk was
a typewriter.

And even from this distance, the machine looked bulky
and odd. It seemed out-of-date and old-fashioned.

She hadn't realized she had been holding her breath.
Now she began to breathe, but harshly, with excitement
and dread. She glanced around, then quickly closed the
door. She rushed across the room.

It was an older Remington machine, but Francesca did

not know precisely how old it was. But it was also a shift-key machine.

Had the note been typed on this machine? Where was the model number?

She glanced frantically around the machine, looking for the model number. She lifted it up, but it was so dusty underneath that she would have to wipe it clean in order to find any engraved writing. She thought she heard foot-steps approaching in the hall. She set it down, jumping away from the desk. She strained to hear.

She heard nothing.

Francesca hesitated, ran back to the door, and opened it. No one was in the hallway. It had been her imagination.

She shut the door and ran back to the machine. Where was paper? She would type the first note, "A is for Ants," and take it with her. And then she would be able to com-pare notes once she got her hands on an original.

There was no stack of paper sitting on top of the desk. Francesca began to open up the drawers, one by one, ig-noring her rising discomfort and even panic. She felt like a house thief. It was not a good feeling to have.

And very distinctly, she heard footsteps. Her hand was on a lower drawer, and as she pulled it open, she saw the neat stack of paper inside. The door swung open.

Francesca straightened, smiling brightly, her heart ex-ploding like dynamite.

And the houseman looked at her. "I am afraid that Mrs. Burton is not receiving today, Miss Cahill. Another time, she said."

Francesca continued to smile, aware of the houseman regarding her too closely—as if he were wondering why she was standing so rigidly there at the desk. With her knee, she pushed closed the drawer, as quietly as possible, keeping the rest of her body absolutely motionless. "What a beautiful old desk," Francesca said, coming around it. "Chippendale, I think."

"Mrs. Burton does most of her correspondence there,"

the young man said. "I believe the desk is Georgian." He smiled at her.

She blinked at him, aware of perspiring now. How would a servant know?

"I beg your pardon, miss," he added as she left the room.

"No, that is fine, I am glad to be corrected. What is your name?" Most servants would not converse with a guest, much less correct one.

"MacDougal," he said.

She glanced at him as they went downstairs. He was a young man, and rather good-looking, actually, with thick, dark black hair and hazel eyes. In fact, some women might find him quite handsome. He had a slim, straight nose and fine, even features. She guessed him to be only a few years older than herself. He also had the slightest trace of a Scots accent.

He was not an average servant, she thought. He was outspoken and good-looking. Then she wondered if Eliza had found him attractive, as well.

She knew she was staring but she could not stop herself. He glanced at her repeatedly now, beginning to flush.

I have gone too far, she thought to herself. Wondering if Eliza would dally with a servant in her employ.

"Is something wrong, Miss Cahill?" he asked as they went downstairs.

Her heart leapt. He was not an average servant, no, indeed. What if he had found his mistress attractive—as all men seemed to do? What if he had fallen in love with Eliza? And had either been actually rejected—or only rejected in his own mind and fantasies?

She smiled at him, aware that she might be grasping at straws. "I have known the Burtons for years," she said cheerfully. "But I do not recall seeing you here. Have you worked for them for very long?"

"About a year," he said with an answering smile. "And

I do recall seeing you here in this house, from time to time."

He was very bold. And he had a good memory, as well. "This is a terrible tragedy," Francesca said as they entered the hall.

He was immediately grave. "Yes, it is. Jonny is a wonderful boy. Whoever has done this should be shot."

She glanced closely at him. He had spoken in the present tense. Did that mean he knew something no one else did? Because by now, Francesca felt certain that everyone believed the boy to be dead. "Poor Eliza," Francesca said softly.

He nodded solemnly. "It is terrible, what this affair has done to her. She is a great woman who does not deserve this."

Francesca could not get a reading on him. The only thing she could be certain of was that he was rather bold and not very deferent to the upper classes. "Thank you," she said at the front door while waiting for her coat, hat, and gloves.

"Shall I tell the commissioner that you are leaving?"

Francesca glanced toward the closed door at the far end of the front hall. They had not had their private conversation yet. Her heart leapt, with excitement, and with dread. What if he did not declare himself? What if he insisted that the kiss had been a mistake?

She wished she did not have such doubt. Francesca sighed, and faced MacDougal. "I don't think we should interrupt him," she said. And as she accepted her garments from another servant, a new and very different dread began to rise up in her. Did she really have to do this? she wondered.

There was only one possible answer.

The first thing she did upon arriving at her sister's house was to inquire as to her sister's whereabouts. She was informed that Connie had left for a luncheon appointment.

A further inquiry told her that Montrose was in the library with his secretary. It was as she had hoped.

As a frequent visitor at her sister's house, she was allowed to find her own way to the library. She did so with growing trepidation. The door was open. Montrose sat with one hip on the edge of his desk in a dapper pin-striped suit. He was dictating to his secretary, a slim, middle-aged man with a bald pate and spectacles. Montrose saw her and halted in mid-sentence.

Francesca could not smile. She was trembling. Could she go through with this? How could she not?

Montrose stood up. "Francesca. What a pleasant surprise. I am afraid you have just missed Connie." He finally smiled. It seemed grim. Or was it her imagination?

Francesca made no move to enter the room. She felt ill. "Hello." She took a deep breath and said, "Actually, I had hoped for a word with you."

He continued to smile, his gaze moving over her. Suddenly Francesca recalled that she had not really repaired the damage done to her appearance by Bragg's heated kisses. It was too late now, however, to worry about her appearance. And who was he to call the kettle black?

"Very well. James, will you excuse us?"

The secretary left. Francesca entered the room, wondering if she was baiting the lion in its den, or if she were on a wild-goose chase. She could only pray that the latter was the case.

Montrose gestured for her to take a chair. He made no move to close the door, left wide open by James. How innocent he now seemed.

Francesca folded her arms tightly across her chest, but that did not still her wildly pounding heart. She told herself to relax, but she couldn't. And sweat beaded her brow. The fact that she had been somewhat taken with Montrose ever since she had first met him was not helping matters. It was hard to think clearly. How, in God's name, should she begin?

"Is everything all right, Francesca?" His brow was furrowed now. "And why, may I ask, are you so pale and disheveled?"

"I'm fine. As fine as can be, given the circumstances," she said hoarsely.

He had not seated himself, as she remained standing, and now he walked directly over to her. She found it hard to breathe. She reminded herself that this was Neil, and he really did seem the same. A big, devastatingly handsome man with flawless elegance, whose gaze now swept over her with penetrating concern. A man who made her tremble when it was not quite right for him to do so. A man who was a wonderful father—but not a wonderful husband, as one and all thought him to be.

"Has someone . . . hurt you?" he asked bluntly.

She thought he referred to his mistaken conclusion that she had a suitor. "No. No. There has been a fifth note, Neil." There. She had said it.

For one moment, he just looked at her, clearly not comprehending what she meant. Then his eyes widened. "You mean, about the Burton boy?" he asked.

She nodded, her pulse continuing to pound. " 'E is for Eternity,' " she whispered.

His eyes widened fractionally more, and then he whirled away, pacing back and forth. When he faced her, he appeared anguished. "Dear God, if only that boy is alive!"

"Yes." God, it was impossible to tell if he was guilty or not. He was acting like Montrose, like the Montrose she had known for four years. Then Francesca reminded herself that even if he was not guilty of Jonny Burton's abduction, he was not the Montrose she had known for four years. He was a liar—an adulterer—a cheat. He was not what he had appeared to be, oh, no. And what about his first wife? The circumstances had been suspicious enough to warrant an investigation. No one in her family had any idea, Francesca was absolutely certain. "The police have a list of suspects. It gets narrower every day. Apparently someone is out to destroy Robert Burton." And Francesca could hardly believe her own ears. How calm and composed she sounded.

"Everyone has enemies, I suppose. But to use an innocent child, it is unforgivable," he said, hard.

"Yes, it is." This was getting nowhere. Francesca sucked in her breath and her courage. "I saw you with Eliza."

He had been toying with a paperweight on his desk. His hand stilled.

His entire body stilled.

Francesca felt paralyzed.

And then, very slowly, he looked up. "I was wondering when you would confront me," he said at last.

Their gazes locked. He had not denied it. But then, how could he? And clearly he had seen her; clearly, he had known that she knew of his affair all along. Francesca could not move, she could not breathe, and she thought, E is for Eternity . . . his first wife had died under suspicious circumstances.

He walked past her. It took Francesca a huge effort not to flinch when he moved by, and he closed the door firmly. Then he returned to his desk, and he sat down calmly behind it, his gaze upon her.

And Francesca could understand his actions. The desk was massive, the chair he now sat in, thronelike. Even standing, she felt dwarfed and rather like a supplicant. "How could you?" she asked hoarsely. "How?"

His smile was slight, the sound he made harsh. "You would not understand. You are still half a child."

"I am hardly a child," she managed.

He did not answer, hands clasped in front of him, his expression grim.

"Do you love her?" Francesca cried. And tears filled her eyes, blurring her vision. She swatted them away.

He was startled.

And Francesca realized the irony inherent in the question. Which "her" had she referred to? "Do you love Eliza Burton?" Francesca asked harshly. Damn it, but she would not cry, she would not.

"No. Not in the way that you mean," he said.

"No! Then how could you?" Francesca cried again.

He looked at her for a long time. "As I said, you would not understand, Francesca."

"Do you love my sister at all?" she heard herself whisper.

He hesitated and he stood. "I am not going to explain myself, not to you, not to anyone."

He had refused to answer her. Francesca's heart sank so hard it was sickening and painful. He did not love Connie. "I imagine that one day you will have to explain yourself, certainly to my sister, and maybe even to your daughters," Francesca said, aware of how high and loud and angry her voice had become. Her eyes felt moist. "How could you do this to your family? How, Neil, how?"

"I am not the first man to make such a mistake," he said flatly. "What is it that you want, Francesca? An apology? Or an explanation? Because you will get neither from me." His blue eyes were dark now with anger.

"I want you to tell me that you are sorry, that you have been a fool, and that you love my sister—that you always have and you always will," she shouted at him, tears falling. "I want you to tell me that it is over, and that this will never happen again!"

He had come around the desk in a single second and he gripped her arm, hard. "Keep your voice down. I will only say that I am sorry you saw what you did—what you had no right seeing." His eyes flashed. His color was high. "One day, Francesca, your spying will get you in terrible trouble, indeed."

She gasped, pulling away from him, certain his big hand had left an imprint on her small wrist. "Are you threatening me?" She was disbelieving, but it had been a threat, she felt almost certain—and she was scared.

Because if Montrose was insane, if he was a madman, then he was capable of harming her.

His eyes widened. "Are you mad? You are my sister! You became my little sister the day I married Connie. I would never hurt you."

"But you can hurt your wife," Francesca said bitterly.

He became still. "What are you intending, Francesca?" he asked flatly.

She inhaled. "I don't know."

He shook his finger at her. "You will not breathe a word of this to anyone, do you understand me?"

She clamped her lips together.

"Not to anyone, and not to Connie. In fact, you had damn well better stay out of my affairs altogether, and out of my marriage, as well."

Somehow, his words truly hurt. They stabbed through her like a knife. "I don't know what I should do. But when I decide what is right, that is what I will do!"

He was wide-eyed and incredulous. "Stay out of my life," he thundered.

She stepped back, away from him. "I love my sister," she said. "As, apparently, you do not." And she wondered if she was insane to fight him, when he might be capable of violence and brutality, with no regard for the mores and laws of society.

He marched to the door and flung it open. "Good day, Francesca."

She did not move. She was drenched now in sweat; her underclothes stuck to her like a second skin. "Where were you last night, Neil?"

He started. "What?"

"You heard me. That last note, it was slipped under your mistress's pillow. She found it this morning." It was a gamble. She did not know when the note had been slipped under Eliza's pillow.

He blinked. "And . . . are you accusing me of something? Good God!"

She hugged herself. "Did you see Eliza last night? Or this morning? When did you last see her?"

His jaw flexed. "You know when I last saw her," he said dangerously. "I cannot believe you. You think me some insane monster just because . . ." He stopped.

"Someone hates Burton. Very, very much. And Eliza makes you insanely jealous." Francesca waited for his reaction.

He stared at her. "What?"

"This is an exact quote, I believe. 'God, Eliza, you make me insanely jealous.' "

He stared at her, his blue eyes fierce.

Francesca felt the barest moment of smug satisfaction.

Until he shook his head. "Incredible," he said. "But as I said, you are half a child. Francesca, when a man speaks in the heat of passion, his words tend to be meaningless. In fact, they usually are meaningless."

She did not believe him. Shaking, she said, "I think you hate Burton. I think you hate him because, like all of her other lovers, you have fallen madly, uncontrollably, in love with her, against your will, against your better judgment." She was out on a limb, one long and weak. Francesca knew it would shear away at any moment.

His face tightened. "I do not love her. And I do not hate Burton. In fact, if you must know, I pity the poor fellow, as I shall not be the last to warm her bed, and I was hardly the first to do so."

Francesca said, "Someone very close to the Burtons is responsible for that little boy's disappearance, and now, for his fate."

Montrose stared. He did not speak for an endless moment, as if weighing whether to reveal himself or not.

Francesca summoned up the rest of her courage. Bragg's words of wisdom chose that moment to pop into her head: "Words once spoken can never be taken back."

She said, "There was an investigation into your first wife's death."

His eyes closed. He turned deathly white. And he cursed.

Francesca flushed, stepping back, prepared now to flee.

Then he said, hard, "Perhaps you had better look closer to the Burton home for your murderer, Francesca."

Her mind scrambled and raced. He was pointing the finger at Robert Burton again? It was as if she and Bragg were going around and around in circles.

And Montrose said, "Eliza hates her husband with a vengeance."

CHAPTER
16

THURSDAY, JANUARY 23, 1902—1 P.M.

Francesca closed her bedroom door and leaned against it. Her mind was spinning.

Eliza hated Burton with a vengeance.

Was it possible? Could Eliza wish to destroy her own husband so passionately that she would concoct such an outrageous scheme as to abduct her own child and then cruelly toy with Burton by delivering a series of clues that all seemed to lead to one inescapable conclusion? That Jonny was dead?

Francesca had to sit down. She cradled her head in her hands. She could not imagine Eliza being so devious, so ruthless and so insane. The problem was, Francesca had always liked Eliza, even if from a distance, and she had certainly admired her.

In fact, even now, knowing that Eliza remained unconscionable when it came to her adulterous affairs, Francesca found it hard to sit in judgment of her. Which made no sense.

Francesca believed in right and wrong. And adultery was certainly wrong.

She closed her eyes, leaning back fully in the chair. She tried to imagine what it was like to be Eliza Burton.

She was intelligent, vivacious, and her joie de vivre was

contagious. When she entered a room, she brightened it considerably, and she always caused the heads of both genders to turn. She had obviously married Burton while young. The twins were six, and Eliza was perhaps twenty-six or -seven. Both boys seemed to possess their mother's energy and enthusiasm.

Francesca thought about Burton, who was a lawyer and a partner in his own firm. She recalled the many times she had seen the couple together, with Burton doting on his smiling, beautiful wife. She sat up, eyes open now. Eliza had a grace and self-confidence that was mesmerizing. Burton, on the other hand, while attractive and dapper, truly did seem to dote on his wife.

Dote, or fawn?

Francesca now analyzed the pair ruthlessly and decided that Burton had neither his wife's charm, charisma, or intelligence. In fact, she was the outspoken one, and he was the one always seconding her opinions. Eliza was the stronger of the two. It was an unusual turn for a couple. Francesca wondered why she had not realized this before.

Just how many lovers had Eliza had?

Unless she was inherently flawed in her character, she would have sought her affairs because Burton failed to hold her love, and perhaps even her respect. And suddenly Francesca thought she understood Eliza, just a little. She was a vibrant woman and her lovers, at least Bragg and Montrose, were exceptional men. Of course she would be drawn to outstanding men. Burton was just not on her level—and unlike most women, Eliza had the courage to go after what she wanted.

But did this mean that she despised Burton enough to want to torture him and drive him insane?

It was far-fetched. Still, no one had better access to the Burton home than its mistress had.

Francesca was thoroughly bewildered.

There were two soft raps at her bedroom door and Francesca's heart sank as Connie opened it and poked her head in. She was smiling. "Hello. I thought I would stop by on my way home. I just had the most fabulous lunch at Sherry's."

Francesca managed a smile. The conversation she'd just had with Neil replayed in her mind. "Hi."

"Fran?" Connie stepped in. "What's wrong? You are very pale. You don't look well. Are you still ill?"

"I guess I must still have a touch of the flu or something," Francesca said, her temples beginning to throb. She could not face her sister now.

Connie sat down beside her, touching her forehead with her delicate palm. "Well, I do not think you have a fever."

Francesca studied her sister, who seemed as radiant as ever. And of course, as always, she was splendidly dressed in a fitted rose silk suit trimmed with ivory lace. Her blouse matched the lace, and rubies dangled from her ears. "Who did you have lunch with?"

Connie smiled. "Sarah Channing and her mother."

Francesca stiffened, thinking, Oh, no. "And what did you think?"

"I think Mrs. Channing is not terribly clever, but Sarah is far more clever than one would ever suspect." Connie stood up. "But she is awfully quiet." She gave Francesca a look and wandered over to the window. "What a beautiful day."

Francesca also stood. "Don't you think she makes a poor match for Evan?"

Connie turned. "I don't know. They seem vastly opposite, but opposites do attract. Besides, he seems infatuated."

Francesca stared. "He's not infatuated, Con. Papa is demanding that he marry, but I suspect Mama is the one behind this . . . this . . . tragedy!"

Connie was startled. "I doubt either Papa or Mama could force Evan to marry against his will." Then her eyes narrowed. "Not unless he has gotten himself into financial straits with his gambling. Please tell me that he hasn't."

"Why is it that I was the last to know that Evan has gone outrageously overboard with gaming?" Francesca demanded.

Connie made a face. "That is one benefit of being married, my dear. Neil, of course, frequents some of the same establishments as our brother. He's told me of Evan's exploits. We've both been rather worried about him, if the truth be known."

"I had no idea until last night," Francesca complained.

Connie shrugged then smiled. "Perhaps you need to get yourself a husband, hmm?"

"Very funny," Francesca said, suddenly recalling Bragg's kisses. She watched her sister turn back to the window.

Connie made a soft exclamation. "That's Neil's coach! He must be calling on the Burtons."

Francesca almost fainted. "What?" And she thought, How could he? How dare he go back over there, and right after our conversation!

"I think I shall go join him." Connie turned to leave.

"No, wait!" Francesca cried, rushing to her.

Connie looked at her with bewilderment. "Fran? What is it?"

Francesca stared at her sister, at a loss. Too many horrible scenarios were going through her mind at lightning speed for her to count. But chief among them was Connie walking in on Montrose and Eliza as Francesca had yesterday.

"Fran? Why are you staring at me—and in such a peculiar way?"

Francesca forced a wide smile. "I need your help," she blurted.

Connie regarded her closely. "In what matter?" she asked.

Francesca stared, her mind going blank.

Connie suddenly frowned. And Francesca thought, but was not sure, that she saw worry flit through her blue eyes.

"Is there a reason you are trying to detain me?" She suddenly glanced back at the window—toward the Burtons' home.

She knows, Francesca thought wildly. Or she suspects! "Connie, I do need your help." She grabbed her arm and led her over to a chair. "Please sit down."

Connie stared at her and sat. "What is this about?" she asked quietly.

Francesca's mind raced. "I need to go down to police headquarters and I need you to come with me." She fabricated as she spoke.

"What?" Connie was disbelieving.

Francesca sank down on an ottoman. "Oh, God, you won't believe this, but I have been helping investigate the disappearance of Jonny Burton."

"What?" Connie said again. Her expression was so incredulous that it was comical.

"I found some of the clues, Con," Francesca said seriously. "In fact, just this morning there was another terrible note."

"What did it say?" Connie asked, now wide-eyed and leaning forward.

"I can't tell you," Francesca said. "Bragg would throttle me if I did. Time is running out. If Jonny is still alive, this case must be solved immediately."

"Do the police think he is dead?" Connie asked worriedly.

"It is up in the air. It is possible that whoever has done this wishes to torment either Eliza or Robert Burton." Or Bragg, Francesca thought silently.

"This is so terrible. But Francesca, how could you be involved and how can I help?" Connie asked.

"It is far too long a story to explain how I came to be involved," Francesca said firmly. "But Connie, it is very possible that the notes were typed in the Burton home."

Connie gasped.

"They have a typewriter that is very old, and it is a

shift-key model. The notes were typed on a Remington 2, one of the first typewriters ever developed. It was also a shift-key model. Con, we need to go to police headquarters. I feel certain Bragg is not there; in fact, he might still be at the Burtons'. You can stand guard outside of his office while I go in and obtain one of the original notes. I saw them in a folder on his desk the last time I was there." Francesca sat back in her chair. She was smiling. Now she had a firm course of action, indeed.

"What!" Connie cried, aghast.

"If I obtain an original note, then sometime later today, I will sneak into the Burtons' home and type a few letters and then compare the notes."

Connie gaped at her. She was flushing. She said, her tone extremely high, "You think to burglarize the office of the commissioner of police?"

Francesca straightened. "Well," she began.

"You think to commit that crime at police headquarters?" Connie continued, in sheer disbelief.

Francesca scowled. "You are making it sound far worse than it is."

Connie was on her feet. "I do not think so! Burglary is burglary, Fran! You have lost your mind! To even think of going into Bragg's office and steal evidence in a criminal investigation. And I shall not aid and abet you in such a crime."

"But a little boy's life is at stake," Francesca cried, leaping to her feet.

"Fran!" Connie cried. "Why don't you just tell Bragg about the typewriter the Burtons have?"

Francesca looked at her blankly.

"I am sure he would like to know about its presence, and he will probably take it as evidence, and he can compare the notes himself." Connie shook her head.

Francesca realized Connie was right. "Why didn't I think of that?" she muttered.

"I'll tell you why," Connie said. "You have gotten completely carried away with this new idea of yours, this new persona, with being some kind of crime-solver extraordinaire! You're enjoying this!"

Francesca sort of smiled. It felt faint. "I want to find Jonny—alive."

"I am sure that you do." Connie sighed, walking past Fran to the door. "I am going over to the Burtons'. Care to come?"

Francesca's heart lurched. She did not answer, because Connie was already in the hall. Instead, she ran after her.

Everyone was in the drawing room at the far end of the hall.

Francesca entered with her sister, her gaze immediately taking in the scene. Eliza sat on a tufted gold settee, alone. Montrose sat in a chair angled toward it. Burton stood behind the settee and his wife, hands in his pockets, as disheveled as he had been a few hours ago. Bragg stood beside him, and it was apparent, as Francesca and Connie arrived, that the police commissioner was preparing to leave.

Francesca stared at Burton, and saw that he was trembling ever so slightly, ceaselessly. She looked at Bragg, and her heart turned over for him. He was so tired, and even though she already knew that, seeing him even after just an hour or two made her newly aware of all that he was facing and all that he was going through. She turned her gaze to Eliza and Montrose.

She was sitting very primly, her hands clasped in her lap. Her face was pale, and blotchy, perhaps from tears. She was so still that she could have been a statue.

Montrose had leapt to his feet at the sight of Francesca and his wife. He was now kissing Connie's cheek and exclaiming over her presence.

"I saw your coach from Francesca's window," Connie said, with a smile.

"I thought to stop by and see if there was any way I

could help," he returned. "Hello, Francesca."

Francesca nodded grimly. She found that she could not look him in the eye, not now, not there, with Eliza—his lover—just a few feet away.

Eliza suddenly stood. "I am sorry. I must go. I am going upstairs to rest." She quickly left the room, her pale green silk skirts rustling as she did so.

Francesca wondered if her precipitous exit had to do with her sister's entrance, or the mere fact that Eliza was exhausted with the burden of her grief. If she was the one behind the abduction, then she was also an amazing actress. Because Francesca had seen sheer hopelessness in her eyes.

Burton wandered away from everyone, standing with his hands in his pants pockets, gazing out of a window at the snowy gardens. Francesca caught Bragg's eye and he came to her. They stepped into a corner of the room, their comprehension mutual.

"What is it?" he asked without ado.

Francesca glanced past him at her sister and Montrose. He had put his hand on her waist. Connie was saying something. Francesca could only see three quarters of her face. Did she see a tension there that she had not noticed before?

"Francesca?" Bragg prompted. He spoke in a low tone, while following her gaze.

Francesca turned her attention back to him. "When I was here earlier, I saw an old typewriter upstairs in Eliza's sitting room. It is in use—on her desk. In fact, her manservant says she uses it frequently. I think we may have found our Remington 2, Bragg." Francesca spoke very softly, not wanting to be overheard. She glanced back at her sister and Montrose.

He was speaking now. Connie seemed nervous, no, she seemed anxious.

"Perhaps that is our machine. Right now, I shall leave it alone, since even if it is our machine, it tells us nothing new," Bragg said. Then, "Francesca. They will have to solve their own problems."

She jerked back to face him. "I suppose you are right," she whispered. "But I don't want her hurt."

"There are too many instances to count in a single lifetime when one cannot control circumstance. This is one of those instances, Francesca," he said with compassion.

She met his gaze with all of her attention for the first time. He had so much on his mind. Yet he had given her his undivided attention—and his undivided compassion—for this single moment. "Thank you, Bragg," she said.

His smile was faint, his regard intent. "Is that all?"

She hesitated. "No." She inhaled, glanced backward, and saw Connie and Montrose staring at them. She flashed the pair a smile and grabbed Bragg's hand, pulling him into the hall. "I confronted Neil."

His eyes widened. Then they flashed. "I wish you hadn't done that!"

"I had no choice."

"You had a choice," he said, hard. "We are dealing with a very dangerous and unpredictable human being, Francesca. I do not want you getting hurt."

His words thrilled her. "He told me that Eliza hates Burton with a vengeance. And that is a quote, Bragg." She did not look away.

And neither did he.

"Why do you not seem surprised?"

"I'm not," he said.

She tensed. "You already know. You already know her feelings!"

He did not respond, but he did not have to.

Francesca was upset. She realized that she was jealous. Even though it had been years ago, Bragg and Eliza had been so close then that he knew her well even now. Then she whirled back. "And is she on your list of suspects?" she flashed.

"Not really." His amber gaze was steady. He did not seem perturbed.

"Not really?" She was incredulous. And suddenly she was angry. "Why isn't she on the list of suspects?"

"Look, Francesca." He sighed. "I know her very well. We have remained friends for all of these years. She is many things. But she is not insane. Many people despise a spouse. Most people do little about it."

She folded her arms across her chest. "I think you want to protect her."

"Maybe. But has it ever occurred to you that Montrose lied to protect himself?"

Her heart lurched unpleasantly. "Yes. It has."

He nodded.

"I have one other suspect," Francesca said, hating that Bragg wanted to protect Eliza, and hating even more the notion that Montrose had lied, tossing them a red herring, in order to protect himself.

He smiled. "Let me guess. MacDougal?"

She gaped. Then she cried, "And for how long would you keep that one to yourself?"

"I think you have forgotten that this is a police investigation. I have no obligation to share any information with you, Francesca."

She sighed with dismay and frustration. "You are right. Connie is right. I have gotten completely carried away." And she thought, crime-solver extraordinaire. It had quite the ring.

"I interviewed the entire staff on Sunday, remember?" Bragg said. "MacDougal struck me from the start as rather unusual."

"Does he have a police record? Has he ever been convicted of a crime? Has he ever been in jail?" Francesca asked quickly.

Bragg seemed to smile. "The answer to all of your questions is no. But two years ago he was abruptly dismissed from his employment and his employer would not say why. A little digging produced some sordid gossip. He might have been involved with the mistress of the house's best friend."

"Touchdown," Francesca cried with unfettered excitement.

Bragg smiled. "Are you a football fan, Francesca?"

"I have gone with my brother three times to watch the Columbia University team. I rather enjoyed myself." She was arch. If MacDougal was the madman, she would be happy and relieved. "What are you going to do?"

"We have been shadowing him since Sunday. The bad news is, he has behaved with the utmost innocence ever since the abduction. If he is involved, he has a partner."

"Gordino?"

"Maybe."

Francesca clenched her fists. "Bragg, we are going round and round in circles!"

"Yes, we are," he said gravely. And she saw the flash of anguish in his eyes.

She touched his hand. "Arrest MacDougal. Give him that 'third degree' you were talking about."

"I may do more than arrest MacDougal," Bragg said. And his gaze moved past her.

Francesca had a horrific premonition and she turned to find that Montrose was the object of his stare. "No," she said.

"Excuse me," Bragg said.

But before he could go, Francesca grabbed his hand. "Not now, not here. Do what you must, but not in front of my sister," she begged.

Their gazes locked. "Then take your sister now, and leave."

There was no mistaking the warning in his tone. And Francesca knew he would not compromise. Frightened, she nodded and hurried over to Connie and Montrose.

Connie was looking at her oddly. "This is interesting,

Fran," she said, her gaze moving between Francesca and Bragg.

Francesca was in a near panic, and she did not have a clue as to what she meant. "Con! Would you come back with me to the house, just for a moment? There is something I forgot to show you."

"All right," Connie said. She glanced at Montrose. "I'll see you at home?" And it was a question.

He nodded and kissed her cheek. "Don't hurry." He smiled. "Whatever the two of you are up to, have a good time."

Francesca couldn't manage a smile in return. She grabbed her sister's hand, and the moment they had their coats, hurried her outside. As they went down the front steps, she flung a last glance over her shoulder. Bragg was speaking to Montrose. Neither man seemed cordial or social; in fact, both seemed angry and ready to do battle.

Oh, dear, Francesca thought as the front door was closed.

But one moment later it was opened again, and Bragg hurried down the steps. "Excuse us for one moment, Lady Montrose," he said with a polite smile at Connie. And he dragged Francesca aside.

"What is it?" she cried, alarmed.

"I forgot to mention something to you. Although I doubt you will be in any danger, I want you to be cautious," he said.

"What happened?" She prepared herself for a blow.

He was grim. "Gordino escaped the Tombs this morning."

CHAPTER
17

THURSDAY, JANUARY 23, 1902—5 P.M.

"Actually," Francesca said, the moment they had stepped inside the house, "I want to ask you something." She was stalling for time and trying to invent an excuse for having dragged her sister away from her husband.

Connie glanced at her, brows lifted. "Francesca, something odd is going on. You are behaving strangely and I almost get the feeling that you are hiding something from me."

Francesca avoided her sister's direct stare. "You are now the one with the imagination, Con," she said, as they removed their coats. She wondered what was happening over at the Burtons'. Was Bragg going to interrogate Neil? Would he take him downtown to police headquarters? She winced, thinking about Kurland and the rest of the press. She could imagine tomorrow's headlines, which would be something horrific, such as "Lord Montrose a Suspect in Burton Boy Abduction." She prayed Bragg would not go so far as to force Montrose downtown. Surely anything he wished to say to him could be said at the Burtons'.

If only Neil were faithful to his wife, she thought despairingly.

"So? What is it?" Connie asked. Then, "Did you by any

chance notice something amiss between Neil and the police commissioner?"

Francesca almost choked. She was saved from responding by Julia, who breezed into the hall, clad in a pale blue jacket and skirt. "Hello, girls," she said, smiling. "What are the two of you up to?"

"We were just visiting the Burtons, Mama," Connie said.

Julia's face fell. "I feel so terrible for poor Eliza. Is there any word?"

Francesca and Connie exchanged glances. "Not really," Francesca said.

Julia sighed. Then, "I have just got in myself. I am going to take a nap before supper. We are going to the opera tonight," she said.

That was twice in one week. They waited until Julia had left, walking into a salon together. A brilliant idea struck Francesca. "Con, I am going to confront Papa over his choice of Sarah Channing as Evan's bride. Would you come with me? And lend me your support?"

Connie blinked. "Fran, if you mean, will I unequivocally state that I am opposed to the match, my answer is no."

"But how can you favor the match?" Francesca cried.

"I do not know that I favor it, either. But this is really Evan's business, and Papa's—not ours. I don't think you should get involved."

"How can you say that?" Francesca said with anger, shaking her head. An image of Montrose and Eliza in a torrid embrace on the sofa in the Chinese-style salon filled her mind. Perhaps Connie did know, but pretended not to, looking the other way. Yet how could anyone pretend ignorance of an unfaithful spouse? For it suddenly occurred to Francesca that her sister liked to mind her own business; keeping blinders on. "He is our brother. We should most definitely become involved, and that means expressing our opinions on the matter of his marriage."

"I love Evan as much as you, but I disagree. Besides, Papa is usually right. And Evan is wild—a wife like Sarah Channing might be the best thing that ever happened to him," Connie said firmly.

"Or the worst," Francesca retorted. "Will you at least give this matter some serious thought? Once the engagement is announced on Saturday, it will be hellishly awkward to get out of. I am hoping Papa will postpone the announcement, instead of rushing forward with it."

"I will think about it," Connie said. She paced to a window, but the view was mostly of the lawns, with just a sliver of Fifth Avenue visible from this angle. "I wonder what Bragg wished to discuss with Neil," she murmured.

"I am sure it is nothing," Francesca said, far too quickly.

Connie glanced at her. She wasn't smiling. "Maybe I should go back to the Burtons'," she said. "I really do have a bad feeling."

"Please come with me while I speak to Papa," Francesca said, taking her arm firmly. "I need your support, Con."

"Very well," Connie said. But as they left the room, she glanced again at the window. "I wish I knew," she began. Then she stopped, shaking her head.

Francesca's pulse was pounding. Only one thing had become clear, she realized. Connie loved her cheating husband, and must be protected from the truth—and any hurt—at all costs.

Francesca did not know if she was strong enough to bear such a burden.

"So, what grave matter brings you both to me?" Cahill said with a fond smile. He sat at his desk in the library, going over papers he had brought home from his offices downtown.

Francesca shut the door carefully behind her sister and herself. "Did you have a good day, Papa?" she asked with a smile in return. There was always something so cozy and comforting about the library when her father was at his desk and a fire was roaring in the hearth. Even the cigar— which he had apparently just put out—smelled wonderful.

"As good as can be expected, I suppose," Cahill replied. "Considering the tragedy unfolding next door. I am disturbed that they have not found the boy and the madman responsible for his abduction."

"We are all concerned," Connie said softly, sitting down in a big green chair.

"It is not an easy case," Francesca found herself saying, in defense of Bragg's efforts to solve it.

"Apparently not. The criminal responsible is clearly sadistic. I saw Bragg yesterday at the Fifth Avenue Hotel. We spoke briefly. I can see that he is beside himself, trying to bring this case to a successful conclusion." Cahill shook his head. "He seems to be taking this almost personally."

Francesca stiffened. Her father was one of the smartest men she knew. He rarely missed a thing. "What are you thinking, Papa?" Francesca asked, perching herself on the edge of his desk. She was as curious as she was uneasy.

"I do not think Bragg will survive as the commissioner of police if he does not find this madman, and the boy— alive."

Francesca stared, filled with dismay. Of course she wanted justice to be served, and more than anything, she wanted Jonny Burton safely home. But dear God, it would be so unfair for Bragg to lose his job if the case could not be solved the way everyone wanted it to be. He was doing his best. He was a man of determination and integrity. Francesca was quite certain that he would be the best police commissioner since Teddy Roosevelt back in 1886.

"What makes you say so? Have you spoken with the mayor?" Francesca asked worriedly.

"I would never pry in such a manner," Cahill said. "But haven't you been reading the newspapers? The press has been merciless these past few days, accusing Bragg of incompetence and, in general, suggesting he is in over his head."

"That is terrible," Francesca whispered, ashen. She had been so immersed in the case herself that she had hardly looked at a newspaper recently, when usually she read one if not two every day. "And it is unfair," she said vehemently.

"The press is not known for being fair," Cahill mused.

Francesca suddenly realized that Connie was studying her far too closely. Francesca recalled the way Connie had been watching her and Bragg earlier at the Burtons', and for some reason, she flushed. Her sister rarely made her uncomfortable, but she was accomplishing that feat now. Then she had to smile, suddenly thinking of Connie's reaction should she ever tell her about *the* kiss. She would swoon.

"So, what is it that you wished to discuss?" Cahill asked Francesca. "By the way, you still seem peaked, dear. Are you not feeling better?"

"I am just tired, Papa. This nightmare concerning Jonny Burton is making it impossible for me to sleep."

Cahill stood and came around his desk. "Darling, you have a bleeding heart. It is wonderful to be so compassionate, but you are taking the misfortunes of others too deeply to heart. You should not be making yourself ill over this."

Francesca managed a smile. "I know." She paused. Then, "Papa, I think Evan and Sarah Channing are terribly mismatched."

Cahill raised a brow, settling back in his chair. "Really?"

Francesca nodded and spoke in a rush. "She is not his type, not at all. You know how he is always attracted to the most beautiful and lively of women. She is so sweet, but my brother needs a woman of fire, Papa. Surely you must agree with me there! Sarah is retiring and timid. He will make her miserable, I am sure, and she will make him as unhappy. I have no doubt about it!"

Cahill smiled. "And you are, I suppose, a woman of the world? That is, a woman of vast experience when it comes to relationships of a personal nature between men and women?"

Francesca blushed. "Papa—" she began.

He interrupted her. "Francesca, I happen to disagree with you—completely. I know how you adore your brother, and how, in your eyes, he can do no wrong. But he is highly irresponsible. His reckless ways must come to an end, my dear. The time has come for him to assume responsibility as my son and heir. I think Sarah is exactly the kind of woman he needs, a woman of substance, not fire, a woman who can steer him in the correct and moral direction. The last thing your brother needs is a wild temptress to encourage him in his frivolous ways. In time, I am sure, your brother and Sarah will become the best of friends. And that, my dear, is what makes for a successful marriage. Not fire, not passion." He smiled firmly at her.

Francesca was dismayed. She was also disbelieving. "Papa, surely you believe in love?"

"Indeed, I do. But I am a realist rather than a romantic, Francesca. And I thought you were, too."

Francesca stared. She was a realist, but she was coming to realize that she was far more romantic of nature than she had ever before suspected. She thought about Bragg and her heart leapt uncontrollably. "But Evan does not love Sarah Channing. So how can you even suggest he marry her—much less rush him into this marriage?"

Cahill sighed. "He will come to love her in time."

"And what if he does not? Because frankly, I cannot imagine Evan ever loving her. I think he may come to despise her in time. Have you considered that possibility?" Francesca asked.

"Actually, I have not. Francesca, my mind is made up. Sarah is the most admirable of women. She is strong and sincere, and the perfect match for your brother. You will not move me, my dear. And I know you think you can." He smiled.

Francesca stood, thoroughly disconcerted. "Is there a reason you must announce the engagement the day after tomorrow? Can't that wait? Why is there such a rush?"

"I see no reason to delay." Cahill was mild of manner.

"Papa. Please postpone the announcement? At least give Sarah and Evan more time to get to know one another," she pleaded with a smile, sure she would gain her way.

He shook his head. "Do you really think that if we delay this, somehow you will find a way to end the union?"

Francesca flushed. "Evan is so upset. He doesn't like her at all," she cried.

Cahill was dismissive. "Francesca, enough. The engagement will be announced Saturday night, and that is the end of that."

Francesca stared, unable to believe her ears. Her father was always kind, and he always kept an open mind. But on this subject, apparently, that was not the case. "Are you trying to punish him," she finally said, "for his gaming debts?"

Cahill was grim. "No, my dear, I am not. I am trying to correct his character. That is all."

"His character is wonderful!" she cried.

Cahill stood. He was flushing. "Francesca, I do not want to beat a dead horse. Enough."

"We are not beating a dead horse, Papa," she said. "We are discussing my brother's—your son's—life."

"Fran." Connie stood. "Papa is growing angry. He is not going to change his mind, and I must tell you, I like Sarah. I think Papa may be right. I think she might be very good for him, a calming effect, so to speak."

Francesca could think of nothing worse than to be forced into marriage for a "calming effect." She turned back to her father. "Tell me one thing isn't true," she said.

"And what is that?"

"That you are not using his debts to force him to wed? Surely that is not the case, Papa?"

Cahill stared. After a long pause, he said, "I have the right to spend my money as I choose. I have worked very hard my entire life, Francesca. I was not born into a home like this. My mother worked in a mill, my father on the farm, and there was barely enough food on the table when I was growing up. I butchered cows with my own two hands. I have worked very hard to be able to provide you, your sister, and your brother a life like this. Why should I make good on your brother's extravagant, reckless debts? I am sick and tired of the way he gambles away all that I have worked so hard for!" Cahill exclaimed.

Francesca was taken aback. She knew all about her father's past, and how poor he had been. But she had never seen him so angry. She didn't know how to respond. She finally said, "But surely you are not using those debts to force him to wed?"

"I am not the first father to deny a son payment of such reckless debts," Cahill said. "Now, if you will excuse me?"

Francesca stared as her father, who was clearly controlling his temper, left the room. He did not march past her, and he did not slam the door, but the sound of it closing had something frighteningly final about it. Tears filled her eyes.

"Well," Connie said on a deep breath. "I think we may rest assured that Evan will marry Sarah Channing."

Francesca folded her arms. She was trembling. "Papa will not listen to reason. I have never seen him like this before," she whispered. "And what is worse, he is blackmailing our brother," she choked.

Connie put her arm around her. "It isn't quite as bad as you are making it out to be, Fran. It really is for Evan's own good."

Francesca felt as if she were collapsing in every possible way—mentally, physically, and emotionally. "But he wouldn't even consider my point of view!"

"I suppose he feels very strongly about this," Connie said. "Come on, chin up. There are far worse things that could happen to Evan, Fran."

Francesca could not agree.

"Anyway, I am going home." Connie kissed her cheek. "If I don't see you before, I will see you at the engagement party Saturday night."

Francesca looked at her. She was beginning to feel numb. Connie was going home. Would Montrose be there? Or was he even now downtown at police headquarters with Bragg? Dear God, she could not worry about her sister's life now. She just could not. "All right," Francesca said.

After Connie had left, Francesca turned to stare out of the window at the back lawns. Twilight had fallen. The sky was blackening rapidly. She realized just how tired she was.

And she and Bragg had still not had a chance to talk about what had happened at his house just that morning.

Her gaze fell on the newspaper on her father's desk. She could not take much more, and she did not want to read about Bragg's failure to solve the case. She turned away.

But a headline had caught her eye. She whirled, grabbing the newspaper. It was the late edition of the *Sun*. A headline screamed: "E is for Eternity."

Francesca gasped, and in that one stunning moment, a comprehension struck her, and it was crystal clear.

It was the madman himself who was leaking information to the newspapers.

Francesca sat down on her bed clad only in her chemise, having let her hair down. Maybe she would take a nap, as well. Otherwise it would be a very early evening, indeed.

But as tired as she was, her mind refused to stop. Images tumbled one after another, leaving in their wake unformed thoughts. Bragg and Montrose, Montrose and Eliza, Eliza and Burton. Evan and Sarah, her sister and

Montrose, her father's grim expression. And then there was little Jonny Burton. She no longer saw him as a smiling imp with a twinkle in his brown eyes and a splattering of freckles on his nose. Now, when she thought of him, she saw him pale and frightened and drawn.

If Eliza was playing a terrible trick on her husband, then the boy was somewhere safe, and he was alive.

Francesca wondered if she could be prosecuted for abducting her own son.

She knew it was far-fetched. No matter how much Eliza might despise Burton, she was not insane and she was not cruel. How easily Montrose could have lied.

But then he would be the insane one, then he would be cruel and sadistic.

Francesca tried to sort through the facts. There was one suspect who was clearly cruel and sadistic and capable of brutality. And that was Gordino, who hated Bragg, who had escaped prison that morning.

Francesca stood and found herself walking to the window and staring toward the Burtons' house. It was Gordino. Of course it was Gordino. How could they even have a doubt?

She turned and retrieved her opera glasses, returned to the window, refusing to acknowledge any guilt for her spying. She trained them on the opposite house.

All the lights were on downstairs. Francesca stared into the ground-floor windows, one by one, but saw no one. She lifted the glasses to the second story. By now, she knew she was looking into Eliza's apartments where she had been just a few hours ago. She still wished she had managed to type a few words on that old typewriter in her sitting room. It certainly would not have hurt.

The sitting room was empty and unlit. The bedroom was not.

Francesca's grasp on the opera glasses tightened and she gasped as she focused on Eliza and Burton in what was clearly the midst of a fight. The two of them were standing almost in the center of the room—Francesca could make out the bed just behind them. They were face-to-face. Burton was gesturing wildly at her. Eliza did not seem to move, her body seemed stiff and set.

So much for the apparently perfect marriage, Francesca thought grimly. She was about to set her glasses down—for this was not her business—when Eliza turned away.

And as quick as a striking snake, Burton's hand lashed out, and he whipped her around to face him.

She struggled to shrug him off.

Francesca knew she should put the opera glasses down. This was one scene she should not be privy to. Their battle was becoming physical and violent. This was another burden she could not bear.

But she could not move; she was frozen, standing there staring into the other house. Eliza managed to break free of Burton, and she said something to him.

Faster than before, his hand lashed out again. And this time, he struck her across the face.

Francesca cried out as the blow sent Eliza falling backward, onto her hands and knees on the floor. And then Burton was dragging her upright, and Eliza was struggling madly to free herself of him. Disbelieving, Francesca saw Burton grab a hold of her hair and yank her head back so hard that it must have hurt as badly as the blow to her face. She became utterly still in his grasp.

He said something to her. And then he lifted her in his arms and an instant later he threw her down on the bed. Eliza scrambled to get off on the other side. Burton caught her, dragging her back to the middle of the mattress, and then he straddled her, covering her mouth with his hand. He bent over her, and before Francesca's wide eyes, he tore open the bodice of her dress.

Francesca dared not watch any more. She threw the opera glasses on the bed, then stared blindly, in horror, out of the window—at the hazy outline of the house.

Oh, God.

Her pulse was deafening her now. She began to shake wildly, trying to think of what to do—of how she could stop whatever was occurring in that bedroom across the street. But what could she do? Burton was accosting Eliza, and unless Francesca missed her guess, he was forcing himself on his own wife.

Should she run over there and demand to see either one of them? Of course she would be turned away. And Francesca knew, with the most awful sinking realization, that there was nothing she could do to stop Burton's violence against his wife.

Eliza hates Burton with a vengeance.

Oh, God! Francesca rushed about her bedroom, not knowing what to do, where to go, what to think.

Eliza hates Burton with a vengeance.

Of course she did.

Francesca trembled. She was ill.

For now she could no longer deny that Eliza had the motive necessary to abduct her own son and attempt to destroy her own husband.

She had the motive. Oh, yes, she did.

And nothing Francesca did or said or thought would make that motive disappear.

She had missed two days of classes. She was quite certain the dean would wish to speak to her when she arrived on campus. It was the following morning, and Francesca had her books in a shopping bag, hidden beneath a newspaper, and she was on her way out the front door. She'd barely closed it when she saw the small figure lying in wait for her behind two large oak trees at the head of the Cahill drive. Joel Kennedy, bundled up in his worn, stained overcoat, a cap pulled down low over his face and ears, stood there clearly waiting for her. Even from the distance separating them, their eyes connected immediately. Francesca felt a stab of unease. She had the worst of premonitions—

he was seeking her out and no good was going to come of it.

She was almost afraid of what it was he wished to say to her.

It was nine in the morning; her mother remained abed, her father was already on his way downtown to the office, and God only knew where Evan was. Francesca wasn't sure he had even come home last night.

She hurried down the front steps, shivering—it was a frighteningly cold morning. And as she walked down the drive, Joel stepped out from behind the trees. He waited for her to approach.

"Joel. This is a huge surprise." Joel fell into step beside her as they went down the drive. Francesca glanced at him. "Good morning."

" 'Mornin'," he said. He seemed grim. "I gotta talk to you, Miss Cahill."

Francesca halted in her tracks. She could not care less if Evan might come up the driveway at that moment, or if her mother might glance out of her bedroom window and see her speaking to the urchin. "What is it? Has something happened? Or have you come to tell me something?" She found herself gripping her tote with unusual strength. She prayed for good news. It was sorely needed.

"I don't know why I gotta come clean," he said, shoving his hands deeper into his pockets. "But I do. I lied to you, Miss Cahill."

"About what? The silver?" But she knew this had nothing to do with the stolen silver, oh no.

He shook his head. "About Gordino."

Francesca felt as if the air had been knocked out of her lungs with one fell blow. "How so?" she asked fearfully.

"He wasn't the one who gave me that note to give to the fox." Joel stared at her unblinkingly.

She shivered and this time it had nothing to do with the cold. Her dread increased. "I don't understand, Joel. It wasn't Gordino? Are you sure?"

"Of course I'm sure," he cried.

"But why would you lie about something like that?" Francesca cried with despair.

"Why wouldn't I lie?" He shrugged. "You give me a real good reason to tell the spots the truth when all they ever done is throw me in the Tombs. As if they don't got worse roughs to pull."

She blinked. She really could not understand him, and now, it had little to do with his speech.

"Besides, he said he'd only pay me if I kept my mouth closed," Joel added.

"He? The person who gave you the note?"

"And I *hate* Gordino. He's a rotten son of a bitch. I was hoping that fox you like would kill him!" Joel cried viciously.

Francesca was frozen. And afraid. "Why do you hate him so much that you would try to pin a crime on him that he did not commit?" she asked in a whisper. How silent the morning had suddenly become, silent, still, frozen.

Joel only stared back at her, his expression twisted.

"Joel?"

He snarled, "He's after my mother, the bastard, and she's so scared of him."

Francesca was horrified. "After her?" she whispered.

"You know!" he cried. "He wants her in his bed and he's been threatening her for weeks now! She cries whenever he comes near!"

"Oh, Joel." Francesca reached for him but he dodged away. "We have to stop this, we do."

Tears had appeared in Joel's eyes. "If your fox friend had locked him up right, he would have been stopped, now wouldn't he?"

"Yes," Francesca whispered, thinking of what it must be like to be Maggie Kennedy, working so hard to feed her children, and then having to deal with a horror like Gordino, as well.

"So, I want to come clean," Joel was saying.

Francesca looked at him in total comprehension. "Who is it? Who gave you that note, Joel? Who?"

"Sort of a nice fella, actually. Name of Mack. A gent's gentleman, I think."

"Is that all you can tell me?" Francesca asked, in more despair. When it clicked. Like lightning in her brain. *Mack.* MacDougal.

"Well, he was Scots. An' a bit of a ladies' man, if I don't miss my guess," Joel began.

Francesca grabbed his hand in excitement. "Joel! I think I know who this person is. Can you come with me? Now? I need you to identify him." And then she would forgo her classes—she was going to get expelled if she was not careful, but she would explain—and go directly to Bragg with this new bit of evidence.

Joel nodded slowly. "I guess."

"It's very important," Francesca cried. They hurried down the drive, Francesca not releasing Joel's hand, her breath hanging in heavy puffs of vapor in the frigid air. Her mind was spinning, racing. "When and where did Mack make contact with you?"

Joel shrugged. "That mornin', I think. On the street. Not far from where I was supposed to wait for the spot."

Francesca paused on Fifth Avenue, staring at the closed front door of the Burton house. Now what should she do?

"Is that where he works?" Joel asked.

Francesca nodded, some of her excitement fading as she was faced with the reality of confronting MacDougal and making sure he was really the one who had given Joel the note. "We can't politely knock and ask for MacDougal. That will tell him that we are close to the truth. Oh, no. I must figure out a way to get inside so we can sneak a peek at him."

Joel chuckled. "Follow me, lady," he said.

Francesca followed him around the side of the house, keeping close to the walls, wondering what he was up to.

She quickly found out. After trying three windows, he found one that had been left slightly ajar. He grinned at her then pushed it open. Then he gestured for her to follow him inside.

Francesca watched him climb over the sill with a small boy's effortless agility, and duck into a darkened room. Her heart was pounding now. She could hardly believe what she was doing, but she had no choice. She lifted her skirts, flung one leg over the sill, and found it harder than she had thought to get her other leg up and over it, as well. She finally scrambled over and in, a small tug from Joel aiding her immensely—hitting her head on the window in the process.

Once she jumped down, the sound far too loud in the silence of the morning, she crouched down with Joel, waiting breathlessly for the door to fly open and voices to accuse them of breaking into the house. Nothing happened.

Her eyes adjusted to the dim light. They were in a small parlor. She had never been inside this particular room before.

But it was at the back of the house. She assumed the library was next door. "Now what?" she whispered.

"Guess we go hunting for your friend MacDougal," Joel said.

It did not sound particularly pleasant, but Francesca nodded. The only positive aspect to their adventure was the early morning hour. Eliza would still be in her apartments. Burton might be taking his breakfast, but with any luck, he was already out.

They crept across the room and cracked open the door. The hall was empty. The door facing them on the opposite side of the hall was closed. Another corridor led deeper into the house.

They strained to hear and heard nothing and no one. "I think the kitchens are back there," Francesca whispered. "Let's go that way."

Joel nodded. They left the parlor and scurried down the

hall. Within moments, voices could be heard, as well as the clanging of pots and pans. They froze before turning the corner.

"I'll go sneak a peek inside. If he is there, I'll come back and then you can do the same. Then you can tell me if MacDougal is Mack or not," Francesca whispered.

"Sounds good to me," Joel said with a grin.

Francesca looked at him again. He seemed to be enjoying himself.

Then she turned the corner and pressed up against the wall beside the kitchen door. Her heart flipped hard, because she could hear him speaking—she was certain it was MacDougal with his silky soft voice and barely-there Scots accent.

Still, she did not dare be wrong. She pressed the kitchen door open an inch, then another inch, and peeked inside.

She saw five servants, including the cook, a big man in a white hat. She did not see MacDougal.

She hesitated, then pushed the door open another inch. And saw MacDougal whispering in the ear of a pretty blond housemaid. She laughed at whatever it was that he had said.

Francesca began to slowly close the door when MacDougal looked right at her.

She froze.

So did he.

And then she closed the door and rushed back around the corner, waiting for his shouts.

But no shouts came. Yet he had seen her, hadn't he?

"Well?" Joel asked.

"I think he saw me," Francesca said, grabbing his hand and hurrying through the house. "We had better get out of here."

"If he saw you, wouldn't he say something and come after us?" Joel asked, glancing back over his shoulder. But there was no pursuit.

"Maybe he didn't see me. I don't know," she cried, her

heart hammering madly. "Now what are we going to do?" she asked in a whisper. "You have to get a good look at him," she said as they turned another corner and entered the front hall.

Joel did not respond.

Francesca stopped short.

MacDougal smiled at them both. "I didn't realize the Burtons were receiving callers at this hour," he said. And he withdrew a deadly-looking revolver from inside his suit jacket and he leveled it at them both.

CHAPTER
18

FRIDAY, JANUARY 24, 1902—1:30 P.M.

Francesca stared not at MacDougal, but at the long frightening black barrel of the gun. She could not breathe, and her knees seemed to buckle. This could not be happening, she managed to think, panicked.

"Turn around," MacDougal snapped, grabbing Joel's arm. "And I do mean you, Miss Cahill."

Francesca met his eyes and saw anger reflected there. "What are you going to do? Surely you—"

He cut her off by jabbing the gun into Joel's temple. "No one in this city will even blink if he disappears," he said.

"Don't," she whispered.

Sweat had gathered on the boy's forehead. He had paled. "Fuck you, you bastard," he spat.

MacDougal jammed the gun harder against Joel's head. "Move down the hallway, Miss Cahill. Now." Urgency laced his tone.

Francesca did not want to obey. Surely at any moment someone would walk into the front hall and find them being held at gunpoint.

"Now," MacDougal gritted.

She despaired and she quickly obeyed. As she walked down the corridor, he followed directly behind her with

Joel, forcing her to an even faster pace. "Where are you taking us?" she asked. Her tone sounded high with her fear, even to her own ears.

"Shut up," he said. "Stop right there."

Francesca stopped in front of a solid, plain door, which she suspected led to the cellars below the house. Her fear increased. Still holding Joel tightly by the arm, he opened the door, then let the boy go, only so he could push him down a steep, dark flight of steps. Francesca could hear Joel falling and she cried out. He jabbed the gun into Francesca's back. "After you," he said.

Francesca stepped down and stumbled. "I can't see."

"I do apologize," he said, not kindly.

She managed to grope her way down to the bottom, using the rough cement wall for support. "Joel?"

"Right here," he said, moving so close to her that his arm brushed hers.

A light came on, from a single bulb suspended from the rafters overhead. Francesca looked at MacDougal, who stood at the bottom of the stairs, aiming the gun at them both. "Now what? Surely you are not so mad as to kill us both?"

"I am not mad at all," he said. "It is truly too bad that you had to involve yourself with Joel."

"I think it is too bad that you are a criminal," she said. "Is Jonny Burton alive? What have you done to him?" she cried. "Where is he?"

He hesitated. "Actually, I don't know if he is alive or dead."

Francesca felt her eyes widen. For one moment, she stared in surprise. But shouldn't she have known that it could not be this easy to solve the case? "Who are you employed by?" And she waited for him to tell her who the monster was.

He smiled. "I am not that dumb, Miss Cahill. Boy. Bring me that rope."

Francesca glanced to her right and saw a coil of rope.

Her heart sank. If he tied them up, how would they ever escape?

"Like hell I will." Joel glared.

MacDougal's nostrils flared. And he took several vicious strides forward, raising the gun. Francesca realized he was about to strike Joel down, perhaps even killing him with such a brutal blow. "No!" she shouted.

But it was too late. MacDougal struck Joel with the gun on the back of his head. He went down and lay prone and unmoving.

"Oh, God!" Francesca cried, rushing to him. She dropped to her knees, cradling Joel, who had been knocked out cold—either that, or he was dead. "Did you kill him? You are insane!" She realized that tears were forming in her eyes. Joel remained motionless. She bent over him, hoping to feel his breath feathering her cheek. She felt nothing.

MacDougal gripped her arm and dragged her to her feet. "I mean business," he said, dragging her over to the rope. A small stool was there by a worktable cluttered with carpenter's tools. He shoved her down on it.

Francesca didn't even think. She kicked him hard in the shin, then tried to grab the gun.

He shouted in pain, and for an instant, Francesca actually got her hands on the gun, and she tried to yank it away from his grasp. He jerked it free, and as he did so, it went off.

She cried out, clapping her hand over her ears, as the shot was deafening. Then she met MacDougal's wide, angry eyes.

"You could have killed me or yourself," he said harshly. Still holding the gun, he picked up the rope and, within seconds, had tied her hands tightly behind her back.

"You will not get away with this," Francesca cried. "Bragg is on to you, you know. You are on his list of suspects!"

"Be quiet." He laid down the gun and pulled her ankles together.

Francesca stared at the gun, lying just inches from her feet, her mind racing frantically. Did she dare make another try for the gun? Would anyone know she was missing? And if so, how long would it be before someone did realize that she was gone? If only Bragg would conclude that MacDougal was involved—but the problem was that she did not think he was close to reaching such a conclusion. And what about Joel?

She found herself staring at him, breathing harshly. He still hadn't moved. Her heart lurched. He was terribly white, and now she could see the small blossom of red beneath his head. "Did you kill him?" she asked fearfully.

"Don't know." He tied her ankles to the legs of the stool, giving them one final, hard yank. Then he picked up the gun, tucking it back inside his suit jacket, and he stood. Their gazes locked. "You can scream all you want. No one will hear you from down here."

"Please don't do this," Francesca pleaded. "You don't have to do this, MacDougal. I can see that you are not an evil person—"

"Shut up!" He gave her such a hard look that she went silent, dismayed and panicking now, while he bent over Joel. Francesca watched him searching for a pulse. And then he pulled Joel's hands on top of his small body and he tied them together, as well.

"He's alive?" she asked, hope surging.

"I think so." MacDougal stood. His expression changed. "I am sorry you had to get involved, Miss Cahill. A beautiful woman like you. I truly am." And he turned to leave.

"Wait!" Francesca cried.

He paused.

"If you are not in charge, if you do not know what happened to Jonny, then you are only an accomplice," she cried in a rush. "I am sure you will not suffer the same fate as whomever it is that you are working for! But if you

kill us, then you are a murderer, MacDougal. And you will
be electrocuted. That, MacDougal, is the law."

He was grim. "Not a bad try, Miss Cahill. But I am in
far too deeply to get out now." He went up the stairs.

"Please come back!" Francesca called.

His only response was to turn off the room's single
light, casting it in darkness. And then she heard the heavy
cellar door slam closed. A moment later, she heard a lock
turning.

Julia found her husband in the library. It was, as she well
knew, his favorite room. He was reclining on the sofa, in
front of the fireplace. He was reading from a folder of
papers he had brought home from the office. "Hello, dear.
How was your day?" She smiled at him.

He looked up, smiling in return. "It was a good day,
actually. Dear, I have decided to build a new wing at
Lenox Hospital."

"That is wonderful," Julia said approvingly. Then,
"Dear, have you seen Francesca? I have been hoping to
have a word with her all afternoon, but no one has seen
her since this morning. Do you know where she went off
to?"

"Don't have a clue," Andrew returned, laying down the
folder and sitting up. He had exchanged his suit jacket for
a smoking gown with satin lapels. "Have you asked
Evan?"

Julia frowned. "He is not home. He went out directly
upon arising this morning, and has not been back since,
either."

"He did not come to work today." Cahill sighed, standing. "If he thinks to punish me with his juvenile show of
defiance, well, he should think again."

"Well, you are rushing the engagement," Julia said.

Cahill stared. "I thought we had gone over this? I am
not changing my mind, Julia."

Julia went to him and hugged his arm to her side. "Dear,

I know you will not change your mind. And you know I like Sarah, although I still think Evan could do better. I only suggest that you delay the engagement and give him some time to come round to the idea."

"Absolutely not."

Julia knew when to back off. "Where could Francesca be?"

Cahill pulled out his pocketwatch. "Hmm. It is almost five o'clock. Knowing our daughter, she could be off anywhere. I am not sure I like this."

Julia exchanged a worried glance with him and went to the telephone on the desk. In a matter of minutes, Connie was on the other line. "Do you know where your sister is, dear?" she asked.

"I'm afraid not, Mama. Is something wrong? You sound worried," Connie replied.

"I am a bit worried. According to Mrs. Ryan, she left this morning at nine, and has not been back since. Where could she possibly be?"

There was a pause on the other end of the line. "I don't know, Mama. I'm sorry I cannot help."

"Very well." Julia said good-bye, but only after reminding her that she would like to see the girls the following day for lunch, as it was Saturday. Both women hung up.

At 698 Madison Avenue, just around the corner on Sixty-second Street, Connie walked over to the huge marble fireplace in the library, and stared unseeingly into the flames. For Francesca to take off for a few hours without telling anyone where she was going was not unusual. But for her to be gone an entire day, why, that was very unusual. Where could she be?

Connie realized she was hugging herself. Francesca had been behaving strangely for the past few days, and Connie knew her sister very well. Something was going on. Francesca was keeping secrets.

Connie did not like it.

Her sister was too adept at prying into other people's affairs. She was too adept at involving herself in noble but difficult if not radical causes. She was too adept at getting herself involved in things that might not turn out the way she planned.

I am helping investigate the disappearance of Jonny Burton.

Connie stiffened. And she was assailed with dread.

Con, I know you won't believe this, but I found several of the notes.

Connie's dread increased. She did not have a good feeling, oh no. But surely Francesca's disappearance that day had nothing to do with the Burton affair. Surely not.

Had her sister also disappeared?

We found another note. I can't tell you what it says— Bragg will throttle me if I do.

Feeling sick to her stomach, Connie walked back over to Neil's desk and sat down behind it. As always, sitting in his huge chair, she could smell his cologne, which was spicy and male and so utterly lovely, and ensconced there in his big chair, she could almost feel his presence. She touched the worn leather top of the desk, a top he had run his hands over hundreds of times, and briefly, she was comforted. This desk reminded her of her husband so much that it was bittersweet. She wished Neil were home now.

But he was rarely at home these days.

Connie refused to think about that. She picked up the telephone and requested the commissioner of police at police headquarters.

Francesca wondered how many hours had passed since she had been tied up. She was desperate. Joel was clearly dead, but she could not cry, not yet, not now. She must plan an escape. Still, every time she looked at his small, lifeless body, she felt sick, and she felt a tide of anguish and anger, which she had to forcibly tamp down so she could remain calm, so she could think rationally. Yet how could she escape?

It seemed impossible. Not only was she tied up, but to make matters even worse, she lay still tied to the stool on her side on the hard cold floor. Hours ago she had tried to hop over to the worktable. Instead, she'd fallen over to the floor.

And her wrists felt raw from trying to work them out of the rope. Her eyes were filled with tears that were partly frustration and partly fear and tinged with the grief she dared not admit to yet. She had to escape. Because maybe Jonny was not dead, and she certainly had no wish to die. God, she was only twenty years old.

Hadn't Bragg warned her repeatedly not to become involved in the investigation? Hadn't her father and Evan said the exact same thing? Of course, she hadn't listened.

At least MacDougal was on Bragg's list of suspects.

She fought for composure. How many hours had passed since MacDougal had locked her in the basement after killing Joel? Had *anyone* noticed that she was missing? Surely someone had noticed by now!

And who was MacDougal's employer? Eliza?

Eliza would never condone murder, Francesca was certain of it.

But what did he—or they—plan to do with her?

A small sound made her stiffen and lift her cheek off the cold floor. What was that?

She suddenly envisioned an army of rats scurrying around the floor, where she lay—scurrying around her—and she stiffened, alarmed. She could think of nothing worse.

Another small sound made her pant with desperation.

And then she froze. The sound wasn't a scurrying one. Had it been a moan?

"Joel?" she whispered, seized with hope. Her voice came out low and hoarse. "Joel?" she cried, more loudly.

And this time, there was no mistaking his moan.

"You're alive! Thank God, you're alive," Francesca cried, bursting with relief and a joy that was impossible to describe. Once again, she tried to wiggle herself into an upright position on the floor, but it was impossible. Worse, she was going to wet her drawers if she was not allowed to relieve herself very soon.

"Miss Cahill?" Then, "Ouch. Shit. I'm bleedin'!"

Francesca's eyes had adjusted to the darkness, and she watched as Joel sat up, touching the back of his head. In the dark shadows his face was starkly white. "Are you all right?"

"Just a bit weak, mebbe dizzy," he said, shaking his head as if to clear it.

"Be careful! MacDougal walloped you on the back of the head with his gun and you lost blood. Joel! I thought you were dead!" Suddenly Francesca began to cry. The tears just streamed down her face and would not stop.

"Hey, are you crying over me?" he asked, gaping.

"Yes," she managed. Then, "Joel, I must go to the bathroom."

He giggled.

She giggled, too. At least it stopped the sudden flood of tears. Then, "We have to get out of here. He might come back and kill us both."

"He might kill me," Joel said, getting onto his knees. "But he won't ever kill you 'cause there would be hell to pay."

Francesca was suddenly filled with hope. Joel was alive and together they would find a way out of this dire predicament, and maybe he was right. If she should be murdered, disappearing, there would be hell to pay. No monster could ever think to get away with such a thing.

On the other hand, the monster was a madman. He was insane.

Joel's hands had been tied in front of his body and his ankles hadn't been bound at all. She watched him stand. He swayed a little.

"Oh, dear. You've lost blood—"

"I've been worse." He walked over to the worktable, and a second later had picked up a saw. "Look at this." He grinned.

More hope surged within her. Then she stiffened as he knelt beside her. "Please be careful," she cried as he inserted the saw between her wrists.

"Don't worry. I ain't going to saw off your hands."

Her heart lurched as he began to saw. And suddenly her arms broke apart. "Thank God." She rolled over and sat up, the stool still attached to her ankles. Within seconds, Joel had severed that binding, too. Then Francesca sawed the rope binding his hands apart. Their gazes locked. "Now what?"

"We get outta here," Joel said. He took the saw from her but did not return it to the table.

"The door upstairs is locked."

"Yeah?" Joel's grin was challenging. He groped around the worktable and came up with a long, thin picklike tool. "Follow me, lady."

Francesca followed him eagerly up the stairs. Joel handed her the saw—which she was afraid he intended to use as a weapon—and she watched him insert the long, thin blade of the tool into the lock. In an instant, it clicked, and Joel popped open the door. "Let's go," he said firmly.

Saw in hand, her heart pumping with adrenaline, Francesca hurried into the hall behind him. They turned the first corner without seeing or hearing anyone, but then, as they approached the library, voices could be heard. And one of them was MacDougal's.

Joel's pace increased. Clearly he intended to bolt past the library door, which was ajar, and make a mad dash for the front door. Francesca gripped his shoulder, detaining him. Pressing her mouth to his ear, she whispered, almost soundlessly, "Wait."

He glanced at her, mouth pursed, shaking his head emphatically no.

Francesca ignored him, inching along the wall toward the library door. Whomever MacDougal was speaking to, she felt certain it was the madman who had abducted and perhaps murdered Jonny Burton.

"Don't worry," MacDougal was saying. "They're both tied up. We got plenty of time to decide what to do with them."

"Plenty of time to decide what to do with them!"

Francesca almost gasped—because the speaker was Robert Burton.

"Francesca Cahill is on to us, MacDougal, and all because of your ineptitude. I cannot just dispose of her the way one would an unwanted cat."

"She don't know about you, sir," MacDougal said. "I never said a word."

"Well, that was intelligent, at least. Goddamnit. What am I going to do with her?" A pause ensued. Then, "So you think the boy is dead?"

"I think so."

"Well, that's one problem, minor though it may be, that is solved." A silence fell.

Francesca touched Joel's hand with her free palm. Their eyes met. She mouthed, "Let's go." But she was thinking, stunned, Burton. It is Burton. Not Eliza. It is Burton and he either hates his wife or he hates Bragg and he knows the twins are not his own and, dear God, does this mean that Jonny is dead?

And what would Burton do to them if he caught them now?

The thought was terrifying.

They dashed past the library door.

"Jesus!" Burton shouted. "It's her! It's Francesca Cahill!"

They ran down the corridor, as fast as they could, pursued by Burton and MacDougal. A shot sounded. Francesca thought the bullet whizzed past her ear. She did not want to die. She had to escape.

"Not here," Burton shouted at MacDougal from behind them, sounding far too close for comfort.

Francesca and Joel slid around the last corner and wound up skidding into the front hall. And as they did so, Eliza Burton stepped out of a salon. She was extremely pale and moving with the odd feebleness of a much older person. She blinked at the sight of them, pausing.

And a hand grabbed Francesca by her collar, yanking her backward, against a hard male body and a warm steel gun.

"Miss Cahill?" Eliza asked, her eyes wide and unfocused, going from Francesca to MacDougal, who was holding her, and then to Burton himself. "Robert? What is going on here?"

"Nothing, dear. A vast misunderstanding." Burton stepped past Francesca, smiling, and she felt the gun disappear, although MacDougal's grip did not lessen.

In fact, he snarled in her ear, "Do not speak and do not move."

Bewildered, so much so that Francesca wondered if she was on laudanum, Eliza blinked anew at her husband. "A misunderstanding?" She shook her head. "Why is Miss Cahill holding that saw? And by the by, the police commissioner is looking for her."

"It's not a misunderstanding," Francesca suddenly shouted. "Burton has abducted your son!" And she whacked backward at MacDougal with the saw with all of her might. As she did so, from the corner of her eye, she saw two things happen simultaneously.

Bragg stepped out of the salon where Eliza had been, and Joel tackled Burton around the legs, knocking him off balance and to the floor. MacDougal howled from the impact of the saw upon his leg.

Francesca met Bragg's astonished gaze and then he wasn't astonished anymore. In fact, faster than any eye could see, he pulled a gun and then she felt the Scotsman's gun jab her between her shoulder blades. The gun went off.

For one horrifying instant, Francesca thought she had been shot and that she was about to die.

Instead, MacDougal's eyes widened and he was flung backward by the bullet, staggering back against the wall. In a flash, Francesca realized that Bragg had shot him. Half of his right pants leg was severed, and his knee was covered with blood. He slid down the wall to the floor. Francesca leapt away from him.

Turning, she saw Burton racing for the front door, past Eliza, who had recoiled and was watching him with dazed amazement. Bragg leapt on him from behind. The two men went down in a tangled heap, and then Bragg was on top, pointing his gun right between Burton's eyes. Burton went still. He did not move.

And Francesca's heart lurched with no small amount of relief.

"This is a mistake," Robert Burton rasped.

There was no mistaking Bragg's smile. It was cold and ruthless and all of Francesca's relief vanished. "I don't think so," he said. And without removing the gun or even turning his head, he said, "Francesca, pick up Mac-Dougal's gun and call the police."

Francesca had been paralyzed. She reacted, darting to the fallen man, and picking up the gun that had slid from his fingers and now lay on the floor. She backed away from him.

"Are you all right?" Bragg asked, never taking his eyes off Burton.

"Yes," she whispered. Then, more audibly, "We are fine."

"I don't understand," Eliza said hoarsely. "Rick, what are you doing? Please let Robert up."

Bragg did not answer her. He jammed the gun harder into Burton's forehead, causing the skin to stretch grotesquely. "Where is the boy?" he demanded.

Burton spat at him.

Bragg slid the gun into the waistband of his trousers, lifted Burton up, and slammed his fist into the other man's face.

Francesca wanted to run to him and stop him from a bout of uncontrolled violence. But MacDougal had ceased howling and he was staring at her with an unnerving intensity. She trained the gun she was holding on him, afraid he might try something. The gun was shaking so terribly— it was her own hand, she realized, that she could not control.

Eliza ran forward as several servants rushed into the hall. "What are you doing, Rick? Surely you don't think . . ." She trailed off.

"Everyone stay back," Bragg commanded the staff. No one moved. "Eliza. Your husband has held Francesca and this boy captive because they were about to discover the truth." Bragg kept a firm grip on Burton, but he did hold Eliza's regard. "Burton is the madman who abducted Jonny."

"No," Eliza whispered, ashen. Tears started to trickle down her face. "No. I don't believe it. It isn't possible. He may be—" She stopped.

"I would never do such a thing, darling," Burton cried. "Ever. Do you think I would hurt our own child?"

Eliza shook her head tearfully. "I do not know what to think," she whispered.

Francesca stared and briefly her gaze locked with Bragg's. *Burton did not know*. Burton did not know that the boys were not his. There was hope. "Bragg."

He met her gaze again, his eyes wide, understanding her. Then he faced Burton. He lowered his face even more closely to the other man's and spoke so softly it was almost impossible to hear him. "You don't know? You don't know why I will kill you with my own bare hands if anything has happened to Jonny?"

Burton stared. "Bugger off," he said harshly.

Bragg's smile was savage. "They're mine. I was your wife's lover seven years ago and I am the father of the twins, Burton. *I want my son.*"

Burton turned white. "You're lying," he shouted. "I know you took her to bed, they all have, but the boys are mine!"

Bragg stood, hefting Burton to his feet and throwing him hard at the wall. Burton hit it but managed to catch himself before falling. He turned and faced his wife. "He's lying, isn't he?"

Eliza stood there, looking from one man to the other, as white or whiter of countenance than her husband was. More tears welled in her eyes and began to fall. "No."

Burton stared and stared and then he cried out, "You whore! You goddamn bitch whore! God, I have had to watch you take lover after lover all of these years—and I was about to break you, wasn't I? Destroy you? Finally, I was so close, finally, the day was mine, finally, vengeance was mine, for all those years of fucking. But the boys aren't even mine? You would deny me even my own heirs? You goddamn bitch!" He screamed, trembling like a lunatic, "You are the one who belongs behind bars!"

Eliza did not cringe. "I hate you," she said, lifting her chin, still crying. "I have always hated you. It was Bragg I loved when I was forced to marry you and I am glad the twins are his. Where is my son? Damn you to hell! Where is Jonny?" she screamed.

Burton roared and rushed toward her. "Never! You will never see him again, bitch!"

Bragg caught him before he could reach Eliza; he grabbed him and spun him back around. And very deliberately, he pointed his gun and shot Burton in the knee.

Francesca's heart felt as if it had stopped; Burton screamed and fell to the floor, clutching his wounded, bleeding knee, writhing hysterically.

"You're crippled for life," Bragg said calmly as Francesca watched with her heart wedged somewhere in the vicinity of her throat. "And you have three seconds to tell me what I want before I shoot off your other kneecap, making it impossible for you to walk."

Burton looked up at him, tears in his eyes. "Fuck you."

"One," Bragg said.

Francesca stopped breathing.

"Two," Bragg continued.

"Let me," Eliza suddenly screamed. "Let me do it!"

"Three," Bragg said, handing her the gun.

"Wait! He's at 208 Fourth Avenue. I let an apartment there!" Burton cried. More tears fell. "I need a doctor," he said. "Please," he sobbed.

Bragg walked away from him. He took the gun Francesca was holding and handed it to a servant. "Do not let anyone move until the police arrive. If they move, shoot them."

"I'm coming with you," Eliza cried, her face pinched with incredulity and desperation.

Bragg nodded. He ordered a housemaid to get her coat. And he said, "Francesca, you can put the saw down now."

Francesca stared as Bragg accepted a coat handed to him by a breathless servant. She glanced down at the bloody saw she held and felt ill; she dropped it immediately. She was still shaking.

Then she watched Bragg put his arm around Eliza and they hurried to the door. Francesca did not hesitate. She ran after them.

Eliza was crying as they paused on the stoop of the tenement on Fourth Avenue where Burton had apparently rented an apartment. The building was old, squat and dirty. Worried, Francesa kept her arm around Eliza while Bragg pounded on the front door; several roundsmen stood behind him, as did two detectives. Not far from where they stood, a train was roaring by down the center of the avenue. The force of the speeding locomotive was so great that the sidewalk where they stood seemed to tremble and vibrate.

The door did not open.

Bragg pounded again. "Open up! This is the New York City police!" he said.

"Why won't someone, anyone, open that door?" Eliza whispered, her face tear-streaked, as the door remained tightly closed.

"Don't worry," Francesca tried, squeezing her shoulders. She expected Bragg to signal the police officers to move in with their clubs and break down the door. But suddenly he threw his shoulder and all of his weight at the door, repeatedly, as if he were a human battering ram. Francesca cried out, afraid he would hurt himself and badly, when the door flew in off of its hinges, causing her to cringe as well.

Bragg barged inside, followed by the cadre of police.

Eliza broke free of Francesca, racing after the men. Francesca lifted her skirts and followed, determined to keep Eliza in sight.

A tall, thin young woman in a servant's black dress and white apron stood by the stairs in the center of the hall, as still as a statue, her eyes wide and bugging.

Bragg gripped her arm. "Where is the boy?" he demanded.

She came to life. Tears filled her eyes. "I knew it wasn't right, I knew he was some kind of crook," she whispered hoarsely.

Bragg shook her. "Where is he?" he cried.

"Where is my son?" Eliza screamed at her, rushing forward.

The Irish girl shrank away. "Upstairs. First room. Don't hurt me," she whispered in fright.

Bragg did not wait. He took the stairs two at a time, Eliza on his heels, stumbling after him. Francesca managed to run up behind the two of them, the police behind her.

She halted on the threshold of a dark, poorly lit bedroom, panting and out of breath. In it was a narrow bed, a dresser and a rocking chair. Jonny lay on the bed, curled up on his side soundly asleep in the day's lengthening shadows. He clutched a frayed and stained teddy bear to his small chest. He was in a shirt and his knickers, and his breathing was shallow and uneven.

"Jon," Bragg said roughly.

But Eliza cried out, rushing past Bragg, as the little boy blinked and stirred. "Jonathan, Jonathan, it's Mother, it's Mother," she wept, pulling the half-sleeping child into her arms and holding him hard against her chest. And she wept.

Francesca felt tears streaming down her own cheeks.

Jonny had awoken and he clung to his mother like a chimpanzee might to its mother's neck. "Mother," he began to sob. "Mother, where have you been? I want to go home!"

Eliza wept harder, rocking him. "I am so sorry, darling, I am so sorry. Are you all right?" She set him back a bit and smiled at him through the torrent of her tears.

But he was crying, and he shook his head no. "Why did Papa bring me here? I want to go home! I'm cold and hungry and I miss you and James. Please, take me home! I hate this place!"

Eliza crushed him to her breast again. "I'm taking you home," she said against his face. "I'm taking you home and I am never letting you out of my sight again."

Jonny's crying eased a little. "I want to go home," he whispered brokenly.

Francesca had been mesmerized by the reunion, and mostly, by the frightened, unhappy little boy. How could a man frighten and distress his own son so? Then she thought about the man standing beside her and she turned to glance at him.

He was trying to keep his expression impassive, but he was not succeeding. Because he was crying, a few small tears slipping unobtrusively down his chiseled face.

Her heart turned over so hard and with such force that the effect was stunning. She reached for and found and held his hand. Startled, he tore his gaze from the mother and his child and their eyes met and locked. Francesca did not think. She only gripped his hand more tightly.

"He will be fine, Bragg," she managed, her own voice seeming husky to her own ears. "He is frightened. That is all."

"I will kill Burton," Bragg returned grimly, his eyes so dark it was terrifying.

"Your son is alive," she said passionately. "And with his mother. And with you. Thank God for that!"

Bragg stared at her for a long moment and turned his gaze back to Eliza and Jonny. His son wasn't crying now, but he remained in Eliza's arms, and she was stroking his hair. She kissed the top of his head and looked up, at Bragg.

Their gazes met and held.

In that instant, as she looked from Bragg to Eliza and back again, something else stirred within Francesca, something dreadful and uneasy and distressing. She had become the outsider. They had a bond she could never share.

She had forgotten that she was still holding his hand. She pulled her palm free.

Bragg suddenly glanced at her, startled.

The look in his eyes was so soft and unguarded, so vulnerable and gentle, that Francesca realized she was hopelessly in love.

And as she felt her heart falling through the vastness of space, the sensation dizzying and wonderful and horrible and terrifying, she started, staring, stunned.

Bragg hesitated, then turned away and moved to the bed. Eliza smiled up at him, moving aside slightly with their son, and Bragg sank down on the edge of the bed with them both.

Not wanting to watch, yet unable to look away, Francesca saw him slip an arm around Eliza, and after a small hesitation, he slipped his other arm around Jonny.

Mother and father and son.

She closed her eyes, hard, against a new wave of tears. She realized that the tableau would haunt her for years.

They had once been in love. But they had been starcrossed, she managed to think. It could have ended so differently for them.

"Jonathan?" Eliza whispered. "You recall Mr. Bragg, do you not? He is your fa—your father's and my friend." Her voice had a tremor.

Jonny Burton looked at Bragg, clearly tentative. "You're the policeman."

"That's right," Bragg said, his tone husky with unshed tears. His hand had somehow slipped into the boy's thick, dark hair. "Are you all right?"

Jonny grimaced. "I want to go home. I want to go home now." Tears filled his eyes.

"You're going home, son," Bragg said, a tear sliding down his cheek. "I'm taking you home, right now, this very minute. In fact, I will take you home in the police wagon. How would you like that?"

Jonny had been staring at him, as if deciding whether he believed him or even trusted him, and then slowly, he nodded and he smiled. "A *real* police wagon?"

"A real police wagon," Bragg confirmed.

And for Francesca, so much pain mingled with her newfound feelings.

It was time to go.

Very quietly, so as not to disturb them, Francesca started from the room. She must not cry. The case had been solved. All's well that ends well, she managed to think, but inside her heart, she was choking on tears she did not want to spill.

A soft voice with a slight Western drawl made her pause on the threshold. "Thank you, Francesca," Bragg said.

Francesca felt more hot tears rise up in her eyes. She nodded without turning to him, and she left.

CHAPTER
19

Where was Evan? He was late to his own party, and Francesca could see that while her mother was embarrassed but hiding it very well, indeed, her father was growing angrier and angrier by the minute.

Francesca stood near the wall in the reception room as the two hundred and fourteen guests who were attending the engagement party arrived and passed through on their way to the ballroom. She was still exhausted from the events of the previous week. Bragg had not let her off easily—her parents knew that she had briefly been captured by MacDougal and Burton and they were so furious with her that they had yet to tell her what she might suffer for her part in the investigation. Francesca thought that Bragg had been somewhat happy to finally tell her parents all.

Her heart fluttered. She would see him tonight. Of course, it had only been twenty-four hours since she had last seen him, but this would be the very first time since they had met that they were meeting under normal social circumstances.

The press was cautiously hailing Bragg as a hero. One journalist had gone so far as to say he might be the next Theodore Roosevelt.

But where was Evan? Francesca scanned everyone present in the reception room. How could he be late? She had the most dreadful feeling, and she had so hoped for some normalcy—and happiness—in her life.

She continued to watch the scene in the front hall. Her parents stood on the threshold of the reception room with Sarah Channing and her mother. Sarah's mother seemed absolutely bewildered by Evan's tardiness, but Sarah herself seemed fine. She smiled at each and every guest politely, absolutely composed if somewhat reticent. But by now, Francesca knew that was her personality. And in her pale blue gown with its ruched bodice and flounced hemline, she was lovely in a small, sweet way.

Connie paused beside Francesca. "Where could he be? He should at least be in his apartments getting dressed."

Francesca smiled worriedly at her sister, who was stunning in a brilliantly yellow taffeta gown that completely bared her shoulders. She was wearing a yellow diamond choker to match. "I am afraid, Con. I don't like this."

Connie nodded, both sisters watching the new arrivals as they spoke. "So am I. Surely Evan will show up?"

"Of course he will," Francesca said staunchly. Her brother might be a bit wild, and perhaps a bit irresponsible, as their father had claimed, but he was not so thoroughly irresponsible as to not appear for his own engagement party. On the other hand, he had never been backed into this kind of corner before.

Francesca suddenly wondered what she would do if she were ever in his shoes. And suddenly she knew. She would never cave in and marry under any kind of threat, she would hold out for true love, or at least, for what appeared to be true love.

She had definitely become a romantic. Or had the sleeping romantic within her been awakened by this week's past events?

She thought about Bragg and smiled, then told herself quite sternly not to get carried away. After all, although they had shared a single devastating kiss, he was not a suitor. Not yet.

She smiled again.

"Well, at least Jonny Burton is at home with his mother and brother, where he belongs," Connie said, sighing.

At that precise moment, Bragg stepped across the threshold, shaking her father's hand and speaking with Julia, Sarah, and Mrs. Channing. Francesca was aware of her heart pounding madly, of her cheeks heating. He was by far the most striking man in the room. He had a charisma and a presence that even now was causing heads to turn his way. And he did not seem to notice. "And Burton is behind bars, awaiting a psychiatric evaluation," Francesca murmured, unable to remove her regard from Bragg.

"It is just unbelievable, that he would do such a thing to his very own wife," Connie said, glancing closely at her and then following her gaze. She smiled.

Still watching Bragg, Francesca said, "He wanted to destroy her mentally. He wanted to break her heart the way she had broken his. That was his vengeance. I was standing there—I heard him."

"He is extremely handsome, is he not? Especially in his evening clothes."

Francesca realized the way she was staring and that Connie had noticed the object of her attention. She felt herself flush. "Yes, he is," she said as evenly as possible.

"So Fran." Connie faced her, smiling. "Let the cat out of the bag. Is something going on between the two of you?"

Francesca felt her cheeks warming even more. "What could you possibly mean?" She batted her eyelashes at her sister and felt absurd a moment later for doing so.

Connie giggled. "Aha. I see," she said happily. "You have finally found someone who interests you romantically."

Francesca did not move. Bragg smiled at her with the slightest incline of his head, from across the room. Her heart chose that moment to perform a distinct series of somersaults.

And then, her elation vanished. Bragg wasn't suitable. At least, not in Julia's opinion.

"Con, Bragg and I have worked together and that is all. We are friends—in a manner of speaking."

Connie laughed at her. "Very well," she said demurely.

Francesca shot her a glance. Clearly Connie did not believe a word she had said. She scowled. The last thing she needed was for Connie to get a bee in her bonnet. Connie was not the best at keeping secrets. Francesca dreaded the idea of facing her mother over the issue of her seeing Bragg socially. "Look, he has not called on me; he is not a suitor. And you know that I am not looking for a suitor."

"Love can change all of that in a heartbeat. He will call on you," Connie said without a doubt. "Sooner, rather than later, I am quite certain."

Francesca's gaze immediately found Bragg, who was shaking hands with several gentlemen who were part of a group that included the mayor. She realized she hoped, very much so, that Connie was right. It would be very pleasant indeed to go skating with him on a starry night in Central Park or to sit through a musical on Broadway. In fact, it would be very nice to wind up in his arms a second time.

Her breath seemed to catch in her chest.

"Oh, there is Neil," Connie said, an odd, high note to her tone.

Francesca had seen him entering the reception room, as well. He was by himself, and magnificently handsome in his black tuxedo. She had already wondered why Connie had arrived alone, then had decided it was because she had come half an hour early to help Julia with any last-minute problems that she might have. But Francesca had only half-heartedly believed her own excuse. All thoughts of Bragg and any possible romance vanished. "Why don't you go join him?" Francesca asked very quietly. She almost despised Montrose. She knew she would never forgive him for betraying her sister, not ever.

"I think I will." Connie's smile was brief as she pressed Francesca's hand. "I've hardly seen him all day."

Francesca managed a smile, not liking the sound of that. Especially as she knew where Montrose had been that afternoon. He had been at Eliza's.

The impossible man.

And just as Connie was about to walk across the room to her husband, Evan appeared on the threshold.

Francesca's instant burst of relief vanished. He was drunk.

"Evan, how could you?" Francesca cried in a very low voice, so as not to be overheard. Perhaps thirty minutes had passed since his arrival.

Evan put his arm around her. "Please, Fran. I am here, aren't I?" His smile was lopsided and endearing.

He was drunk, but not miserably so. Francesca wondered if everyone could tell that he wasn't sober, or if it was only obvious to those who knew him well. They were now in the ballroom, standing on the fringes of the crowd. A few couples were waltzing, and waiters in white coats were passing trays filled with flutes of champagne. Well, at least in a few more hours Evan's state of inebriation would hardly be unusual. "Where have you been?"

He smiled at her again. "Ever the inquisitive Fran. You would not like it if I told you the truth, so accept a small lie. At my club."

Her mind sped. An image of the ravishing redhead she had seen him with last summer flitted through her head. "Surely you don't mean . . . ?" she began, not completing the question.

"Ssh," he said, hugging her briefly. "I am here, the ever dutiful son. And being so ever dutiful, I shall claim a dance with my beloved."

Francesca winced at the way he spoke, and watched him stroll away. At least he had dressed before arriving. But she was worried now; how could the evening conclude pleasantly? She had a distinctly bad feeling, one she did not like.

She wondered why, after the turmoil and tragedy of the past week, this night could not be a splendid celebration. That would be so very appropriate. She sighed.

She watched him pause before Sarah, who was standing with a group of young women, listening to the animated conversation around her. Sarah turned to face Evan, who bowed over her hand, gallantly kissing it. There was nothing inappropriate in his behavior, and Francesca watched Evan smile at her. She smiled back and a moment later Evan was waltzing her across the dance floor.

Francesca realized she had been crossing her fingers behind her back; she exhaled and relaxed. Evan might be furious with their father, but he was a kind man and he would never take it out on Sarah. If they married—no, when they married—he would be amicable, she felt certain.

She glanced past the dancers and her gaze locked with Montrose's. She stiffened.

He looked away, turning his broad back to her. The slight was obvious.

Her heart began to pound. He was chatting with three other gentlemen. Francesca stared at his broad shoulders. What should she do? Their relationship had become damnably awkward. She almost regretted confronting him over his affair with Eliza. She grimaced, reminding herself that she was not the one at fault—she was not the adulterer. And what about the fact that she had, briefly, suspected him of being the madman responsible for Jonny Burton's abduction? Francesca winced to herself.

That had been a terrible faux pas.

Montrose left the group of men, and was momentarily standing alone, the gay, festive crowd swirling about him.

Connie was not with him. Francesca wondered why as she glanced around the room. She saw Connie standing in the midst of a group of couples, laughing and smiling, but she kept glancing in the direction of her husband. And Francesca knew her so well. Something was wrong; she was anxious and worried.

Francesca sucked up her courage, reminding herself that this was Montrose, her brother-in-law of the past four years—the doting father of her nieces. She walked over to him, refusing to allow her courage to fail her and trying to tamp down her anger at the very same time. "Neil?"

He turned, halting. He did not smile, although he bowed. "Good evening, Francesca."

"Good evening." Francesca realized she was so nervous that she was wringing her hands. She fought to still them. Damnable images of him with Eliza kept trying to creep into her mind. "Can we have a . . . a word?"

He eyed her briefly. "Of course."

Francesca stiffened as his hand touched her waist, moving her through the crowd. He was very angry, she realized. But what did she expect? She had to be even angrier, she thought grimly. And she wished he would remove his hand from her body, it was just too large, sitting there on her small waist. She did not like being so aware of it. As they left the ballroom, Bragg entered it. Their gazes instantly met.

Her eyes widened slightly; so did his.

Montrose nodded at Bragg. "Good evening, Commissioner. Congratulations on a case well solved." His tone was level. Any remaining hostility that he might have harbored was well disguised.

Bragg's gaze lowered and Francesca realized he was noticing Neil's hand on her waist. "Thank you. Miss Cahill? Will you save me a dance?"

She felt her cheeks burst into flames. "Of course." The pressure of Neil's hand on her waist increased.

They nodded at one another and Montrose guided her

into the hall. They walked into a large room used for recitals. Montrose dropped his hand and leaned one broad shoulder against the doorjamb, folding his muscular arms across his chest. "Well?"

"I owe you an apology," Francesca said simply, then realized she was grimacing.

"You do," he said flatly.

She crossed her arms as well, thinking about the apology that he owed her sister. "I am sorry I ever thought, even for a moment, that you might be involved in the abduction of Jonny Burton."

He regarded her. "Are you? And are you also sorry for spying on me?"

She felt her own temper rising. "I wish," she said, choosing her words with care, "that I had never seen what I did. I wish I did not know what I do."

"Then why don't you just forget about it?" he asked bluntly.

Her temper got the best of her. "And how can I do that?" she said, too loudly. "I mean, it might be helpful if you ended things, wouldn't it?"

He levered himself off the doorjamb. "Once again, you are butting into affairs that are not your concern."

"Why did you have to go over there this afternoon? You just could not stay away!" Francesca could not control herself.

His eyes widened. "I don't believe it! You were spying on me again?" He was disbelieving. "Can you not mind your own business, for God's sake, Francesca!"

"It was an accident," she said, meaning it.

"I somehow doubt that," Neil returned.

Francesca almost hesitated, then demanded, "Why, Neil? Why did you have to go to her today? Why?"

His gaze blackened. "She is my friend, not that it is your concern. Francesca, one day you will pay for your insufferable prying. And one day, when you are older, you will understand that relationships—that marriage—is hardly simple or easy."

She did not take his words as a threat. "Prying is hardly a sin. Lying is—among other things."

He turned to go.

"Why are the two of you arguing?" Connie asked, standing on the threshold in the hallway. She was pale, her gaze going back and forth repeatedly between her husband and Francesca. Her blue eyes were filled with anxiety.

Francesca felt her heart skip too many beats to count.

"Ask your sister," Montrose said harshly, and he moved abruptly past his wife, striding angrily away from them both.

Ill, Francesca met her eyes.

"What have you done?" Connie cried. "To upset him so? What is going on?"

Francesca could not think of a reply. It crossed her befuddled mind that she could tell her sister the truth. The evening was going to turn into a disaster anyway, and would there ever be a good time? She said, "Montrose has discovered that I have secretly enrolled at Barnard College, and we are fighting because he thinks I have gone too far. He thinks I should tell Mama and Papa," Francesca said unhappily.

She could not tell Connie the truth. Not yet. Not so precipitously. Bragg's words returned to her now, full force. Words once spoken could *never* be taken back. She did not know what to do; she would have to think carefully about it.

Connie's worried expression had eased. "How did he find out? You don't think that I . . . Fran! I did not tell him, I swear!" she cried.

"I know you didn't," Francesca said, stepping to her and putting her arm around her. She did not want to add to Connie's woes. "He guessed himself. He is a smart man. Shall we go back to the party?" But even as she spoke, even as she forced a smile, she was thinking, Doesn't my sister have a right to know?

Dear God, she was caught between a rock and a hard place!

"Let's," Connie said, finally smiling in return. "We don't want to miss the announcement."

Francesca just looked at her. And she knew, with every instinct that she had, that one day, soon, Connie was going to find out about Montrose's philandering ways. If she did not already suspect the truth.

"You do not seem to be enjoying yourself, Francesca."

Francesca started and met Bragg's gaze. He had come up behind her, catching her unawares. She smiled happily. "I am not the kind of woman who is truly fond of parties," she finally said.

He smiled in return. "And why does that not surprise me? Let me guess. Attacking ruffians with saws is more your fashion?"

Francesca laughed. "The saw was Joel's idea. But it did allow us to cut the ropes and free ourselves."

"Thank God for small miracles," Bragg said, still smiling, but slightly, his gaze very intent upon her face.

In fact, it was so intent that Francesca was aware of becoming increasingly nervous and flustered. Why was he staring? What was he thinking? "And how is Burton?" she asked as lightly as possible, given the nature of the question and her nerves.

"Ah, shop talk," he said. His golden eyes moved slowly, deliberately, over her face. "I personally believe him deranged. But he has actually lapsed into a monumental silence ever since being locked up at Bellevue. He refuses now to speak. Still, we are working determinedly to build an ironclad case against him." He then sighed. "At least there were over a dozen witnesses to his confession yesterday in the foyer."

She studied him seriously. "What is it? Is it Eliza?"

Francesca plucked his sleeve. Trepidation had risen within her. He and Eliza shared a past. They had had a love affair and two wonderful boys. The fact was somehow frightening.

His gaze met hers. "You are so astute. Yes, I am worried about her. Whether or not Burton is insane, the odds are very high that he will be found mentally competent, enough so to stand trial. I would not wish for the world to know the details of their marriage."

"You do mean, the details of her personal life," Francesca said, worried in spite of her slight jealousy. Eliza did not deserve such a fate. She had suffered enough. Somehow, Francesca was still fond of her; somehow, she still admired and liked her. "She would be ruined."

"Yes, she would."

"That is probably the last thing on her mind right now," Francesca said, imagining that Eliza was at this moment at home with her two boys, resolving never to let them out of her sight.

"She has yet to think of it, I am sure. I was reluctant to intrude, but I did stop by this morning, to see how everyone was faring. Jonny is fine, of course. He hasn't a clue as to what happened, he believes he and his father were on some kind of holiday."

"Thank God for small miracles," Francesca said, and they both smiled at her use of his words.

"Eliza still seems shaken. I believe she is blaming herself for driving her husband to such madness. In any case, time does heal all wounds."

"Oh, Bragg. Such a cliché," Francesca said lightly, touching his arm.

His gaze twinkled. "As you know, I am hardly infallible."

"You are a wonderful crime investigator," Francesca said staunchly. "And I suspect you will be a superb commissioner of police."

His smile faded. For a moment, he said nothing, his

gaze searching, and Francesca knew she flushed. Then, "She is planning to take the boys out of school immediately; she is making arrangements to spend some time in Europe."

"That is a wonderful idea," Francesca cried.

He did not smile. He stared. He stared with such intensity that Francesca began to fidget. But more importantly, there was one question she just had to ask. And suddenly he smiled. "What is it, Francesca? What is bothering you?" His words were whiskey-soft and laced with his slight Texas drawl.

She wet her lips. "You still love her, don't you? Eliza." And she found herself holding her breath.

His slight smile vanished. "No. I do not."

She blinked. His words were so flat, so firm, that there was no doubt that he meant what he said. "I am sorry," she managed, thoroughly flustered now. "That question was so inappropriate, given that—"

"Was it inappropriate?" He cut her off. "Considering my behavior in my house with you, the other day?"

She froze. He was referring to the passionate, astonishing kiss that they had shared. She could not speak.

"About my behavior," he said. And he stopped, flushing darkly, as if the sun had somehow scorched his high cheekbones.

She looked at him, afraid of what he might or might not say. Carefully she said, "You do not have to apologize."

His jaw flexed. "I do. I was hardly a gentleman." He winced then. "Francesca, I treasure our friendship. I would never do anything to jeopardize it."

Francesca's heart sank. She looked at him, filled with dread and a new, rising hurt. He only thought of her as a friend?

"I should not have let you in," he continued, "not when I was in such a state. I am sorry for putting you in a damnably compromising position."

She had to turn away, blinking back sudden, hot tears. What a fool she had been! To think she had expected some kind of chivalrous declaration of love!

"Francesca." He turned her back around to face him. "Why are you upset? I behaved abominably. You deserve an apology. You deserve more than a stolen kiss on a secondhand sofa in the middle of the day."

She smiled at him, knowing she must appear miserable, as she felt several tears sliding down her cheeks. "Apology accepted," she said as brightly as possible.

"Why are you crying?" he asked in his police commissioner's voice.

She had no intention of obeying him by answering the question. "I have an allergy," she said. "It is the time of year."

Both dark brows slashed upward. "In the middle of winter?"

"It is a very unusual allergy," she replied.

Their gazes locked. It was an endless moment, Francesca incapable of looking away, her heart feeling trounced upon. Suddenly he said, "Shall we dance? I do believe you promised to save me one." And he smiled.

She met his golden eyes, knowing he was being polite, knowing that Connie was wrong, and wishing for so much more. But of course, it was better this way. She did not want a suitor as she did not want to marry, and Julia would never approve of him anyway. "Why ever not?" she managed lightly.

He swept her into his arms and onto the dance floor.

Nothing had ever felt so right—other than the kiss they had shared.

"Hello, Francesca," Sarah said somewhat shyly after Bragg had escorted her off the dance floor.

"Hello, Sarah. Have you met Bragg? I mean, Rick Bragg, the commissioner of police?" Francesca was breathless and flustered and confused. Bragg lightly held her arm. It was bare, and she relished the feeling of his fingertips on her skin even though he was only her friend, even though she had decided she wanted it that way.

"I don't believe we have been formally introduced," Sarah said, extending her hand.

Bragg bowed over it. "May I be premature and congratulate you on your forthcoming engagement?" he said with a charming smile.

Francesca studied him as Sarah replied. His mother might be a woman of ill repute, but he was certainly a gentleman. Then she felt eyes upon her and she turned and met her mother's direct stare. Julia wasn't smiling.

Francesca turned away, her pulse racing. There was no mistaking her mother's disapproval, and it wasn't fair. They had only shared a single dance and Bragg should not be blamed for the facts of his birth. Besides, he had made himself clear and he was not courting her. Oh, no.

Bragg excused himself. Francesca made certain not to watch him go. "How are you, Sarah?" She had recovered some of her composure at last. It had not been easy.

"I am fine, thank you. And you?" Her brown eyes held Francesca's.

"Fine. Are you nervous about the announcement?"

"Not really." Sarah smiled. Then, with excitement, "Have you given any thought to my doing your portrait?"

Francesca was startled; she had completely forgotten about it. "I . . . actually, I have been so occupied, I had forgotten you wished to paint me."

"Oh." Sarah's face fell with disappointment. "I was so hoping we could begin with preliminary sketches this week."

Francesca was surprised. "Sarah. You are about to get engaged to my brother, but we are discussing your painting."

Sarah regarded her evenly. "What does the one have to do with the other?"

Francesca bit her lip. She could not point out that Sarah

did not seem very enthusiastic about her upcoming engagement. She hesitated.

"What is it, Francesca? I can see that something is on your mind."

Francesca hesitated, then decided, Why not? "Sarah. You must be one of the happiest women in New York. Evan is considered one of the city's best catches, and you are the one who has ensnared him."

Sarah blinked at her. "I am very pleased to be marrying him," she said.

Was it possible? Was it possible that Sarah really didn't care one way or the other about her marriage? Was it possible that she was not smitten with her brother? But she would never land another suitor like him. "Sarah, do you love my brother?"

Sarah's eyes widened.

Francesca wanted to kick herself. "That was a horridly rude question! I do apologize," she cried.

Sarah took her hand. "I find your honesty refreshing, Francesca. Do you know, with all the gossip flying about town about Evan and myself, that you are the only one who has asked such a question? We have only just met," she said. "We hardly know one another."

"But . . . you are to become engaged. The two of you are making a commitment to spend the rest of your lives together," Francesca said.

Sarah shrugged. "I know. It is a good match. It is good for him and it is good for me. I do mean, we both must marry, sooner or later. And I believe that, in time, we shall become fond of one another. Are you so romantic, Francesca?"

"I had never perceived myself that way, but apparently I am," Francesca said, remaining astounded. Sarah was not in love with her brother. It was almost unfathomable to Francesca.

"Would you please think about the portrait?" Sarah said, rushing her words.

Francesca realized why. The orchestra had gone silent, and her father and mother had taken to the podium. Evan was about to go up the steps. Julia was waving at Sarah to come over.

"I don't have to think about it," Francesca said. She squeezed the hand of the woman who would one day become her sister-in-law. "Of course you may paint my portrait."

Sarah's eyes brightened and she smiled and then she hurried through the crowd.

Francesca turned. Evan was waiting at the bottom of the steps of the podium for his fiancée. He took her arm and helped her up, following behind her.

"Everyone. May I have your attention, please? I have an announcement to make," Andrew Cahill said loudly.

The crowd began to hush.

Someone came to stand beside Francesca. She did not have to look to know who it was. She glanced at him. He smiled at her. "A very big day," Bragg said.

"Yes, indeed," Francesca agreed, pleased in spite of herself to have his company again. One of them shifted slightly, and Francesca did not know if it was he or she herself. In any case, their arms brushed, as did their hands. Not even an inch separated their bodies. Francesca wondered if he noticed; if he did, he gave no sign. Neither one of them moved away.

"I am very pleased to announce the engagement of my son, Evan Martin Cahill, to Miss Sarah Beth Channing," Cahill said.

Everyone clapped.

Aware of Bragg watching her from the corner of his eye, Francesca also applauded. She prayed the match would turn out far better than she had thought it would.

Then she thought about Bragg's apology, and she felt sick inside of her heart.

Evan was taking a jeweler's royal-blue velvet box from his breast pocket, and he opened it. He held up a huge ruby ring, flanked with large diamonds. The women in the crowd oohed and aahed. Even a few men gasped. The ring was worth a fortune. Evan smiled, grimly, Francesca thought, and slid the ring on Sarah's finger. She smiled politely back at him and he kissed her briefly on the lips.

More applause rang out.

Francesca imagined what it would be like to receive a ring like that, but to receive it out of love, not duty. She wondered what it would be like to be so loved by a man that he would declare himself and want to spend the rest of his life with her. Acutely aware of Bragg beside her, she just could not move. She could not even breathe.

What was wrong with her?

The gathering was breaking up. The orchestra had begun to play. Francesca turned to move off the dance floor, but instead she bumped into the man at her side. She looked up.

Bragg was staring at her. Very intently. So intently that she felt herself flush.

She smiled, hoping all of her thoughts and all of her anxiety were not written there on her face.

"I am going to call it a night," he said, his gaze never wavering. "It has been a very long week, Francesca."

"Yes, it has," she said, not daring to move.

"I will see you soon," he said.

Francesca watched him leave.

CHAPTER
20

Francesca stepped out of Tiffany's, feeling quite pleased with herself. Five days had passed since the engagement had been announced. Five days that were rather boring, if she dared be honest with herself. For life had gone back to its normal routine. She was attending classes and studying at the library every day, while trying to hide her studies from her mother, who seemed as suspicious as ever about her activities. And then, of course, there were the evening engagements, which she just could not avoid. In fact, last night she had attended the ballet, and Mr. Wiley had been a member of their group.

Francesca had put off having that discussion with Julia. She grew grim at the thought. It could not be put off for much longer, for Julia had actually invited Wiley to dine with them at the house tomorrow night.

She paused on the corner of Fifteenth Street on Union Square. Some of her satisfaction over the morning's endeavor wore off. She hadn't seen Bragg since the engagement party, and she missed their sparring, their conversations, and their crime-solving together.

He hadn't called. But then, Francesca had known he wouldn't, even if his last parting remark to her had been that he would see her again soon. Connie hadn't been right, but Francesca refused to think about it or even to be disappointed. She refused to be hurt that he had not noticed her as a beautiful and intriguing young woman. She had courses to take, classes to attend, charities to do. She had everything she wanted in her life.

She was on her way to drop by police headquarters before going home.

Not because she was still romantically inclined toward him, oh no. But they had become friends; he had even said so. So why shouldn't she drop by? And as they were friendly, how could the action then be considered forward on her part?

All she wanted to do was share her good news with Bragg.

It was as simple as that.

How nervous she was.

"Miss Cahill! Hey!"

Francesca started at the sound of Joel Kennedy's voice. She smiled, her day brightening considerably, as he came rushing toward her, appearing out of the crowd of milling pedestrians. As usual, he was wearing his shabby brown tattersall jacket and a gray cap pulled low over his forehead and ears. His chin was blotched with dirt. He grinned back at her.

"How are you, Joel?" Her spirits lifted considerably at the sight of the small boy.

"Right fine, Miss Cahill. Shoppin'?" he asked, hands in his pockets. He was shivering. He glanced at her shopping bag.

"Yes, indeed. It's a beautiful day, but terribly cold. Can I give you a ride?" Francesca asked.

Joel accepted eagerly. Jennings was double-parked just up the block, and they started toward the coach. "What brings you to Union Square?" Francesca began, and then she knew. She halted in her tracks. "Joel! I hope you"— she lowered her voice—"are staying on the right side of the law!"

He avoided her eyes. "Of course. I learned my lesson, I did."

He was lying. He was strolling about Union Square, picking pockets, Francesca was quite sure. "Come on," she said. They climbed into the coach and she instructed Jennings to go to Mulberry Street. "I am going to stop briefly at police headquarters; you may stay in the coach. Then we'll drop you at home."

Joel sat in the seat facing her, legs outstretched. "I see." His grin was wicked.

Francesca ignored that comment, refusing to decipher its meaning, and inquired after his mother, his brothers, and his sister. A few minutes later Jennings had halted the carriage in front of the brownstone she had become so familiar with. "I'll be right back," she told Joel.

He winked, somewhat lewdly. "Take your time," he said.

Little boys, she thought, hurrying up the building's front steps. In the lobby she approached the policemen behind the front desk, her nervousness increasing. She reminded herself that this was a proper social call; she was not making advances on anyone and certainly not the commissioner of police. There was a captain behind the desk whom she did not recognize. But she did recall the other burly, bald man. "Hello, Sergeant," she said with a smile.

He glanced up. "Miss Cahill." He smiled. "Go right up."

Francesca felt a thrill and she smiled at him, about to go. Then she paused. "Sergeant? What is your name?"

"O'Malley," he said.

She nodded and hurried up the stairs, as the elevator was in use.

His opaque glass door was closed. Francesca hesitated, heard him speaking, and wondered if he was on the telephone or with his men. She knocked and was told to enter.

She did. Bragg was standing behind his desk, his hands on his hips, his expression grim. As usual, he was in his shirtsleeves, which were rolled up. He was not alone; a gentleman in a dark suit with dark hair stood with his back to the door and Francesca. Looking at Bragg made Francesca's heart skip a series of beats; she realized she was so glad to see him again.

Today he was cleanly shaven and it did wonderful things for the planes and angles of his strongly sculpted face. She took another look at his set expression and knew that something had happened. Another thrill swept over her, followed quickly by concern.

His eyes widened; he had seen her. The gentleman he was with turned and Francesca saw a dark, swarthy, good-looking man who somehow had a dangerous air about him. Their gazes met.

Francesca looked away as Bragg said, "Francesca?" He smiled then. "This is rather unexpected."

She hesitated upon the threshold of the room. "I hope you do not mind." She twisted her hands anxiously.

"How could I possibly mind a call from you?" he asked with a small smile. Then his smile faded and a ruthless expression replaced it. "Besides, my . . . guest . . . is about to leave."

Her eyes widened, her smile disappeared, and for one instant, she was speechless. Was Bragg flirting with her? Was it possible? And suddenly the dark gentleman strode past her, nodding to her as he left. Francesca turned to stare after him, forgetting all about Bragg's flattery. He had not introduced them; it was the height of rudeness.

She turned and met Bragg's cold eyes. "Who was that?" she heard herself ask.

"That," he said flatly, "was Calder Hart, my stepbrother."

Calder Hart? The stepbrother he despised? She stared. A dozen questions raced through her mind.

His expression softened. "So? What brings one of this city's most beautiful and adventurous women calling?"

The questions got lost, muddled up inside of her head.

She blinked at him. "Are you flirting with me, Bragg?" she asked cautiously. *Was* he flirting with her?

He set one hip down on the edge of his desk, knocking a newspaper to the floor as he did so. "And if I am?" His smile reached his amber eyes.

His gaze was so direct, his smile so promising, that she was once again briefly at a loss.

"It is hardly a crime, Francesca," he said, a tad more softly than his usual tone. "And it has been a while, hasn't it?"

She knew, or she thought she knew, that he meant it had been a while since she had last seen him. Was it possible that he had also felt that the past five days had crept by at an excruciatingly slow pace? Undone, Francesca bent to retrieve the newspaper. As she handed it to him, their hands brushed. She knew she was behaving like a schoolgirl, and then she saw one of the smaller headlines on the front page of that morning's *New York Times* and she forgot all about her nervousness. "Masterpiece Stolen from Socialite's Home."

Francesca glanced up at Bragg wildly. "What is this? Is this your latest case? A painting was stolen?" And even as the questions spewed forth, even as she had visions of the two of them traipsing through the city, attempting to find the stolen artwork, she glanced down at the article and read that a Rubens had been stolen from the home of the art collector Mrs. Lionel Carrington.

The levity in his expression vanished. "Francesca, have you not learned your lesson? You are not a policeman, or should I say, a policewoman?"

Francesca just stared at him. Her intention had been to become one of the country's first and leading female journalists. But what if she became one of the country's first police*women*?

Then she thought about that morning's endeavor. And she was torn.

"Francesca?"

"Oh, dear," Francesca said, glancing up at him. "I do not know Mrs. Carrington, but my mother does, and well. Of course, I have been to affairs where she has also been present—"

He made a sound. It wasn't pleasant. She looked closely at him. "Bragg?"

"No. No. Absolutely not. Stay out of police work, Francesca. I mean it." He was standing, facing her, his arms folded across his chest.

She debated numerous replies and decided that none of them was sufficient. "Bragg, I only want to help."

"I give up!" he cried, throwing his hands into the air.

He gave up what? She just looked at him.

Abruptly he put his arm around her. The gesture was unnerving, and it scrambled Francesca's thoughts as he led her to the door, their hips brushing and bumping repeatedly. She quite forgot her next question. "I am glad you dropped by, Francesca," he said. "I have been thinking about you."

She almost stumbled in the hall in front of the elevator. "You have?"

He smiled a little. Then his gaze became serious, indeed. "Of course I have. But I have a police department to run, and frankly, since I took this appointment, I have not had a single day off, or any time to myself in which to enjoy the finer things in life." He rang for the elevator without taking his eyes from hers.

She felt a rush of pleasure. "You must find time for yourself," she admonished.

"You are right." His eyes held hers, then moved over her face. "When can I take you for a drive in the country? Long Island is beautiful at this time of year."

Her heart seemed to stop. The elevator door opened. They both walked inside and it closed and the cage began descending. *He is inviting me for a drive in the country,* she managed to think, dazed. "How about Saturday?" she said, a tad hoarsely.

"Saturday it is, then." The door opened and he walked her out of the lobby and down the front steps. "I hope I am not being rude, rushing you out like this. But I have so much work to do, and I doubt I will finish before eleven or twelve tonight." They paused on the curb before her carriage.

She suddenly realized he was standing there in his shirt, the sleeves rolled up to his elbows, and it was eighteen degrees out. "Bragg, you will catch your death!" she cried. Then, frowning, "Wait a minute. You have rushed me out because there is something about the Carrington case that you do not want me to know."

He looked up at the sky, as if asking heaven for mercy. And then he looked at her. "The investigation is *classified*."

It was classified. Thrills swept over her. She smiled at him.

He groaned. "Please, Francesca, try and stay out of trouble until Saturday, at least."

She smiled again. "Of course I shall stay out of trouble." She decided a social call upon Mrs. Carrington was the very next order of business. Surely Mrs. Carrington could use her new services—now that she was prepared to offer them.

He guided her to her waiting carriage. "Shall I pick you up at noon? I know a wonderful inn where we can stop and have lunch on Oyster Bay."

Francesca was exhilarated. A new case for them to solve together and a drive in the country on the weekend. Perhaps he was courting her after all. And to hell with Julia! "Noon is perfect," she said happily.

He opened the carriage door for her, when she remembered why she had called in the first place—or at least, one of the reasons, and not the primary one, for now it was safe for her to be honest with herself. "Bragg! I forgot. There is something I must show you." She smiled at him as she dug into her purse and produced a pile of ivory calling cards, which she had just picked up at Tiffany's. "Fresh off the press an hour ago," she said triumphantly.

He read, his eyes widening more and more. " 'Francesca Cahill, Crime-Solver Extraordinaire, No. 810 Fifth Avenue, New York City. All Cases Accepted, No Crime Too Small.' " And he looked at her with sheer disbelief and absolute astonishment.

She beamed. "I must confess that Connie came up with the 'crime-solver extraordinaire' part."

He just stared at her, clearly speechless.

"Bragg?"

"Francesca!" He was turning red. "You are not a detective! We have trained detectives on the police force and then there are the Pinkertons! You are a woman!"

She was not really surprised by his antiquated male reaction to her new profession. "Bragg, I refuse to be held back from my true avocation merely because of my gender." She was calm.

"Merely because of your gender," he sputtered.

"I think the cards are lovely," Francesca said, meaning it.

"And what do you mean—your true avocation?" he cried.

"I shall offer my services to those in need of crime-solving," she said.

"And what about your parents?" he demanded, gesturing wildly.

She shrugged. "Oh, you know my parents. Papa will say I shall soon enough grow out of it, not to worry, dear. Of course, I do intend to hide this from them for as long as possible."

He continued to stare at her as if she had come down from the moon in front of his very eyes.

Francesca climbed into the coach and waved airily at him. "Until Saturday then, Bragg," she said, but now she was not envisioning their interlude in the country, she was thinking about poor Mrs. Carrington who was mad about her collection of art, and she was wondering just when and how the painting had been stolen. Did Bragg's mug book contain art thieves as well as burglars and pickpockets?

"Until Saturday," he said, closing the door. He seemed to slam it a bit harder than was necessary. Seeing Joel, he shook his head. "And what is he doing here? Oh, God. Do not tell me he is your . . . your . . . sidekick!"

Francesca grinned. "Joel is very handy to have around, as he is so familiar with the world of crime."

Bragg stared and stared and then he signaled the driver to proceed. "Francesca," he said, warningly. "Do *not* do anything rash. Stay *out* of the Carrington case."

"I promise." She smiled widely at him and the coach moved forward and she settled back in her seat. Her contentment was vast. She uncrossed the fingers of her right hand.

"Whoa!" Joel exclaimed, laughing.

Francesca smiled at him. "What is it?" she asked mildly, her mind racing with too many possibilities to count.

"Do you see the way that bleedin' fox looks at you? That spot's in love with you, Miss Cahill, the rotten sod!"

Her pleasure knew no bounds. "Balderdash," she said.

NEW YORK TIMES BESTSELLING AUTHOR

BRENDA JOYCE

THE THIRD
HEIRESS

The tragic death of her fiancé in a harrowing car accident plunges Jill Gallagher into a dark mystery. His final words to her, "I love you . . . Kate," force her to realize she neither truly knew this dashing British photographer, nor understood his true motives for being here in America. When she brings his body back to his English family, she enters a world of hostility, suspicion, and closely guarded secrets. Then she finds a century-old photograph of an American heiress named Kate Gallagher who looks remarkably like herself—and who disappeared nearly a century ago. What legacy of scandal has she unearthed? Who is so desperate to stop her? And can she trust the handsome, enigmatic stranger who may be her greatest ally . . . or a dangerous foe?

"Sexual intrigue, betrayals, and century-old cover-ups . . . A page-turner." —*Publishers Weekly*

"A tense and atmospheric thriller. *The Third Heiress* adds gothic and ghostly overtones to a story of one woman's obsessive quest for truth and justice."

—*Romantic Times*

**AVAILABLE WHEREVER BOOKS ARE SOLD
FROM ST. MARTIN'S PAPERBACKS**

Experience love at its most dangerous,
and pleasure at its deadliest.

The FRANCESCA CAHILL Novels

DEADLY LOVE

DEADLY PLEASURE

DEADLY AFFAIRS

DEADLY DESIRE

New York Times Bestselling Author
BRENDA JOYCE

Brenda Joyce has enthralled millions of readers with her *New York Times* bestselling novels. Now, join us in the next chapter of her unforgettable storytelling: the Francesca Cahill novels. Travel back in time to turn-of-the-century New York City, where a metropolis booming with life also masks a dark world of danger, death, and daring desire…

"Joyce excels at creating twists and turns in her characters' personal lives." —*Publishers Weekly*

"Joyce carefully crafted a wonderful mystery with twists and turns and red herrings galore, then added two marvelous, witty protagonists who will appeal to romance readers…Add to this a charming cast of secondary characters and a meticulously researched picture of society life in the early 1900s. I can hardly wait to see what Francesca and Rick will be up to next." —*Romantic Times*

"A delight!" —*Reader to Reader*

THE
CHASE

—

BRENDA JOYCE

NEW YORK TIMES BESTSELLING AUTHOR

CLAIRE HAYDEN has no idea that her world is about to be shattered: at the conclusion of her husband's fortieth birthday party, he is found murdered, his throat cut with a WWII thumb knife. He has no enemies, no one seeking revenge, no one who would want him dead. But the mysterious Ian Marshall, an acquaintance of her husband's, seems to know something. Because someone has been killing this way for decades. Someone whose crimes go back to WWII. Someone who has been a hunter . . . and the hunted. As Claire and Ian team up to find the killer, they can no longer deny the powerful feelings they have for one another. Then Ian makes a shocking revelation: the murderer may be someone closer to her . . .

**"Joyce excels at creating twists and turns
in her characters' personal lives."
—*Publishers Weekly***

AVAILABLE WHEREVER BOOKS ARE SOLD
FROM ST. MARTIN'S PAPERBACKS